Nightflower Of Comanche Mound

Katlyn Bates

Adventure & Quest LLC

To James, in whose shade I write.

Nightflower of Comanche Mound

When things change inside a house,
things change on the outside, too.

By KATLYN BATES

Chapter One

Nothing other than Mim's death could've taken my mom back to West Texas. She didn't make excuses why I couldn't go too, just boarded a plane from Seattle to Lubbock to bury her mother. She was back after two days. I think she and Pap rehashed how he blamed her for everything from the time my dad convinced her she was better than Texas and took her away all those years ago. I'd grown to question a Grand-pap who could sacrifice a relationship with us, yet draw to himself a gentle soul like Mom professed Mims to be.

"Charlotte Kensey?"

A flutter of uncertainty skipped my heart. I stood, stepped around the sprawling legs of other passengers whose sleepy eyes didn't even look up. Mom followed at my heels, soft mumbles bruising my neck.

"Charlotte?" The ticket agent's daisy-crisp smile settled on me.

"Charley," I corrected. "I go by Charley."

Her fixed smile froze unnaturally. She snatched my voucher, scanned quickly. "I'm afraid there's been a seat change." Mom met her *I'm so-busy* attitude with one of her own, her face fretful. The agent drew a bright breath. "But I'm going to make it lucky for you!"

Carefully manicured nails raked the keyboard. Eyes raised with the hand that flipped the ticket over the counter. "There you go, Charlotte. You can board any time."

I wheeled into Mom's brooding eyes that begged me not to go, and wished we were parting on a happier note. Why did she have to ask that security guard for permission to see me off at the gate? We'd already said our goodbye's. Like I can't do anything by myself—

She reached out and threaded her fingers through my hair... picking, pulling, as if I was three instead of practically an adult. I didn't usually wear bangs. "Tell Pap—" The sentence broke. She drew a deep breath.

I willed my heartbeat to slow, but it hammered impatiently. I looked past her through the tall glass to the waiting plane parked on the Seattle tarmac. Pilots were seated in the cockpit behind large windows, their hands stretching, busy with their pre-flight checklist. They laughed over something that must've been a good joke.

"Tell him..." Tongue flicked over dry lips, another anxious habit she'd developed since Dad took off. I heaved an exasperated sigh and pulled away from her plucking, away from the mangled words that hung in the air. She shook her head and her words flew away. She dropped her eyes to the floor. "Things *will* get better, Charley."

When, Mom? When will things get better? Give me a date, I didn't say. How much worse could Pap be than sitting alone in that dank little apartment all summer while her work schedule stretched into unimaginable hours? Of course I still resented moving away from our home. Away from my friends, away from my school.

Away. Away. Away.

Spring break had been no break at all. I'd determined my summer wouldn't be the same. How did I know she'd freak when I told her I'd found Pap's number and called to invite myself to his sheep ranch for the summer? I didn't think it was reckless. She didn't have to go ballistic.

"I want to do this, Mom. You might be scared of Pap—" I said of the man she'd disowned my entire life. "—but, I'm not you!"

"I'm not scared," she hissed in my ear. I rolled my eyes. About Pap, Mom had always been vague and illusive. "I'm not afraid for me. I'm afraid for you. You don't know—"

Of course I didn't know. Didn't care. Didn't smile. Gotta go.

"It didn't cost you anything," I reminded her gently. I didn't want another melt-down like when I told her Pap had consented to pay my airfare. There wasn't any other way.

She didn't talk to me for two days after.

I hustled a breath and took a deep dive. "With Mims gone, Pap needs his family." Pap had never actually said that. In fact, he'd hardly said anything at all. I did all the talking. Although I hid my disappointment through the uncomfortable silence that stretched like earwax over the phone, Pap didn't bother to conceal his indifference. I would've felt better if I'd heard even a shred of enthusiasm from this man I'd never met, never even talked to, hardly knew anything about.

Maybe if I'd thought it out a little first—

I blinked up at the plane. The engines were starting. One pilot wiped his sunglasses. Truth was, I needed Pap. I needed a *whole* family. Especially now.

"He'll be...he's glad I'm coming." I knew my call had caught him off-guard. Maybe I'd wanted it that way. What could he say to his only granddaughter? I wouldn't mention that.

The attendant stood over us nodding reassuringly, waiting patiently, cutting her eyes back to her laptop. She had no business eavesdropping. She didn't know the whole story...that it was Dad who never allowed us to visit the *'ol coot,* as he'd tagged him. All because he hated the smell of sheep?

But Dad's not here any more. Everything's different. While he could've stopped me from going to Texas, Mom couldn't.

The attendant said, not to me, "Don't worry. There's one stop-over but no plane changes. I can ask a crew member to see that she's met when they land in Lubbock if you like."

I might've been a lanky suitcase standing between them.

"Good grief!" Instructions had dogged me all my life:

Don't talk to strangers.

Don't be a bother.

Don't interrupt.

Until everything changes. When things change inside a house, everything on the outside changes, too. A new parental guidebook shows up: *Divorced Parents, Single Moms—After the Fallout.* I knew the rules by heart:

Don't leave the apartment.

Don't let anyone in.

Don't watch too much television.

Don't forget to do your homework.

And stay off the internet!

Rules lose their fire when nobody's there to enforce them.

I hoisted the heavy canvas backpack and slung it over my shoulder. "I think I'm old enough to find him myself." That ancient, crackled photo was practically kicking a hole in my pocket. Mom expected me to recognize Pap from a picture taken before I was even born? I doubted he would look anything the same.

She tried one last time. "There's always next year. You'll be a little more mature. More able to—"

"Sixteen in a month, Mom. Sixteen candles. My life is wasting." The plane was ready to jet. I was antsy to get away.

She polished her boots with a glare and wagged a hand. "I'll call you tonight...to be sure...in case. Um—"

I knew what she meant: So she'd know Pap showed up at the airport to get me. And what did she suppose she could do about it if he didn't? I didn't know what *I* would do.

I raised my eyes to hers without lifting my head. "It's a little late to worry over the what-if's." It would've been the safe thing to do to have a Plan B. Too late now.

She fidgeted with the top button of her shirt; I knew that she knew that I knew she'd lost. I tenderized a smile. "Please understand, Mom. I never had a chance to know Mims. I can't let Pap die off, too, and lose my one chance ever to get to *know* him." I kissed her cheek, reached out and gave her arm a squeeze. "It'll be okay," I said like to a child. "Pap and I will be a ton of help to each other."

The ticket-taker straightened, drew a sharp breath. Tight lips turned up, stark blue eyes sparkled. She scrunched a shoulder and said with all the confidence of one who'd tossed plenty of kids to the wind, "She'll be fine."

I boarded the flight from Seattle to Texas at five o'clock in the morning. Settling into the window seat, tension built in my bones. A handful of others filed on. Nobody sat on the same row as me. Good...I didn't have to talk to them, although it wouldn't have been hard since nobody cared to chat up a teen-*er* anyway.

The heavy metal door thunked shut, locked with a flat *clunk*. A flight attendant test-tapped the microphone. I dug through my knapsack, pulled out my phone, and with it the photo of the towering man who'd made Mom's life miserable.

Across the years I'd absorbed every snippet my mother ever spoke about West Texas—the ranch, the sheep...Pap and Mims, and laced them together into pictures for my mind. But I could never fix in my head how bleak and radiant could run together. How the Llano Estacado—the Texas Staked Plains—might erupt in magnificent sunsets to form a vast and colorful prairie sky streaked in long fingers of pink and orange and gold. So I'd carefully sliced off the parts I loved best: wide open prairies, spring lambs, the running tumbleweeds. Her stories often broke into parts of a circle, expanding and collapsing like deep breaths when she talked about a life she came to loathe.

I dropped Pap's picture in my purse, skimmed the tunes I'd downloaded...I didn't figure he would have my favorite music. Fixing my ear buds, I turned up the volume, leaned back in the huge humpback seat, and closed my eyes to the rush of revving jet engines that vibrated through my feet. Tonight, I would see a West Texas sunset. It wasn't lost on me that for all Mom's bitterness toward Pap and the ranch, I was running into the very existence she claimed to despise.

No matter about Dad—I would *love* the smell of sheep.

Chapter Two

The plane touched down in Lubbock a little after three in the afternoon. Jet engines shut down immediately so I felt the scorching afternoon heat before I ever stepped onto the Staked Plains. The passengers had all filed off, but I sat rigid in the upright seat, a cynical thought sweeping over me, not for the first time: I'd made a colossal mistake.

The flight attendant was eye-balling me. I checked my hair in a mirror, dotted on faint-pink lipstick Mom had warned me against bringing. Drawing a deep breath, I held it in, thinking it would help settle my jitters. Time to get this show on the road. Pap will be waiting. Or he won't. Either way, I had nobody to blame but myself.

* * *

I spotted him through the glass barrier, hands clasped casually over an ample belly. We locked eyes as I rolled through the revolving door. *Did he have a picture of me?* My grip tightened on the cheap ten-dollar flute Mom had given me to practice; she was proud I took an interest in music, and wanted me to keep my lips stuck to a version of flute that was less to lose. It suddenly felt more a lifeline than a companion.

It's not true that all people shrink when they get old. Pap stood straight and tall under a light-colored, broad-brimmed hat that rested low on his forehead just above white, bushy brows. Deep grooves ran around his mouth and down a chin he hadn't bothered to shave.

I didn't exactly expect a warm snuggle from him—Mom had prepared me for that. Still, deep down I couldn't help thinking she might be wrong. I had imagined I would run and throw my arms around him and all my doubts would fly away when he pulled me into a tight squeeze.

Instead, we squared off and studied one another, eyes never wavering.

I stuck out my hand. "I'm Charley."

Weight lifted from my shoulder as he took hold of my backpack. "Heck of a name for a girl." With a quick nod to the long cement aisle, he said, "Go that way."

I'd like to think he held out hope that he'd passed inspection, as did I.

Pap walked fast. I scuttled to keep up alongside the man who'd once sent me a birthday card when I was eight that read, Happy Anniversary. I could still see Mom's grimace. She said nothing about it, though Dad said plenty—none of it made sense to me at the time.

Pap steered me through the baggage claim area where we waited without niceties, like, 'So, 'bout time you got to meet me. Haven't we both missed a lot of years!' Nope. Nothing like that. The awkward silence made watching for my luggage on the carousel an exaggerated event.

* * *

The double glass doors hissed open and poured me into the breathless heat of summer when Pap finally spoke. The words came out pointed and sharp, like a bark. "Don't know why any mother would let...a girl go off alone." Like that made her a bad mom.

"Kids travel without parents all the time. Younger than me."

Pap tossed my bags into the back of a truck. "Load up."

I stood in the sweltering heat in the middle of the parking lot perched on one leg like a blue heron, the slender plastic purse fixed like paste under my arm. "I'm sorry, what?"

Eyes squinting hard on me, his mouth bunched with thoughts he had no plan to share. He mumbled, "Get in."

I blew out the lungful I'd been holding back, cut an uncertain glance to the parked plane that would leave me on the Texas tarmac, and climbed into the rusty green truck swept with dents and smelling like flammable solvents baking in the sun.

Pap threaded the long length of his body under the steering wheel. Raising his hat, he ran a palm over the surprisingly thick white hair, his frown passing over me. "You're kinda boney. You a picky eater like your mama?"

I wasn't sure how to answer and paused to think. "I don't much care for Brussel sprouts."

He twisted the key and the engine roared. "Brussel sprouts," he repeated, as if trying to picture such a thing. "Good. We don't have any."

Gears grinding, a distinct knock under the hood, Pap coaxed the truck forward, eased through a stop sign without stopping, and away we puttered until Lubbock Municipal Airport grew small behind us.

I scanned the roofs, every last one. Buildings began to feather out, and, soon, it seemed as if we'd left civilization behind. The long, flat road stretched like a ribbon between panting, dogged trees so unlike the tall evergreens that lined the

Seattle highways and the entire Pacific Northwest, a shimmer reshaping it, making it wobble.

Miles rolled past in painful silence, reigniting my concern: What had I done? Hot air funneled through the open windows, blowing my new haircut to smithereens. The back of my knees stuck to the vinyl seat.

I shouted over the engine noise, "You don't have air conditioning?"

"Nope." He was quick to answer, without so much as a glance at the perspiration beading my face.

"I thought everybody in Texas had air conditioning."

"Makes a person lazy. Then you wouldn't want to step outside."

I glanced at the instrument panel, at the button labeled AC, and propped an elbow on the open metal window frame, like Pap, to hook a drift of air to my face. "Yeow!" I recoiled. "That's hot!"

"Yep. And dry. Everything's hot and dry. And dusty." His gaze flickered over my blue rayon blouse and short springy skirt. "Your mama knows better than to send you here dressed like that."

I rubbed the sting off my elbow, inspected the welt that reddened my arm, smoothed my favorite skirt flat across my legs. "I've been able to dress myself for quite a long time." There was an edge in my voice I tried to smooth away...probably left-over from the airport. Noting Pap's long-sleeved white shirt, I added some reasoning. "I checked the weather conditions for Texas on my phone, and packed for the heat. I didn't bring anything with sleeves, like you're wearing. Who'd think in the summer you could even wear anything so heavy!" My stomach gnawed against my belly button. Maybe I was hungry. Or maybe I was more fond of the apartment than I'd thought.

* * *

Pap's silence kept me muffled. I followed mile after mile of fence stretched tight between an occasional gate, and studied the desolate, snaking road—its color more asphalt than concrete, the stark, sandy ground more craggy than stony, the distant terra-cotta hills more chipped than broken. I could've been on the moon for all I knew, everything so bleary.

"How far are we from your ranch?"

"A ways," he answered.

I leaned back, fingers gripped, gulping in the heat, the dry, and the dust, glimpsing Mom growing up under this kind of drill. She'd never bothered to make me understand why coming here was a bad idea. It didn't make sense—she should be glad I wanted to meet my Pap, get to know him.

A billboard rose out of the ground: *Welcome to Quitaque.* As if a million people had asked, beneath, it read: Pronounced *Kitty-Quay.*

"Kitty Quay?" The name suddenly connected. I straightened. "This is Quitaque? Mom talked about where she was born, but I don't remember ever seeing it spelled." The sign was the size of a semi-truck trailer, so obviously nobody else could pronounce it right either. "Who would name a town something you can't even spell?"

"Comanche."

"Comanche? Like Indians?"

"Like Native Americans."

"I guess lots of people get stuck on that name."

"Guess so." Pap leaned into the steering wheel and stretched his back. "Folks can't say it right, that's their problem. If they say it right, they can't find it on a map 'cause they can't spell it right. Fine by me." He cut his eyes upward to a single swish of cloud that floated all alone in the vivid blue sky like a bird that had lost its flock.

The highway funneled through the tiny town of Quitaque, a bold double-line splitting one side from the other like a long, yellow arrow: north side, south side, left side, right side. Pap slowed the truck to a crawl even though there were no other vehicles either coming or going through the scant cluster of buildings.

He drove poky past stores with no shoppers, their windows dusty, freshly painted parking slots, unoccupied. We passed sidewalks with no pedestrians, rolled through the one blinking light that never turned red. If he would stop in the middle of the road, I could hop out and run—no! walk around the truck three times, and not a soul would see.

I wrinkled my nose. "It's a ghost town!" I'd never met a ghost town. No wonder Mom left. She'd never described it *this* harsh. I'd never considered Dad might be right. Maybe he thought, What the heck is there to come back for? Maybe it was a kind thought; I was running out of excuses for him. "This doesn't look anything like where I live."

"Guess not."

"Did my mom go to school in Quitaque?" I didn't remember her saying. I couldn't picture a big-city girl like her growing up in a little no-where place like this. It didn't fit. I grinned, imagining a line-up of girls with pompoms: Gimme a Q, gimme a U—.

"Nope."

"Quitaque." I reworked the word in my mouth. "Kitty Quay." The help-sign definitely made it easier. "Where then?"

"Yonder." I looked into yonder where he flung a hand. "That school's not around anymore. It's gone." Pap turned grass-stained eyes on me. "Everything's gone—"

I peeked down the fringe streets at houses with fenced yards and stunted trees and brown grass, no matter that the first day of summer wouldn't arrive for another week. "People here should water their grass." Were these the scrappy trees Dad hated? "Is there anything good in Quitaque?"

He let the question linger. "You'll have to decide."

Just as I thought the plane had plunked me down on another planet, that Mom was right—Nothing to see here—two trucks pulling long trailers inched toward us down the main street like cattle, slow and deliberate. I said, "Those trucks, for instance. Where could they be going? There's nothing back there." I threw a thumb over my shoulder to where we'd just passed through the nothing.

"No tellin'." He lifted four fingers from the steering wheel as they passed and they did the same.

The heat was exhausting. My skin felt like rubber. The hood of the truck winked with heat that poured from the engine.

"The truck's not overheating, is it? If we're going to break down, I hope we're in walking distance to that hamburger place." I glanced longingly at the Dairy Blast as we passed...the only action in town was centered there. Four trucks and one car parked on the gravel lot, a kid stood at a window. "Not in the middle of—" I flipped my hand over the dashboard. "—all this."

Pap floored the gas peddle. The old pickup lunged like a laugh before settling back into the same knobby crawl. I pressed my lips tight so as not to irritate, remembering what Mom had once said, that Pap had difficulty in the real world. Society's ways didn't appeal to him. While she had learned to walk in it, he had not. I sensed an emptiness, something other than land that grew no flowers, no bushes, no trees, and set my mind to what the coming six weeks might look like if Pap turned out to be crackled as old shoe leather as Dad had described him. I chuckled. "Mom says you're kinda like an apple pie without the apples."

He spit out the window, wiped his mouth on his sleeve and turned back to really look at me for the first time. "Don't let first impressions fool you."

"Exactly!" I shuffled to face him. "That's what I've always said! We probably both should look a little deeper. I'm afraid I don't make a very good first impression." I mopped my sweaty hands across my skirt. "I feel better already, knowing it runs in the family." Thick brows puckered, settled over a firm frown. "I mean, I think there's definitely more to you than just crust. You strike me as a survivor, like those scraggly trees...just dried out and in need of a good watering."

Pap's lip curled but not in a smile. "Those trees aren't dried out—they're mesquite trees. We don't laugh at any tree that grows in Texas."

"I'm not laughing. It's a figure of speech. Those trees are probably the most solid thing around. Maybe you are, too. Anybody who can live in this heat, and keeps a ranch with sheep—" I folded my hands neatly in my lap. "I know stories about the sheep. I love, love," I steepled my hands. "—love animals."

"You obviously don't have to take care of any."

Wind whistled through the window, whipping, coiling my hair. I pushed it back and strapped it down with the elastic band I kept bound to my wrist. The old truck sputtered. Pap ground the gears, and we started climbing. The highway wound like a wiggle-worm past a cut of red rock, over a large stone embankment, around bends that held a surprise behind every curve.

I looked down into the canyon's stark belly where erosion had scratched out crevices and filled them with thin colors of green: flat-green, gray-green, stark-green...scrub-brush growing in every deep-pocket gully or rut and every shaved cranny.

We reached the crest; the valley floor took my breath away. A wide plain unfolded, stretching as raw and far as I could see. Nothing prepared me for the wild colors and jagged textures, as if over all the miles behind I'd seen them with one eye closed. Even the air felt different. Distant bluffs rose from the ground like deli-beef, deep red at their root, changing layer by layer up hills in variegated tones, an assortment of colors from brick-beige to soft pink. I'd seen an oil painting like this once.

"Thank you for bringing me down here."

"I didn't. Plane did."

"Same difference. You paid for my ticket. Thank you." I was pleased he'd wanted to meet me as much as I wanted to meet him. "What kind of things did my mom do when she lived here? I mean, I know she loved the sheep, but, because you live so far from town, what else?"

"She—" His chin quivered as if tugged by a string. He turned his head to the side window. "She...she did ranch things."

It was probably more of a question for Mims, if only she were still around.

The cloud speck drifted ahead of us, racing its shadow over the hills, muting large swaths of rock in shade, as if concealing the hills were its duty. From the hill's cap, the engine whined to cut loose. Pap started down, down, down, slow, slow, slowly through a twisting, rocky canyon the color of clay pots. The road leveled out as if we hadn't just passed over such a mass of buckled earth. Fences once again separated the two sides where yet more miles of sun and barren land splayed out before us.

Something moved in the road. I strained to make out the shifting image, thinking it one of those trickster floating mirages.

"Oh—" I cried. "It's a horse! A *Texas* horse!" Pap seemed not to hear. "A horse! A horse!" I yelled over the engine noise.

A horse the color of soot clomped purposefully down the

lane where we sped. Its head swayed with each step, like how a swing moves...never wavering side to side or faltering from the heat.

I unbuckled my seat belt, leaned into the windshield, and clutched the dashboard with ten fingernails. "You see it? Just ahead? It's an Appaloosa! I think it's an Appaloosa!" The horse was a perfect shade of gray, with vivid rump markings in splotches and speckles.

Pap didn't act concerned in the least, but kept his speed steady, his eyes brassy.

I whipped eyes on him. "Do you?" I stabbed the windshield. "It's in the road!" We were coming up on it. "He's outside his fence! What's he doing outside the fence? Somebody might hit him!" I twisted. "Pap, slow down. You're going too fast!"

Pap didn't slow. The truck gained momentum.

I shifted to the edge of my seat, braced my knees against the glove box, and dug my fingers into my thighs. Any closer and I'd be splayed out on the dashboard.

"Pap! Pap!" The wind fought for my words. "We're getting close! Slow down! What if he jumps into the road, right in front of— Don't hit him!" My heart beat wildly as the truck spewed past with an oily stench.

I spit out the hair that stuck to my lipstick and launched from the window as we shot past no matter that it was hotter than a firecracker. Clinging to the window frame, I watched the horse settle back into its same swaggering gait.

The truck picked up speed. I crawled back to my seat. "Sure glad that horse was traveling in his lane—"

Pap sliced eyes at me.

"Really, shouldn't we stop and check? Maybe put him inside the gate?" though there hadn't been a gate for miles.

I adjusted the side mirror and tried again, my eye on the horse. "I think we should find out where the horse belongs, don't you? It's not safe for it on the road. Maybe it's lost. Maybe it's just wandering around in the middle of nowhere."

"It's not the middle of nowhere. He knows where he is. You act like you never saw a horse before."

"Well that's plain silly. Of course I have," I bothered to answer. "I know more than you might think I know about horses. Mom probably told you I'm a horse lover, right?"

"Nope."

I checked the mirror, watched the gray grow smaller and smaller until, finally, it was reduced to a tiny blob in the road. "Well, I am." I flipped in my seat, flushed, and a little sullen about the horse. "You sure live a long way from Lubbock."

"Yep."

"And from Quitaque."

His mouth bunched. "Do you always talk this much?"

I winced, feeling the weight of Mom's warnings. "Since I've never been here," I said, poetically, "—there's things I ought to know." He didn't ask. "Like, do you have horses?"

"No."

I slapped the flat of both hands to my heart. "You mean—aw, crap. No horses?" That took a stink of a time to sink in. "Who has a ranch and no horse?"

"Me."

Digging words out of Pap was like prying gum from a shoe. I smelled a long, boring summer ahead. It coated my mouth with a different flavor. Did Mom know he didn't have horses? She should've told me. It might've swayed my decision to come. I checked the mirror again, but the gray had vanished in a curve. *Maybe he has four-wheelers.*

"Do you have a four-wheeler?"

"Yeah. You're riding in it."

I rolled my eyes. "You still have your sheep, right?"

He took his time answering. "A few—"

The road turned to gravel. "I would love to take care of the baby sheep. Do your sheep have any babies?"

"The ranch hand takes care of the animals."

"Oh! Sabion." Mom had couched a tip: Remember, you can always count on Sabion if you need help. I was beginning to get a glimpse how she might think I might.

No air stirred. I'd never considered heat could be so dead. I studied the hole where a radio once sang, thought about Sabion, the other old fella who lived on the ranch. "What else does Sabion do?"

"He—" he shouted, almost angrily. "—he fixes things."

I wiped the perspiration from my neck, peeled the limp skirt loose from my sticky legs, and cringed to ask, "Does Sabion have a horse?"

"No!" Pap snapped. "He has a stupid, backwards donkey that makes trouble and I have to waste good feed on."

"Can I ride him?"

"No! You can't!" He slowed. The brakes cheeped. He turned the truck a little too quickly and squealed to a stop. "Go open the gate."

"We're here?"

"You've been on ranch property for the past two miles while you've been yapping."

I jumped from the truck, swept the property with a quick eye. The small house at the bottom of the hill was set with countryside rocks in shapes and colors like the squares on a giraffe. It sat beneath a bare, sparse hill that rose rounded behind it.

But the barn! Ooh, the barn was ancient and tall with sharp corners and wide wings of boards bleached by the sun—just the kind of barn I'd always imagined would be cool to explore; the kind of rickety 'ol' barn I'd loved in the horse movies. If it were a ship instead of a barn, I could imagine it would be a pirate ship. I would've painted it red.

Something else caught my eye: a cowboy on a leggy, brown horse. A dog barked from somewhere inside the cluster of noisy sheep.

I threw the gate handle, stepped on the bottom rung to ride it open, then ran, squealing, back to the truck. "Yes you do have a horse!" I yanked the door open, jumped in the truck, leaned across the long seat, and playfully slapped Pap's arm. "And you said you didn't have a horse—" I teased. "I knew it! You were joking all along! And a cowboy!" I felt giddy. I'd never seen a cowboy in real life! It was like seeing a celebrity in the middle of nowhere. Maybe this summer would have some pop after all.

He squinted through the windshield, scanned the long driveway. "That's no horse. That's that crazy, lop-eared mule."

A whisper tickled my cheek. I brushed it away like shooing a mosquito. "Close enough. People ride mules. My friend Anna said her cousin knows somebody whose whole family rides mules on the trails going up Mt. Rainier—that's in Washington. They said—"

"No!" The force behind the word drained my smile away. His eyes cut hard to mine. "You're not riding it!"

He floored the gas pedal; I fell against the seat and the door slung shut. But I was happy, locked on the horse...mule, whatever.

Chapter Three

P ap culled his herd from over five hundred sheep to a flock of only fifty when Mims got sick. She died in January, when the ground is hardest and the wind coldest; where five strands of barbed wire—the devil's rope, Mom said Mims called it—were the only thing left to block the North Pole winds from the West Texas Plains. A few dilapidated windmills brought water up out of the ground. Now I could see why Mom said the sparse prairie grass doesn't grow in the winter. It survives.

Pap hurried the truck down the dirt road dividing the sheep left and right, and pulled to a stop under the spreading tree between the house and the corral. Sheep folded around the truck, their heads tilted up.

"Look at them all!" Tiny black eyes shined like black glass beads, thin mouths pressed closed, as if waiting for instructions. I wiped the blossom of sweat that mustached my lip and inched the door open. They caught a whiff of me and scattered.

"Humph. Not so many—" Pap said gruffly, but I'd already darted from the truck.

The brown-skinned cowboy waving a gloved hand sang from his mule, "Hola, Carlota!"

Carlota? *Me?* A dragonfly soared past my face so close I had to duck. I returned the gesture, my grin as broad as his hat.

He swung the gate wide and lodged off a series of short, shrieking whistles that grew in my ears. The dog dashed among the flock, moving them through the gate, leaping and pushing the slow ones with his forefeet as if they could never find the gate without him.

I took it all in: the decrepit old wood barn, the rustling herd, the splotchy-colored dog with the flapping tongue. When the last one filed in and the gate clinked closed, the dog raced to me and skidded to a stop as if to show himself to be the best trained in the bunch.

"Hey, fella!" I scooped his head in my hands. The panting tongue fell limp out the side of his mouth. His black-white-brown-gray hairs parted down the center of his back and fell to either side.

"No, no, Rowdy!" The cowboy threw a leg over the mule's neck and slid to the ground. "This is no way to greet our guest," he scolded. "It is a very fine day when our young Carlota come to the ranch." He shoved his round hat back to reveal a mop of black ringlets damp with sweat.

"It's okay. I love dogs." He wouldn't know I'd never had one of my own.

He squared his shoulders as if to lift himself taller and slapped the hat to his chest. "I am Sabion Severo and I welcome you to the ranch of your grandpapa!"

His words were sing-song, one word riding into the next like the full notes I forced through my flute. I smiled at the formality. It sounded rehearsed, but genuine, and erased the long, tedious drive from Lubbock and the cranky man who rode with it.

"Thank you. Actually, my name's not Carlota. It's Charlotte, but my family has always called me Charley." I cut a meaningful glance back to Pap who'd never yet said my name.

He chuckled. "What kind of name is Charley for such a girl?"

I was used to the question. "My Dad shortened it. It kinda fits." I stretched out a hand to a short-clipped ewe who leaned in to sniff. When it didn't run away I slid my palm down the crop of wool, the touch leaving dank traces of silk on my hand and a strong, heady scent in my nose.

"Ah, si," He wagged his head. "—but in my language, you is Carlota like my grand-mama." He made a fist that punched the air. "It mean strong!"

He and Pap were just alike: thick, coarse jeans, long-sleeved white shirts, snaps instead of buttons. Their hats were different, but both wore chunky-heeled boots that came practically to their knees. I could never wear anything that heavy.

I stuck out a hand. "I'm glad to meet you, Mr. Severo." We were much the same size—small and wiry, except he had short legs. He'd looked much taller in the saddle.

He yanked off the sweaty gloves and clasped my hand with both of his. "I am Sabion." He wagged a finger. "Only Sabion. You do not call me mister." His eyes were dark, the corners creased, as if he'd squinted into many suns.

I nodded. "Well, you can call me whatever you want. My mom told me about you." She'd called him gracious. I bet he could teach Pap a few manners.

"Oh, si. If only she would come, also. It was very good to see her last...when—. And how is our Miriam?"

So he didn't want to touch on Mim's funeral? "She's okay." I wouldn't think of the wild eyes I'd left behind.

He nodded slowly.

Sabion didn't worry that he smelled of mule and sheep and sweat. His was a pleasant face—a chin without hair. The kind of face you couldn't pin down in years, though I guessed him to be every bit as old as Pap.

Drawing the bridle off the mule, he grabbed the halter and walked her to the water trough at the corner of the corral. I followed him. The dog followed me.

"Rowdy?" I scratched behind the dog's ears. "He's friendly?"

Sabion laughed. "He is very happy. His job is to boss the sheep."

I had to listen closely to follow the strong Hispanic accent that enunciated words differently. He opened the faucet where the flock was gathered. The sheep rushed forward, never minding that I stood between them and water. "But, also he is bad. Bad to jump on you. Bad to eat you food when you do not look. Bad to not mind." Sabion clicked his tongue as at a naughty child. "Friendly. Happy. Just bad." His squint beneath the round hat made something of a grin.

I climbed the rail of the corral and leaned toward the herd, my chest swelling with the scent of them. "I love them. I love them already! They smell good!" *Mom was so right about them!*

He threw back his head and howled, his teeth showy against his sun-weathered face. "You think? I believe you are the only one to think so."

"Can you teach me to be a cowboy while I'm here?"

"Miss Carlota," His eyes held a smirk. "You do not want to be a cowboy. It is hard work for such a girl, no matter you have a name of Charley." He walloped the leather chaps that covered his jeans and dust flew. "Mira. You see? A dirty job."

Ha! That's exactly what I wanted to be.

"I can help herd sheep. I'm a hard worker. A little dust doesn't bother me."

He chuckled. The mule turned her head to me. "What's her name?" I reached for the tall, brown mule with the crazy eyes, but Sabion moved quickly to block my hand.

"Best you do not touch this an-nee-mahl." His pronunciation broke the word into syllables. "Tessa is not the same as the caballo. Not the same as the donkey." He tapped the side of his head. "On her thinking. She is very smart. She watch good over the sheep, but this mula—" He shook his head. "She is sly. And teeth! You do not want to see the teeth. This one, she bite. She is not bad...she is mean." He slid the bridle from Tessa and turned her loose in the corral.

The truck door slammed, Pap leaned hard against it. "Mean as a snake. Stay away from her."

"You mean I can't ride her?"

"That's right," Pap said.

Nothing was what I expected. "Ranches need horses. I pointed to the small donkey poking its head from the barn. "How about that one? I'll ride a donkey!" I'd ride a tricycle if they had one.

Sabion flashed a look at Pap. "Jennie—" He shrugged. "She love everybody. She will let her ride."

Pap said, "The donkey follows the herd."

"Perfect. I want to follow the herd!"

Pap glared at Sabion. "If you two are done jabbering—" He jerked his head to the house, clomped past me, and disappeared into the barn.

Sabion lifted my suitcases from the truck. I grabbed the backpack and flute and followed.

* * *

The condition of the house surprised me. It didn't look like a house Mom would grow up in. From what I knew of Mims, I didn't think she would've left her house in this kind of chaos. But then, I could already see what Pap could sabotage in six months.

Sabion's spurs jingled through the kitchen, the living room, down a short hallway, and stopped in a little pink room, small and square, with dusk-rose wallpaper and no closet. The pale lace coverlet on the bed matched the thin, ruffled curtain that hung across a single window. A four-drawer dresser stood along the wall. I knew immediately this was once my mother's room.

Sabion stood in the middle and rotated. "Is a good room, no?" His eyes twinkled as if he'd built it himself.

I nodded. "Yes. Thank you."

He set my suitcases on the bed carefully; it stirred up a musty odor like a room closed for many years. As if reading my mind, he jolted to the window and threw it open. A hot wind stalled at the screen.

"What do you do here, Sabion?"

He rapped his chest with a thumb. "I am vaquero!"

"What is vair...quero?" I twisted the word on my tongue until it came out like he said it.

Opening his hands and thrusting them at me as though I should know that, he said, "I take care of the ranch. I take care of the sheep. Vaquero! You now say cowboy, but vaquero is the cowboy from long, long ago." The emphasis made the word sound older, wiser.

I thought about that. "Then, you taught my Pap how to be a cowboy?"

Sabion chuckled dryly. "Oh, no, chica. Your Papa, he is already the cowboy." His eyes grew wide, his voice rhythmic. "Very big man, this cowboy Pa-pa of yours. No, Carlota, vaqueros come into this country before Texas is young and wild

—vaquero is the cowboy from South America. But, I am a Mexican vaquero, from *Texas!*" He smiled. "So, you see? Vaquero is still here!"

I smiled, plucked up a soft-bodied doll that sat on a chair in the corner by the window. Its cherry-pit eyes and puckered lips stared up at me much like the ewe I still smelled on my hands. The glaring pink cheek color looked out-of-sync for its sweet baby face.

Sabion clutched his hat in both hands. "It is very good you come," he said quietly. "You bring much happiness to this ranch." He fanned his hat in a wide arc that included the house, the hills, the rocks, and the fence that shaped the driveway that ended outside the window.

"Thank you. Mom has said many good things about you."

He nodded. "Si, Carlota. I know Miss Miriam from a very young chica, younger than you now. You look very much like her when...she was...that young. Look—" He swept a framed photo from the dresser and held it out to me.

I'd heard it many times before. What did it mean? Who was Mom at my age? I traced a finger over the old snapshot. She couldn't have been but twelve or thirteen, perched on a rung of the rail, sheep gathered beneath her. Mim's arms wrapped her tight.

I wound a mousy curl around a finger and stared into dense, thinking eyes that lapped up the sunlight...at the high, rich-colored cheekbones she had inherited but didn't pass on to me. All my life I'd grasped for something, any unique quality I could claim, because, in myself I saw no particular nature or strength or grit. Just fifty-two freckles I worried over, and counted each week.

I studied Mims, whose character I was told I possessed, and felt the same longing I'd always known at the mention of her name. Her hair was long and straight and black as her eyes. I'd lost my chance to know her, never learn who gave me my temper and traits. Would never map the lines in her face or smell the cooking in her apron. She was gone.

I shifted my eyes to the young, strong-looking man who sat on a broad-shouldered horse, a new white lamb slung over the saddle in front. It wasn't too late for Pap.

I pulled the old snapshot close to study the towering man who'd met me at the airport. Here, he held himself different. His face shone with pride at the small boy in boots and shorts who straddled the railing, elbows poking the wind.

"You see," Sabion chirped. "Once a child as you, but now she is a grown woman."

I stroked the doll's coarse baby hair absently, stepped to the window that panned over a yard that grew little grass and one lone tree. The splintered barn leaned menacingly into the corral. "Was she still the same?" I asked. A dry breeze squeezed through the murky screen.

"What do you mean, still the same?"

"Like you remembered her?"

Sabion drew a breath that filled his cheeks, and searched for the words. "Such sorrow last winter when your grandmama die." He lowered his eyes, shook his head apologetically, his perpetual smile turned downward. "My heart was very, very happy to see Miss Miriam." The question still lingered between us. His shoulders froze in a shrug. "Everyone must change. Must grow."

The muggy room strained to catch a breath. I knew the answer—she hadn't been the same in three years. Sabion had just caught a glimpse of it when Mom returned last January.

I set the frame on the dresser. "Who's the little guy?" I asked of the kid in the picture.

Sabion backed to the door. "I will go. You will find me tomorrow and I show you everything." His boots banged away, spurs like ornaments on the hardwood floor. The screen door slammed.

The house felt hollow, empty...abandoned, like weeds that lay dormant in the ground.

Like the apartment. I recognized a shell when I saw one.

My shorts, flip-flops, all the summer clothes I could never wear out in rainy Seattle—where I never broke a sweat—everything fit in the four drawers.

I searched the picture again, the photo of Mom that could've been me.

But, the boy? "Who's he?"

Chapter Four

Almost seven o'clock. My answers would be simple: Yes, Pap met my plane. Yes, we were at the ranch, though now I could see why she might worry he may not have shown up. He didn't exactly show me the kind of family tenderness I'd witnessed from friends whose own grandparents were practically draped around their necks. I wouldn't mention that, for supper, he'd laid out a couple sleeves of crackers, two cans of tuna, and a glass of milk that I wasn't sure I should drink.

I could've heard the telephone blast from the barn. I lifted the grip to my ear, unsure which end should go where.

"Hi Mom. I tried to call you on my cell, but Pap doesn't have that kind of reception on the ranch." Her muffled voice wafted through the phone. "Oh, that's right. Yes, I guess you would know that." It was a good thing I'd downloaded some music. I would practice my flute to it.

I scrolled through the photos I'd already snapped: the sheep,

Jennie, the donkey with the white nose. There was a great shadowy shot of the barn, and one of Tessa, Sabion's mule. I stretched the long cord to the kitchen screen door. Sabion was chanting to Jennie as he brushed her down. *Was he telling her about me?*

"You're right about Sabion. He's nice."

"Yes, very nice," she answered. The washing machine played in the background. "Good company for Pap."

"Maybe." I lingered over the picture of Sabion leaning over a rail in the corral, arms dangling like tree limbs, one I'd snapped of him as he checked a mama ewe's hoof, and a selfie of me hugging the smallest of the spring lambs. "Probably." I lowered my voice, found a chair. "Though I don't know how much company Pap is for *him*." Short, clipped breaths rattled through the earpiece, and I knew she stifled a giggle. I doodled a smiley face on a pad that lay at my fingertips. "Somehow I don't think Sabion needs company. He seems very content."

"What a good virtue to have," she said quietly. "Maybe you can learn from him how to do that. And teach me."

I knew what she meant—she'd had no peace since Dad took off. Always rushing, almost at a trot. Always short of breath like she might forget to do something. "Why didn't you tell me Pap doesn't have horses?"

"Mm."

"He doesn't talk much, does he?" I said of the man who asked no questions and offered nothing of himself. "It's like he lives in his memories."

"Memories—" She paused.

"I'm sleeping in your old room. I'm sure it's exactly like it was when you lived here. Mom, everything so—" I chuckled. "Somehow, I never figured you for pink!"

I had to strain to hear her. "People change. Some things never do."

A shadow of her face flickered back at me. I knew that. Did I ever. I'd learned how suddenly life can go from green light to red light—no yellow. "We ought to get a warning, anyway."

"Maybe we do, and choose not to see it."

I didn't want to say it, but it came out anyway. "Have you heard anything from Dad?" My heel tapped through the silence.

She took her time answering. "No." There was a long, lagging stretch of quiet where neither of us spoke.

"Just wondered."

* * *

The sun slipped behind the hackberry tree that shaded the porch. Pap turned in after Mom called. No satellite television, no cable, no cell reception—the only thread that connected him to the world was that go-nowhere telephone, a bulky piece hardwired to the wall. Pap told me straight up it would cost long distance if I used it. I got the message—so don't use it.

I washed up the two cups and two plates, and crept through the rooms like a mouse, a finger on everything: the orange kitchen chair cushions, the knobby texture of the couch, a clock that had lost one hand. Our house in Seattle was never this quiet. Even the most tranquil days were filled with barking dogs, screeching tires, rain thrumming the window. But the apartment noises—they were different.

I'd never been able to imagine the sound of the wind that Mom had described from her childhood: sweeping, gusting, howling.

I stole to the porch, plunked down on a step, drew my knees snug against me. The sun had fallen over the hill behind the house. Mims would've sat with me to explain the veined sunset, the warm illuminated arc that stretched over the sky moments

before twilight yawned and the last hue fell away into one—
when the last draw of light would squeeze every shadow from
the sky and leave the hillside only an outline. At least the night
took some of the heat with it.

I tiptoed into the house, careful not to let the screen door
slam. I brushed my teeth, washed the heat off my arms and legs,
slipped into a pair of boxer shorts and an oversize T-shirt. I shuffled clothes from one drawer to another, picked up my mom's
silly doll, and flopped hard onto the bed. The mattress curled
around me like warm skin.

Too restless to even close my eyes, I opened my ears to the
guitar playing. The sound came from the barn. Sabion.

If only I could start the day all over again. I would explain,
calmly, in a civilized adult-to-adult manner to Mom that coming
here really had nothing to do with her. I wasn't trying to deny
everything she'd ever said or felt about the ranch. Or about Pap.
I was older, and I understood things better. It's different for
me now.

So I tapped out the numbers on my phone, knowing it
couldn't ring, but pretending she answered.

I whispered into the phone all the things I'd already learned
in a day: how fences went on and on forever over the empty,
swelling land. How the occasional stubby, poking plants looked
like no more than splatters of paint in the desert until you saw
them closer. How the heat wavered in the road far ahead, uncertain of its place.

How odd to see Quitaque, a town without people; how
Pap's old truck seeped choking fumes through the window at
every curve in the road. And the thing I would have to grow
into: heat that took my breath away.

Yet, I was drawn by the raw, rugged beauty that rose from
the folds of broken hills, and wondered how Dad could hate this

place so much. How could he think the ranch held nothing at all, when it filled my eyes and excited my heart?

Now that I'd seen this barren landscape, felt the lifeless heat, my imagination could easily braid together the puzzle of why it would be special to sprint across the unproductive ground to collect iridescent wildflowers that explode in a rainy spring. I rolled onto my tummy and realized in the quiet hush how completely I'd left Seattle behind.

"You're right about one thing, Mom," I murmured to the dark. "Pap will be a challenge. He's a deep well that I want to pour something into."

A full moon cast an eerie glow through the window. I tugged at the doll's soft body...its fat, round face with lips that sucked in, and recalled how Mom's silhouette filled my doorway, her fingers strumming the door jamb like a twisting nerve... exactly how she looked the night she told me about the sheep— the night she sensed something somber in my silence and crept to my side...the creaking sound the bed made when she sat on its edge, before she cradled beside me and meshed her body next to mine.

When I threw the blanket over her and said, 'Tell me about the sheep'.

We'd huddled deep under the covers, her voice a bit husky as she whispered about the gentle, trusting ewes. I'd snickered when she showed me how their mouths swirled in gracious circles as they nimbly chewed the grass.

She had no words to describe the strong scent of their skin where she'd bury her hands and toes against their soft coat, '— and soak up the lanolin from their wool.' She stroked and patted my hand with a finger to show me the way Mims would spread the sticky wool-fat on a cut or a burn '—the best kind of medicine to soothe and heal. Mims could mend a sore almost by willing it so.' I recalled her rooted sighs as she remembered that feeling.

I knew now. In spite of the washing, sheep scent still clung to my skin.

"But the babies—" She'd stopped, sipped a quick breath. "—sweet, pure, fuzzy babies...I had my own lamb, you know." I couldn't see her sad smile, but felt it, and finished the story she couldn't: "A coyote killed the mother and you raised the lamb on a bottle. I liked that story." I knew she would skip the part about Pap throwing it out in mid-winter. She'd whispered me to sleep with the clatter of noisy hooves clamoring over my dreams, her own swift feet in tow.

I wanted her back—my old mom. Not the wreck that snapped or cried or sat silently stirring her coffee until it was too cold to drink. I wanted her like she was before. *That* mother—I wanted *that* mother back.

I murmured to nobody, "The lambs were born in March. Sabion calls them teenagers, now." His soft song filtered through the night. I strained to hear the occasional pluck of a guitar string that kept the long notes in harmony. I didn't understand the words, but it sounded sorrowful, and I thought of Dad.

The curtains billowed inward like a spoon. Each gust filled the room with cold. How can the night be so cool when the day is so hot?

I flipped onto my side, curled in a ball under the covers, spun in the blanket until it tightened around me, but still my feet felt like popsicles. I didn't want to move from my niche, the warm sunken spot in the middle of the bed, but if I didn't get up and close that window I would never get to sleep. I could just see Pap finding me frozen between the sheets in the morning, and saying, "She had no business being here anyway."

Just get up and shut the stupid window!

I rolled out of bed. A board squeaked under my feet. I

grabbed the ballooning curtains and pressed them behind me, latched onto the frame to slam the window shut, but the stark night stopped me.

The stars!

Mom never told me about the stars.

I was locked in a world of twinkling life—winks and flutters, one movement backlit by another, while Sabion sang softly from a place near the barn. I searched every faint flutter where fissures gathered and rifts collided, so distinct as to stem my breathing. Cold blew through my shirt, but I couldn't be moved from the glimmering sky, one star tapping messages to another.

I'd never paid much attention to the sky at home—not in Seattle, where clouds patrolled the sky. How can you miss something you've never known? I wanted to push my bed under the window and rake in the night, but reluctantly pulled the window closed, and crawled back to bed where I dropped in and out of the same drizzling, fitful dream that never had an end —scenes I'd packed away but sometimes thundered at me when the night took over and the air was still—the ones where Dad yelled and Mom cried. The ones just before he went away. It woke me. It always did.

How could sheep be a reason to leave Texas? How could he hate them so? Maybe he just didn't give them a chance. Sudden whammies can stop a life in a huge way. I'd never imagined it would come to divorce. It took a while to realize he wasn't coming home, that he had cut the country bumpkin loose, and the kid.

Maybe that's how Dad felt about West Texas and the sheep. I wished I could tell him to look for what he couldn't see, that West Texas might be a lot like the sky. Not so empty after all. What's he doing now?

I hope he's lonely, too.

Chapter Five

Rowdy snarled under my window.

"Go away," I grumbled as his guttural growls shifted into snappy, pitching yips. Crunching my eyes tighter, I willed myself back to sleep, even as the dream began to fade. One swift roll furled me into the blanket that turned with me. Rowdy's growls grew hostile. Pap's cough hit a strangulation note.

"Great. An alarm-dog." I cracked one eye. A faint hue flushed the room. "Why does it have to be *my* window?" Chucking back the covers, my feet hit the floor. I slid the window up, and my gritty morning voice lashed out. "You're just not gonna quit until I get up, are you!"

Rowdy turned his face up to me and fanned the air with his tail.

"Don't smile at me!" I wiped the sleep from my eyes, drew a breath. "You can be very annoying, you know that?"

The stars had vanished behind the gray milk of morning, the field was subdued in its pre-dawn blur. No air stirred, yet I shivered. "Okay, okay. I'm up." I shushed him. "Don't bark. Pap will eat you for breakfast."

Rowdy perked his ears to the driveway. I leaned my fore-head into the heat-scorched screen that smelled of grunge and rust. A pale ray of color nibbled the fence. "I agree. It's pretty."

Two, three quick barks, he shot across the yard and disap-peared in a pallid haze that painted everything murky: the long row of fence that wound with the driveway, the crooked gate Pap had left open, the horse the color of smoke that clomped through the stillness like vapor, as if the morning had mythically breathed out.

I swiped the screen, took a step back.

"Horse?" I scouted the corral where Tessa munched from a feed bag outside the pen, where Jennie stood among the sheep, ears flickering like fishing rods.

"Pap doesn't have a horse!"

Soft gold exploded over the hill glossing the world with the first rays of morning. I dove over the bed, shoved my feet into flip-flops, burst through the kitchen and out the screen door where Rowdy met me, whining, whooping, leaping.

"Sit!" I commanded with as much force as I could whisper. Adrenaline pumped as I raced past the tall tree that stood guardian over the yard. Rowdy pranced on my heels, yelping like a foghorn in my ears.

"*Grr—*" I spun, hissed, "Rowdy! Don't spook him!"

Slowing, stealthily, as if gliding on wheels, I shuffled along the fence. A strong pulse hammered in my temples, the crunch of gravel echoing so loudly I felt it could've been heard on the moon.

A dark gray horse stood motionless like a vertical column pushed up from the ground. I stilled my panting, slowed my roll, held out my hands, my breath so shallow there might have been none. I took ten inching steps forward, gulped air through a mouth moist with drool.

The horse reeled his head toward me and pitched his ears.

I took a step closer. "Tell me you're not a dream—"

The black tail swished and I knew...I *knew* it was him. I tiptoed delicately, not wanting to startle him. "You're the horse Pap and I passed in the road." A tremor shook my voice. "You found me."

The first shaft of sunlight streaked over the hillside to burn away the haze and gobble up the night's cool. I shuffled three steps more, while Rowdy jumped wide loops in and out and around us both.

My breath quickened. *Almost there.*

His right fore-leg shuddered. He rolled his neck—deep-shadowed eyes skimmed mine and moved on.

I flipped a hand, palm up, as if to say, *Here, kitty, kitty.* The flat of my hand met the velvet of his nose—soft as a new-born puppy. "I've always wanted a horse like you." A light rumble rose from his throat, a vibration that spilled through my hands, and I thought my heart would burst.

He didn't flinch when I cupped his satin chin. Neither did he shy when I traced a hand along his face to the rigid cartilage of his ears. He didn't brace or turn away when I smoothed a wrinkle of soft neck skin, but stood patiently while I slipped a hand under the weight of tangled mane that hung like jewelry and sunk a handprint into the deep, swarthy coat still cool with night.

"You've come a long way fella." Two days, he'd walked.

From the corner of my eye I saw the silhouette step slo-mo from the sheep pen. Sabion lifted a curl of rope to his shoulder, shoved the other hand low in his pocket and sauntered unhurriedly forward. The horse between us, Sabion motioned me back with a slice of hand.

I whispered with as much calm as my crazed, whooping-up-and-down insides could muster, "Did you see? He walked right to me!" I beamed meaningfully, nodded warp-speed, but

Sabion's face conveyed nothing. "He came right up to me and let me touch him!"

The horse pushed the length of his face into my shoulder and nudged me off balance. Joy rushed through my veins. "He's not even frightened!" I chuckled. "At all!"

Slowly, Sabion slipped the lariat loosely around the horse's head.

"I already know what I'm going to name him. Radar. He'll be an excellent horse."

Sabion's mouth drew a tight line. Grave eyes peered across the horse like pinpoints. "Radar," he repeated, his voice a quiet monotone.

I nodded. "Because he came right up to me, like he has radar! And it wasn't even actually completely all the way light yet!"

Sabion shook a finger. "Carlota, you give this horse a name but you cannot claim him. Where he belongs, we do not know. Somebody come—" His hand snatched the air. "—and he will be gone. You will be too sad." He smoothed a hand down the horse's neck.

Radar muffled my palms. "I'd be happy for him to find his home. I'd never want to lose such a beautiful animal." The thought was bittersweet, because I was already building visions...feed him, comb him, ride him. I couldn't *wait* for full daylight and I could take him all over the ranch.

I combed Radar's forelock with my fingers. "I always knew I'd have a horse someday. My friend has a horse that some-times...Oh, never mind." Pap didn't want to hear it and neither would Sabion.

"What you know of horses?" He pushed a flock of dusty hair back under his hat.

Now *I* was indignant. "I've been around...them. Some. And I've read everything, *everything* about horses." I'd never owned so much as a goldfish, but of horses I'd always fantasized.

Sabion shook his head. "Stories—"

"I took a subscription to a horse magazine for two years. Two!"

"Mm." He shook his head, a warning. "Do not start to love this horse."

"You like him, too. I can tell."

Sabion tightened the lariat, hesitated to appraise him. "Where you come from, big fella?"

Radar's blowbacks fell across my neck. "I bet he's thirsty." I suggested, gently. "And probably very hungry,"

Sabion clicked his tongue, tugged slightly. Radar obediently followed him to the sun-bleached barn that wore no color. He never once pulled back or tossed his head or stomped his feet.

I pranced after them like a six-year-old birthday girl.

He drank heavily from the sheep trough. "We should give him some of what Tessa's eating."

Sabion nodded. "For now, Tessa will share." Pulling the feed bag away from the mule, he spilled a portion of oats into a pail and set the bucket on the ground in front of him. Tessa slapped her ears back and cut her eyes sideways. Radar wavered his head and sniffed the ground, while sheep milled at the gate.

"If you have to go, I'll keep a good watch over him." I jerked back as the bucket of oats toppled. Sabion looked from me to Radar to the spilled oats. "I guess he doesn't like buckets," I chuckled.

Sabion pulled Radar's head up and stared hard into the face that paid him no mind, never blinking or flinching or bothering to look back. He clapped his gloved hands together and parted them outward to either side, then billowed his arms like jumping jacks.

Nothing startled the horse. I laughed. "What are you doing?"

"This caballo, he do not blink. He do not shy from arms that move like that." Fumbling with his hat string, he whipped it off and flared the air.

Radar found the oats on the ground and nibbled hungrily.

"I couldn't hope for a more calm horse." I stroked his dusty neck and gauged his height. Measured my own.

Sabion picked up a rock the size of a golf ball, clasped onto the rope, and threw it hard against the barn.

Radar staggered in a flash of panic. I spun at Sabion. "What'd you do that for?" I could practically hear Radar's heart hammering. "Were you *trying* to scare him?" I lunged forward to steady something...myself maybe?

"The horse," Sabion reached and patted. "—Radar, he do not blink because...because este caballo es ciega."

Cupping an elbow in each hand and tucking my arms fast against me, I asked, "What?"

"¿No entiendes?" He took a step back. "The horse, he is blind."

My heart lost a beat. "Blind?" The words clanged behind my eyes. "No way. Ridiculous!" *Cruel, even.* "How can you say such a thing? He walked right up to me. To me! He saw me and walked—. He did!" I pointed down the long, meandering drive, picked the word from my ears, sucked back the loose breaths that escaped through the hiccups that exploded in my chest, met the narrowest slice of Sabion's vacant gaze with a fist in my gut. "You're trying to take him away from me!" My jaw ached from the clench.

Sabion eyes dropped over the hat he held rigid in his fists, to the small stones that littered the ground.

"Pap and I saw him on the road on our way back from the airport." I pointed the way to Lubbock, and wished away the pity that waited for me to understand. "He followed me! All this way! How can you say he's blind? You probably saw him, straight down that—" The words floated the way pollen drifts.

Sabion shook his head sadly. "Si, Carlota. He walk to...to Rowdy. He walk to the bark of Rowdy." The sadness in Sabion's eyes made hearing it worse.

My tongue felt like a marshmallow, so full in my mouth. I shut my eyes, but Sabion repeated as if I hadn't heard. "The horse, he hear Rowdy. He follow the barking noise. Yes, like radar."

I focused on the white pebble under Radar's left hoof. I'd noticed the dullness in his eyes. I could manage only a whimper. "Are you sure?"

"Si, little sprout. I am certain. I am very sorry, Carlota. But I know this caballo, he cannot see."

Even now I knew he was right, perhaps had known it all along. The horse had moved toward sound. I folded my hands around Radar's muzzle and watched our summer slip away, because, in the breath of time since Radar stepped to my hand, I'd already planned our exploits, our long, loping excursions.

I drew a new thought. "So what if he did make his way to the house because of Rowdy's bark, first he had to find this blasted ranch. And that has nothing to do with a yapping dog." No long, dry road could stop Radar from finding me.

I wiped my nose on my sleeve. "We'll call a vet!" I yawped.

Pap stepped from the barn's shadow. "You're not calling no vet."

I whipped. "But, Pap—"

"He got here, he can get somewhere else." Pap discarded the horse with a swish and a hand joggle. "Take him away," he told Sabion.

Heat stung my eyes. "Pap, don't you see? He came to...to get help! Let me help him. You never know." Pap's gritty glare gagged me. I brushed the tears aside. I was running on empty. "We can *try.*" What could make a man so hostile that he wouldn't help a helpless animal?

"Turn him out when you take the sheep. Maybe those coyotes will leave the lambs alone for once."

My chest held a scream. It was coming loose. Pap locked eyes on the speckled rump, and that seemed to anger him all over again. He turned back to Sabion, his mouth bunched. "Or, share a bullet—"

My knees caved. "No!" I grabbed his arm and jerked it hard. "You're not going to shoot my horse!" I was incredulous that he would think the horse's life is worth nothing just because he's blind!

He ripped his arm free, clamped a thick paw on the top of my head. "Your horse?"

"Yes! This horse came to be mine. I know it. He chose me. I won't let you shoot him." There was gravel in my voice.

Sabion looked down, away.

Radar's breaths warmed my neck, making me even more determined. Maybe Sabion was right, Carlota means strong. I'd never felt strong. Did an instinct to protect a defenseless animal make a person strong? It all made sense now: Saving Radar is what brought me to Texas...to stand in the way of Pap's bullet. What a bold test.

"You don't know what you're doing," he whooped, eyes flickering from me, but pausing on Sabion. "Just what do you expect to do with a blind horse?"

"I—I—I'll train him!"

Pap's face turned flushing red. "To do *what?*"

"He...he can herd sheep!" I blathered without thought.

The laughter hurt. A stream of tears ran hot over my cheeks. Pap jerked his head to Sabion, his expression full of meaning. "Get rid of him."

Every passion I'd held in check for the past six months exploded in this dry hole in Nowhere, West Texas. Fire broke in me. I plugged my ears with my fingers hands, as if *that* would squash the shriek that made Radar throw his head back so that Sabion had to grab the rope and hang on. The sheep excited.

My heart pumped so savagely I thought my brain would explode. There it was, all over again—no control. I never had control. *Over anything.* When I'd cut and run for Texas I'd felt just as helpless, in just as lonely a place. Now I could see—I didn't leave helpless and lonely behind. I brought it with me. I knew what surrender looked like. It had changed me, but not in the way anybody had in mind. Now I saw Pap as a threat... maybe what Mom had tried to warn me about. I wouldn't surrender again.

Pap and I squared off like how we met at the airport. But this time, my teeth were clenched and my toes made a fist. Like when Dad walked out. The words unraveled, words with no regret. "You're a miserable 'ol fart—just like Mom said! No wonder she left this place and never looked back."

Sabion cut shocked eyes away from me. He'd be no help after all.

Pap's finger curled like a mustache over his lip. He muttered, "I s'pose a miserable 'ol fart is some better than a bad f..."

"So, why did you even pay my way to Texas?" He raised his chin as if to answer, but no words came out. "If you kill my horse I will go home, and I will always think of *this* when—no, *if* I ever think of you again! I mean it. Mom didn't even want me to come here. I'm old enough to stay by myself. I'm the one who wanted it. I wanted to get to know you, who you were. I—"

"The horse has no life."

"That's plain silly."

"I don't have a choice." He gnawed the inside of his cheek.

"There's always a choice."

"He's blind as a brick-bat."

"And I'm short. I hope you're not around if I need glasses—you'd shoot me?" Radar was tall and intimidating but he didn't frighten me. Pap did.

Two fingers twitched on Pap's thigh. Steely eyes held mine in a challenge that I returned with iron. "Don't be ridiculous. A blind horse can't protect himself. A mountain lion will take him down—it'll happen, you know." There was a tic in his jaw. "How will you feel then, knowing your horse couldn't get up while gristly teeth chew into his ribs? Shooting him is a far cry more compassionate than getting ripped to shreds piece by piece."

My feet tingled as if I were standing on stobs. I blinked through the wait, grappling for an answer to that.

His arms flared. "The country's wild. A lamb wouldn't last an hour before it'd be chops in a coyote's belly. Even its mother would run away, knowing it couldn't survive. How'd you put it when you saw this country from the safety of the truck for the very first time? Only the fit? Looks like you understood that right away."

He had more excuses than me. "Maybe somebody's looking for him, right now!" I offered. "Maybe he's lost. How would you feel if your pet got lost? Wouldn't you want somebody to help him and bring him back home?"

"I don't want a horse to begin with, blind or with six eyes." He turned his back dismissively, and I knew I'd failed.

But he took no steps.

A slender breeze tickled the spreading tree making the thin leaves rustle like dry paper.

"One week," Pap said. "Find somewhere else for him to go."

Close to hyperventilating, I steepled my hands over my mouth. "A month!" I countered. When he hesitated, I bawled,

"I just got here. I don't know where to begin. It might take a day, it might take a month! Just...just give me a little time."

He bent, stretched a hand to his knee and kneaded the knob of it. "Find where that horse belongs, quick. If nobody claims him, then that's it—I have my way. In the meantime, you best keep him outta my way." He hobbled to the house, fluffs of dirt swirling and settling. The kitchen screen door squeaked open, slammed shut, wood on wood.

The breath I'd been holding poured out. "Okay then!" I shouted after him, on tiptoes. "I'll show you!" I wiped the crust from my eyes. Sabion scrunched beneath his hat like a turtle tucking into its shell. "I'll show him."

A blue dragonfly settled on the tip of Radar's ear. Long wings wagged the air, just enough to keep it balanced. It stared at me, dark eyes shiny and flickering and fascinating.

Sabion's cough broke the air. "Um. Señor, he is a hard man some days."

"The way I've always heard it, he's a hard man every day."

I ripped my phone from my pocket and scrolled through the calendar. "One month...July 28th—a Thursday." Did Pap even know that? Sure he did. Probably has a poster-board size calendar hanging over his bed with big, fat, red checkmarks ticking off the days until he gets to drive me back to Lubbock. 'See ya, kid!'

I had to find Radar's owner by July 28th, or convince Pap that Radar was worth saving. If I didn't, I'd return to Seattle in hate with Pap.

No time to waste. I would find someone who would help. "Wait and see, Sabion." I shoved the phone in my pocket. "Radar will be the best horse on the ranch!"

Sabion rolled his eyes. "Ah, si. He is the only caballo on this ranch."

"Well, until I find the owner, I'll take care of him!" I

plunked my hands on my hips and twisted enough to aim my big mouth at the kitchen window from where Pap was probably watching. "And if something happens to him," I shouted. "I'm outta here!"

* * *

Rowdy sat ready. The donkey fished her way to the front. Radar's ears pricked to the noisy sheep packed tight at the gate. With a skip and a hop, Sabion flung onto Tessa's bare back, and the shrill whistle punched the air. One well-positioned kick and the gate sprung open.

The herd rushed for the gate. Jennie brayed, loud and bossy. Radar startled to the pounding of so many stammering feet, as from a start line. He stomped, smashing Tessa's feedbag flat. Rowdy circled the pen until he'd pushed the last ewe out.

Sabion gestured for me to lead Radar into the vacant corral. "You will find oats in a barrel in the barn. Give the horse a little more for his breakfast. What he ate is not so many." He urged the mule forward with a modest thrust.

A whippoorwill called after the dwindling sheep. I gawked after the retreating man Mom said I could count on, the man Pap told me fixes things. The one who knows everything about animals.

"Wait!" The tightness in my lungs forced the word out like a shriek.

Sabion spun Tessa to face me with a look as if confronting a wounded animal. "Que?" he asked, not impatient, but the word landed with such weight that my request stuck under my tongue. "What?" he repeated. A pregnant glow of sunlight lifted from the hilltop and formed a glowing halo around his hat.

I swilled a breath. "Fix this." An ache welled in my eyes as he regarded me with understanding and pity, unease and misgivings. "This horse needs me," I said. "And I need you."

He cut his eyes to the house, then to the scurrying flock. A gloved hand splayed open and closed around Tessa's reins, while I counted the seconds like guilt on my shoulders and wished for a breeze, a shade, a cloud—away from the grief that filled Sabion's face.

His head dipped beneath the oversized brim. "I do not know, Carlota." His head shook slowly. "I do not think this horse can fix. I am very sorry."

Heat prickled under my arms. I took a step toward his stained leather chaps, the split toe of his boot, the snap torn from his shirt pocket. "Help me train him. I'll do all the work if you will just get me started." My lips were dry. "I will never again beg Pap."

Sabion hesitated, just long enough.

"Besides, he didn't say I couldn't. He just said I didn't know what I was doing." I sought the eyes under his hat. "He might be right about that." A slip of perspiration slid down my spine.

Tessa stomped a hind leg restlessly, and I stepped away. Fidgeting, his shoulders hunched, his words were careful. "Perhaps you papa do not keep this caballo so long to teach. Who can know? What if this horse go home today?"

I nudged a toe in the stony soil. "That would be best, but, I have a doubt." I looked up. "And Pap does, too, or he wouldn't be so eager to kill him."

Sabion's eyes were on me, thoughtful and still. I searched his face for a signal or warning...a clue that I might be right.

"Even I can see that Radar's been loved. I promise I will try to find his owner."

Rowdy barked in the distance. The heavy sigh that filled Sabion's mouth slowly seeped out. He pushed back the broad rim of his hat.

"Okay, Carlota. I will keep the sheep not so far today. Tessa will stay to watch over them, and I will return for a little time. We will make a plan."

I clasped my hands.

With a nod and a press of his kerchief to his brow, Sabion twisted the reins and spurred Tessa after the wheeling dust from the fading herd.

I climbed the sheep pen rails and shouted, as if from this height my voice would reach him. "Thank you!" I waved. "We'll be waiting!" I cupped the silk of his chin...his whiskers like pinpricks on my palms. The contact, like holding hands.

Radar blew a breath with no flutter. I raked the dirt-crusted forelock away from his eyes and drank in the silence the herd left behind.

"Oats!"

Chapter Six

Old barns hold great stuff, and I'd been antsy to get in there. Chips of by-gone paint clung to the sun-bleached sides giving it a strangled, uncared-for look that matched everything else on the ranch. The barn was so cool I would never have ever painted it in the first place!

The wide doors yawned open, slapped shut behind me like a shotgun firing. Splintered light cascaded through a towering rooftop that plummeted down and outward over shadowy compartments to either side. I waited for my vision to correct to the din.

The air was still, the place stuffy,\no air moving. Jennie's stall lay to my right, just inside the doors. Tessa's big bay stood directly across with a view of the sheep pen if the doors were propped open. A flagstone corridor anchored the two halves down the center, like a backbone. I couldn't imagine this building had ever known a new-barn smell; the rancid tang of deterioration whooped with proof that I might be right. I pinched my nose.

My footsteps left no sound as I followed the littered pathway cased with plugs of dried sheep muck, many hearts beating at once. Donkey and mule leavings gave the barn a pulse.

I ticked off the compartments I passed: tools, fencing supplies, hay bales stacked to the ceiling. Empty feed sacks lay in a scatter. A layer of dust covered everything. The next berth was wide and deep and filled with barrels as clunky as minion soldiers. The oats would be here.

Wiping the hair out of my eyes and shooing a fly, I pushed the gate forward, but it stuck. Jiggling the latch, I leaned into the handle and almost laughed. The gate's locked? "Afraid somebody's gonna steal a bucket of oats, Pap?" I grabbed a flyswatter, kicked off my flip-flops and climbed, pausing to let my eyes wander over the stall. A tangle of turquoise-stained leather hung from a hook at the narrow doorway at the rear of the stall. I knew what it was.

I was alone. *Sabion said—*

I knew what I was going to do. I wouldn't ask. I'd let Pap see Radar wearing that beautiful halter before he whooped out a resounding, *No!* Sabion's mule and donkey didn't need it. And the blue-green would look perfect on Radar's mottled coat. More important, I could get rid of that stiff lariat before Pap decided to hang him with it.

I dropped to the cool sand below and began shoving and pushing my way through the barrels with a singular thought: Get that halter!

My fingers resting on the frame of the small room before me, I leaned through the door for a quick peek.

A cozy space unlike anything else on the ranch I'd seen. A long wooden plank the length of a car formed a countertop of a workbench built low to the ground. A workroom? For Sabion? I left the halter hanging and stepped through the doorway.

Paint splatters gave the space a good vibe, as if somebody had just stepped out of their shoes. A five-drawer column dropped down one side from the counter. A pair of cabinets hung so high overhead they might as well have been nailed to the rafters. One of the cupboard doors hung loose on a broken hinge and a spider had sewn a cobweb the size of my head across the opening. Blowing wind had smeared everything with dirt and grim, and birds and mice had left their scatter all over the workbench.

I smacked the ratty droppings onto the ground with the flyswatter and swung the cabinet wide, severing the web anchored there. A sprinkling of feathers fell on the counter.

Miniature paint cans lined the bottom shelf: red, yellow, white, black, blue. The lids were rusted shut though the colors were still vivid on the paper wrappings. I shook a yellow can. Powder. Why didn't he just throw them away? The same colors dappled the countertop.

I lifted a handful of paintbrushes from an old tin coffee can. The bristles were soft, so at least he knew how to take care of his brushes. I rapped the swatter on my knee, *tap...tap...tap.* They didn't know I'm a good organizer. I could see where I might be of some use. It was just the kind of go-to place I would love to call my own. Obviously, Sabion didn't use it any longer.

I raised on my tip-toes to get a better look at a display case on a higher shelf. Belt buckles. The kind cowboys win in their rodeos. I couldn't reach them.

Radar bumped against the doors; he was moving in the corral. The taste of dust was growing in my mouth. I turned for a last look, helped myself to a curry comb, swung the cabinet door closed. Snatching the halter off its hook, I backed away. I would check this place out later—a summer project. This might be a good place to stay out of Pap's way. One day he would find it all cleaned up and remember me long after I'm gone. I tucked the floppy loops of halter against me.

* * *

I parked Radar beside the fence and started combing the grit from his mane. His coat was healthy beneath all the road dust, only a hint of ribcage showing. "No telling how long you've been walking." I freed a knot on his forelock, looked into eyes that couldn't see mine.

I mimicked Sabion. "Where you come from, big boy?" His brows knitted at my words; deep rumbles bubbled from his throat. I chuckled. "What? You know what I'm saying?"

Nothing about Radar frightened me. He felt like an old pal, uncannily familiar, as if I knew he was coming. He never shied from my touch, but closed his eyes and basked in my touch. "That mess this morning, with Pap, that was all just a big misunderstanding. We might be outcasts around here, but we're not renegades."

I climbed the rails to get to his haunches and found myself eye-level with his back. Leaning in, I stretched to reach the top of his tail. It wasn't even a step. I couldn't *not* do it, balanced as I was. Seizing a handful of mane, I cocked a heel over his rump.

Radar's head jerked up, swung backwards. Nostrils squeezed something in, poured it out noisily. I wheeled with him, a foot dangling mid-air, and caught my breath. "Pap!"

Pap regarded Radar as though he wished him dead through eyes that might well be empty except for the dank fog that filled them. "Don't get close to that horse." His voice was deep and raspy, as though he'd just woken.

"I didn't hear you. I thought you were—" I glanced at the kitchen screen door I hadn't heard bang. "—somewhere."

"Where's Sabion?"

"He left with the sheep. A little late...so much...going on."

"That won't happen again." He bent his head to the corral, along the fence, as if looking into the meadow.

"He'll be back soon. He's coming back to help me with—"

Pap made no move toward me, or Radar, or away from us either. He offered no advice, or help. He didn't pretend to be busy in the corral.

I scampered down, reached for an excuse. "I...there were so many flies. I was..." I shrugged. "The flies."

He chewed his lip and mulled the lame comment. "That's a load of crap. Something a ten-year-old might say."

"I was combing him and got carried away," I said weakly.

"You think this horse is yours because you found him? You're like one of those gullible lambs. There's a reason Sabion told you what he did."

Pap was an imposing man. No wonder Mom never talked about him. I just didn't realize there was so much of nothing to talk about.

I raised my chin; my voice got louder. "Animals are like people. They need love, too. They know who cares about them."

He blinked through the squints, while crickets scratched in the corner. "Humph. That's something your grandmother would've said."

I scurried down from the rail, wiped the wild forelock that fell over Radar's eyes, and swiped the bangs from my own.

"Go eat your breakfast," he said gruffly. His brows folded. "And, by gosh, why aren't you dressed?"

I looked down at the shorts and shirt I'd slept in and shrugged. "This really isn't much different from what I'd change into. Sabion's going to help me—" His look stopped me. "I don't eat much breakfast. A yogurt, maybe."

"A what?"

"Or a banana. A banana and peanut butter sandwich sounds great. I'll make you one, too."

"We're fresh out of bananas," he snapped. "We have oats."

I glanced at the bucket Radar had licked clean. "Thanks, but I'll pass."

"No, you won't. You're not in Seattle anymore. We eat breakfast around here. It's on the stove, getting cold." His tone was gritty and halting. "What're those things on your feet?"

"Flip-flops."

He squinted, as if seeing with his ears. The gate squeaked open, sprung closed.

"It wasn't my fault that—" I hollered after him, trying to recall exactly how that had worked out. I threw down the comb and followed, reciting to myself in my head: I'm not afraid of him. I'm not afraid of anything! Hadn't I made that promise to myself before I ever left Seattle: I would form my own opinions, not draw from the blueberry answers Mom had rehearsed all my life. Hadn't I determined I would make a difference in this family? Mom might've disowned him...I wouldn't.

But now, I could see where keeping that promise might be like climbing Mt. Rainier. How long would I have to protect this horse?

* * *

The screen door smacked my heels. Pap pulled a pan from the oven with a dishcloth wrapped around his hand. Char filled my nose; my hands flew to my mouth. "You burned the toast!" My stomach turned over.

Pap shooed the smoke away with the dishrag. A plate hit the table and clattered to a stop. "Sink toast," he snapped. "A little scrape and it's perfectly good."

I opened the refrigerator: A half a sack of potatoes. One onion. No fruit. Nothing green or yellow or red. Not a single vegetable, fresh or frozen. What had he been living on since Mims died?

I could fix it with a few groceries. I imagined six months ago Mims would've dried her cooking hands in the apple-speckled apron Mom said she always wore, wrap me in a doughy hug, and ask me what I wanted for lunch.

A peanut butter and banana sandwich.

In the pantry I found tuna...crackers...tea bags. Nothing with electrolytes. That's what's wrong with Pap. He needed electrolytes.

I sunk to the edge of the chair, gawked at the black bread smoking in front of me. A little scrape and it's perfectly good? That's not what Dad said when Mom burned the toast! when he stomped out and left everything behind: Mom and me, a car that guzzled gas, and the pile of bills in a stack on the counter that meant Mom would have to work all those extra hours just to steer clear of the desperation I saw in her eyes. The memory blistered up.

It took me a long time to realize he wasn't coming back.

Pap plucked the crud off my plate like a lion reluctant to share his booty, carried it to the sink, and scratched the layer of burn off in the basin with the flat of a knife.

"There!" He tossed it back on my plate. "Haven't had to do *that* in a long time." He plopped an oversized bowl of oatmeal beside it. The spoon stood straight up in its middle, as if in a vat of ice cream.

I looked past him out the small, square kitchen window above the sink—only slightly larger than the airplane's tiny pane where Mom didn't know I saw her standing behind the tall windows in her snug jeans and wild honey-colored shirt that shimmered against the black, black shine of her hair. She couldn't know the ache that washed over me when her forehead tipped against the glass and she closed her eyes.

I might've been back in that tiny apartment where I chose to ignore her when she finally did come home from work. Glad that she had to sit in the same empty silence. Frustrated that there was nothing I could do to change it.

I never asked what it did to her.

I never let her see me watching.

I tried not to know. She thought I didn't care?

Pap looked from the bowl, to me, to the window, back to the table. Maybe he was more like Dad than anybody knew: Sit here. Be a meek little princess.

Princess, pffft! I'd outgrown that that shiny, pink, gleaming, plastic phase in, like, a week. It worked until it didn't. My feet never really fit in those shoes.

I flecked a crusty edge from the toast. "Burnt toast runs in the family?" I felt the scowl change my face, pull my mouth in a knot, and inched the plate across to Pap's side of the table. "You shouldn't have burned the toast!" Dad wouldn't be stomping out of our rooms anymore, with his new life in a new place nobody knows about.

Where would I stomp to?

Pap tossed the dishcloth six feet to the sink. It landed like a sour thing.

I dug the spoon from the bowl. "Are there raisins?"

He glared at the bowl. "Probably not."

"Never mind." I waggled a gummy bite onto the spoon and scraped it off with my teeth. It grew on my tongue. My stomach made a fist. I laid the spoon down. "I'm really not hungry."

"You'll get that way."

"Where's yours? Aren't you eating?"

"I already did."

"Whose belt buckles are those in the barn?"

His eyes glowered over his coffee cup.

I frowned across my milk, slapped the empty glass down with a clunk. "Why do you hate Radar?"

His expression blurred to static. "Radar? How do you know

his name?" His eyes were hard, the green centers piercing...the whites a shade hazy.

I had to turn away. "I named him."

Neither of us smiled, my stomach in knots. I pushed my chair back. "I'm going to make my bed. If you'll write down the names and phone numbers of your neighbors, I'll start calling."

I took the oatmeal and toast to Rowdy's bowl and dumped it, rinsed my utensils, turned and faced Pap, arms folded. "And if you don't give me a chance to find this horse's owner and somebody's pet gets shot, I'll make sure everybody in Texas knows who did it!"

I stopped in the doorway. "Ha! Dad doesn't even know we don't have burned toast anymore. *We* got bagels." I dashed away to a long eruption of breath escaping.

It was his.

Chapter Seven

Snitches of white streaked the Texas sky. The air smelled different from ever-drippy Seattle, with none of the blooming mold that grew in the Northwest...no drizzling rain puddling from the roof, no screeching cars sliding to a stop, no lawnmowers shouting at my window.

I'd squeezed one name and number from Pap and made the call. Though the lady was pleased to meet me over the phone, she had no information about a blind horse. She was much more interested in my mother: Was Miriam with me? What was she doing nowadays? When was she coming back? "We all miss her," she'd said.

Good. I really didn't want to find Radar's owner, anyway. *Yet.*

Sabion's eyes winked over the halter Radar wasn't wearing when he left. His head tilted like when he'd first seen Radar.

"I found it," I rushed to explain what he hadn't asked. "Tessa and Jennie don't need it. Radar does. He can use it, right?"

The corners around Sabion's eyes softened. "Hm." He

rubbed his jaw with the back of his hand. "I think I know where is a lead rope like the same pretty color."

I followed Sabion down the corridor, his musical spurs clicking, my flip-flops popping on the stones. He swept the barn with the broad of his arm. "Is a big place, heh?"

We stopped at the gate where I'd found the oats. "We feed two times a day." He raised two fingers. "Grain. Hay. Morning...afternoon. And this—" He wagged a finger at the gate. "—this, you must keep locked always, because this is the place where Jennie like best. She like to knock over the feed barrel and eat too much the oats. So much make her very sick."

He bent, motioned me close. "The unlock number," he whispered, as if Jennie might learn something. "—is two...one...two...one." He threw the bolt from its latch. Metal pinched metal, like a buzzsaw in my ears.

Sabion looked back and grinned. "Eh? What I tell you? Jennie know this sound!"

Jennie lumbered toward us as though summoned, eyes cemented on Sabion, her white muzzle pinched as if she might sneeze.

"She is very clever to get inside. She can loose a knot with her teeth, or open a latch if it is not locked. Oh, yes!" He answered the question I might've asked. "I do not teach her that." He tapped the side of his head. "My Jennie is muy intelligente. A little oil, I think this lock need."

But my eyes were on Radar, who was following Jennie, his nose pinned to her hip. "Sabion, look! She's leading Radar!"

He nodded. "Oh, si. Jennie is muy friendly." He opened the gate, motioned me in, slammed it closed quick, and threw the bolt.

"I mean...that means—" An idea blossomed. "Radar follows Jennie. I'll ride Jennie—you said I could—and lead Radar. That's how I'll train him!"

"O-kay," he said indifferently.

"But it's perfect! With Jennie's help, Radar and I can herd the sheep with you."

"Mm, no, Carlota. You think too far ahead. First is first. I plan that you make a stall ready for the horse. Even though you may find where the horse belong," He shrugged. "the stall will be clean! In case." He made a path through the kegs and returned with a loop of turquoise rope that matched the halter exactly.

"Were you a rodeo cowboy, Sabion?"

He grinned bashfully. "Si. What do you think? With my mula, and the sheep, I rodeo every day."

"I mean, did you compete?"

He shrugged. "Cowboy is the work of life. Rodeo is the glitter."

* * *

Dry manure lay like fossils strewn across the stall floor, splintered boards like broken teeth along the back wall. *"Where do I start?"*

"Ah!" Sabion took a step sideways. "The shovel. The rake. There, the wheelbarrow for to move the...the...mm...you know. And when there is no more of that—" He hooked the claw end of a hammer over a board. "There can be nothing sharp for the horse to bump on. No wire on the ground to catch a foot." He pounded a board. "You must hammer in or pull out all the popping nails so a blind horse do not get stuck with one. Nothing to surprise or frighten. It is most important to protect a no-see animal so he can feel safe."

"And when I'm finished cleaning the stall, then I can ride?"

"You have much to do. When you are ready to begin, I will show you—"

"I'm ready!"

His face made a scowl. "You are *not* ready." He swished a hand at my legs. "What do you have to cover your blank legs?"

I looked down, shrugged. "My shorts? This is what I brought! I packed for hot weather. You sound like Pap. I've got one pair of jeans but I'm saving them for when I need them."

He nodded. "You need them. You do not have the kind of skin for the hard sun. Inside you, there is no blood. No sunshine in you bones. You are very white, like milk."

"Am not." I stretched out an arm. *Er! Now I'm growing freckles on my arms?*

"You must have long pantaloons." He popped out a leg. "Long sleeves to cover you..." He stretched out his arm as if calculating its length. "A hat to swoop down over your head. And boose!"

"Boose?"

"Si." He kicked a foot up on the rail. "Boose!"

"In this heat? Why can't I wear a T-shirt?"

"You can. Under the long sleeve. You skin do not go brown," he said dotingly. "It go very, very red, and we both be in very much trouble." Grooves sunk across his forehead, a look as if to say, In this, you must listen. "You only wear that—" He pointed to my shorts. "— when you sit on the porch, or in the house, or under a tree, or...or...ride in the truck."

"Or work in the barn?" I chuckled.

"Hm. No. There is much here to get hurt with. Now, you go to put on you long pantaloons."

* * *

I dug through the drawers, shoved on the jeans, changed to a rayon blouse with three-quarter sleeves, and hurried back to the barn. "Okay?"

He slumped, leaned on his shovel, a look as if weighing the heat. "Miss Carlota—"

I bordered on frantic. "Well, I don't have any boots!"

"Okay-okay! Is okay." He palmed the air, tapped his lips. A gloved knuckle scratched a brow. He shook his head. "Mm...is no okay."

"Sabion!" Pap banged through the gate. "Go get that dumb donkey. Can't you control—" I dug my hands in the cargo pockets and struck a pose. Pap's eyes knotted over my Army-Navy camo jeans. "You going...huntin'?"

"Hunting? These aren't— Sabion said I had to wear long pants. So—" I kicked a heel in the dirt to show off my fluorescent lime-green sneakers...that I had on something other than flip-flops. "They're running shoes." I bit a fingernail.

Pap grunted. "You running somewhere?"

Sabion rolled a shoulder, cut his eyes sideways to Pap. "Is better, no?"

"Hell, no!"

My face flamed, but not red like Pap's.

Wrenching his neck, he told Sabion, "Go get that stupid donkey. She's opened the gate again and is making a mess at the trash can." then whirled back on me, slicking the air with both hands. "This won't work."

Sweat bled through my silky shirt. "Well, I didn't know I needed...then I don't have any clothes that are okay." I dodged the fly that buzzed my head. Pap quietly stewed. "Maybe you have some old overalls I could cut off?" I asked. "And very big safety pins?"

Pap blew a breath and noisily sucked up another. He studied his watch, lips pursed. "We're gonna have to go to town and get you some decent clothes. Gotta see that blasted vet anyway."

"Yes!" My hands clutched. "A vet will know who's lost a blind horse."

Pap flashed me a look that, were it a hand, would've made a fist. "Not about that! I gotta pick up worming medicine for the sheep."

"But I can ask—"

His jaw clenched and I knew—he didn't have to say it. Just when I thought he'd go to any lengths to make Radar disappear, he balks at helping make it happen. What's his problem? Did he mean to kill my horse after all, as soon as I leave? I wouldn't let that happen.

"You want Radar gone but won't do anything to help me? This is a lot of drama for one lost horse." A suspicion crossed my mind. "Do you know something about Radar that I don't?"

He took a step back, eyes narrowing, his voice low and cloudy. "You're chasing a dream. Young and stubborn will only get you in trouble."

"If that's how it starts, I know how it ends: Old and obstinate makes trouble for everybody else." A stupid fly landed on my sweaty forehead and I defied to move a single finger to shoo it off.

"We'll see about that." He stomped away; smut that kicked his heels may as well have been smoke.

I'd already bluffed him once and it almost melted my spine. About clothes, I'd have to give a little. I mean, who's going to see me? Heat or no heat, I'd be much less picky.

I'd have to be. There wasn't a shopping mall for a hundred miles.

* * *

One leg slack, a dip in his hip, Radar's ears either doled or flattened with each scrape of my shovel or squeak of the wheelbarrow that hauled the dingy hay. His head whipped when my cart tipped; he grumbled with me when I had to shovel poop twice.

I brushed dirt-dauber nests from the studs, pulled every jagged or rusty nail from the boards, mangled or crumpled stabs of wire back onto themselves like embroidery. Whoever invented rayon didn't know squat about Texas heat. The fabric sweated to my back, the sleeves clung to my arms. I heard a rip and looked down.

"My jeans! That does it!" I ran to the house and changed back into my shorts.

* * *

Sabion stood in the middle, hands to his hips and silently examined the floor, traced the rails, inch by inch. Finally, he gave me the nod.

I carried a water bucket into the stall and hung it from a hook, led Radar through the gate and closed him in, then planted myself beside Sabion, a death grip on the rail.

Radar stumbled into the pail at once and water sloshed everywhere. He plowed a circle, colliding with every wood panel, whacking the planks hard.

"Maybe he needs more space," I whispered.

"Wait. This horse make a map in his thinking."

Radar backed across and planted his rump against the rear wall. Boards creaked where he leaned. Sabion squalled, as if nails were popping out the other side.

Just when I thought this wasn't such a good idea, Radar dropped his head and started moving in a steady pattern, sniffing each step like a hound and blowing puffs through his nostrils.

"How long do you think he's been blind?" I asked. Sabion shrugged. "Do you think something happened to him?"

"Things go wrong, Carlota."

"Do you think he's in pain?"

He splayed his hands over the stall. "This horse, he is used to living like this. This horse, he is not sad. This, I can see."

"Do you suppose Jennie and Tessa know he's blind?"

Sabion looked incredulous. "Oh, si. You think animals do not know? They belong in the world as much as you and me. Maybe even, creatures are a test: if a person cannot take care of an animal who must depend upon them to survive, then maybe that person will be given no more good things in life to love." He shook his head as if shaking stupid from his ears.

"Phhft. Now you're talking about Pap who doesn't mind having a mean mule around, but won't take responsibility for a horse who really needs help."

Sabion's face folded. "Jennie, Tessa, they are mi family. Tessa, she is good to herd the sheep." He thought about that. "—except when the little lambs are born. Then I must watch her very careful. She is bad to cut the babies from their mamas and do not let them go back." He shrugged. "Maybe she take the little lambs because she need something of her own." A finger pressed back a smile. "She take very, very good care with them."

"Nobody's even stopped by to ask. You can see he's been well cared for. We know he's used to being around people. How could a blind horse get all the way here without water or food?"

"Very good grasses grow on the prairie. He eat like the sheep eat. And he find water to drink along the way, because, you see —" he chuckled. "He is still alive!"

Now Radar had a sense of the boundaries, and shifted around the stall easily. He came to a stop in front of me.

Jennie plowed through the gate of her stall, propped her nose on the top rail and pressed one eye to the slats. Long ears waved. Curling her lips back, she broke into a loud bray. Radar crossed his stall, flung his head over the rail that separated them and nuzzled the slope of her back.

Sabion chuckled. "See, I tell you my Jennie is happy. She likes her new buddy. She will help him."

A buddy, I thought. That's cute.

"Okay," I said brightly. "Now, I'm ready to ride."

Sabion laughed. "Tomorrow, you must do the same in the corral."

I balked, but he shook his head. "There is much responsibility with any animal, especially a horse like this one. He must know always what is where. Remember, nothing to catch the foot!"

Chapter Eight

I cubed the onion and potatoes and set them on to boil. The house smelled good when Pap came in and parked his hat on a kitchen hook. "What's this?"

"Lunch."

He glanced at the door. "Somebody here?"

"No. Why do you ask?" I ladled soup into two bowls. They looked pretty on the table.

"Who made this?"

"I did."

"You?"

I nodded. "I would've made something else—soup is kinda hot for a day like this, but," I opened the pantry door. "—you don't have much of anything. Potato soup is what you get."

He sat hard. "Where'd you learn that?"

I guffawed. "You're surprised? Good grief, I'm almost sixteen! Mom works. She can't do everything, you know. I can make lots of things. If you take me grocery shopping, I'll do better than this."

He picked up a spoon and dipped. The knotting in his

brows relaxed. "Tastes like your Mim's potato soup." He spooned another bite.

"That makes sense since it's Mims recipe and she taught Mom and Mom taught me." I shoved a tray of crackers toward him. "Why do you hike up that hill every day?" It was just a hill like all the others—brown and gristly, that grew nothing but rocks. "It's a long way up and down with that knee of yours." It wasn't really the walk that alarmed me, but the dead eyes that returned.

He didn't answer.

"I'm sorry. I don't mean to pry, but—"

"Then don't."

"It's just that if you fell—"

"I'm not gonna fall."

"I wouldn't know where to look if something happened."

"If something happens, just leave me lie."

I recognized in Pap the same fixed, vacant gaze I'd seen in Mom. It always sat me silent. Someday, I'd follow him and see for myself. Someday.

* * *

I couldn't wait for the phone to ring. At straight-up seven o'clock, I grabbed the receiver on the blast . "Hi, Mom. Guess what...I have a horse!"

"What?" The word rolled fluid through the phone.

"A horse!" I blurted. "A gorgeous gray Appaloosa. Maybe only for a little while, until we find his owner, but Sabion's going to help me train him so I can herd sheep. I wish you could see him. He's smart and gentle and gorgeous."

She cleared her throat. "Sabion?"

"No, not Sabion." I rolled my eyes. "Radar. The horse. I named him Radar. It's too bad there's no way to send pictures.

This phone is absolutely worthless—no reception anywhere out here at all. And believe me, I've tried." My words rushed together. "We're going to Quitaque tomorrow; I can send them then."

"Do you mean—" Her words were clean and measured. "Pap bought a horse?"

"No. It's the weirdest thing. The horse just showed up on the ranch all by himself. Which is mysterious, because he's blind. That's why I named him Radar, like a bat." I gulped a breath. "So, I've got a horse until I find his owner! He's beautiful. I love him. I've checked with a couple neighbors. So far, nobody claims him. Personally, I hope they never find him." Mom didn't respond so I added, "Pap's taking me to town tomorrow. Clothes shopping. He doesn't like mine. Said they're not appropriate."

The phone was silent—no sound, not a peep.

"Mom? You still there?"

When she spoke, I had to strain to hear. "I want you to come home."

"Home?" It wasn't what I expected. "I just got here. Why?"

"I think it's best."

"No! I just told you. I have a horse, even if it's only for a month! You know what that means to me." I glanced at the porch where Pap sat behind closed eyes, and stretched the cord around the doorway, lowering my voice to match hers. "Okay. I know, at first I had my doubts and wasn't so sure I wanted to stay. But now—" How could she even say that?

"I'll get your ticket."

"No!" I shouted, and held my breathe to the count of five to settle my beating heart that was pounding quicker and quicker. How could I explain what I didn't even understand myself?

"I can't." I cupped the mouthpiece and whispered, "I can't leave now. I have to be here. *Because* of Radar."

"Frankly, I'm surprised Pap allowed the horse to stay." Her voice sounded farther than the miles.

I pressed my forehead into the screen that smelled grimy. "That's why I can't come home." I squeezed my eyes, tight. "I... Pap wants him gone, all because he's blind. He said he'd shoot him."

The quick, breathy intake clipped her words. "Maybe it's not...because he's blind."

"Yes, it is." It came out hissy. "He thinks he's just another mouth to feed. I guess he feels that way about me, too." I imagined her clutching her throat—a breathing habit, like a pause. I rushed to add, "Radar is counting on me. Pap agreed to give me a month to find his owner. A month! If he shoots him before that, I'll walk home!"

"Stop this!" She didn't shout, but I heard it that way.

She *never* listened to me. How could I convince her to just *hear* me! "I can't! Pap will kill him. He means it!" She probably thought I was being melodramatic, but I was serious.

"Pap—" Her voice cracked. "—will kill him anyway." She sounded tired. "He won't let you keep that horse. Not after—" She blew her nose; it fluttered through the phone.

"After what?"

It was a real hesitation this time. "Let me put it this way, Pap and horses don't get along. Come home." The edge filled her voice, the edge I knew so well traveled the distance loud and clear.

I slapped the Formica counter. "That's not true. There's a picture of him on a horse in my room—your room. You and Mims and Pap with a horse and the lamb, and that cute little boy in the—"

She cut me off. "Honey, stop talking!"

"What? Why?" It had only taken four minutes for the chat

to turn sideways with the kind of gravity that had come to define her these past several months.

"We'll talk later."

"Wait!" I forced a swallow and chose my words carefully, asking the question that lay sour in my throat. "Has Dad called?" I already knew the answer but couldn't make myself not ask.

"Just wondered."

But she had hung up.

I slammed the phone back in place, untangled the long cord coiled around my legs, dropped ice cubes in a glass—the first clink, final.

What did I miss? She could barely talk. She didn't have to go. I knew she didn't. I didn't get to tell her about the halter that fit Radar so perfectly, that Sabion found the lead rope that matched it exactly. I had questions about her growing up in this house. I wanted to tell her I'd found a special place: Sabion's cubbyhole.

I poured tea over the ice, finished it off, poured a second. Pap's lifeless body was slumped in a chair on the porch twenty feet away. His rocker didn't rock. His eyes were closed, and it gave me a thought: What if he were dead? He was so still. What would I do if he were?

Sabion could figure it out.

Gathering my tea in one hand and my flute in the other, I slipped out the door, pausing behind Pap's rocker to look for a sign of his breathing: a twitch of a finger, the rise and fall from his chest. The thin night air had already muscled the heat from the day.

What did he care about? Certainly not that I'd come to Texas just to get to know him. If I evaporated—poof!— He wouldn't know it for a week.

He never talked about Mims, or of Mom when she was a

girl, or gave me any reason why horses were evil. Drawing him into a conversation was like dragging my feet through concrete. Though I asked the questions and could see by his expressions that he was thinking the answers, he never voiced them. His was a miserable life. It scared the bejeebers out of me that I might be anything like him.

His foot jerked, and I felt a relief.

Fireflies twinkled between the branches like flickering lanterns, as if dangling on silk threads. I couldn't recall ever hearing about lightning bugs. I tiptoed to the far end of the porch and perched on the top step.

The flute at my lips, my fingers poised over the air holes, I breathed out a simple tune to their soft dance. Pap's chair began to rock to the tempo, the night so quiet I felt like I were entertaining the moon as it sat on the horizon waiting to be called. The lighted tails twisted, colliding and clasping one onto another like drifting embers.

My notes quickened. Pap's chair changed as well...the rocker runners crunched, adding a dimension to my music. I closed my eyes and pushed through notes that fixed the dark, uncertain mood of wood groaning on the plank porch—and replayed my conversation with Mom in my head.

Why did she want me to come home when I just got here? Nothing had changed in Seattle: she would still be working unimaginable hours, I'd still be home alone watching soap operas and lying that I didn't. A low grumble reverberated through the windpipe. A young lamb bleated from the pen. I worried how this house might have arrived at the place that it smelled like baked bricks, and blew out a long, halting note that abruptly ended. Pap's rocker stopped with it.

We sat in silence. It occurred to me that he didn't hate my music. Even if he'd never say it, my flute had a calming influence.

I know! I'll play it for Radar! If it comforted Pap, maybe it would work on Radar, too. I would keep my plan to myself. Pap would never understand.

* * *

I was dreaming of a house made of ice. My feet were cold. A distant, haunting wail drifted through my dream, mysteriously beautiful, as if a mirage—a single, lonely howl. I half-listened, half-awake, to the dark, soulful moan in the desolate night. Could I hit such a note with my flute?

A choir of complaining, high-pitched shrieks broke through the howl, and Rowdy erupted beneath my window. His barks turned hostile.

I raised in the bed and yelled, "Pap! Paaaaa-p!" as excited yips rose and fell like an out-of-whack siren.

He snarled, "What?"

The crescendo intensified. It was close! I clutched my pillow as if it were a shield. "Do you hear that?"

He didn't answer right away. "Coyotes," he shouted back at me. He could've been Dad, growling that way.

"*Coyotes*—" I whispered, and pulled the blanket tighter. "They're outside!" I shrieked.

"Good!"

The freakish cries sounded closer and closer, as if circling the house. There were so many...must be *a hundred!* Now Rowdy barked from a different direction. *He's chasing them?*

"What are coyotes good for?" I wasn't sure I wanted to know.

"Nothing!"

Rowdy yowled from the barn. The medley split from a chorus of short, sharp yaps into long, yawning, lonesome arcs that strung the howls together—painful cries that grew to a frightening concert, then broke.

They were everywhere! I needed a flashlight. I wished Pap had street lamps. "Pap?"

He cleared his throat. "Now what?"

I wrung my hands, but had to ask, "What, exactly, is a coyote?"

"Aargh!" he belted through the dark. "Wild dogs. Now go to sleep."

I flinched. *Wild dogs?* I burrowed down in the center of my bed, wide awake. A wild dog could be very ferocious. "So they're really mean?"

I heard him grumble. "Everything's mean."

I covered my head, yelled, "Can they get in?" Was my question muffled?

"No! Go to sleep!"

Wild dogs. My eyes wouldn't shut. I waited as long as I could, tried not to ask, but, "Will they hurt Rowdy?"

"No! He'll hurt them if they come any closer. Now, that's all. Go...to...sleep!"

I stared at the ceiling without seeing it.

Chapter Nine

The plan seemed good to me: I would ride Jennie, and Radar would follow on the lead rope, though I wasn't exactly sure what that would teach him.

Sabion watched from the rails as I snapped the clasp-end of the lead rope to Radar's halter and waggled it to get his attention. Tying the other end around my waist, I threw a leg over Jennie, and flapped my legs.

Jennie had never moved so fast. She lunged, lifting the ropes' slack, then dashed, which stretched it tight. Radar didn't follow.

"Carlota, Carlota, Carlota." Sabion laughed. Shaking his head, he offered a hand and pulled me off the ground. "This caballo already know what he can do. It is you who must learn. It is you who must think different."

He dusted my back with his hat. "To train a horse such as this is a very big responsibility. Before you ask him to trust, first you must show him you are trustworthy. Any animal—not just the blind one—must feel safe. To feel safe, he must believe you would never hurt him."

"I'd never want Radar afraid of me! I want to be his partner."

"Then be a good leader. You must tell this horse what you want he should do. Do not be bossy just because you hold the rope. Be kind. Speak with your voice gentle. Talk to him as with a friend."

"If you want this caballo to go, ask polite. If you want this caballo should see, be his eyes. As you walk, tell him what you see, where you want he should go. There is nothing wrong with his ears! Show him the way so he can learn what is here, what is there."

Sabion pointed to the water trough. "You say, 'Big horse, this is the water for you to get a good drink. This is the door where you go into your stall.' You must teach signals: a sound you make with your mouth and a tap for him to feel, and a word to get his attention. He will soon learn what the sound or tap or noise means."

Sabion curled his bottom lip under his teeth—I covered my ears. Radar threw his head back at the shrill whistle.

"I can't do that."

Sabion shrugged, backed away. "No matter. You decide the signal." He smacked his lips like throwing kisses and Radar twisted to the sound. "See? A word with a signal. Same word, same signal every time. The horse will learn what each signal means."

I brushed Radar's forelock aside as if that were blocking his vision, flapped my tongue—a series of clacks. Radar cupped his ears. He stretched his neck to my hands and inhaled a deep whiff of me. I took a step backwards to the trough. "C'mon, boy. Water." I clacked and pulled and clacked and pulled until he stretched his neck and took a step.

"Wa-ter," I said, as if to a toddler. I opened the faucet a

trickle and splashed, spooning palmfuls over his muzzle. "Waaa-ter."

He fished in the stream with his lips like a kid at a fountain. I cupped dollops over his neck and combed dribbles into his back. "Wa-ter." then washed the smutty nasal crud off my shoulder.

"Now, Carlota, walk the horse so he will know how big is the corral."

"C'mon, boy." I clicked my tongue and turned him to the tree's spreading canopy. He followed, stabbing my neck with needling whiskers, though I didn't cry out or slink away.

Sabion jumped from the rail. "No, no." He spun a hand in loopy whirls. "Take him around and around until you come to the center from the circles that you make."

I understood that Sabion meant I should lead him around the rails and spiral inward to the tree so that with each rotation Radar could feel the space in the way he'd sniffed out the stall.

"Now, let him drop his head and smell his way as before." I unclasped the rope and backed away. Radar's nose did the work. "Soon he will know how to find the door, how to find the water by himself."

Sabion raced to the forgotten wheelbarrow left in the middle of the pen and wheeled it to a corner. "Always, always, we must put things back in the very same spot so he will not tangle in it. We must not change anything about."

Just as I'd never considered obstacles in a sheep pen as any kind of calamity, I'd never considered the tree, the railing, the side of the barn, its doors or gates—certainly not a wheelbarrow!—as things that could injure. Now I looked on everything with an eye of disaster.

Jennie marched up to Radar and raised her nose to his.

Sabion chuckled. "Horses and donkeys are herd animals—they find one another. My little Jennie like this big horse. She feels muy importante to make a new friend. She will give to him confidence." He hung his head. "But I do not think Tessa will be his friend. Tsk Tsk Tsk. I do not know."

* * *

Pap honked. My legs were raw and needled with Jennie's choppy hair. I couldn't go to town like this. I trotted past the truck, signaling just-one-minute...gesturing a stop in the house.

Swiping my arms and legs with a washcloth, I changed my shirt, and leaned into the mirror. My nose was blistered, my cheeks, red. No wonder my face hurt. I would be peeling like a snake in a few days. I would buy sunscreen.

I jogged back to the truck.

"Now?" Pap said gruffly.

"Can we go to the grocery store?"

"For what?"

"Uh, bacon? Eggs? Lettuce?" BLT's? Peanut butter...something other than oatmeal and tuna.

"If you're cooking—"

"I'll cook. Can I buy what I want, and you'll eat it?" Pap grunted. "Do you have enough money?"

"What kind of question is that?"

I gave him an exasperated look. "Every question doesn't have to be difficult."

* * *

We drove in silence, Pap fixed on the road as though at nothing. Hot air funneled through the truck. He removed his hat and tossed it on the seat between us. Wind ruffled his white hair. He looked different without the hat.

The shirt tag stabbed my neck and I knew it was sunburned,

79

too. I dangled an arm out the window—a thin slice cut from a cardboard box to protect my forearm from the heat of the metal frame.

"Mom says your family came from Ohio." Old German. I didn't know how that was different from new German, but that's how Mom had summed him up when I was nine years old, when I asked the probing questions that she only vaguely answered.

He punched out a short, cursory nod.

"Where in Ohio? Really!" I answered the doubtful flicker of his brows. "I want to know." I had questions. I knew next to nothing about him. About Mims, or about Mom's childhood.

His eyes pinched as if the inquiry were painful. "Cleveland."

"You were born in Cleveland, Ohio?"

He drew his shoulders up in a what-difference-does-it-make shrug. It was the most cordial exchange we'd had all week. "But you've been here all your life?"

He bobbed faintly.

I sucked a breath and let it seep through my teeth. As long as we were locked together on this drive, we might as well make the most of it. I leaned against the door to face him. "So, how'd you end up in Texas? Mom said you—we—come from a railroad family." I deflected the glance. "So your dad worked on trains? I've always wanted to ride a train."

"Rail," he mumbled. "Working on the rail is a lot different from working on trains."

"How?" I asked, optimistic. Nonchalant.

He drew a deep breath. "One is an engine, the other is tracks."

"Oh, right." I processed that. "So your dad helped build rail tracks?"

"Father, grandfather, four uncles. Followed the rails into

Texas, followed it out." His voice was tight, like the barbed fence that shaped the road. "Hard work." His brow crimped, the thought lingering on his face. "Nasty heat. Bitter cold."

"You worked on the railroad, too?"

"For a while."

"You retired?"

His eyes flickered over the road. I waited for his answer. "You could say that. The rail moved on. I didn't. I'm the only one who stayed." Pap had a deep voice that was nice to listen to when he wasn't angry. Just listening to him stirred me like a wooden spoon muddles gravy.

The road curled, dropped around a rock ridge, cascaded into a valley that fell away on either side. "That must've been lonely, to watch them all move off." I could imagine the whole bunch of them sitting for a photo shoot a hundred years ago—hard-looking, crusty men, greats and grands. "I've never seen pictures of any of your...I mean our family."

"I'm not surprised."

"Where are they all now?"

His forehead puckered. "Six foot under."

"Oh. Yeah. Duh." The sun shimmered through the windshield, sucking the life from the truck. "Where did you all live, back then?"

He glanced off in the distance and pointed out the window. "At the base of those hills." There was weight in his voice.

He didn't ask about my life. Surely there was something he wanted to know about me. About Mom. Something, after all this time?

But if he didn't, I was happy just to keep talking about him. "Mom said you had hundreds of sheep. What did you do with them?"

"Don't have time to mess with 'em."

I chuckled. "Don't have time! You have nothing but time."

"Don't know why I even kept the ones I got."

"Because Mims loved them?" I offered. "With them, you still feel a touch of her?" I knew I did. Mom's stories had always been just that, stories. But now that I saw, Mims had come to life. I could feel what I could never see. I felt her on the porch, in the corral, in the wind. She would have loved Radar. I know she would've.

My phone blinged. The surprise made me jump. I pulled it out of my back pocket. "I have a signal! Mom left a message!"

Pap frowned, said nothing.

I tapped a reply: *Mom, call me when you get this text. I'll be in town and can finally use my phone.*

* * *

We entered Quitaque from the opposite direction of when I first saw it. Nothing had changed except the trucks parked at the Dairy Blast. A woman in a flowery skirt was hustling her two little cowboy-kids into one of the trucks.

My mouth watered. "Can we stop for a hamburger? I brought some money. I'll buy."

Pap blew past Dairy Blast without a glance. He whipped left and lunged into a curb of Larry Littleton's General Dollar Store.

"What do we need here?" A large sign plastered to the window advertised potato chips on sale. "Is this the grocery store?"

"Clothes." Pap opened his door.

"Here?" The word came out punchy, the way my Dad would've said it. "I mean, what kind of clothes do they have?"

"The sort that cover your body so you're not sick with sunburn."

I touched the raw on my nose. "I need sunblock."

He slammed the door, stopped at the curb to rub the knee that made walking difficult, peered through the windshield. "You coming? Or should I pick out something?"

Oh, geez. No!

Pap held the door open; bells clanged as I walked through. I stopped, an idea blossoming.

"Morning, Fred!" the clerk said.

Pap nodded, grabbed a basket.

The old building smelled stale. Large fans rotated slowly, winding off a steady hum and an occasional out-of-sync thunk as they turned slowly in the high ceiling, like horizontal wind turbines.

"Do you have any of these bells for sale?" I asked, pointing at those above the door.

She straightened, looked me over. "You can look in the holiday section." She speared an arm down an aisle. "Last row. Might have to dig."

I pulled a shopping cart of my own and started off down the aisle. *Christmas? Cute.* Who'd think, a little town like Quitaque sold holiday relics in June. To bring in shoppers?

Pap went straight to the clothing racks. I shot past him to the bins, nothing sorted or labeled Thanksgiving, Christmas, or Easter, and started digging. I found ten sleigh bells the size of golf balls sprayed with silvery glue. Holding one out, I flicked my wrist. It had a nice musical jingle.

The clerk leaned across the counter and looked.

I rubbed off a spot of glitter and was satisfied that the gunk would all drop off, and tossed them in the basket along with a small flag on a stick. No one knew I was having a birthday July 4th. For ten cents it would add a small flavor to the cake I planned to make.

Pap circled the racks. He pulled out a white shirt with long, draping sleeves, and snaps rather than buttons. Its pointy collar matched the toes of his pointy boots. *Not* his size! He held it up to me.

"Uh, Pap—" I stuck it back on the rack. "Too outdated."

He picked it back out. "Why change what works?"

Meh. "Fine. I'll try it on if we can get a hamburger. Is there a dressing room?"

The saleslady settled in a chair behind the counter. She giggled before answering, "No."

I ripped the shirt from the hanger and slipped it over my T-shirt. The sleeves fell six inches over my fingertips. I slouched for the mirror, cut Pap a *I told you so look.*

"Roll 'em," the cashier offered.

It was a dress on me. I turned so Pap could see how ridiculous I looked. "All you want is something over my arms, right?" I would wear it open over my T-shirt. Pap tossed five more just like it in the shopping cart, then headed for the jeans.

I raced ahead of him. "I can find them, Pap." They, too, were all the same: western style, boot cut, deep pockets all way around. I flipped through the sizes, and finally asked the clerk, "Do you carry petites?"

"Sure do." She plopped her elbows on the counter and rested her chin on her fists. "Look o'er there on that little boy's shelf."

Boys? I mouthed the word.

She shrugged. "Honey, we just sell what folks wear. If they don't fit, you can sure bring 'em back. Save the tags. And maybe your receipt in case they go on special, but I'd remember you got 'em, sweetie."

I held pair after pair against me. The legs either hit my ankles, or they were so long I was walking on them. I folded each neatly and laid them back on the stack. I told Pap, "I won't wear them."

Pap pulled the long ones out of the pile. "This is what we came for. You'll wear 'em."

It was suffocating in the little attached building out back. The boots were half a size too big, but Pap said they'd work, with socks. "Then you'll have a good fit."

I set my basket beside his: bells, sunblock, candy bars. I asked the cashier, "Do you know anybody who has a blind horse?"

Her lips twitched. "Why? You want one?"

I smiled faintly. "I *have* one. A dark grey Appaloosa. I'm looking for the person who lost him."

Pap stood by silently.

"Can't say as I know of any." Her eyes twinkled. "Do you, Fred?"

He tossed the jeans and shirts on the counter. "That's Miriam's daughter. From Seattle."

Her eyes worked up-down, down-up. "What's Miriam up to these days?"

He didn't answer, only laid out sixty dollars for a wardrobe I didn't want and probably wouldn't wear even for the month I'd be here in this place.

Chapter Ten

The grocery store was tiny, like the parking lot, the town, the population—nothing like the supermarkets I was used to. Four pair of eyes turned to watch me snatch potato chips from the display.

"Hey, Fred!" The clerk's eyes shifted to me. Same scene, different store.

Pap touched his hat, nodded. "Abby."

A couple weeks in Texas and it was like I'd never seen a bulb of fresh garlic—it made me so happy! I threw it in my basket. Pap looked at it as if a mouse had crawled in the cart. A head of lettuce, tomatoes, onions, zucchini. "Fresh peaches!" *Cucumbers, parsley, and a watermelon.*

Pap tossed two boxes of crackers in the basket.

"You sure like crackers."

"Bread spoils. Crackers don't so easily."

We worked our way to the meat department. Hi 'ya Fred." Pap grunted a reply.

"You don't have fish?" I asked.

"Aisle five. Tuna...sardines." Nothing fresh. I really wanted fresh. I scratched salmon from my list, and chose chicken from the meat counter. Pap picked bacon and hamburger meat. I made a mental note to go for eggs, buns, and pickles.

The rows were crammed together with hardly any freezer section. Pap watched me fill the grocery cart. "You gonna eat all this?"

"You bet." I threw in a carton of plastic zip-bags. By the time I finished shopping I had the ingredients for some good meals. "How long before we come back?"

"Don't know if we'll ever need to."

* * *

I slurped my drink. A burger and fries fit just right in my stomach. Pap threw the truck into gear, shifted one block west, and pulled onto another gravel parking lot.

A vet clinic? He'd changed his mind?

He re-wrapped his hamburger and tossed it on the dashboard. "Stay here." He jerked the door handle. "Got to pick up some worming medicine."

No-no-no-no! I had to get in there. I'd never get another chance. "Eat your sandwich, Pap." I dropped my drink in a holder, said overly-cheery as I whipped my door open. "I'll get it." I jumped out, ran to his side of the truck before he could twist in his seat. "You said you needed to gas the truck. I know you're in a hurry to get home. You do that, and I'll do this. It'll save time. We'll meet back here when you're finished." I snapped his door closed.

"I expect it's ready. I called ahead."

"No problem. Do I need money?"

He shook his head. "They'll bill me. Never've missed a chance to send one yet."

* * *

The receptionist looked up when I pushed through the door. I smiled at the large man who cuddled a tiny dog wrapped like a sausage-in-a-blanket, and trooped to her window.

"I'm here for some worming medicine for my grandfather, Fred Kotes."

I'd never had a chance to say that before.

She rolled her chair forward and leaned heavily on the fleshy part of her arms. "Oh, so you're Charlotte!" She didn't try to conceal her surprise. "Or, it's Charley, isn't it?"

I nodded, dumbstruck. "How did you—"

She grinned, shrugged, reached out and patted my hand. "Small town, dearie. I hoped you'd come in."

I felt my face flush, and swiped my lip, as if catsup were smeared there. "Um, first," I looked around, glanced out the window but Pap's truck hadn't moved. I lowered my voice, as if he might hear. "—would it be okay if I talk to a vet? Right away," I pleaded. "Before...please?" Surely it wouldn't get back to Pap.

"Certainly."

I straightened. "Really?"

"Sure. I happen to know there's somebody who'd love to meet you." She chuckled at my grimace. "Follow me."

She led me through the office, past a block of examination rooms, through a swinging door that opened into a large metal barn. "Wait here." She scuttled across the concrete floor to a man in a bright red shirt who was kneeling over a young calf laid out on a tarp, the little fella sound asleep. I stretched on my toes to see better. A long gash ran down the calf's chest.

"Young Charley Kensey needs to speak with a vet," she said, then leaned over to add, "Fred's granddaughter."

His back stiffened. The arm holding the threaded needle froze mid-air. It took a couple seconds for him to glance over his shoulder. Nodding, he motioned me forward, the needle still working in and out of the dozing calf.

I approached the middle-aged man with large ears, round glasses, and thinning hair.

"So you're Mariam's daughter." It wasn't a question.

"I know. I mean, you know my mom?" Why did everything in Quitaque come back to my mother?

He chuckled. "Sure do. She's the gal who broke my heart." I couldn't think of anything to say to that. His eyes brushed over me in an dissecting way. "You look like her." He pushed the needle through the calf's ugly wound.

"Yeah, but the way I hear it, I act like my grandmother."

He threw his head back and belted out a bubbling howl. "Lucky gal. Then you got the best of both worlds." Sobering quickly, he looked around me to the door. "Did your mother come with you?"

"No. I'm alone."

His hands got busy, the shot of laughter forgotten. "How is she? Your mother?"

"Divorced."

Something dropped, shattered in another room. Heavy brows drew together, throwing some shade to his eyes. "Oh. Can't say I'm sorry to hear that." He shifted on the stool. "The guy blew out like he blew in, huh?"

"Whatever that's supposed to mean. Now you're talking about my dad!"

He dropped a shoulder, gave me an apologetic nod. Twisting, he spun the rolling stool to one side. "You're right. I'm sorry. That was uncalled for. I don't have any business saying such as that." The calf lay motionless between us. He tied off a final stitch, wiped his hands on a stack of towels, dug with his boots and rolled the chair to the sink where he stood, a towering man.

I followed, watching quietly as he washed away the muck. We locked eyes as he dried both hands, between each finger, and up thick arms. I grabbed a fresh towel and held it out for him.

Unrolling his shirt sleeves and buttoning them down, he swam his eyes over me. "Let's start over." He stuck a hand out. "Hello. I'm Dr. Lund, but everybody calls me Ben."

I grinned, shook his hand, hard. "Hello, Dr. Ben, if you mean me, too. I'm Charley Kensey." I chuckled and he did too.

"I'm very glad to meet you, Miss Charley. Now, how can I help?" He had a nice smile when he wasn't working on a slashed-up calf.

My arms dangled uncomfortably with no place to settle, so I folded them tightly across my middle in what I thought of as a business-like pose. "Now we're getting somewhere."

He laughed. "Yes, I can see your grandmother in you. Ok, Miriam's not here with you. Is she in Texas?"

"No."

"No—" He shifted his eyes to the floor. "I see. Got that out of the way. So, how about your grandpa?"

I slung a thumb over my shoulder. "He's getting gas in the truck, and I have to make this fast or he'll be suspicious." I pressed my lips tight, not sure how deep I needed to go into this.

"Now I'm suspicious. And what do you want to see me about that you don't want your grandpa to know?"

"A horse."

"Ohhh—" The word stretched like a rubber band. His squint traveled up the wall, landed on the ceiling. "Yeah, obviously Fred didn't send you in here about a horse."

"I'm supposed to pick up the worming medicine."

"Let me see...you want a horse and Fred won't hear of it."

"Yeah! How'd you—" I bit back the question and started again. "Wait. It's like this: I have a horse because it found its way to the ranch."

His eyebrows lifted, then folded. He tilted his head a beat. "How's that?"

"The horse is lost. Here. I have pictures." I whisked out the phone and opened the photos, stood by while he thumbed through them. "Do you know this horse or where he belongs? Pap's been pretty awful about it." It all came out in a breathy rush. "Another thing, Sabion says...you know Sabion, right?" I gave him time to nod. "Sabion says the horse is blind."

That made his mouth drop. "How in the world did—"

I straightened taller, until the top of my head came up to his top button. "I know what you're going to say: How is it possible that this horse could make it all the way out there? We first saw him on the highway on our way back from the airport—just clomping along the road. And that was a long way from the ranch." I looked Dr. Ben squarely in the eye. "He knew I would help him. I have to find his owner. I figured a vet is the first place somebody'd come. The horse is absolutely friendly. You can look at him and see he's been well cared for."

"Hm."

"But worse than that, Pap says he'll shoot him." I almost lost my hamburger just saying it. "He said a blind horse won't last long anyway." I shook my head. "I can't reason with him. I might as well be talking to the wind."

He handed my phone back. "I believe you. I know Fred quite well."

A weight lifted...somebody was listening.

"Your Pap is right about one thing—that horse won't survive left to himself. A predator will single him out."

"I can't let that happen. This horse came to *me*. I know it! Sabion thinks he might have some Appaloosa blood."

"Could be. Appaloosa's can have a tendency to blindness." Dr. Ben's shoulders were broad, and each time he spoke, he seemed to grow taller. "On the upside, a blind horse can do very well in a domestic environment."

"I know! I mean, I figured as much. I've been working with him." I glossed over the part about training him to herd sheep. That didn't go over so well the first time I said it. "Pap gave me one month to find his owner. Then, he—" I glanced away, the words mushing in my mouth. "—he assured me what he's going to do. He *means it.*"

He shook his head and mumbled, "Fred, Fred, Fred, you 'ol coot. Are his eyes clear?" he asked.

"I wouldn't know, always with that hat—"

The vet chuckled. "I mean the horse. Are the horse's eyes clear?"

"Oh! Well—"

"Any swelling, or blood around them, like from an injury? Could be he ran into something."

"No"

"No." He tugged an end of his mustache in a thinking way, sneaked a look at his watch. "Brett!" he shouted. "Brett, where are you?"

"Almost finished." The voice came from outside the building.

"C'mere. Now!"

A lanky kid, squinting from the sun, strolled through the large roll-up door at the rear of the building. He scanned the shadows, lifted the sweat-stained straw hat, and wiped an arm over a messy crop of blond hair before plunking it back down. Slips of perspiration glistened on his sideburns. He smiled when he saw me.

I touched the tips of my hair, swiped my bangs to the side.

He lumbered forward wiping his palms on his jeans, and extended a hand. "Hello! Brett Littleton."

Littleton, as in General Dollar Store?

The hand was rough and dry. I didn't think I'd cringed, but he apologized as if I had.

"Sorry. It's the work Ben makes me do." His T-shirt was drenched with the muck of a workman's hard labor. Stains on his hat matched the wear on his boots, both the color of pecan shells.

I was unsure where to look...directly, as he did? or indirectly...as in, anywhere else. "It's okay." I managed, conscious of the warmth of his lingering touch. "I'm Charley."

Dr. Ben pushed hurriedly through a swinging door and disappeared, while I stood tongue-tied, aware of my splotchy red face and peeling nose.

"Where did you come from?" Brett asked. It wasn't an unusual question, but the way he said it made me flush, as if I'd dropped in from the moon, which was almost true.

"From Seattle. I'm—"

Dr. Ben blasted back through the door with a bark, "Where's your manners? Charley is Fred Kote's granddaughter." As if that explained anything.

Brett whipped his hat off again. "Really? Then is your mother was the one—" Brett stuck his hand out and clutched mine tighter in an awkward second handshake. "I'm especially pleased to meet *you*! We have a lot to talk about!" He stared, unblinking, smoothed his dusty crown of hair that matched the shadowy scraps he wore on his chin.

I blushed. I couldn't imagine what.

His jeans were faded, frayed at the boot. Maybe he was around my age, maybe just a tad older. A large rodeo buckle yoked his belt to his....were those Larry Littleton's General Dollar Store jeans he was wearing? I had them in the truck. Maybe there was some hope for mine.

"Find me an equestrian mask," Dr. Ben told him.

Eyes never leaving me, Brett shuffled backwards in a kind-of toe-trot—all elbows and feet, a tease on his lips. Dr. Ben was talking, but the voice faded in my ears as Brett tangled in a water hose and tumbled.

I clasped a hand over my mouth, felt myself color as he crashed into a cart, and took a header. Startled, Dr. Ben shook his head and rolled his eyes as Brett popped up speedily and scuttled through the swinging door.

The pulse stayed in my ear. I stuttered over my words. "Wh...what were you saying, Dr. Ben?"

"I *said,*" he said indulgently. "—I'll come out to the ranch in a few days and take a look at the horse."

He had my full attention now. "Pap won't like that. He wouldn't let me call you. He doesn't know I'm even talking to you." I added plainly, "He won't pay for it!"

Dr. Ben chuckled. "Let me worry about that. It's about time I made a visit to that herd of his anyway."

Brett returned, holding the hat in his hand. His hair was groomed, sideburns still wet, his face as if scrubbed.

Dr. Ben whisked a notepad from his pocket and made a few quick notes. "Until I can get there, cover the horse's eyes with that—."

Brett raised the black, stretchy fabric and made a big show of swathing it around his own face. He winked the one eye that protruded through a hole. I tried not to grin.

Dr. Ben whipped the mask away from him and handed it to me, breaking a connection and pulling me back. "It'll help keep the flies away as well as give him some sunshade. You want to protect those eyes as much as possible. These rubber pieces are blinker cups, kinda like they use on race horses."

He scribbled some more on the pad, flicked it closed, shoved it in his shirt pocket. "And, if you had a mind to, don't shave his eye whiskers. They're like feelers...they provide information, like how close he is to things."

The mask was elastic in my hands, but I knew I couldn't walk out with it. "If Pap sees this he'll know I did exactly what he told me not to do—talk to a vet about Radar."

"Hitch it around your waist like a belt. Pull your T-shirt over it. Use it when you can." He shrugged. "I usually carry one of these in the truck anyway. I'll explain when I get there; he won't know I didn't just show up with it. Maybe I can come sooner. Day after tomorrow?"

I folded it in two and stuffed it in my waistband, then covered the bump with my shirt like Dr. Ben said. My cell phone rang. "Oh, wait! Wait! I'm sorry but I *have* to answer this." I yanked out the phone, gave Dr. Ben a grin.

"Hi Mom! Guess who I'm talking to!"

Dr. Ben's face turned as bright as his shirt. He gawped, open-mouthed, as if trying to decipher Morse Code.

"Nope," I said. "I'm with Dr. Ben Lund! Hello? Hello... Mom? Are you there? Oh, there you are." A glance, a shrug. "I've got a lot to tell you, but can't now. Pap's waiting in the truck and I've already been in here too long." I listened a moment, and repeated, "Sunday. I promise I'll tell you everything. I'm so excited!"

Dr. Ben wiped his mouth with the back of a hand, sank onto the stool.

* * *

Brett held the office door for me, then followed me out. Pap was watching. Brett stuck a hand in the window. "Hello, Mr. Kotes."

"Brett. Pap shook his hand. "If you get any taller you won't find pants to fit."

"Yes sir. That's what my mom says. Can't stop it." He leaned to the window. "I'm glad I caught you. Will you bring Charley to the Fourth of July Rodeo? I'm roping. You know it's a big competition. Maybe Charley can bring me some of that Kotes family luck."

Pap grunted.

"Kotes family luck? I need some of that." I wasn't sure I'd even found the Kotes family yet. *And a rodeo! On my birthday!*

Pap started the engine. Reaching for my hand, Brett led me around to the passenger door and opened it for me. "I really hope you can come." The crinkle at the edge of his eyes made what he was saying, probably, more important. It was a natural smile.

"I'd like to, but—" I shrugged.

The door shut with a clank, his hands on the window frame. "I hope you can. " Snapping the lock down, he backed away. Pap threw the truck into reverse. Brett waved from the sidewalk. "You remember, Mr. Kotes, You know where."

Chapter Eleven

A week on the ranch had really transformed me. I looked the part, like I'd lived here all my life. Before jetting from Seattle, I had an expectation of riding a fast horse over a wide prairie, the wind whipping my hair. Never had I imagined myself in baggy-butt jeans with pockets that sunk to my knees. They were heavier than any I'd ever owned, and fastened high on my waist, as if pulled up with suspenders. The shirt tail draped my back, and I had to roll the sleeves five times.

But the boots! Oh, I loved how they made me taller. They fit like clamps, as if my feet were growing in bark.

I clomped to the large picture window, plunked the sombrero Sabion gave me on my head. "Eesh."

I look like a mushroom.

If Mom had told me from the beginning that Pap didn't have horses, maybe I wouldn't have thought twice about coming. I had the idea of wearing the giddy-up home—I would walk right past her at the airport and she wouldn't even know me. But then, what would've happened to Radar?

No. Destiny had brought me here.

Pap's boots stammered on the porch. I couldn't resist a cocky stroll past him—long, lanky strides that thunked my foot heel to toe. He sipped smugly from his coffee mug. Well, of course—nothing unusual to him. Just a set of sensible clothes.

Oh, well...as long as he's happy—

* * *

Sabion's smirk held a snicker. "Ah, si. You look...now you look right."

I rolled my eyes. "Glug—"

Radar was pungent with horse sweat. Was it his timid nature that made me brave for him? A fearless front to give us both courage, like a parent protecting their child? Well, *some* parents. He sniffed my pant leg, and blew a snort that spewed junk on my knee. *Now they're broken in...*

"How much time do I have today?" I asked. Sabion had honored his agreement to let me use Jennie half a day for training, but I'd already wasted a slip of his morning trying to make the blasted blue jeans work.

He looked at his watch. "None today. I am here too long already."

"An hour?" I pleaded.

Sabion shook a finger. "Yesterday you say to me, 'This day I will make repairs to the corral.' You forget this? Now you say, 'Este día voy a hacer reparaciones.' Mas importante."

I tried not to laugh. Sabion could never scold. Though he tried to sound tough, it only made him look leathery. It was kinda weird that I was beginning to understand him when I didn't even speak the lingo.

"But you're here already. I can make the repairs when you leave." My plan today wasn't to repair the corral; my plan was to string those blasted bells together while I had the workbench to myself. Then I'd reveal my fun training plan to Sabion when he returned.

His shoulders caved, the argument lost. "One hour okay is all." His words netted altogether.

The sun was particularly bright and hurt my eyes. I'd forgotten to look for sunglasses at the general store.

I snapped the lead rope onto Radar's halter and lined him up behind Jennie. Now that I knew what could happen, I'd be watching. If Radar didn't step off with Jennie this time, I would drop the rope instantly.

Hitching the suffocating pants, I mounted, cringing as the coarse jeans raked my sunburned knees. Sabion shoveled dung at the wheelbarrow, an eye on the orbit we were making around him.

Radar's mask bunched in a wad in my waistband. I needed Sabion to be an ally, but just as I was about to confide in him, Pap ambled across the yard, and I parked my tongue on the roof of my mouth.

When Pap turned to the hill without so much as a nod my way, I said, nonchalantly, as if reading a droning news report, "I met Dr. Ben."

"Eh?" Sabion replied indifferently. *Scrape...toss.* The muck hit the wheel barrow.

"I showed him pictures of Radar." Sabion looked up, his face grave. "He doesn't know him," I answered quickly.

"Si." He shoveled...pitched, shrugged. "Nobody know this horse I guess."

"He's coming to the ranch to see him." There! I said it. Split-splat.

"Huh!" The sound came out hard, like a punch. *Scoop... fling.*

"Yeah," I said merrily. "He said he had to check the herd anyway, so while he's here he'll take a look at Radar. He gave me this to protect his eyes—" I whipped the rubbery eye mask from my waistband and dangled it for Sabion to see. "Pap doesn't know yet."

Sabion's sidelong glance quickly shifted away. "Mm-*hum*," he clucked, and chucked another shovelful at the wheelbarrow. "Tsk. Tsk. Tsk. I guess you never mind what you papa say." His dark eyes held an alarm.

"Well, how could I when he wouldn't even allow me to *talk* to a vet!" I sputtered defensively. I thought Sabion understood better than that.

"And what will you papa say when he know this?"

"You make it sound deceitful, as if I was trying to trick Pap." I slid my leg over the donkey and climbed off. Jennie wandered to the barn. "Pap was the one who stopped at the vet clinic, not me! I just took advantage of an opportunity that presented itself. Besides, Dr. Ben said he'd make it tight with him." The thought made my scalp itch.

"Tight? What do you mean, tight?"

I couldn't read his expression, and dismissed it with a hand wave. "Just, explain things. Make everything all right."

He drew a breath that filled his chest and poured out slowly. "Hm."

The humidity was tough, not a cloud in sight. A bird skimmed through the air above our heads; it had no color. "Don't worry," I said, a little snippy. Sweeping back the dark forelock that hung like a mop halfway down Radar's face, I wove the mask around his face and cinched it under his jaw. "I'll take full responsibility. If I have to tell Pap before Dr. Ben has a chance to make him understand, then okay." I adjusted the eye disks evenly like Brett had shown me. Radar didn't seem to mind.

Sabion leaned on his shovel. No breeze stirred. "I worry you reach too far."

I scraped the hair from my neck, turned the sleeves another notch. "Dr. Ben said he'd ask around about Radar. He'll probably have some news when he gets here." Part of me didn't want news, even if it might be good news for Radar. At least I had Dr. Ben on my side.

I stepped back to scrutinize the add-on. "If only I'd known, I would've named you Bandit!"

* * *

The hazy halo surrounding the sun left the sky weak and watery-looking. The heat would be formidable today. Sabion and Jennie were gone, so I let Radar free-rein in the corral while I walked the rails. Not so much to do after all. It wasn't dingy like the stall. No telling how long *that* had sat empty.

I jammed the barn doors open as wide as they'd go, unlocked the gate—two, one, two, one—clicked the padlock, and pulled the bolt. I shoved the metal drums this way and that to forge an aisle to the little cubbyhole. The bag of bells lay on the counter where I'd flung them. The cabinet door dangled open like a broken wing, the buggered spiderweb drooped. I thwacked the door shut, but it drifted back, hovering at just the right angle to be dangerous.

A spiderweb held those doors closed all this time and now it's my fault they can't stay shut?

I swiped the perspiration from my lip. The corner was suffocating. Clothing meant to protect me was hulking and weighty. I rolled the long shirt sleeves another notch, emptied the bag of bells onto the counter, and rifled through the drawers for anything I could use to lace them together...string or yarn or...okay, *twine'll work.* Cutting two long lengths, I threaded five bells on each piece and fashioned them into sections I could hang on Radar's halter.

Not pretty, but at least they would jingle.

A squatty brown jar sat alone in the bottom drawer. *Lanolin,* the label read in smeared-ink scribble. I knew about lanolin. Mom called it sheep fat. Maybe it would soothe a sunburn?

I peeled off the over-shirt, slung the bell-loops over my head, lifted the jar and unscrewed the lid. A bird startled from its roost; the sudden flapping gave me a fright. A pungent odor filled the space...not unpleasant. Medicinal. Antiseptic. Familiar. Tapping two fingertips in the buttery goo, the density and warmth surprised me—the balm like too-old glue too thick to pour, too gummy to smear on skin too tender to rub. A whisper filled my hands.

"Mims—" My heart raced. My hands had a tremor.

I gulped air, but all the oxygen seemed to have lifted to the rafters. The boots were choking my feet. I couldn't catch a breath, as if my belt were cinched too tight. A slow, rolling blink didn't refresh the heat in my face or clear the distortion in my eyes. When my skin prickled, turned clammy and cold, I knew I was in trouble. The counter blurred as if melting.

I have to get out of here. Need to cool down.

I couldn't make myself turn. *Go to the house. Now!*

I raised a reflexive hand. *I should go to the house.* I staggered, swayed with an over-exaggerated step...reached for the counter, even as I felt myself going down.

Down, down, down as if spiraling through a tunnel where sudden vivid flashes revealed unexpected curves that I had to swerve into at a lightning speeds like a wild ride. I couldn't see far enough ahead to plan! An image rose in my mind—a powerful impression too persuasive to dismiss—*windows in a cliff.* I felt rather than heard dismissive voices of a drifting language, drumming like the beat of a heart.

Clouds will be watering Seattle this afternoon. As yesterday. As tomorrow. Pap would never believe the huge flourishing flower baskets that decorate every Seattle corner—under every street lamp, at every store front—exploding nests of yellows, reds, pinks, and blues...mismatching flowers all blending together like fruit cocktail.

I couldn't open my eyes, couldn't move, couldn't speak. Couldn't twitch a finger, yet I was conscious of the coolness of the dirt where I lay, hyper-aware of earthy sounds, as if they were barking from a treetop: the methodical hoof-steps that hammered the flagstone...the annoying fly that zipped back and forth, back and forth. The far-away shriek of a hawk as it complained through the air.

I fought to wet withered lips with a beefy tongue too thick to revive them. I attempted a sound, but my mouth only parted like a fish trying to gulp water. There was no spit to swallow.

The barn stopped spinning. The muddle in my head began to clear, just a little. Enough to wonder why I was lying on the ground in the barn.

The spilling quiet gave me pause: What if nobody could find me...never looked back here in this little room. Or worse.

What could be worse?

If the sneaking coyotes discovered me first, and dragged my lifeless body into the desert and Mom never knew what happened to me— *Ooh. I can't think about that.* She'd experienced one kind of death and it about took her out. She could never handle that kind of loss.

I worked to pry one eye open. Woozy, I closed it. My head fell to one side. I blinked both eyes open again and willed my vision to focus.

There! Where a string of sunlight strained at the cavity under the workbench.

There! Where feet would gather and knees would bend.

It was a barrel shoved deep underneath. A barrel unlike any other, with odd etchings such as a child would make. I rolled to my side heedless of the sand that powdered my hair, managed to raise a hand gummy with lanolin, the salve smelly on my nose. I labored to haul myself to my knees and cling tight to the countertop. When I felt I could make it, I staggered to the house.

Dousing my face and neck and T-shirt with water, I downed two glassfuls, then hurled it all back into the sink.

The pasty lanolin still coated my hands. With no paper towels in the house, I closed my bedroom door, shucked the jeans and rubbed the goo—dirt and all—on my raw, red kneecaps. I would wait for the mid-day heat to burn off before going back to make the repairs I had promised.

Pulling the pillow off the bed, I stretched out on the cool, hard floor, fixed my gaze on the dusty ceiling fan, and tried to draw out the shy memory that lit deep behind my eyes.

Something important. Something.

I wouldn't tell anybody, especially Mom. She'd make me come home. Definitely-especially I wouldn't tell Pap! He would answer nothing, but his biting glare would accuse. I imagined Sabion's stubby finger pointing straight at me as he scolded me tenderly.

I would drink more water.

I closed my eyes. Winks and flashes strained to resurface—a gut feeling of dread, the deep burning between my shoulder blades just before I fell. *Something about Mims—*

Nothing I could throw a dart at. Something that didn't belong, something that lived in the shade. Blasted Texas weather behaves badly when the wind doesn't blow.

Who questions a breeze, until you don't have any? Dad never took the sailboat out without a wind to toss it.

Sailboat—

A hot tear slipped from my eye and ran into my ear.

I sensed the heel of a gentle wave as I slept in the cabin below, and blinked away the blur, suddenly homesick for the taste of sea-spray on my face, the squawking seagulls that begged for a treat. I hadn't thought about the little white boat since...in a while. I hadn't been in it since last summer. That chapter had closed. Another had opened.

I covered my eyes with the crook of an arm. *I have to heal.* I couldn't blame my life on Pap. The decisions that steered me happened months before he'd ever stepped into it. West Texas was a different kind of ocean—an ocean of sand. I could see how life might easily slip away. The land didn't command respect...it was demanded! Such a place had survived with its own set of rules long before I got here. If I didn't learn them nothing might save me.

I felt myself drift.

Nope, Pap would never believe the flowers in Seattle.

Chapter Twelve

I glanced at the phone...almost three o'clock. Sabion would be back soon. I had to get something done in the corral, show him I'd at least started the repairs. I rolled, raised to a sit, discovered the twine loops of bells wrapped around my neck. My stomach wasn't right. My head felt fuzzy. This suffocating heat—it had gotten to me.

I opened the faucet, drenched my face, my arms, pressed the scratchy, sun-dried towel against my eyes and breathed in the tang of strong soap a moment too long. A wave of nausea gushed through me. *I missed my Mom.*

My jeans lay in a puddle on the floor. I kicked them aside and pulled on the shorts. I didn't care if Pap got mad! I still hadn't found the flip-flops Rowdy had stolen. 'Guess you're gonna have to take better care of your things,' Pap had said, his lip in a curl. Now the little thief had taken a green sneaker! I had no choice—I looked like the kid in the picture: shorts...boots.

* * *

The day was still hot, but not as swampy as morning. Bubbles of clouds had built, offering a welcome shield from the sun. I tied the loops of bells to either side of Radar's halter and walked him in circles, but though his head dipped and lifted, the bells made no sound. His gait was too smooth?

So much for *that* idea. At least I'd had the foresight to remove his mask, though I had no memory of doing it. One less chance of a face-off with Pap. I lobbed the hoops onto my shoulder. If only Dr. Ben would hurry and get here and bring this mask-hiding screw-up to an end. Everything about this horse had turned into such a big deal. Pap was upside down, and I was edgy.

Radar followed me to the tree. I fluffed some hay at his feet and went to work. The gloves Pap gave me fit like handprints as I ran my hands along the rail feeling for anything loose or poking or stabbing. The catch of bells clattered from my shoulder as I crimped a wire backwards like a pretzel, tapped a nail flat with a ping-sized hammer. Something tickled my neck.

"Radar! You can't stand here. You might get hurt." I moved down the fence line to a different section and started again, the twine of bells a noisy nuisance. Radar started toward me. I stopped and watched. He swung his head each time the bells jangled. Then it dawned on me.

"So that's it. You don't need to *wear* the bells, you need to *hear* them!"

* * *

I shifted around the small workroom conscious of the fading umbra of afternoon sun, how the barn hid its shadows in different corners, and knocked back the thought: *What* was I doing when the lights went out? I regarded the muddled ground, two knee-prints notched in the dirt. A scatter of bells lay between them.

I recalled the helplessness just before keeling...a breathlessness as if a blanket were thrown over me. I remembered reaching but not falling.

And the odd barrel under the counter...I couldn't get it out of my head. Had I hallucinated it, too? Of all the barrels that filled the compartment—rusty metal kegs, heavy plastic ones—the memory didn't match any of these. The barrel I saw was bulky, sturdy...stashed as if *meant* to be hidden.

The *chirp, chirp, chirp* grew louder.

A hard grip on the rough-hewn plank that formed the work counter, I hesitated briefly, then plunged to a squat and hung, suspended.

It was just as I remembered it: old and clunky, built from wooden slats, painted a soft shade of blue with markings and scrawls—decorative little squiggles with busy lines and geometric circles and squares that somehow formed pictures.

I dropped to a sit. I'd never have seen it if I hadn't been lying on the ground.

Whose?

"Not Pap's." Pap wouldn't paint anything such a wispy shade of blue. Not Pap, who lived under a rock and didn't know wispy from gristle.

"Mims?" *Maybe...probably.* Someone unflappable, like I'd grown to believe her to be. Likely all the stuff she'd packed away to preserve for the next generation.

Me!

I crawled under the worktable, into the deep cavity, tilted the barrel onto its rim, and muscled it out.

It stood tall as my waist, was plump enough that I would've fit nicely inside. It didn't look like something that belonged to the ranch, though it was apparent it had been here a long time. *Forgotten? Discarded?*

I raked away cobwebs that stuck to my gloves, tiptoed a slow circle around it, dragging a finger across the top. I examined the scratchings, pressed a finger into the nonsense symbols, rapped a knuckle on the rusted lid—no, not rusted, but painted a biting crimson red, dull and dark, the color of blood turned blunt by time. Such a stark contrast to the soft, pale body. Care had been taken to seal the drum-like lid firmly—a narrow metal band, round like a Hula-hoop, cinched it down tight.

To keep things out? Or protect what was in?

I mopped the lid with my shirt, blew enough breath to snuff out sixteen candles. A face brightened. Two long, blue parallel lines the length and width of a school ruler swept the lid like a feather, and came together in a sharp, arrow-like point. A mottle of blotchy black specks ran between them, giving the outline dimension, like a spine. Six incision-slit legs kinked out from the torso like elbow joints.

"A beetle? Ha!"

A spit to the finger, I rubbed oversized eyeballs that stared back at mine. Human eyes...bold, with long lashes and arching brows. Two sets of glistening wings branched side to side across the lid giving it a burnished look, as if shining from the inside out. I pulled back, drank in my breath. "A dragonfly!"

I knew better. This wasn't mine. It was none of my business. I flashed a quick look behind. Digging my fingernails under the rim, I inched them around the band feeling for a fastener or clasp, and when I found a short, flat, dogleg clutch I bent it the way I thought it should go, giving it a good, hard twist. The flimsy metal broke off in my hand. I felt a stab of fright, and tossed the broken piece on the counter, but plucked it back off again and hid it in a drawer.

"Okay." My voice had a quake.

The cinching band didn't loosen, but I saw where the lid would come apart so thrust the heel of my hand hard against one side, and jiggled. The ring snapped off with a loud *pop!* The lid burst free.

I yelped, as a grizzly mop-like fluff exploded in my face like a children's toy meant to surprise...I thought it something *alive!* The Hoola-hoopish band bounced away like a spring through the barrels. I felt I'd broken a law.

I got up the nerve to touch the knobby, wig-like blob... gurgled, "Sheep wool!" *I'd felt the guilt of sheep wool—*

Radar bawled from the corral. *The sheep! He's back!*

Panicked, I slammed the lid back in its place but had no way to latch it closed without the banding ring.

Rowdy's barks grew closer.

I punched and shoved the natty wool, but the pelt was having none of it. I threw my weight over the top to push it all down. The gate yawned on its hinges. Tiny feet hammered through. The pen filled with soft mewls.

No time!

Throwing the lid cock-eyed over the barrel, I bolted. I'd get it all tucked away before anybody knew different.

The sheep rushed to be first at the water trough. I opened the water spigot full throttle, as though I did that every day when they arrived.

Sabion turned Jennie loose in the corral. "I see you have been busy," he said, scanning the rails as he led Tessa in.

I nodded gleefully, sweating profusely. "About half done," I fibbed.

He cocked his head, his face crumpled. "Why you do not wear the new clothes?"

I brushed dust and hay and who knows what from my T-shirt and shorts. "I did. I was—" Dodging his darting glances, I babbled, "I was just about to do that. It got so hot. Shorts and a T-shirt are fine for what I've been doing." *Right: red neck, chapped lips, sore, angry knees...*

His finger flapped at me. "You are...how I say," He pinched my arm. "Delicata?" I yawped, scrunched my nose in a meaningful way. He cocked a heel on a rail, flashed up-down eyes over me, around the pen, to Tessa who was sucking up water like an elephant, and said to the sky, "And I see you do not have the hat,"

"It's a cap." I smoothed the rim.

"Mm. You do not care that you face get all burned? You freckles run altogether?"

They already had. "I'm using sunscreen." *Did I?*

"The horse must wear his mask for protection, but you do not? Okay for you. You will be sorry."

I already was. If I'd learned anything it was that the West Texas sun did not play nice with Seattle skin. Even Mom thought I'd packed jeans.

Jennie plodded to her stall as if sent to her room. I heard the gate bang shut. Sabion turned toward the barn. I hit overdrive.

"Okay, then," I said brightly. "Let *me* get their feed ready!" Trotting ahead, I cleared the doorway, raced down the corridor, pounced through the gate, and down the barrel-cluttered path I'd so handily cleared, and worked the barrel back in its hole. I followed up with a quick look around. No sign of the banding rim.

I heard the familiar jangle of Tessa's bridle coming off, the thunk when Sabion hung it on a hook beside her stall. Seconds later, a hideous wail stopped the blood in my feet.

I bolted through the barn, scanned the corral for Radar, who was cowering in a corner where Tessa had him boxed in. A bright stream of blood trickled down one leg and pooled in the dirt. His tail wrung, he swung his head wildly. Moans filled the pen—distressed sheep with no place to escape spooled together in a tight circle, their head rammed together.

"Oh my gosh, oh my gosh!"

I rushed Tessa, shouting to move her…darting in and out of the place where she stood, ears flattened, one hind leg dangerously cocked. I flailed my arms and charged, but Tessa stood staunchly between me and my horse, glaring, wavering her head low to the ground…a warning to back off…while blood streamed from Radar's wither.

"Sabion!" I screamed, and tried to sprint around her. "Sabion!" He dashed across the yard, pieced everything altogether with a quick, *Uh-oh.* "Get her!" I hollered. "Get her!" I whipped wide. "Get Tessa away! She won't let me near him!"

Ears pinned and hindquarters tucked, Radar turned to my voice, but stumbled into the wheelbarrow I'd forgotten to put away.

Seizing Tessa's halter, Sabion scolded, "Very bad girl!" as if speaking to a naughty puppy.

"Bad girl!" I cried, incredulous. "Bad girl? Is that all you can say?"

He halted, surprised. "*Very* bad girl, do you not hear me say?"

"Look what she did!" I rammed a hand at the bloody, flesh-torn gouge. "*Do* something!"

"What you want I should do? She is Tessa."

"Ss…Spa…spank her!" I sputtered.

He looked back at me, shoulders hunched. "Mm. Maybe I do that." Looping an arm around her neck, he muttered in her ear as he led her away, the halter tucked tight in his hand. "Why you do such a thing to that nice horse? He just want to be a friend."

Tessa cut me a narrow glare as I jogged around.

"The horse, he do not know he get in your space." Sabion hitched her to the fence rail, combed a hand down her neck, gave her a final pat. "Do not worry about ese caballo. You know my pockets are full of love for ever-body."

I groaned.

Spreading my arms wide, I approached Radar slowly. "Shh. Shh." The bleeding shoulder quivered as I slipped a hand slowly down his neck to the torn wither. "It's okay, Old Man." Tiny muscles strained at his eyes. "It's all right, now." His head swung to my hand, the breath hot on my arm. "It's going to be okay, Radar. Let's get you cleaned up." I clicked my tongue to move him, but he wouldn't budge. "Okay, Bud. I'll bring the water to you."

I dragged the hose across the pen and ran a thin trickle, first on his hoof, then to the knee, raising the hose slowly until a soft stream of water dribbled over the wound. The bite was ugly, even more torn than I'd thought.

Sabion leaned over my shoulder, hands braced on his knees. "Tessa, um—Well, you know, she maybe feel just a little jealous," he mumbled apologetically. "She do not know she is jealous. She just know what she feels."

It was Tessa Sabion comforted, not Radar. And I was supposed to accept this rangy excuse? "She's *mean*."

Sabion whirled, shook a finger at Tessa. "You is a very mean mula." He shooed flies away with his hat. "These two, perhaps we should keep them apart for some time."

"Really?" I said sarcastically.

"Oh, yes, I think it best for now." I rolled my eyes. "It is the only problem I cannot break of Tessa. I never break her from the bite habit. Of that, she is bad." He reconsidered. "Um...she do not bite the sheep. Nothing bad come to the sheep."

He bent closer, appraised the blood pulsing down the leg. "Hm. I see it do not need stitches, so it is not so terrible."

That made my feet boil. "Well, there's nothing good about it! And *I* can't talk to a vet!" I peeled the hair back, examined the raw chunk the size of Tessa's mouth. "Tessa probably just undid all the progress Radar's *made*." I bit off the last word. "She's a bully! Just what a bully would do."

He growled half-heartedly over his head. "Do you hear? You are a very naughty *bully* girl!"

Metal groaned, a creaking that turned our heads and a slo-mo whole-body twist toward what could make that awful grating racket. Tessa was leaned back almost in a sit. The rope that tethered her to the fence was stretched taut, and the top rail was straining. Her front legs were spread for leverage.

"Ai!" Sabion clutched his head. Leaping, sprinting to the rail, he palmed air and shouted, "Alto! Alto! No, Tessa! Do not pull out the fence! Oh, *please*. No!" He caught hold of her halter with both hands and managed to slack her off, swiped his brow with a kerchief, said, "She can do that, you know. Contessa do not like to be scolded. She can pop up every fence post, this mula can, if she is not happy."

I threw my hands in the air. "Oh, great! Pap wants to shoot him, Tessa wants to eat him. I'm not going to worry about a pouty mule. I'll worry about how I can keep this horse safe when everybody wants to blame him for something!"

The bleeding eased. I cleaned the wound, inspected the gouge. There was no way to bandage such a tear. "This needs— Never mind. I know."

To the barn, to the work counter, I pulled it from the drawer—.

"Yes, yes. Very good." Sabion stood over me. "Maybe you know healing like you Grandmama? She teach you that?"

"Mims? I don't know about healing, except that this will

keep the wound moist and dirt and flies out." Common sense was a strength, too. For things to be believable, they have to make sense—not the nonsense I'd been living with for these weeks.

I plunged my fingers into the jar, gathered the goo on my fingertips, and slathered the tear.

Chapter Thirteen

"I have a surprise," Sabion crooned with a mischievous grin and his left arm hidden behind his back.

"Oh, yeah?" I leaned to glimpse the hand.

"These jingle bells make me a very good idea! Because you have found the horse cannot wear the bells, I arrange it all a little different for you."

Uh-oh.

"I put them on my Jennie!"

"*Jennie!*" I choked.

Taking a step back, he tucked his bottom lip and lobbed off a whistle shrill enough to reshuffled the roof shingles. The donkey stepped from the barn, *my* bells swinging from a rope around her neck. Stretching her mouth wide to reveal large, chalky teeth, she peeled back her lips and loosed an ear-splitting bawl that fluttered Radar's ears. Something passed between them, almost like a handshake, and he passed me in a trot.

"Wait a minute—"

Sabion raised a hand. "I know. I know already what you will say." A plucky grin, he whipped his hand around ceremoniously and opened the fist. "See?"

In his palm lay a thick, black bracelet of hair. A turquoise cord ran through it with five bells braided into it, each separated by knots, as if they were pearls. "What I make for you is a far better wristlet. I use the long tail hair."

"You braided this? From Radar's tail?"

"The horse, he do not mind." He slipped the bangle over my hand and wagged my wrist. The bells tinkled, a chink rather than a clank. "It make a different sound, you see. Like a tiny tambourin. Radar will follow the big bangle noise from my Jennie's necklace where they clunk altogether. And this sound," He jangled my hand again. "—the horse will know it is you."

I twitched my wrist. Radar's head swung. "It's beautiful. Thank you, Sabion."

He beamed. "Si, I think this will work very much."

Like Rowdy's barks announce the sheep are on the move, and the squeaky barn doors alert Radar the way to his stall, this bracelet would direct him to me.

A mockingbird's crisp call startled me. I'd never paid much attention to birds—they'd always been just a part of the sky and the trees and the telephone lines. Here, I saw them as agitated little creatures, anxious and troubled...constantly moving back and forth, back and forth, as if to show that where they were going was more important than where they had been.

I'd played Brett's invitation over and over in my mind. I wished I could see him again. He was so nice. His eyes were so green. He wore cowboy so well: tall and tan with long, clumsy legs, like elastic. I liked the way the brim of his hat curled up from his ears, as if he'd slept in it.

Did he actually invite me to the rodeo? Or did he say, like Texans say—Y'all come? I tried to recall his exact words. Did he mean, as his guest? Was that what Dr. Ben meant when he said, 'Mind your manners?' *Be nice to Fred's granddaughter?* One of those Texas things, like when a man tips a hat?

The guys in my school wouldn't even know what that was about.

He could've stuck a flyer in my hand on my way out the door: *Fourth of July Rodeo.* But that's not what he did. I looked for the logic in that. Maybe I looked attention deprived—a few weeks with Pap and anybody'd be talking to themselves.

Was I talking to myself?

He didn't have to walk me to the truck, I reasoned. Silly. He'd simply asked Pap to bring me to a rodeo. Nothing more. Everybody was invited, probably as far away as Lubbock. Brett didn't know that Fourth of July was my birthday. Nobody knew.

Sixteen.

And they wouldn't. Birthdays always flustered me. I didn't like the attention; I hadn't since I was ten.

"I'd love to," I answered, my voice small and mousy, pretending Brett had just asked it again, wondering if he meant, like, a date. I pressed the hand he'd held, his touch rough and calloused. Calloused, but warm and intentional. My head went there.

"I've never been to a rodeo," I started again, comfortable talking to the fence post. "What do I wear?" I shook my head....I couldn't ask that! But how else was I to know? Pap? Sabion? *Never!* Pap wouldn't be picking out any more clothes for me, no matter now practical. The sombrero shaded my face. Definitely not wearing this, that much I knew. I ripped it off—the air on my sweaty hatband was cooling.

What *could* I wear? Maybe I'd try mending the rip in my camo pants. Mims had thread. *Camouflage that!* And the blouse I'd worn on the plane? Camouflage with a striped blouse? *Eh, no.*

I would wash the jeans from Littleton's—wash them over and over to give them some fade. *Was that clerk Brett's mother?*

All I brought were T-shirts. I couldn't wear a shirt Pap bought for me. Not only did they hang to my knees, they bunched in my pants if I tucked them.

Boots. *Of course boots.*

"I would love to!" I punched the words to force some confidence into them. I was getting ahead of myself. Pap never said he'd take me.

* * *

I filled a water bucket, washed Radar's bite, dressed the wound, left him in the corral so he could move about while he had it to himself. I'd spotted the metal hoop-band leaning between a couple barrels and vowed to get the lid tightened down on that barrel today while everyone was gone. Nobody even knew that I knew that the barrel was there, and Mr. Nobody had disappeared *again.*

The spiderweb was smashed in the cabinet door. Pap's warnings tingled my ears—all the things that can bite or sting while standing in one spot doing nothing: Snakes and scorpions and leggy spiders. Inhospitable sticker-burs that pierce your feet and won't turn loose, he'd named a few.

He didn't know I'd made a list of my own: scratchy jeans and biting mules. Prickling heat...severe sunburn. Oh! And don't forget heat stroke, though he wouldn't hear about that either. I'd be home, in my other remote existence soon enough. If it weren't for Radar, I'd probably be there now. Except for him, there'd be nothing for me at this ranch. At least at home I could create some diversion: phone, music, television, Wi-fi.

A welcome breeze nipped my neck. I walked the barrel out from under the counter and raked a hand across the bulging fleece. The wool was suspect, that it was so worth saving that Mims sealed it up in the barrel. I dropped the barrel on its side and rolled it to the corridor where the light was some better.

Radar's methodical footsteps slogged across the flagstone. I settled on the ground, the wool mushrooming into my lap, and braced my feet on the rim. Grabbing a fistful with both hands, I pulled. A heavy cigar-shaped pelt as long as my legs slipped onto my lap like a big, rolled-up tortilla. Dust leached up my nose. Radar's head lolled over the rail.

I whistled. "Look, Radar. What is it?" Nostrils flared as he pulled in deep breaths and blew them back in fluttery snorts. "Yeah, makes my nose wrinkle, too." I burrowed my knuckles, smoothed a hand over the fleece, flipped a corner and skated a hand across the velvet underside. Warm, like cream. Soft, like Mom's best gloves.

Unfurling a measure, tattered fringe thronged around my knees like talons. It had no particular shape: angular, uneven... more oval than square, with rangy ends and corners. I lingered over the worn center, tilted a piece to the light where a row of dragonflies were cut above the fringe. Lots of dragonflies. But not like the cute little bugs painted on the barrel.

These dragonflies were hard and grim, like warriors, their long bodies a puzzle streaked with hatch marks or cross-cuts or slashes. Some were daubed with speckles and splatter, others with circles painted inside circles like a bulls-eyes. Each tapered tail had a long, stabbing barb.

The paint must've been imperishable as the colors still dazzled. What did something like this have to do with a sheep ranch? It didn't make sense. It was out of wonk with this place. Why did Pap even have this? I pushed it away with my feet. It clunked as it rolled.

I ran after it and dumped the barrel. Long black straps fell at my feet. I clapped a hand over my mouth, fighting not to squeal.

"Why didn't Pap tell me he had a bridle?" Did he have a saddle, too?

The bridle was black leather, stiff and dry. Nothing a good scrubbing wouldn't clean up. Flashy silver accent strips decorated the cheek pieces and noseband. They were all badly tarnished, though I could see an engraving on each. I spit on one and scoured the gunk away with my shirt tail. "Dragonflies? What's the deal with dragonflies?"

A bright beaded thing was snarled in the bridle's straps. I picked it apart, turned it in my hands. Simple. Beautiful. Handmade. I'd seen enough of Mom's handiwork to know basting stitches: Tiny glass beads the size of BB's stitched on a soft length of leather. The background was beaded in solid white, except across the center was imbedded a large turquoise dragonfly. Opaque beads the color of ice made the dragonfly's wings.

A part of the bridle? A head piece? Did it cinch to something? I fiddled with the tassels...a way to tie it, but couldn't make it work. I hung it on the hook from where I'd taken the halter, flopped the blanket over the rail of the feed stall, and wheeled the barrel back to its hiding place.

I wasn't prying, I would say. *It was just there!*

Chapter Fourteen

Radar snuffled the bridle bunched in my lap. It was cleaning up nicely, the silver conchos shined. His head suddenly swung back. Ears dished.

"I hear it, too. Somebody's coming!" I hurled the bridle at the empty bucket and rushed from the barn as a large diesel truck raced down the road barely staying ahead of the dusty rooster-tail that billowed up behind it. It blew through the gate and sped down the driveway. I buried my face in the crook of my elbow as a choking cloud of dust swirled over me. When everything settled, Dr. Ben stood at the gate behind bronze sunglasses. I ran to meet him.

"Hi, gal." I reached to shake his hand, but his arms wrapped me like an elevator instead. "Got here as quick as I could." He grinned happily—not like the brooder I'd first met in Quitaque. He lifted the shades; eyes swept the yard, the house, the barn. "I haven't been here since your grandmother died."

"My mother came for Mim's funeral."

He nodded, shrugged. "I was late. They told me Miriam had just left." He dusted his jeans with his hat. "Must've been in a hurry."

"Mm," I puzzled. "I don't think she and Pap got along so well. I didn't know why at the time, but now I'm beginning to see things more clearly."

He laughed. "Where is Fred?"

"He's," I brushed the hill with a hasty glance. "—somewhere. Pap might be back before you go, but Sabion will be gone all afternoon."

"No," Dr. Ben drawled the word out. "They'll likely be back very soon. There's a storm brewing." He appraised the sky. "Folks in these parts don't leave it to chance when those kinds of clouds build. We like to celebrate the rain under shelter."

"I would welcome a little shower." I scrutinized the gathering clouds with a fresh eye. "Maybe it won't get this far."

He chuckled. "When it gets here, it won't be like your rain in Seattle. You'll know it!"A tailgate dropped. A shout, "Where do you want this?"

I twirled, dragged a hand through my hair. "Brett!" He rounded the truck with a large cooler, grinning his surprise. I licked dry lips.

"On the porch," Dr. Ben answered. Brett hoisted the cumbersome container to one shoulder, and staggered to adjust. "Don't drop it!" Dr. Ben yelled.

Brett corrected; the shifting weight knocked his hat off. He hesitated, as if unsure whether to set the cooler down and go for the hat, or deliver the goods and come back for it.

Bolting, I swooped to grab the hat and settled it on his head with a decided tap. "There!" Brett winked against the sun. I fixed on the vacant air between us, breaking the eye-lock that left me frazzled. "Follow me."

He joggled the weight. I extended a hand to steady the load. "I hope you're hungry."

"Are you kidding? Around here, always. What'd you bring?" He set the cooler in the shade and fanned the lid with a sidelong look that challenged me to guess. I sipped the spit that watered my tongue. "I didn't see a barbecue restaurant in Quitaque."

"Made to order. We have a saying around here: Give folks a reason to come back." He snugged the lid down. "Ben thought you could use some meat on those bones." He poked me in the ribs and I squeaked. "I didn't say it!" His eyes twinkled over my mess of hair. I smoothed an unruly wave behind my ear. He combed his own with the tip of the hat's brim before adjusting the hat properly. He was even more handsome than I'd remembered, looking so fine in the fresh-ironed, button-up shirt...boots, jeans and the huge cowboy buckle. The blond snaps of brows matched the shaggy chin-growth, but he'd shaved the scatter of hair that grew over his lip.

"I didn't know you were coming." I shucked the long-sleeve shirt down to my tee and tossed it on Pap's rocker. My arms were like lobster claws compared to Brett's deep tan. *Why did I have to get my dad's goober complexion?*

"Wait!" Brett said. "This is just the hot food." He jogged to the truck and hauled back another cooler just as large. "The cold stuff."

* * *

Dr. Ben studied Radar from the gate, hands drawn to his hips, as if appraising art. "He's a beaut!" he said.

"Do you know this horse?"

"Nope." His head wagged slowly. "Never laid eyes on him."

"But you know most horses around here, right?"

He nodded. "I did some checking with other veterinarians in the neighboring counties. Nobody claims to know of a lost Appaloosa. It's odd that he even showed up. Blind horses don't generally take off down a road by themselves." He yanked the latch, peeped cheeping noises as he approached Radar.

"I've kept the mask on him whenever...as much as I could. He doesn't seem to mind. Maybe even likes it."

"It's a comfort." Dr. Ben dragged a hand down Radar's torn shoulder. "What happened here?"

"Sabion's mule bit him. She won't leave him alone. I have to keep them apart."

"Animals are no different than some people in that way— they'll bully whomever they can." Doc probed the wound. "Did you dress this?" I nodded. "Where'd you learn that?"

I shrugged. "Nowhere. I just did it. I had to do *something*. It was pretty ugly."

He gave me a sharp look. "Maybe you're a healer like your grandmother?"

That's what Sabion had said. I shook my head. "No. I just remembered something Mom told me. Does it need stitches?"

He prodded the skin around the tear. "Probably could've used a few, but it's too late now. I think he'll be okay. It'll heal. You did good." He slung a stethoscope over his shoulder. A stain of dried blood coated a cuff. I hoped another calf hadn't been sliced by a fence. Or now that I know, maybe...barbecue sauce?

"I work with Radar every day," I said. "He catches on fast."

The tight smile bundled his lips. "He's got a good teacher."

I shaded my eyes. "That tree's a problem. I'm always afraid he'll run into it."

"Throw something around the base so he'll know when he's close."

"Hay?"

"Sure. Anything that changes the texture for his feet." He tromped a wide circle around Radar; I followed in lock-step like a shadow.

"Hey, Old Man—" I jiggled my wrist and Radar raised his head. I flashed a look at Dr. Ben. "Not you. I call him that sometimes to let him know I'm here. I know better than to walk up on a sleeping horse."

"Exactly right. A blind animal relies on other senses. He'll catch any infliction in your voice, every tone, every pitch and read your mood."

"Sometimes I run out of things to say," I said, grasping for something to say.

"You can always sing!"

I laughed, a vision of it. "I better stick with my flute."

"Sure, why not?" Yanking the scope from his shoulder, he stepped in and laid a hand on Radar's neck, concentrating on a wristwatch with the intensity of a heart surgeon. The hand traveled unhurriedly across Radar's chest, then shifted to his center to prod his girth. I lost him to the beats and sloshes of stomach sounds. Brett watched from the rails, one leg cocked on the bottom rung, one arm folded over the other. His eye caught mine and he grinned. I looked away quickly.

Had I smiled first?

Dr. Ben's hands moved over Radar's ribs, one lifting over the other like hands on a piano, swiping left to right...right to left. "A continuous touch lets this horse know exactly where I am," he said. "Helps keep him calm. The idea is to do whatever you can to ease your horse's anxiety. A blind horse doesn't need the added fright of a sudden poke from out of nowhere." He slid a hand down a foreleg to the knee and pressed. Further down, a squeeze. Down, squeeze, down, squeeze—a smooth motion. Lifting the hoof, he pressed its soft center with both thumbs, then set the leg down carefully. He opened Radar's mouth and examined his teeth, lifted the fleshy lip and rubbed a finger across his gums.

"I pound on the barn siding when we walk by," I said, as if he needed that information.

"Uh-huh."

"That came out weird. I mean, Radar knows the difference. The door has a hollow sound and he's learned it leads to his stall."

Radar stared straight ahead, empty eyes measuring as Dr. Ben moved right and slipped a hand to the throat. I watched the doc's face for the slightest suspicion or hesitation, and Radar's, whether he would yield or flinch. Both remained immoveable, motionless, steadfast.

He finally got to Radar's eyes. Hitching his hat back, he wiped first one, then the other, peering steadily...steadily. I clenched my hands, waiting, waiting. He turned to me, his expression complex. "That's what I figured. Uveitis. Moon blindness."

I clenched my hands and plonked them under my chin. "Moon?"

"An old disease. Ages ago, people thought it was related to the moon because it seemed to flare up so regularly." The ground felt harder under my feet. "Has nothing to do with that, but the name stuck. It's actually an auto-immune disease...recurrent, aggressive. Each case is different."

Splaying a hand protectively to Radar's shoulder, his muscle flexed under my palm. "Can you fix him?"

Dr. Ben shook his head. "Sadly, no. I'm afraid it's too late for this guy. His sight is gone. A disease like this must be caught early. I'm not a veterinary ophthalmologist though—you may want a second opinion."

Pap had never agreed to one vet, he certainly wouldn't let me go to another. "I'd hoped—" I looked away. Dr. Ben couldn't make a difference after all.

"I'm sorry, Charley. Believe me, I wish I could help. Your horse is healthy in every other way."

"How did he get it?"

"People blame it on any number of reasons. When something confuses the immune system anything can set it off: wind and dust...poor housing or pasture, you name it. Stress...flies...an injury—. Infection often spreads from one eye to the other, and it's usually too far gone by the time it's discovered their horse has a serious problem."

I drew a slow breath that filled my cheeks. "Is he in pain?" I couldn't stand it if he were hurting.

"I'd say, no. He doesn't act out like a horse in pain." The hand combed Radar absently. "Keep his eyes clean. Watch for redness or weeping, bleeding...discoloration." "You'll learn what's normal for him."

"He's beginning to trust me. That's what I'm working for."

He nodded. "Good. But you have to have confidence in him, too. Don't doubt his instincts. Animals don't have to think like us to be smart, but, as their care-givers, we have to think like them. Recognize their fears, their frustrations, their anxiety. They express them with signs: vocal sounds, body gestures. Pay attention. Soon, you'll be able to read him, realize what he's trying to tell you."

I rubbed Radar's flapping lip.

"Blind animals can have a perfectly good life. But be careful. Any horse can panic. He's a big, strong animal. Making him feel secure is one thing, but keeping yourself safe is another. He won't mean to hurt you but accidents happen—all the time." He sank his hat back on his head; it folded the tips of his ears forward. "The more he trusts you, the more he'll rely on you to be his eyes."

It wasn't the outcome I expected. I didn't want Pap to be right.

* * *

Barely noon, the mewling sheep tromped over the hill. "Here comes Sabion with the sheep. You're right."

The sheep scattered along the fence and nibbled the thick undergrowth where Sabion left them. He threw Tessa's reins over the rail without tying her, clapped Brett on his back as he passed, slipped off his gloves, and locked hands with Dr. Ben.

"Hola, Doc-tor Ben! Miss Carlota, she say you will come to see the horse."

Dr. Ben chuckled. "The horse, the sheep...the dog."

Sabion brightened. "My Jennie, she like to wear the bells Carlota bring to me! Thank you." Dr. Ben cocked his head uncertainly.

"Sabion, Dr. Ben doesn't know about the bells. *I* bought them. " I explained the unasked question on Dr. Ben's face. "We're using bells to train Radar."

"Oh! Good idea."

I held up the bracelet. "Sabion made this for me so Radar will know where I am. He made the necklace for Jennie. Watch." I jingled my wrist and whistled. Radar looked up, tossed his tail.

"I knew Sabion was resourceful, but didn't know he was crafty, too!" He chuckled.

"Dr. Ben, don't you think I've worked hard enough to be able to ride? Radar is trusting. Sabion agrees he's docile and patient and willing. There's not a mean bone in him. So why can't I ride?"

Dr. Ben looked at Sabion. "You've been on this horse?" he asked.

Sabion gave me a furtive look before answering. "Si. He is a good horse, Dr. Ben. No meanness."

I shook a finger. "You did not tell me you've ridden Radar."

Sabion shrugged. "Sorry, Miss Carlota. I cannot leave a horse with you that I do not first know."

"He's right," Dr. Ben said, his mustache twitching. "Maybe there's something we can do."

"Brett, bring the sheep in, one at a time. Wait until I'm through with one before you bring the next." To me, he blurted as casually as if asking the time. "Is green still your mother's favorite color?"

I had to stop to think. Of all the memories for a grown-up to cling to, it struck me funny. "Ha. She liked green way back then? What's so special about green?"

Brett led a large ewe in.

Dr. Ben pursed his lips thoughtfully. "Maybe we appreciate that color around here because there's not much of it." He forced a smile. "You know how we all wish for the thing we don't have."

I had wishes, too. I wished I'd found Pap to be a different Pap. I wished Dr. Ben could fix Radar. But wishing didn't change anything.

"Who knows. Maybe that's why we live in Seattle—lots of green."

"Does she plan to stay up there?"

I shrugged. "I suppose. It's where we live. Where she works. Where I go to school."

Eyes on the ewe, attention on me, he shook his head. "I never figured Miriam for anything but this country."

I fixed on the scrappy hills with stumpy brush, gray with thirst. At rocks on the hillside the color of ripening cherries that grow so abundantly back home. "Why?"

"Humph. I could never visualize her any other place."

"Why?"

He tilted his head, a slow, spreading smile. "You look so much like her when she was your age. Seeing you with Radar is like seeing Miriam with her horse."

That landed like a rock on my head. "Her horse?" I

repeated, a half echo. Mom never had a horse. Pap didn't have horses.

He dropped the stethoscope in the bag. "Sweet Sal! Miram's Appaloosa. What a trooper. Radar kinda reminds me of Sal." He mulled it over a moment, his eyes turned down. "I guess...being...Appaloosa."

I lost him to a brooding reflection of a distant memory. A rip in my throat kept me silent. I blinked, not seeing.

"We used to ride all over this countryside." He waved an arm at the hills, shook his head at the manure under his feet. "Nobody could ride like Miriam. They were one soul, those two. And barrel racing...she made history."

Pow! That hit me like a kick of thunder. He was confused. He was talking about someone else. I would know. She would've told me.

I glanced at Brett as if for confirmation. He nodded, thumbs plugged under the belt buckle. "There's pictures in the county library."

The sun scorched my head...my confused, bewildered, befuddled head. Dr. Ben was mistaken. He's nice, but I didn't actually know this man. How can he know anything for real about my mother?

She had a horse?

"She sure could put on a show—that pony painted head to tail. I can still feel the energy when she exploded through that gate!" He brushed horse hair from his shirt. I watched the strands blow away like nippy seeds. "Yep, the best barrel-racer this part of the country ever saw, before or since. She still holds the record, you know." He pulled another large ewe to him. "You've never seen the trophies?"

Never seen. Never heard. As horse-crazy as I've always been, Mom would've mentioned that...*that she rode barrels. No. He's wrong.* Why, I'd have been all over it.

"Does she still ride?" he asked.

The words spilled like a waterfall in my ears. It took a while to answer. "I...guess...not—"

Tessa stood at the rail as if sleeping. Dr. Ben ruffled the ewe's head and turned her loose.

"How...how old was she?" I mumbled, the image of the fancy bridle behind my eyes.

He sucked a breath through his nose, spewed it out his mouth. "She rode up until Kyle's accident. I guess she was thirteen...fourteen." He shook his head, a *tsk...tsk* on his tongue. The long bushy mustache hid his lip.

Kyle?

Chapter Fifteen

A battle was raging inside me. *Barrel racing?* The best barrel-racer from this part of the country and she never bothered to tell me? Everybody knew my mom as a hot dog barrel racer, except me? How's that any different from a Dad who professed to live one way while he actually lived another? It stung my eyes.

Liars! Cheaters! And this...this Kyle—

I needed space....to be alone. Alone to soak up the crazy trivia, categorize it fiction or fact. Alone to think how Mom could have had her own horse in this place, but couldn't have shared it with me.

Brett hustled another ewe into the corral; Dr. Ben fixed her between them. I took a step back...backing, backing until I could turn. I ran blindly to the barn. Running to what? *From what?* I hurled Radar's gate open, slammed it shut, stood in the center of the stall flashing anger everywhere. I'd never heard any of this! Mom never mentioned a Dr. Ben, or barrel racing, or riding across the plains. I wouldn't have forgotten. My stomach was in a knot. I'd have quizzed her with a gazillion questions.

What upset me most, that she had a horse and did all the

things I'd only wished I could do, or that she'd hidden it from me? I took a ragged breath. Because she did! She hid it! She didn't forget! She didn't think it was unimportant!

I flipped the bucket. The bridle dropped at my feet. My palms were sweaty. I kicked it across the stall. It landed like a horseshoe in the dirt. I tried to recollect a name like Sweet Sal. She'd told me stories about the sheep, so why couldn't she have talked about her horse, when she knew horses were my dream? She *knew* that! I lunged for the bridle, snatched it up, hugged it to me. It felt different in my hands. Calculating.

I flopped the pail upside down and sunk down, slumping against the stall. How did she always put it: Deceiving and concealing a truth is like a lie. What else did she lie about? *That Dad was never coming home?* It scared me that, suddenly, I couldn't even remember the good.

* * *

A hand combed the top of my head. I flung back, blinked hard. "You all right?" Brett asked. "Are you hurt?"

How long had I been sitting here? I chuckled dryly, sniffed. "Just my identity."

Brett pressed through the gate and towered over me. He looked confused. "Did I say something?"

"No! No, of course not. It's just—" How could I explain? "I don't handle surprises very well."

"What surprise?" he asked.

Serious? He wouldn't understand. I bet *he* didn't come from a deceitful family. He couldn't know how the divorce had colored every fiber of my life: one parent gone, the other... absent. When she was there, it was only halfway.

"I just..." I pegged Brett as a kind, sensitive guy, and shook the suspicion from my head. He was being a friend. I confessed, "I'm hurt that my mother never told me about...any of this—" I flicked a hand. "—barrel racing. That she even had a horse." *Was that pity in his eyes?* I dug a boot in the dirt. "And don't say she forgot! Nobody forgets something like that. She *chose* not to tell me."

The brim of his hat touched a shoulder in something of a shrug. "There's probably more to it."

"Sure there is." My voice warbled. I felt the tear trail my face. "I think I'm starting to get it." I shoved the bridle at him.

"Hey! Nice one." He picked the bridle out of my hands. The straps drooped through his fingers, the silver conchos glowed in his hand.

"Lots of good that does. Pap let my mother run barrels and he won't even let me *sit* on a horse!"

"Cheer up." He pressed his hat onto my head. I raised my face to him; the brim fell over my brows. He smiled. "Looks good on you."

"I'm sorry. I know I sound like a brat."

"Naw. But don't you see? This is your ticket!" He reached a hand out and pulled me up. "We're finished with the sheep. Let's go talk to Ben."

Mom would call tomorrow. I would have lots of questions. She better have the right answers.

* * *

Dr. Ben took the bridle like a delicate thing. I couldn't see his face for the hat that shadowed it. "It's Miriam's." He pulled on the straps, tugging their strength. "She won it." He looked up. "I told you she was good."

The silver flashed in the sun. With one hand Dr. Ben offered Radar the bit. With the other, he unlashed the halter and handed it off to me. He swiped a sleeve across his face and gave Brett a nod.

Brett flung onto Radar's back and propelled him forward with a modest tap. I held my breath to see him ride Radar, watch them circle the corral. Radar's gait was smooth, his tail arched.

Dr. Ben opened the gate and Brett trotted through. They loped to the end of the driveway, then Dr. Ben whistled, and Brett turned Radar around. He stopped beside me. I wanted that sparkle on *my* face.

"C'mon," Brett said. "Let's go for a ride."

The words mushed in my ears. I steepled my hands over my mouth and twisted, searching the porch, the barn, the path from the hill. Dr. Ben's eyes followed. "It won't be a problem."

Brett extended a hand; Dr. Ben laced his hands together to make a footstep.

"Not the hand," Brett shook my hand aside. "Lock wrists."

I clutched his wrist and stepped a foot into doc's knotted palms. He tossed as Brett lifted and swung me like a wave onto Radar's rump.

Radar shifted under me, and my heart laughed. His saucy scent hit my nose—a smell I loved even more from where I now sat.

I could already imagine the silent treatment I'd get from Pap, but all the barbs I'd taken from him just washed away. Who cares whose bridle it was...it was mine now! I'd rescued it from the barrel. It, too, was meant to be mine! All the years of tacking horse pictures on my bedroom wall was just school play. I shuffled into position and sat tall.

"Hold on," Brett yawped.

I chuckled nervously. "Where? There's nothing to hold to."

"Me!"

Swigging a breath, I clamped a hand over each shoulder.

"No. Put your arms around my waist." He waited for me to shuffle closer and wrap my arms around him. His shirt was slightly damp and wore the tang of sheep scent. I was conscious of the curvature of his back, the stone slab of his middle, his stiff hat that shaded my nose, and felt my whole body flush. Could he feel my heart throbbing through my skin? It felt so natural. "Here we go!" He tapped Radar gently.

Radar stepped lively; the thrill sent me chirping. The power of him left me feeling tiny on his back. I'd waited and waited and waited for this moment!

"He trusts me to lead him, but I'll let him set the pace." Brett gave him rein, and Radar lunged. My head jerked back, my grip tightened. We trotted all the way up the driveway, through a fence that led the way the sheep left every morning. Radar pranced...his happy-tail swishing with each step. He responded to Brett as well as any horse with vision could have.

"My stomach is doing flip-flops," I said to Brett's ear.

"Probably 'cause you're hungry. I know I am."

Radar moved into a trot, holding his head high as we circled back from the hill and down the long drive that led back to the barn. "How long are you going to be in Texas?" Brett asked.

He couldn't see my shrug. "I didn't know I'd even make it here this long." *But now—*

Dr. Ben opened the gate and we pranced through.

"What a great horse." Brett leaned over and patted Radar's neck, then pried my hand from his middle. His profile was turned—I saw the grin. "Throw your legs over the side, grab my elbow, and slide off." He cocked an arm. I wrapped my hand through it and slid to the ground.

Dr. Ben reached in his pocket and held his hand open to Radar who lapped up the sugar lump. "Maybe you'd like me to take you on a real ride?"

"Yes! Yes! Of course I would!" I sounded childish, hopping

so eagerly on the offer, but I couldn't hide my excitement. I couldn't have wiped the smile off if I got bucked over the hill Pap walked every day.

"How about me?" Brett said. "I can come! I mean, can I come?"

"Sure." Dr Ben turned to me. "Thursday. We'll bring horses."

"And I'll ride Radar!" I said breathlessly.

"Mm. We'll have to talk about that. There'll be rules."

Rowdy burst through the gate in a billowy dust cloud and flopped at my feet as if dead. Pap rounded the pen, a scowl on his face. Dr. Ben spoke first.

"Hello, Fred. You don't have anything to worry about with this horse." He slapped Radar's hip with a resounding smack that raised Radar's head. "Beautiful animal. He'll be a good friend."

"Great," Pap answered, as if it weren't. "Then you came to collect him none too soon."

Dr. Ben shifted a look back at his truck. "Hm. Seems I don't have a trailer back there. Guess you'll have to hang onto him a while longer." He reached into another pocket and sunk a needle into Rowdy's hip, then gave him a dog biscuit and a good shakedown.

"If you expect to charge me for this visit, you can forget it."

Dr. Ben laughed. "Now, Fred. There's no secrets in Quitaque. Everybody knows you have more land and more money than all the people in three counties put together. I know you're not concerned about a little bill from me. But, nope, except for the sheep, I'm doing this as a favor to Charley." Pap's eyes drifted to me. Dr. Ben laughed. "I will squeeze you for the rabies shot I just gave your mutt though."

"Humph. I didn't order one."

"Well, we have to keep Rowdy healthy, now don't we?" He winked at me.

Pap threw his hands in the air.

"Can we eat?" Brett said. "I'm starving."

* * *

"The horse doesn't have a wary temperament," Dr. Ben was telling Pap as I scooped ice in cups and pretended I wasn't listening. "Doesn't exhibit a fight-or-flight response. He'll be a good fit for her."

"No!" Pap boomed, stabbing a sausage link from the plate of barbecue.

"I wouldn't say it if I didn't believe it."

"Bah! Then you ride 'em home. The horse has no business here." He dragged the sausage through the sauce and chewed with his front teeth.

Dr. Ben toyed with his fork, weighing his words. "Fred, Charley's not seven years old. You can't deny it's in her blood."

"What's in my blood?" I asked.

Pap blew an exaggerated breath, let his knife fall. Cole slaw spilled. "Sure! Fine!" He wrangled sticky fingers over his jeans. "Take 'em all! Just take 'em all why don't you?"

Dr. Ben ignored Pap's thunder like he ignored the grumbling sky. "Sabion and I agree, Charley has to learn to mount before she can ride."

Sabion nodded, chucked a piece of brisket fat to Rowdy.

Pap clucked, "She's not strong enough to pull herself up on a horse and you know it. If she grew two more feet she still couldn't do it! Stay outta my business."

I slammed my tea glass on the table...*thwack!* "I'm stronger than I look. I just rode bareback!"

Brett leaned in. "They mean you have to mount without help. Mount bareback."

I shrugged. "If that's what I have to do, I'll do it! I can learn."

Pap glared. "You think you're too young to die?"

"Die? We're talking about riding a horse, Pap." *For this, I will pretend he's a loving Pap.*

Sabion groomed the potato salad with his fork. Rowdy's eyes followed his hand with every bite. "I have no time to teach—"

"I will!" Brett shouted. All eyes turned on him.

Pap's face flushed. Knife angled at Dr. Ben, he jiggled the tip. "Alright, Muttonhead. You don't know what you're unleashing. I'm holding you responsible."

Dr. Ben bent over his plate. "I can carry that weight."

"Tomorrow!" Brett said. "I don't work tomorrow. I'll be here by nine and we'll start your first lesson." He tipped his hat. "Mounting is just a technique. You'll catch on quick."

Dr. Ben turned to Pap. "I have another reason for coming, Fred. Maybe I can talk to you and Sabion privately?"

Brett helped me carry leftovers into the kitchen. Indistinct jabber—sheep and lost and ravaging—drifted through the window. I washed forks and knives and glasses. Brett dried. I wished there were more.

* * *

It rained this evening in Texas! Heavy clouds rolled over the ranch, changing the landscape, coming down hard in large, sloshing drops that muddied the ground and pinked the dusky hills. It rolled past as suddenly as it began.

Pap had gone to bed. A glint of light burnished in the barn where Sabion sang to his donkey—the ill-mannered lassie who'd never seen a swift kick to her rump. They were a comical team, Sabion and Jennie, and I was so glad they were here. I couldn't imagine a summer alone with Pap, a man I wanted to steer clear from like bugs under the bed.

I slipped off to my room. The scratchy limbs of cicadas sang from the trees. If I were back in Seattle, it would still be light. I would probably be deep in yackety-yak with old friends from my old school. What were Sharon or Alex doing right now? Making plans for the weekend? Did they ever ask Mom about me? Wonder why I didn't text?

Changing to my night clothes, I picked up the picture of a happy-looking Pap from the dresser—evidence he wasn't always this way. So much isolation couldn't be good for him. Of course he was sad after losing Mims. I could relate, from a little different perspective. I hugged the pillow. "You don't know this, Pap, but I won't give up on you like you gave up on Mom, like Dad gave up on me. I want to be the one who makes things different."

I was trying hard not to make mistakes. I could vividly recall every single thing I regretted. Things I couldn't change. I didn't want my visit to be Pap's regret.

Chapter Sixteen

The kitchen was smoking. I reached across Pap, popped the blackened toast, gave the tiny knob a good, hard, counter-clockwise twist. "This little button controls how light or dark you toast the bread," I said testily. "You don't *have* to burn it."

He contemplated me smugly over the steaming mug poised at his lips. "Well, see now, I didn't know that."

I plunged in two more slices and rammed the lever down. A truck backfired. Gears shifted on the incline. I dashed to the window, a hand to my throat as Brett made the turn down the drive.

"Oh! He's two hours early!" I flailed my arms at Pap. "I'm not dressed...haven't brushed my—" I stomped a circle. "Pap, go meet him! Tell him—"

Pap slurped the coffee, snowy brows tethered like matching paintbrushes. I exploded, stamped a foot. "Argh! Do something. Tell him...tell him I'm almost ready! Tell him I'll be right there!"

I snagged a piece of bacon and sprinted to my room, pausing a nano-second at the living room window to yelp, "Oh! He's almost here!"

No time to shower.

I brushed the night scrum off my teeth. My hair smelled like burnt toast. *Maybe he won't notice.* I scrubbed my face, doused on some sunscreen, shucked the shorts, stumbled into my jeans, and drew my newest T-shirt over my head.

There were voices in the kitchen.

Er— Boots! I turned a circle. "Boots! Where are my boots?" Blood pumped through my head like oil through a machine. "Rowdy better not have...*grr!—*" I spread out on the floor and smacked the bed skirt aside. There they were, pressed against the wall at the head of the bed. I had no idea how they got there.

Buffing the floor grime off my clothes, I grabbed the long-sleeved shirt on the way out the door, stopped just outside the kitchen to take a deep breath, and strolled leisurely through lobbing the shirt casually over my shoulder like a forgotten thing. Brett looked up with his wonderful smile. My stomach did a flip. It might've been ages instead of hours since I'd seen him.

* * *

Radar's expression was drawn, as if he felt himself concealed. Jennie nestled beside him, the two like an old pair of sneakers.

I said, "I can't imagine why Sabion left her behind today. Shoo, Jennie. You can't come this time."

Brett cleared his throat. "Actually, he left her here for you."

"Really?" I snorted. "I'm riding Radar. You can have Jennie."

"You're having a lesson today, remember? The mounting?"

"Of course." I scratched the narrow crest of my nose where a thick blob of sunscreen blocked a corner of my inside vision.

"Mounting bareback is a technique," he began, all business-like.

I turned a buoyant, but serious, all-ears look of concentration to him, student to instructor. He was so cute. What luck that he'd volunteered. He was everything I couldn't have imagined a cowboy to be.

He brushed eyes over me, away, back to me as if he couldn't quite decide if I'd spoken. "That means we start small."

"Small," I repeated, nodding all my attention at him.

He cleared his throat. "You have to learn from the ground up before you can work from his back down." His eyes flashed to Jennie, where they lingered before blinking back to me.

"Of course. Ground." I said, almost giddy, and stabbed the dirt with my toe. He gave a head jerk to the donkey. I followed the Jennie-wag. It all curdled together. Pinning my hands to my hips, I spun, and gawped at Brett. "What?" He nodded. "No way! Jennie?" Jennie yawned. "Seriously? I can practically step over her."

Brett grinned. "I started on one her size."

"But...but you were probably only a kid." Who'd obviously grown some legs.

"True. But that little pony of mine looked ten feet tall at the time. The technique is the same."

A chair scraped the porch. Pap settled his coffee on a side table and molded himself into the rocker.

Great. Just great. When I want him here, he disappears. When I don't, he lines up like it's a lemonade stand. *Always ready for a good laugh?*

Brett called me back to my task. "When you learn to swing onto Jennie, you can do it on Radar. It's easy, once you find your mojo. Watch."

Facing backward at Radar's wither, Brett grasped a fistful of mane with his left hand. "You watching?" He swiveled a look to make sure I was. "A tight clutch here, a little skip-hop, then leap quickly, like springs live in your boots. Hurl and hoist." Brett sprung easily onto Radar's back, adjusted his posture, then dropped back to the ground. "See? I'll do it again."

He did...again and again, adding a frisky little shuffle before extending like a grasshopper, swung his right leg wide, hooked a boot, and adjusted, sitting tall in the dip of Radar's back.

"Easy. Now you try." He pointed. "On Jennie."

Jennie eyed me. Pap was feasting...his neck bent. There was no turning back.

I grabbed a handful of ragged mane and lunged, but my feet didn't lift. I fell against her like into a brick wall, and felt myself blush. "That was just to get the feel of it, like measuring." I said to Brett.

Pap leaned back in his rocker and shoved the slice of his hands under his armpits.

This time I hurled at Jennie with the intensity of a jack hammer, willing my feet to fly, which they did. I curled over Jennie's thick body and right off the other side.

Jennie hawed in my face, sucking air and blowing back as if she were gagging.

Brett stifled a laugh, offered a hand. He'd made it look so effortless. Graceful, even.

I lined up for another hop, flicking a discomforting glance back to the porch. Pap wore no expression at all, but planted his boots on top of Ben's cooler. I flung at Jennie with a pretty good leap, but she side-stepped—I vaulted over her head and plunged to the ground. I shook the dust off. "Did you see what she *did*? She did that on purpose!"

Brett chuckled, offered his hand to haul me up again. "Oh, you know donkeys, how they like to show you who's really in control. I told you it wasn't easy."

I brushed the tiny pebbles from my hands. "You told me it *was* easy."

"It is, once you learn it."

I scrubbed my chin with the back of a hand, tried a common sense approach. "Shouldn't I be working this jump out on Radar since there's a good, mm...three feet difference?"

Brett shook his head. "Doesn't matter. Sabion's no taller than you, but he gets up on Tessa the same way every day."

"Sheesh." I rolled my eyes. "That's not fair."

I marched up to Jennie, stood in her face and shook my finger. "Listen up, you little shrew. Don't do this to me. I need all my energy to tackle that four-legged tall boy that you're so fond of. We're going to do this until we get it right. So be nice, and the day will go smooth." I positioned for another hoist.

* * *

It didn't come right away, or even on time, but the moves finally came together. At last, I was sitting upright at the end of my leap, having landed on Jennie just right.

"I did it! I did it!" Brett high-fived me. "You're right. It's the tempo! I felt it! Like learning to ride a bike without training wheels."

I pivoted, but Pap was gone.

"I knew you'd get it. Now, try it on Radar. Don't let his height fool you. It's the very same, just more lift, a little more pull." He gave me a sly look. "Unless your Grandpap's right...you're not strong enough."

"I am! It's...*difficult*." I stood beside Radar, a clutch of hair in my fist, and calculated his height. I couldn't fail.

Determined to show everybody, I leapt, frog-kicking, twisting and eating dirt...performing the awkward dance of skip-hop, jump-hurl...mid-air kick with a slight body twist in a perfectly timed vault, while Brett called out each step.

"You're making progress." He urged me on. "That was...uh...better." He'd shout. He wouldn't let me quit. After two hours, he began harassing: "Charley, you've got to get up on this horse or you'll never get to ride! And you've got to do it all by yourself. I can show you a thousand times, but you're the one who has to do it. Push everything out of your head. Repeat each step."

By noon, my muscles were screaming. I hung upside down from Radar's neck like an opossum, my feet flapping in the air.

Brett laughed. "Stop clowning. This is serious. Ben's going to be here in a few days. If you want to ride Radar, you've got to learn to do it."

I felt faint. My hands were raw. Good thing there wasn't a hole in my head or all my brains would drain out. "I'm...not clowning!" I huffed, no arm strength left. "I'm—" I spit hair. "—trying to get up... here." Radar stood rigid and patient as I slipped down his leg.

Brett pulled me out from under him by my boots. "One more time."

"Why can't I climb from the fence?" I'd entered the whiny stage of the day. "I just want to sit on him...ten minutes."

"Sorry. Ben said you had to learn this."

"But, why?" My joy was melting. I was failing.

"What if you're off someplace by yourself with nobody to help you? No rail or stool to stand on? It'd be a long, roasting walk." He whipped off his hat and dusted the back of my shirt like Sabion would've done. "You need a break."

We raided the refrigerator, carried sandwiches and drinks to the tree that shaded the yard. Radar was parked at the gate swishing flies away with his tail. Jennie stood nearby, her eyes closed, as if exhausted.

"Bareback riding is completely different from using a

saddle." Brett lectured. I peeled waxed paper away from my sandwich and nibbled the beef that hung from its edges. "You connect with your horse and he with you. He can sense your ability. Fear even. Your composure sends messages as well, like if you get unbalanced." The sun stabbed my eyes. "The more you ride, the more your horse knows how to adjust to you, or knows to wait for you to adjust to him. It might feel funny at first, but soon you'll see, Radar can tell what you want him to do by your posture, how you use your body."

"If I ever get to."

Brett ripped into his sandwich, popped the top on his cola, tipped the can back and drank long, squinting into the bright sky. "You never said when you have to go home."

I sighed. Chewed. Swallowed. "In a couple weeks." I didn't even want to think about it. Before I found Radar, before I met Brett, it felt as if I'd been here a year. Now I had a purpose.

"How come you've never been here before?"

Brett was easy to talk to, but not when the subject was me. I didn't know why I'd never been here. I mean, maybe I did, but I couldn't confess to a nice Texan like him that my folks wanted nothing to do with West Texas. Maybe he'd think I wasn't even worth knowing. And yet, Texas and family was the very reason for my coming—to see for myself. Now I knew. I'd stepped onto the Staked Plains just to pull the cover off their lies. I shrugged, crammed in a mouthful of chips, and suffocated the answer: "Uh-jegum—"

He asked, "What's Seattle like?" Our fingers met over the potato chip bag.

"Beautiful. There's so much water, of course." *We have to wrap in sweaters and jackets, even in the middle of summer.* "The sky is incredibly blue." *When we see it through the constant current of cloud that track to the mountains...rain clouds in summer, snow clouds in winter.*

"The Puget Sound is a large inlet from the Pacific ocean." *The water temperature doesn't change more than five degrees winter to summer, so, not much on water sports.* "It rains a lot, which is why we have so much green...flowers, forests!" *Then fog from October through...* I turned a smile on him. "Not so many flies." I shooed one from my soda can.

He stared off, as if visualizing the place. "What kind of things do you do with your friends?"

I thought about that, my *before* friends, Sharon and Alex. Not so many *after* friends...just curious faces at a new school. "The usual. Movies. Shopping. Baseball in the summer."

Nothing.

Brett leaned back on an elbow and scanned the long drive, as if gauging its length. "Too bad we couldn't have met earlier."

"Um-hum." I wadded the napkin in the waxed paper and rolled them together in a tight little ball.

"I guess you feel better? After yesterday?"

Brett was so self-assured, such a planted person, while I was guided by a broken compass.

I asked, "Did you buy all that stuff Dr. Ben was saying...that the bridle belonged to Sweet Sal? That Radar could be her offspring—even her offspring's offspring?"

He shrugged. "Yes. It's possible."

"Well, I didn't." There'd been too many arrows flying at me at once.

"Did your grandpa say anything about the rodeo next week? Whether y'all are coming?"

I shook my head. "He hasn't mentioned it." He'd been making himself kinda scarce. I didn't mention to Pap that the Fourth of July was my birthday. *Sixteen.* Even if he knew, it would only be false glee. I'd keep it to myself. That way I wouldn't be disappointed when he disappointed me. That went for Brett, too. I didn't like spotlights.

"I'll talk to him before I leave," he said. "If he'll let me, I can drive out and bring you back to town, except I'd have to pick you up really, really early. I'm on the set-up committee. And, then, I won't even be free until after it's over."

Did he like me? Or was he just being nice, because...he's nice?

"Are you trying for another belt buckle?" I asked.

"Sure. It would be my seventh for team roping."

"Do you keep yours in a display case?"

He chuckled. "I suppose I do. I wear them occasionally."

I nodded. Where was I going with this? "I found some buckles in the barn."

"Really? After we get through here, show me. It's cool that you found that bridle."

"*Glurp*—" I sat up, swept my hair back, a gag in my throat. "I think I swallowed a fly!"

"It won't hurt you." He clapped me on the back. "Especially if you don't know for sure."

* * *

I closed my eyes and concentrated on timing the mount. "I'm visualizing the leap," I murmured, as if hypnotized. Reaching high, I grabbed a thick swath of black mane for what felt like the thousandth time.

Radar turned his head back to my leg, as if to prod me on. I buckled my knees and bounced on the balls of my feet until I felt the leap rise up in me, like for a pole vault. I was surprised when my toe snagged Radar's rump. Inching a boot, then a knee over his hip, afraid to pause, afraid to smile, I wiggled into the sink of back and arched in a sit that fit my hips like a triangle over Radar's backbone.

"You're right! You're right!" I laughed down at Brett. "I get it now! It's a process! Not so complicated."

Brett smiled. "What'd I tell you? It's just RPM's...rhythm, pace, and—" He raised a brawny arm, bent at the elbow. "—muscle." He clutched my boot. "Without the struggle, you'd never have known how it feels to do it right."

I whipped my phone from my pocket and snapped a picture: the view from Radar's back! "Now what do we do?"

"Practice until you can do it every time."

"I won't forget. I'm ready to ride."

"Where are your reins?"

The bridle straps lay slack on the ground. I leaned over Radar's neck, stretching to reach them. "Hand them up to me, please."

His mouth jerked sideways in a smirk. "No, Charley." He shook his head slowly. "What good would that do if nobody's around to get them for you? You have to get down and get them yourself."

I didn't want to get down. It was a long way to the ground, and an even longer way back up.

"Brett." I said with as much business-attitude as I could muster. "It took me all afternoon to get here. Just—" I motioned a gimme.

"Nope. Once more."

I rolled my eyes; he raised an eyebrow. Slinging my leg over Radar's rump, I slid to the ground, my mouth clenched. I wrangled the reins in a handful of mane, but rather than a leap, my forehead dropped into Radar's shoulder. "I can't," I cried.

"Sure you can. You did it once. You can do it again."

I shook my head. I knew better. I had no energy left.

"Okay," he said. "That's it for today. You know what you have to do the rest of the week: practice, practice, practice." He intertwined my hand with his and raised our hands between us. "Show me the buckles."

Maybe Brett could make some sense of the rest of the stuff in the barrel.

Chapter Seventeen

The spidery cabinet door dangled on its hinge. I swung it wide, but the box was not there.

"They were here. In a—" I squared my hands the size of the box. "—a wooden curio case."

He stepped back to look. "There's something on the top shelf. Is that it?"

"I don't know." I rocked on the balls of my feet, straining to see that far up. "Might be. Wait!" I ducked under the counter, wobbled the old barrel out, dropped it on its side, and started to climb.

Brett stopped me. "You're not tall enough to reach even if you stand on the counter. Let me." He stair-stepped from the barrel onto the counter and pulled a box forward far enough to ooze a low whistle. "Wow." He looked down, forced a smile.

"What?"

"You're not gonna believe this." His hand stirred in the box. "It's not the buckles."

"What, then?"

"Trophies!"

I startled. "Trophies? What kind of trophies?" Images of little sheep awards came to mind.

"Rodeo, what Ben was talking about." He lifted a figure, paused to read the inscription on its base. A pencil of sunshine lit the golden bling of a horse statue, the rider's head broken off. His eyebrows arched as he handed it down. "Take a look. From way back in '92." He looked up. "I wasn't even a kid yet. Neither were you."

The metal was warm in my hand. My lips moved over the words. *First Place Quitaque Barrel Racing Competition, 1992.* I tried the word on, her name strange on my tongue. "Miriam Kotes and..." My hand went to my throat. I looked up. Brett's eyes were on me. "And Sweet Sal."

I felt my face go flamingo. It wasn't that I'd *completely* doubted Dr. Ben. I just couldn't believe it real. But this...*this?* This just cemented the slice of denial I'd been clinging to. "Dr. Ben's stories are true, then? Sweet Sal was a real horse?"

Brett nodded. I scrubbed a finger across my cheek. *She would've told me* flew right out the window. "Here's another."

I reached, turned the inscription to the light. It was like the other, but a different year: *First Place Quitaque Barrel Racing Competition, 1993, Miriam Kotes and Sweet Sal.*

"There's more," he said. "A *bunch* more!" He dragged the box off the shelf, lowered it to the counter, whipped off his hat and stooped over them, pulling out one after another. "See? '94, 95. Not only that, she got First Place at the Tri-County Championship. She took Championships four years running...and State! Miriam Kotes and Sweet Sal, 1995."

I may not know the significance or difference of the rodeos, but I did know what State Champion meant: The difference between skill and art. I scratched the itch on the back of my hand. *This, too, best kept secret ever.*

His hand stirred in the box. "They're all broken," he said

apologetically, as if he'd taken a hammer to them himself. "These ought to be in the house, not the barn. Then they wouldn't be broken."

My eyes met his, fluttered to the glitz in his hand. I felt the urge to scatter the trophies he lined up on the counter like Legos while he picked through the broken heads trying to match one to its body.

"Here's something pretty cool: Best of Show, 1996, Miriam Kotes and Sweet Sal."

I smacked the trophy on the counter a little too hard. He startled, cocked his head. "I don't know this Mom!" I snapped. "All the years...the things she could've taught me. Why didn't she share this part of her life? Why did she hide it?" His eyes skimmed mine and slipped away. "She didn't *want* me to know."

"I had no idea you didn't," he said quietly. "Your mom is a legend around here. Everybody knows who she is. Ben's right. She has a reputation for being the best horsewoman this part of the country ever produced, before or since." A trickle of sweat ran down my spine. "Like he said, she still holds the records. Those photos I told you about in the library are framed and hanging—professional pictures. I'll take you there and you can see for yours—"

"Stop!"

Brett cocked his head. "Okay. Well, except," He shifted awkwardly, bunched his lips respectfully. "—there's some pictures you will probably like to see."

Raising to the top shelf, he swept up a handful of photos and spread them out on the worktable. I caught the warning in his eyes, felt the weight of something urgent pressing, and let my eyes drift to the young teen sitting tall and statuesque on a sorrel appaloosa with the composure of someone confident, proud, serene. Strings from the horse pad tangled around her foot.

I'd never seen pictures of my mom as a kid, never seen her

hair plaited in braids or her young body poured into leather leggings with tanned moccasins reaching for her knees.

I fixed on her knowing smile. She could've been me.

Sweet Sal, larger than life in the stunning bridle was flamboyantly painted with symbols and figures, scrawls and squiggles, a great white circle painted around one eye. The distinguishing appaloosa splotches were enlivened with paint that blended them together like red, white, yellow polka dot bubbles. The braided tail was intertwined with turquoise ribbons.

I could see why Dr. Ben might suggest Radar could be her offspring.

I brought the photo close to my face. The beaded thing I'd found with the bridle was lashed around her waist. What I'd guessed to be a decoration for Radar's bridle was actually a belt?

The work space suddenly looked very different. The low-built cubbyhole and paint-splattered workbench...the pale blue barrel with the fuzzy mass I couldn't shove back inside, now the barrel made sense. I pressed a thumb and forefinger to the bridge of my nose, and pinched. It belonged to Mom.

The wooly skin was Sweet Sal's horse pad. The bridle, the belt, the whole darned paint-smeared room, I saw my mother there, and felt shafted all over again. I'd have never imagined a Pap who would build his daughter a space of her own. Things couldn't have been so bad as she'd claimed. And the missing belt buckles? I guess they were hers too?

She didn't want any of this for me.

"This place," I started. "How can you live with someone all your life and not know the things they care about?" A slurry of emotions washed over me. I *knew* there was a reason I had to come to Texas.

Brett nodded, shrugged, shook his head regretfully. "I

couldn't honestly say, but look at this." He pushed a photo at me, an action shot of Mom leaning hard into Sal's neck as if their bodies were welded.

I felt humiliated that Brett knew what I didn't. What must he think?

I picked up a worn, stained photo unlike the others—the face of a woman, ancient and wrinkled and brown. A breeze had caught her flowing white hair in the frame. She wore a congealed expression, as if squinting over the sun. Her feet were bare except for the leather band around one ankle. The picture tore at my throat. "This can't be Mims."

Brett peered over my shoulder. "She's definitely Comanche."

"Comanche? What's it doing here?"

"In the South Plains, are you kidding? You see a lot of stuff like that around here."

I flipped it over. "Little Old Woman." *Hidden like everything else. What else is Mom hiding?*

Like a scent at my back, my fingers had a twitch, as if waiting for a decision to be made.

"Put everything back!" I whooped.

"Huh?" Brett raised a brow at the sternness in my voice.

"Put the trophies back just like you found them!" I raked the broken pieces into the box. "If they're important enough to hide, then I'll pretend I don't know about them." I gave a heartless laugh I didn't feel and pushed the box at him.

He shrugged. "Okay."

"Except for the photos! I'm keeping these." I gathered the black and white picture of Mims, the faded sepia photo of Little Old Woman, the color-filled picture of teen-Mom with Sweet Sal and shoved them in my back pocket. "I'm sure Pap won't mind." *Who else is there to carry out the legacy of lies?*

Somebody had some explaining to do, but I would choose the time.

"I'm certain," he said. "If your grandpap is anything like my folks, he probably has hundreds."

I almost laughed.

He'd barely slipped the box in its hole when an explosive *Cr-ack!* made me twirl.

"Oh, geez!" Jennie's front leg had punched through two of the barrel's wooden slats. She shoved her face into mine. "You... you...you broke the barrel! Get off!"

I shoved, but trying to move her was like pushing a freight train. She jerked her leg loose but brought two more jagged pieces of wood with it, leaving behind a big, ragged hole in the antique barrel.

Brett hopped down and thwacked the counter with a smacking good sound. Jennie backed.

"How'd she get in here? " he asked.

I whirled, and spotted the gate I hadn't thought to close. Jennie stuck her nose in the barrel, sank her teeth in the heavy, wooly brown mass.

"No! Drop it!" I hollered as if scolding Rowdy.

Brett caught an ear and held firm, tugged her down the path I'd so handily cleared, and shooed her though the gate. "Git!"

Jennie stopped in the corridor, rolled her lips back in a sneer, walked away swirling her tail and laughing through teeth too big for her mouth.

I slammed the gate and threw the latch. My insides were upside down. I couldn't hide this much damage. How would I explain it?

A lot can change in a week. I felt like somebody else. Not new...just different. There was too much I didn't understand. I wanted to know, wanted to know everything, but I'd settle for a little.

Yet, when Mom called, I managed to be unavailable.

159

Chapter Eighteen

"Training must begin in your heart," Sabion had cautioned. "Do not use the bridle to yank or pull, to clench or snatch his tender mouth. He is a partner. Let him know what you want. Show him that you will not teach with anger or hurt. Let the horse be calm."

I worked out cues and signals to steer Radar around obstacles, learning I could shuffle him sideways a step or two with a tap of my heel when I didn't need to turn him: one tap to move one step, two taps to move two steps. Any more than that, I used the reins. I combined the foot signals with hand nudges and verbal commands: clacking and clicking sounds, words and whistles, and the wrist bells. I found I could control a giant with few words, anticipating each leg as it raised, each foot planted.

Radar was attentive and obedient, and aware that when I pressed both legs flat against his ribs, it was a signal to increase the pace. He discovered quickly that every command had a meaning: Move here, move there. Pay attention! A slow walk. Now trot. Break into a slow lope. To stop, I simply raised the reins and let Radar slow at his own pace, Sabion's prescribed method.

I was circling the corral in a moderate trot, stiff and jarring, when Sabion waved me over and wagged a finger. "This up-down, up-down is no good. You will not sit tomorrow. You must use these." He plonked his hands on his buttocks. "Shift back to forth, side to side. Not up-down, up-down, boom, boom, boom! This caballo, he will know what you ask by how you shift. Sit the horse to let him know how you want he should go. Use the leg, the toe, the reins, your voice, to instruct where. Everything belong altogether."

He crooked my knee in a measuring way so that my heel aligned with my hip. "Here to here. Now go." He spun the air with a hand. "Take him again. This time, sit tall. Sit flat. Breathe like when you play the pretty flute. He feels you on his back like a little bird would feel in your hands."

That's the same thing Brett had tried to explain. I paid better attention to my position, shifting with Radar, careful how I leaned, netting my fingers through Radar's mane and lashing the reins between my fingers like puppet strings, communicating through my hands. Always, I talked to him in a reassuring voice.

"Move with him!" Sabion shouted, hands perched on his hips, as I circled past.

I shifted, sat taller. Radar sprang forward in a smooth, long-legged lope. I giggled to my toes, wishing Sabion would open the gate and cut him loose. I felt Radar wanted it, too.

Sabion bobbed his approval, signaled me to halt. I raised the reins, shifting flat. Radar responded to the relaxed position and slowed to a trot, then a walk, and halted short of the tree trunk when his feet touched the hay.

Sabion's brown face lit beneath the hat. "You have done well."

"You said when he learns basic commands we'd take him to the pasture. I think he's ready."

Sabion winked.

* * *

I gave Radar a sugar clump and led him to his stall. Pap swept in as I was brushing him down, brows knotted over a squint. He'd become impossibly withdrawn and cranky. Though he said nothing, tension had built between us. He didn't like that Sabion was helping me, and yelled at him for taking time away from the sheep. He didn't like that he'd lost the agreement, that I could mount without assistance.

Why couldn't he just step out here and help me? Take an interest. Give me pointers like I was sure he'd given Mom to turn her into such an expert rider. Everything I was doing with Radar should show him I could be that way, too. I wanted to make him proud. I'd never had a dad or a grandparent sit in the stands. I wanted him to like that I cared for this horse.

Instead, he moved about the porch, pretending he wasn't watching me work Radar, and stomped through the barn ten times a day, as if he had pressing business there only to exit out the corral, and back to the house. I never mentioned the trophies, or pictures, or what Dr. Ben said to me.

He paced the corridor, snorting heavy, raspy breaths rather than a greeting. Stopping suddenly at the rail, he gripped it tight with both hands. His jaw churned. "You're gonna end up getting hurt on that horse!"

Radar threw his head. I lowered mine and kept the brush moving, balling my elbows close to my body. *Silly me, to have thought Pap might've come to heap a few praises.* "You make him nervous when you growl like that."

"I do, huh?" he boomed louder. The opaque in his eyes made me flinch. "You don't have to talk with sugar in your mouth to make a horse listen!"

The other side of fear is success? Who'd said that? Did that make the other side of success, fear? I would wait out the anger. I turned my back, fumbled awkwardly with the bridle, the neck strap, my fingers trying to distill the tension I was getting from Radar.

"A Seattle slip like you don't know nothing about how to train a horse!" My heart skipped a beat. "Don't know the things that can go wrong!" A lick of froth settled in a crevice on the corner of Pap's mouth. He stomped through the gate and slammed it behind him with a crash.

The compartment felt over-weighted, as if gravity had filled it. He'd been acting out ever since I found the bridle. That's what I get for trying to avoid a confrontation. I should've asked his permission to use it. But, why? Sabion had no problem with Radar having it.

Radar pawed the floor with the tip of a hoof—an elastic sound, like rats building a house under the hay. I glanced up. "I can take care of him, Pap. He minds. He's doing great."

I didn't have the sense to be wary.

"You call that training?" The grave eyes made me shrink. "You gotta *show'em* who's boss!" Pap wiped the spittle from his mouth with the flat of his hand. "You don't ask *pretty* please. *Make 'em* listen!"

Radar's stewing brows gave me a worry-ache. To reassure him, I pressed two hands on his ribs to shove him back, away from Pap, but he side-stepped and pinned the toe of my boot under his foot. I lost my balance and fell backwards.

Pap jolted, but I kicked. Radar shuffled enough to free my foot. I rolled, and popped up between them. "It's alright! It's alright!" I said brightly. "I'm not hurt. See?" I wrangled ten fingers, brushed the dirt from my britches so he could see how good my fingers and feet worked.

Pap's anger only snowballed. He snatched the reins from my hands. "So you wanna train a horse?"

I smelled fear, and feared it came from me.

"*I'll* show you how to train a horse!" He clenched the leather straps tight, brought Radar's head down and threw a right punch to Radar's nose.

Radar recoiled, even as his rear legs folded. His eyes rolled back in a flash of alarm.

I shrieked, "Pap!" and clawed at the hand that tethered my horse.

"*Show* 'em who's boss! *Show* 'em who's boss!" Ligaments and muscles bulged in Pap's face.

"Let go!" I screamed, prying at the clenched hand. "Turn loose!" I screamed louder, but his eyes were lost to me.

He braced, his beefy, orange face ablaze, teeth clamped. "Blind or not, he's going to learn to do as I say!" His right hand locked in a fist.

I yelped at the clamp that pulled Radar's neck toward him yet again. "Stop it! Let...him...go!" But the arm plowed into Radar's fleshy chest.

Radar's ears pinned flat. Jolting from the shock, he spread his legs wide to hold himself steady. Every muscle quivered. His teeth clacked unnaturally.

I bawled and squawked, but the stall was a'flurry, dust swirling in my face...arms and feet flashing everywhere at once. I doubled my fists and pounded Pap's back, but that didn't affect anything. Panicked, I grabbed a rake and threw it with all my strength into the side of the barn just to change the direction of the noise.

Tail clamped, hindquarters tucked, the frightened bellow tore at my heart, but only made Pap's rage burn sharper.

Heaving, his face wet and raw and red, his eyes glazed, emotionless, manic, narrowed to mere slits. A low, guttural growl brewed in his throat so that when he yelled, "If my words won't correct you, this *will!*" it wasn't Pap's voice at all. He moved rapidly. His fist found a broken two-by-four. I didn't see it coming. He threw it, catching Radar above his left eye.

An otherworldly scream filled the cracks in the barn—I didn't know a horse could scream! I was close to the same. I couldn't see through the tears as I jumped on Pap's back, hooked my hands through his elbows, and wrenched his bulky arms to stave off the blow, but he shook me off. I threw fist over fist, arm over arm and wailed and wailed, and wailed.

If only I could strip the bridle out of his hand, I would turn the straps on Pap as hard as I *could!*

Radar reared back on his hind legs, lifting until I thought he would fall over. His mouth opened so wide that I gaped at the tongue flexing between his teeth. His head jerked side to side, his feet came down dangerously close to Pap.

Rowdy dashed under the rail and came at us, jumping, jumping, jumping...yapping, yapping, until I thought my head would explode—it confused everything! I held tight to Pap's shirt until I heard it rip.

Twisting, Radar crashed into the back wall. Boards spit apart, the sound like a crack of lighting.

Rowdy sprinted circles around the stall, leaping, leaping, the flag of his tail flashing, flashing as he ran, barking, barking, barking. He wouldn't shut up! I plugged my ears, doubled over, and screamed like my blood was on fire.

Pap raised the chunk of wood to throw, arm cocked, but Sabion dashed in just in time to block it, and snatch the beam from his hand.

Pap made a fist and swung wildly. Sabion stopped Pap's fist mid-air. Pap grabbed the lead rope off the rail and brandished the metal clasp, but Sabion ripped it from his hands...while I bleated like one of those mama ewes.

"What d'ya think you're doing?" Pap snarled in his face. "You two want to train this horse, right? We'll do it my way!"

"No, Señor," Sabion said with a calm I couldn't understand, his chest heaving as heavily as Pap's.

Pap's fists flexed open, closed, open, closed, fingers stretching and contracting. "Get outta my way," he warned. "This horse is—"

Sabion's jaw jutted. He shook his head, his black hair drenched. "No." He met Pap's glower. "This horse is not the problem," he said coolly. "This horse, he do nothing to you." He folded his arms—a crossing guard trying to stop a bull. Enough for Pap to break, and walk away.

I sobbed as I watched him go, trembled with a fear I'd never known before. "I *hate* him," I said between clenched teeth.

"No, Carlota." Sabion shook his head. "Hate is dark, like the night. Dark can only attract more dark."

It wasn't what I wanted to hear. "You always defend him!" I cried. "He's mean! He's even mean to you!" I tasted salt and dirt and rage. "No wonder Mom—" I held back the black thought.

Sabion opened his mouth, but changed his mind and clasped it closed, studied the dirt on his boots. "Your Papa, he is not the same."

"Yeah, well maybe somebody ought to knock the crap outta him with the broad side of a board!" I laughed spastically, uncontrollably, humorlessly, but I wanted to puke.

"No, no, no. You will feel very bad for it to happen like that."

"He deserves it. Give him a dose of his own medicine!" *Bully!* I took a deep, ragged breath, wiped my nose with a grimy hand that smelled like chaos.

"You Papa, he is lost, like this horse, *more* than this horse. I know it is so. You know it is so." He steepled his hands together and said prayerfully. "But, you Papa, he do not know it. He misses his life, the way it was."

Hysterics melted into hiccups. "It's not Mims fault he wants to beat my horse."

"Your Papa, he does not make the time to adjust."

"You make too many excuses for him." I clung to Radar—this horse who had chosen me. "Pap will not get the chance to hurt you again. I won't let that happen."

Never, ever, would I trust him with Radar, *ever* again.

Chapter Nineteen

P ap's boot-shuffle echoed on the hardwood floor. There was a knock at my door. "You getting up today?" he called.

The smell of bacon frying made my stomach ping, but I didn't want to even *look* at him after his reckless behavior yesterday. His total disregard for a defenseless animal was unacceptable. He'd never warm to Radar, that was clear. I'd created enough divide with my own presence, but rescuing Radar had sunk the house. I *had* to find Radar a home. I whipped the door open, wrapped my arms around my middle and gripped my elbows in a defiant pose.

Pap took a step back; eyes grazed me. He cleared his throat and muttered, "You're dressed."

Yes, I'm dressed. So? I didn't bother to reply.

"Breakfast in five minutes." He looked past me, into the room, blinking...blinking, then away. "Uh—" He locked his fingers together and folded them at his waist. "I've been thinking...and thought...I ought to say..." His mouth fixed in a hard line. "I won't hit *that* horse again."

If he thought that skinny hiccup of an apology would work, he'd have to think again.

"Radar is more than *that* horse!" Good thing I wasn't a foot-stomper because I was wearing the boots and my aim was pretty good. "You bring out the worst in everybody, you know that, Pap?" I swung at a fly, swooshing it back to the kitchen where it belonged.

His face reddened. He ran a hand through the blooming stock of disheveled hair and stared down through discerning slits.

"I can't imagine why my dad didn't like you," I said sarcastically. "You're both just alike!" *Maybe that's what Mom tried to tell me. Or rather, hide from me.* "He kicked our neighbor's cat one time for absolutely no reason. Animals have feelings, too, you know." It was me who had to make that whopping apology to her mother. My friend wasn't allowed to come to our house for three months after. Sometimes even an apology had to work itself out.

He fished for a response. Something started to come out, but I cut him off. "The bacon's burning—"

He hurried to the kitchen. I banged out the front door.

The sun had already baked the cool from the night and a nice breeze whipped from the South. Perfect day for Radar's first outing. "We will go slow," Sabion cautioned. "Pay attention! Keep the rein slack, but ready."

The sheep danced forward as if on tiptoes; a jumble of ewes shuffled for position. Sabion kicked the latch, and the gate sprang open. His hand raked the air. Rowdy burst through the herd, pushing every last one out.

"Okay Boy," I called, the verbal signal that a command

would follow. Shifting, I sat taller, raised the reins in my hand. Radar's ears cupped, so I knew he felt the change. He brought his head up, carried his tail high, a sign of excitement.

The sky sparkled like a bright blue umbrella. Rowdy drove the herd ahead. If a young lamb stopped to snap up the resilient June grass, he sprang at it with both front feet, nudging it on.

Jennie chose the path carefully, skirting the scrub-brush, stepping around stubby, lemon-sized rocks for her friend rather than over them. We followed, Radar's nose plugged to her hip, but it wasn't long before he backed off, a sign he was comfortable moving on his own.

The pasture gave way to a vast, barren bowl warped with rippling waves of tawny grasses that spewed us in and out of imploding ravines visible only at our approach, as if the earth had buckled.

Radar's head worked rhythmically left and right as he caught a sound or a scent. I couldn't smell what he smelled, but acting as his eyes made my own sight sharper.

We followed a limestone ridge that stretched north and south like a long, boney leg, picking our way across the broken hillside at the sheep's pace, around the greasewood and tumble-weeds, over gullies and ruts.

I reminded myself not to grip the reins. If Radar pulled, or tried to drop his head, I would simply show him I wanted something different, that he must follow my lead, the cues we'd practiced.

Sabion rocked with each step; the broad sombrero dancing on the dips. I tried to mimic his easy to-fro style, the way he rolled like a sack of sand on Tessa's back. From my shadow I looked the spitting image of a Mexican vaquero.

· · ·

They weren't the pancake plains I'd expected. The unfamiliar quiet was foreign to my ears. To the quick eye, the land paled sparse and uninhabitable, but the further we moved away from the ranch another life began to emerge: Lizards basking on the rocks scuttled beneath to hide as we approached. Jack rabbits rushed under thick tufts of tall grasses locked in the ground by deep roots tight as fists. Prairie dogs, posing on hind legs, gawked and squeaked: *Alert! Alert!* What did they possibly find to eat on this packed ground?

Radar's ears fluttered and dished like moth wings. A click and a bounce, a faint stroke behind his left foreleg, I swung Radar around Jennie and caught up with Sabion, leaving plenty of width away from temper-tantrum Tessa. Sabion glanced, nodded.

"Jennie's a very patient guide," I said. "Did you train her to do that?"

"No, no," he laughed. "Jennie train me!" He tapped the side of his head. "She is many smart."

I chuckled...*many smart.*

The morning was heating fast. Cotton clouds hung over a hill away in the distance like something stirred up by a finger. *And to think, the ocean once lived over this land.*

"Where are you from, Sabion?"

"Mejico! You know that. Far, far south. It is a tiny town on a big mountain."

"Were you ever married?"

"No, I never marry."

"Did you have a girlfriend?"

"Mm—" He thought on it, pointed finger to the sky. "Ah, si! Long ago, a beautiful señorita! She look at me, and I like the way she look at me." He jiggered his eyebrows and I chuckled.

"What happened?"

"Eh." His shoulders sank. "I come to her house one nice

summer night and give her a good serenade." He posed, hands like picking a guitar. "But her mama, she do not like a vaquero for her little one. 'This señorita no can live like a cowboy!' her mama shout. She open the door and out come a very big dog. Vamos!" He shot one palm over another. "Sabion move very fast away."

I laughed at the vision of a handsome, young Sabion sprinting down a long, dark road, a savage dog nipping his heels. "Did it make you sad?"

He nodded, shrugged, flipped a hand to the air. "I do not find another Maria to look at me that way. But this mama is right. The vaquero life is not for everybody." He cast his eyes over the sheep. "Sometime it is lonely, but life is bueno." The gap had closed between Tessa and Radar, and now we were matching her steps.

"Mi Tessa, mi Jennie, they are mi familia. And, you Papa..." He whipped his hat away and wiped his forehead with a sleeve. "Your Pap is a good man to me for many years. He just have a bad time to be happy. Not always. But now."

Sabion knew my family. I did not. It was a curiosity to believe Pap hadn't always been this way—unforgiving. What kind of man would I have found if Mims was still alive?

"What happened to all the sheep? Pap didn't say."

"*Tsk. Tsk. Tsk.* It is a hard time when your grandmama die. Your papa no longer take time with the sheep. He sell—" He nodded to the herd ahead, his expression grim, "—but for this small number."

Sure he did. Pap could barely keep himself going. A herd doesn't know their owner lost a spouse. Do they?

Sabion plopped the hat back, fixed the draw string. "You cannot turn this life on and off. A short moment it take for things to go bad."

"Don't I know it! I wonder why I'm still here when Pap doesn't want to mess with me either."

Sabion wagged a finger. "Shh. Shh. Shh! Words you speak into the air, though they fly away, they must land somewhere." He stirred a finger. "They sink into the skin and settle into the heart, be it for pain or delight." Sabion always had a way to shut me up. "You are young, like the little spring lamb we carry home and set beside her mama. Take to heart, we say to the lamb. It will get better."

"Mm. I don't think so. I'd know."

"You do *not* know. You are not old enough or have the experience of life to understand. Misery of the heart, it makes gloom on the outside, too. Lines of worry here." He traced a thumb and forefinger down each side of his mouth. "And here—" He touched an eyelid. "No-expression eyes mold a face wooden. Hope is very powerful. So is a feeling of hopelessness. Powerful bad."

Did my eyes look dead? My face wooden? Sabion didn't know it was hopelessness that brought me to Texas. "I thought we were talking about Pap."

The sheep knew their destination and hurried to the tank, its metal base half-settled in the dirt. A creaking windmill churned overhead. The ground was hard, with large chunks of terra-cotta colored rocks broken and scattered, as if they'd had a long way to fall. The hills looked far, far away.

I shaded my eyes against the sun. "It's really very pretty, in a dreadful kind of way. One minute the hills look pink, the next they look gray."

"Mm. Drought is in the ground. Dust in the air." He removed Tessa's bridle. She drank deeply, then rambled after the herd.

I dredged my hands through the water, allowing my sleeves to sop up the cool, while dragonflies darted and skimmed the top. Colorful orioles flittered to the ground like orange slices, then rippled back into the sketchy mesquite tree as if pulled up on a string. There was life in these rocks after all.

"You ought to see how pretty it is where I come from." Sabion smiled. I led Radar to the water. "I thought Texas grew cows. Did Pap and Mims have cattle?"

"A few, for beef. But your grandmama, she always like the sheep. It is hard to keep cattle with water so scattered. Sheep do not need so much." He pointed to Tessa. "The mula...I must be careful to take Tessa where water is enough. It is why we are here today."

Sheep nipped the ground with sleepy eyes, their mouths stirring in neat little circles. Tessa meandered through them, head to the ground as if plowing, refusing to be ignored.

"So this has always been sheep country?"

"Oh, no Carlota. This is Comancheria territory."

"Comancheria? You mean Comanche?"

"Si. The Comancheria is a very powerful nation. They did not have sheep. They had fast horses!"

"Wild horses? I'd love to see that!"

Sabion laughed. "I mean Comancheria from long, long, long ago. Fast warrior horses make the Comancheria very strong. They fight the other tribes—Apache, Kiowa, Ute—this people who hold the land so tight. Once, the land had much water: rivers, springs. Good water! The ancient Comancheria protect such a possession. The Comancheria once roamed even into Mejico. They were bad to take what they want." A hawk's scream broke his story. Was that a rabbit in its talons?

"Where are they now?"

"Eh." He winched up a shoulder. "They are still among us. The land today is very different. No more such springs on top of the ground. The water is now used to grow cotton. The wind-mill must bring water from far under the ground for the sheep to drink."

The sheep munched the hillside, heads bent low. Tessa followed, alert for any ill-mannered lambs. Rowdy found a spot of filtered shade under an old mesquite tree. Sabion settled beside him. I climbed a craggy pile and hopped rock to rock… back down, down, down. "Did you hear the coyotes last week? Creepy." I thought to scan the horizon for any wild, howling dogs.

"Tessa do not let anything bad happen to the sheep. Sometimes it is good when she is mean—good for the sheep. She kick and bite, and bye-bye coyote.

Rowdy jumped to his feet, the ridge of hair standing like a mohawk. Growls spilled from deep in his belly. The sheep had stopped eating, their heads now raised. Tessa held her head high, on full-alert. Thrusting her head forward, she moved to the herd.

Sabion bounded to his feet. "Uh-oh. Fear is in the house." His tone sent prickles up my arms.

"What is it?"

He scurried up a rock. Rowdy paced and whined. I shaded my eyes over the folds and pleats of earthen floor, not sure what I should be looking for. Coyotes? I felt a rush of panic. "Wait for me! Don't leave—" I scuttled after him.

"It is the *cat!*" Black, darting slits lingered on the tall, stalky grasses that barely swayed in less than a breeze. I strained to locate what the sheep smelled, what Rowdy sensed.

Ewes dashed together from where they were grazing. From the corner of my eye I was certain I saw something sprint, sudden and swift, the color of sand. It was gone before I could get a fix on it.

Young lambs raced to their mama's sides as a loud bawl blew among the rocks. A long tail splayed the air. Two white legs spilled over a rock, dragged like a toy. Splashes of red smeared the wheat-colored stone like a grim smiley mouth. The scene locked in my head. Sheep circled, parting for the young ones who moved to the middle. Mamas banded around them, and the entire herd shifted sideways, like a swarm.

"*Come!*" Sabion jumped rock to rock. "We must get you home." He scooted me down.

Radar snuffled the air; his head snaking left to right. Sabion snatched Jennie's bridle, shoved it over her gristly ears, like pushing mittens on a child. He scooped me up like sack of potatoes and threw me on her back. "I do not know if that cat is one alone, or if it is one of a pride, but either way, I do not have my rifle. I will ride the horse. You cannot. We must go fast." He yanked Radar's bridle from its mooring.

"What about Tessa!" I cried. "What about the sheep?" The place was parched, desolate, uncivilized. Every kind of thorn lived here!

"Tessa will not be hurt. She will care for the sheep. This cat already have enough for her tummy. It is the friends I must worry about. Vamos!"

"Rowdy?"

"He will follow."

My feet bristled. They knew to be scared.

Chapter Twenty

I sat on the porch with my flute. Pap stirred in the kitchen. The warbling phone broke the silence. He listened a couple minutes in silence. "I'm on my way." The screen door opened, slammed shut.

I cupped the flute under one arm and caught up with him at the barn. "Less than a mile," he shouted to Sabion.

"What's happening?"

Sabion threw the barn doors wide...opened the water spigot and filled a large container, even though the sheep were settled for the night. Pap knocked around in the feed stall and came out with a bucket. He jerked a piece of rope loose, knotted it, and handed it to Sabion.

Sabion pulled a young male from the pen, from its mother, cinched the noose around its neck. The gate clinked, a sound like crystal breaking. He dragged the squalling baby to Pap's truck.

I shuffled alongside Pap. "What's up?"

Without glancing sideways, he said, "It's getting dark."

I trotted to keep up. "I know." They seemed in such a rush.

"Where are you taking the lamb? Is somebody going to buy him? Did you sell him?"

"No." He lifted the bleating baby into the truck bed, climbed in after him, and tied him to the rack behind the cab. The lamb's dark eyes scanned the ground with confusion.

"What, then? Are you giving him away?"

"I guess I am." He jumped down and scooted behind the wheel. I ran around the truck and climbed in on the passenger side. "What'da you think you're doing?"

"I'm going with you."

"No you're not. Get out."

"Yes, I am. I don't have anything to do. Where're we going?"

"No place for a girl."

I looked down at my mucky boy jeans and overgrown man shirt, the tail hanging loose. "Look at me. Do I look like a girl?"

"Yes. Now get out."

I slapped the seat hard enough for a burst of dust to explode between us. "Everybody treats me like I don't know anything, like I'm too stupid to understand. Mom does it. Dad did it. You've been doing the same thing ever since I got here!" I threw my back into the seat. "You have no idea what all I know!"

Pap started the engine. The motor purred like a cat in my arms but for the knocks and bouncing behind us. The lamb cried pitifully.

"Does that lamb have to be tied so tight?"

Pap stared through the window, knuckles white on the wheel. "Twenty livestock have been killed this week across our neighbor's pastures. A mountain lion's been spotted. Tracks the size of your shoulder. We're baiting a trap."

"How can you catch a mountain lion?" Though I had the image of Sabion's fear in my head.

The mother's bellow from the corral made my skin crawl.

"What do you mean baiting? How big is a mountain lion?" I flipped in my seat. "What does the lamb have to do with it?"

The night shrugged off the last to the sun. It was a simple question, but Pap reacted like I'd asked how to interpret the wind.

The lamb lunged against the rope—the clanging and bracing like cymbals in my ears. Two tiny raisin eyes bled through the dirty back window. Cicadas rubbed in the tree. I stifled a cry. "This lamb is your *bait*? You're using this baby to catch a mountain lion?"

Pap suckered a breath, his eyes on mine. A whiff of sheep scent whirled through the window. "You plan to leave that baby out there, all alone so the—"

"We have to. At Morgan's place, the cat jumped the corral and slaughtered five of his herd right inside their barn."

Gripping my knees, I blinked through the grimy swab the wipers had made. I looked at Pap, incredulous. "Why don't you just tie me out there? Won't that solve *all* your problems! Better yet, bring Radar, too—you want to get rid of both of us anyway."

"Go in the house," Pap said firmly.

I saw red. I jerked the door open and slammed it hard, pointing the flute through the window at Pap. "You're hopeless! In real life—"

Pap lunged from the cab and stomped around from the truck to boom in my face, "You want real life? Here's real life: A mountain lion is a predator. He'd just as soon kill *you* as one of those sheep!" I shrank at the weight of his anger. His bulk made the last shadow of the day.

"Life out here is *very* real. A cat will follow his prey for quite some time." His eyes flashed...stabbing, stabbing. "If you were out there with the sheep, you wouldn't want his eyes on *you*. Don't think you're too big for him."

I tried to separate the hiss from the words but it only made my chin quiver. "I believe I would hear him and run!" I quaked.

"*Really?*" Something in the heckle sickened my stomach. "That's the worst thing you could do. I suppose you already know the first thing you'd hear, if you hear anything at all, is the low grumble." He gave that time to sink in. "And that," he said quietly, "—would be your only warning."

He leaned in, his voice so low I had to strain to hear. "It pours from his throat. Birds hear it and scatter. If you were to hear, it'd already be too late."

The words scraped on my ears and burned my eyes. I didn't want to look at him but my eyes were trapped. I locked on the third snap of his shirt.

"It scrunches close to the ground, head down, eyes up, waiting to pounce. It lunges quickly!" His hand came up in a fist. "It goes for the throat. Crushes the muzzle." The fist hammered into the side of the truck like a ball of lead. "Pulls his prey to the ground."

I squeezed my eyes, wiped away the moisture that oozed from their sides, the image of that lamb pulled over that rock.

He straightened, added matter-of-factly, "You would die quickly. A mountain lion can kill lots of sheep in one run." My heart was pumping. I dropped my eyes to the colorless ground.

"Even in Seattle you have to be aware of your surroundings. You think you're so dog-gone grown up when really, you don't have a clue what's real and what's not. You're simply too young to have life-experience. Good for you."

An owl cried in the tree. I was still reeling from the bluntness when he turned, one swirling mass, climbed into his truck, and sped away. A trail of dust kicked from the wheels like a small tornado.

The white lamb bleated and wobbled, struggling to keep its balance, it's smallness too delicate for the belching, angry old pickup. Glaring taillights took an off-road left across the pasture. The cry grew fainter and fainter, until I could hear it no more.

My insides trembled as if the glue holding me together was coming undone. Now I knew what Mom felt when Pap ripped the lamb from her arms.

I slipped through the gate, huddled in the stoop of the barn. There was no other possible place for me to be. How could I soothe its mother? I knew the one. Her cries echoed the lamb's. The ewe paid me no mind, her dark eyes reserved for the space beyond the rails.

I raised the flute to my mouth but notes fell sideways—no color, no flavor, no taste. The lamb would be left, abandoned in the dead of night, tied to a rock with a bucket of water to keep him...what? Fresh?

I closed my eyes but found no peace from the lamb's gaping terror or those smoldering red taillights. Who can understand this kind of life? *This* kind of death?

The light of the moon crowned in mama's eyes and broke my heart. I laid down my flute and wiped the weep that filled my eyes like sap. What would Mims do? Just when I'd come to believe Mims lit my way, Pap moved quickly to block it. A puffy breeze cooled my skin. Stars strained to be released to the night.

Why did everything around me have to break? I wished the phone hadn't rung, that I hadn't followed, hadn't asked...didn't know. I ached for something tranquil. Something perfect. Something all-okay. Something to absorb the senselessness I felt inside. Ranch life was far from tranquil or perfect.

Sabion stole quietly through the herd, gently coddling heads of the mothers who inched near him. He knew his animals. They knew him. He knew he couldn't save them all. He stood at the door, not speaking. I couldn't see the texture of his face or the wrinkles that pressed the edges of his eyes, but I knew they were watching, and sniffed back the wet in my nose.

"That lamb—" I started, but I was thinking of myself.

Sabion leaned into the doorway. His voice was full of kindness. "There are commands in the earth—even the hunter must eat. But this one, he is greedy and wants to make new rules. So he must be stopped. You must trust you Papa. He knows what he must do."

I took a ragged breath. "How did you keep up with five hundred?" I couldn't imagine how many they must've lost.

"Before," he said quietly, as if life had an after. "Before, with Jennie and Tessa, I would stay out all week for there were so many to care for. Now, I bring them back each evening and pen them up safe for the night, for your Papa want me at the house. Not that he asks that of me, but I can see where I am needed. So, sometimes Tessa...she is left to watch over them."

"It's so harsh."

He answered gently, "Would you rather it be Rowdy? Would you rather it be Jennie?" I shook my head—not an answer. "Pain builds a roadmap of the soul. Every scar has a story." I glanced up but Sabion looked away. "Of what do you dream, Carlota?" he asked tenderly.

"Wha...what?" The question flew around me like a mosquito...it made no sense.

"What do you want?"

Want? How about need? I wiped my nose on my sleeve. "I don't understand."

"What is important to you?" He tapped the pocket snapped over his heart. "The bloom that gives you a longing to experience the day...the satisfaction that guides you to sleep in the night? The quiet voice that speaks to you—to you alone?"

The mama ewe hadn't moved, though her bleats drained into occasional pauses that lasted only long enough to listen for the only voice of any importance to her.

"For me," he offered. "It is the land. This land brings me

happiness. I love knowing that I walk through the dust of a civilization that has come and gone and left its mark. I love the animals. They look to me for everything. It brings me joy to share their life. I could never be happy if I could not care for the animals. Even though my brothers and sisters all live very good lives inside a large city in Mejico, and though I was born to the same, it is not for me. I know the difference. I am nothing to this world, yet I am worthy of this purpose." He pulled the hat loose and held it in his hands, a silhouette against the rising moon.

He waited, but I offered nothing. A spider dropped from the doorjamb, its thread cast in an iridescent glow. I veered away. A splintered board stabbed my back.

"How can you know what is right if you do not admit what may be wrong? It is hard enough to find your way in the world, but how you see your life dictates how you will live it. So I ask again, what do you need from your earth?"

"I want—" A whimper crawled up my throat and gathered like a storm in the soft tissues behind my eyes, the dark memory of Dad compressed to the very back of my mind. My grip tightened on my flute. If I thought of him at all, it was to pour him out through the notes with my breath. I stopped the words from forming in my throat. How could I tell Sabion I knew how it felt to be discarded. Abandoned. Deserted. Brooding thoughts of Dad only swept in when my eyelids closed to the night.

"My dream—" I started again, but stopped. The idea of it collided with the big empty in me. "I don't know how to answer that." In fact, I'd never spent a single moment thinking about what was important to *me*, or that I even had a right to consider it. That seemed a thing for other people. What I wanted, what I hoped—somebody else had always answered.

What do I want? What do I need? I shut my eyes, shook my head. "I don't know. I'll think about it, and tell you before I go home."

Sabion bowed his head and all I could see was a dark splotch of hair. But he nodded. "It is fair."

* * *

I was still there, in the doorway, when Pap returned two hours later. I didn't get up, or ask a question, or cry over the lamb. When I knew he was in bed I tiptoed to my room. The ewe's baying bled through the walls as she cried for her stolen baby. I wrestled the blankets, packed the pillow around my ears, struggled to be reasonable: the mountain lion had to be caught.

Did it have to be a lamb from *this* ranch? Did it have to be a *baby*? Did its mother *have* to stand motionless at the railing watching for its return?

She bawled only occasionally now. She'd moved to the far side of the pen, I could tell. I held my breath through each intermittent silence, until she began again, and the fist in my stomach swelled.

Did life have to be so cruel?

Would anybody cry for me?

Not my dad. He didn't miss me.

Chapter Twenty-One

The sheep were still in the pen, Sabion at work in the barn. I stomped in and out of Radar's stall, whacking the gate each time.

Sabion stopped, leaned on his rake. "You are wearing two different flops today, I see." He pointed to my feet, the blue right flip-flop, the pink left one.

"And there's two more just like them out there somewhere." I could feel the difference in the strip that ran between my toes. Somehow, I'd picked up a sand bur. *Nice. Goes perfectly with the clothes.*

"Then it is good you have two pair to share the loss—"

I gave him a sour look, hoisted the water pail onto the hook. "Rowdy steals them. This is all that's left. If you find either one will you pick it up, please? Where is that mutt, anyway? And Dr. Ben—I'm definitely disappointed in *him*. Radar picked one heck of a ranch to show up on. Kill the horse! Hitch a lamb to a rock and feed a mountain lion! I'll be glad to go home."

"Such a wounded spirit you have! What give you so much of that? Perhaps you look too far down the road." He chipped at my blunt edge as he raked Jennie's stall. Then paused to add,

"Even the truck lights shine only so far. I don't think you know enough to judge."

I ripped a bale apart, tossed handfuls into each stall. "I didn't get much sleep last night." I could never be mad at Sabion. He was the only one with a shred of sense around here. Where I thought I could change Pap's mind, I only made him disappear. I grabbed the shovel leaned against the post; I would be mucking the corral today.

"Too much sweet honeybee words make you think too good of yourself!" He nodded, as if to convince. "Too many bumblebee words...they sting, and make you think too little of yourself."

Honeybee...bumblebee—and I gave him credit for common sense? Pap and I ran hot and cold, but my freak-out last night was over the top. I hadn't changed my mind, but I didn't have to kick sand all over the place. I came to Texas believing I could make a difference. If I went home angry, how was that any different from Mom staying mad for seventeen years?

"It's his own darned fault he walks like he has warts on his heels—he doesn't have to charge up that hill every day." Had that bad knee turned him into the miserable 'ol coot that he was? I felt sorry for him, it must be hard. I drove the wheelbarrow through the door, but felt the bumblebee's sting for shouting Pap down. After all, it was his life—his ranch. *His lamb.*

No, I had to be the one who cared enough to apologize. All the *sorry's* were becoming obnoxious. Sorry this, sorry that—I needed to fix it. I needed to leave on friendly terms. I moved Radar through his exercises: walk, slow trot, fast trot, canter—out the gate, around the barn, down the drive...always an eye toward the ridge.

Time to spread some honey. I counted to four hundred with little thought about whether I should.

* * *

The hill was more rugged than it looked. It took longer to climb than I expected, the path steeper than I'd imagined. The hike would've been peaceful but that I now knew what fearsome things roamed the hills.

Half-way up, Radar stumbled. I dismounted and pulled him along, tripping more than once, scraping my knee. Picking the stickers off my shorts, I started again. With each step I rehearsed my apology, changing the words, scratching out the oath, pulling in a new one.

Radar grunted with every foot he planted.

We stopped at the hill's crest. The desert held its breath. The air had no scent, as water has no taste. Clean. Pure. Perfect. The expanse left me giddy, the feeling of falling through a conduit of nothingness clouds. The scene stole my words. Sabion had said it: Words must find a place to land.

I swept the dizzying view beyond—sloping basins and rising hills painted in crusty, broken shades of salmon, yellow, and a color of coral that sometimes bent toward red, sometimes to orange. Banks and bluffs and craggy pink ridges pressed by the sun and carved by the wind unfolded in every direction. The silence left me feeling small as a grit of sand.

A gentle current moved over the hill like an old man exhaling his sleep, tickling my hair with a whirr and a shush, over and through me as though exclaiming, *Who is this child?*

I'd never considered wind a living thing. It moved without notice, pushed from behind. Where had it been? Where was it going, these invisible microscopic strings of floating silk? The air was tranquil, like water lapping a seashore.

Sheathing a hand over my brows, I searched for Pap below, but there was so much openness, so much sky, so much color, that it all melted together. Behind one ridge, another rose.

I chose a slivery trail and started down the scruffy footpath. The explosion of rocks in the path challenged me. Clumps of fawn-colored grasses clung to the ground here and there, the tops rippling and swaying like the flowing hair of runners rushing for the finish.

Fifty yards down stood a huge, bulky tree, the only one of its kind on the entire hill. Thick branches and dense limbs full of gray-green leaves canvassed shade over a large patch of bright, healthy grass. The grass was stomped down enough that I could see the chair placed against the tree where Pap sat alone, upright, one hand on Rowdy. His head was bowed as if he were sleeping except that the other hand occasionally reached out and snatched the air, as if he were explaining. His mouth worked in brooding silence. It looked like a place where he would disappear.

Just as I had decided to turn back, my boot slipped, sending loose rocks sliding. Rowdy jumped to his feet and wagged his tail.

Too late.

Pap glanced sideways—head down, eyes up. I led Radar down slowly. The reins sweated in my palm.

"I worried about you," I called out, though we were easily within speaking distance.

Pap's blue eyes narrowed. He took his time drawing a breath, his mouth grim. "I'm fine." It rushed out in a blowing, gruff sigh.

I blew a breath. *Why did it have to be so hard?* Radar lowered his head and pinched off tips of green grass that seemed so out of place here. "It looked like you were limping more than usual."

Pap stared blankly into the sky over the rise beyond the basin. "It's only a body." He didn't chase me off or shout me down, so I came under the tree.

"Whew! That climb is a workout! You must be in better shape than I thought." *That didn't come out right.* "I mean, I guess I'm not quite as tough as you."

I shouldn't have come.

I wished I'd brought water, my mouth was so dry. I said, "I should've brought you some water."

Pap didn't answer, just dropped his hat on the large rock beside his chair, exposing an untanned band-crease around his forehead. "Still," I patted his leg. "—that knee's got to hurt. When my dad had—"

He raised his hand and cut me off. "I don't wanna hear... about it."

Glancing left and right, I studied for a way to escape, while Radar yanked off mouthfuls. The live oak tree looked like a life that didn't belong, so out of place in its surroundings. How could it grow so big when nothing else did? Perhaps a spring ran underneath the ground? I lobbed a pebble down the stone-speckled slope, aiming for the deep gulch I wished were a wafting river—perhaps this land would've promised a yard of green if only it had a drink.

"Actually," I took an uncertain breath and started again. "I came to apologize."

He didn't ask why. We both knew.

There was something familiar about the way the trunk split in two to form a V. Thick horizontal limbs sprouted like muscles from either side. I could tell from the scars that the tree had been pruned and carefully shaped. Then I remembered the photo: Mims, standing in the juncture of two strong trunks. Mom sat on the limb above, her feet dangling over Mim's head.

I leaned into the place they had shared as if I, too, could be a part. Pap locked on a hawk flying high against the blue. Neither of us spoke for an endless time. Even Radar waited, impartial to the grass. I scoured the ground for lizards, hoping against hope there wasn't a snake, and gathered the nerve to begin my regret.

"I'm sorry I interrupted your...task." I couldn't interpret his silence, but broke the intense rock-gazing by sitting on the rock in front of him and whispering like a snail, "Are you mad at me for coming?"

Whether he thought I meant coming to this hill, or coming to his ranch, I wasn't sure I knew myself. I would have liked an answer to both.

Without looking up, he shook his head slowly.

"Then, please talk to me." The boulder was large—grey-pink, red-beige— protruding from the ground at the base of the tree. There was writing on the stone. "What's this?" I kicked off my boots and climbed its smooth roundness. I bent, traced the lines, and read the chiseled words aloud: "She reached out and took me by my hand, and led me like a blind horse." I nipped the last words. I couldn't unsee it, and sought Pap's eyes, but his lids had folded to close me off. His mouth worked in brooding silence but nothing came out.

I touched his knee. "What does it mean? Is this...a grave-stone?" I meant it kindly. "She's buried here, isn't she? You come up here to sit with Mims?"

His eyes blinked over the rock. "She's not here," he answered grimly. Wild, wiry white hairs sheltered his eyes. I'd never taken the time to study him, but he was a handsome man for his age. I wished, again, I'd known the Pap that smiled.

"Come home," I said, a new softness in my voice. "I'll walk with you. I've got plans for supper."

"A home is its people." His voice was gritty, deep, gruff. "Without its people, it's just an empty...just a house. Go away."

That day I found Pap without knowing I'd lost him.

Chapter Twenty-Two

Metal screeched. The ramp crashed. The truck gave a final heave as Brett backed the horses off the trailer and led the animals around. My legs went to jelly. My eyes shifted away, bashfully.

"Meet Dolly." Dr. Ben patted the red sorrel. I drew a hand down her white star face. He settled an arm casually across a brown gelding's back. "And Madden-the-Younger." They were already saddled and ready to ride.

"You ready?" Brett asked. "Where's Radar?"

"Almost. He's in his stall. I have to put his mask on, and get the sandwiches."

"I'll do the mask. You get the sandwiches."

"Grab some long sleeves, too," Dr. Ben hollered before I could dash. I waved. "Wait!" Dr. Ben called again. "I'm bringing something back to you." He disappeared inside the trailer. A small lamb ran out.

"The lamb! How'd you—?" I dropped to my knees and scooped him against me. "Just wait until your mama comes home and finds you!"

Pap cut his eyes to the vet. "I guess you got 'em?"

"It took a while for that big cat to show up. Wasn't very comfortable either. I'm still getting over the all-nighter, but it worked out like I figured."

"The mountain lion's gone?" I asked. "You killed him?"

"Gone, yes. Kill, no. Didn't have to. We have different methods for handling animals who develop bad habits like that one. Shot the 'ol boy with a tranquilizer gun, put a transmitter on him, and trailered him off to a wildlife reserve where he can eat groundhogs for the rest of his natural life. An animal doesn't have to die just because he's hungry."

Pap mashed his eyes at me. "Some people think they know better."

"I said I was sorry, Pap," I mumbled. Of course they couldn't have a mountain lion slaughtering sheep all over the country. What more did he want me to say?

Pap yawped at Dr. Ben, "I don't suppose you brought my water bucket back?"

He chuckled. "Sure did, Fred. And the rope."

"Humph."

"I'll just...go...the sandwiches—" I scooted off.

Dr. Ben shouted after me. "And long-sleeves! Don't forget the long sleeves."

* * *

I shoved the wooden flute down the shaft of my boot and handed the sandwiches off to Brett, who dropped them in a saddle bag, then threw the colas on top of them.

"There's a sandwich in the refrigerator for you, too, Pap," I said. "Oh! And I left a chicken on the counter to thaw. It's already in a pan with a piece of aluminum foil loose on the top. Will you put it in the oven...300 degrees, at about 3:00?"

He nodded.

Leather creaked as Brett and Dr. Ben pulled up into their saddles. I wrangled the reins over Radar's head and began the awkward process of mounting.

They looked away—to the house, to the barn, to the sky, while I wrestled.

* * *

It was a beautiful day. Arching clouds floated like parachutes overhead. Dolly set the tempo of a tortoise pace, her gait rolling while Radar stepped flat. We headed east into the rising sun, over a trail that tiny sheep hooves had hammered bare. Brett trailed behind on Madden the Younger like a rear guard.

Our steps turned silent once we hit the sandy soil. I thought myself a seasoned rider, a familiarity with the plains since I'd already ventured into them. We rode in the direction of the long ridge. I didn't know where we were going and didn't care. Maybe to the windmill? At least I didn't have to worry about the mountain lion. It was gone.

"Give Radar plenty of rein," Dr Ben called over his shoulder. "Let him drop his head if he wants to—get the scent of a new place. Blind animals use senses a seeing horse can't even imagine. You've done a good job in such a short time."

"It's all this guy." I patted Radar's neck, wiped the sweaty hand on my jeans. "He's worked hard these last weeks." I didn't mention how I'd held Radar's head up, riding with Sabion.

* * *

The desert was immeasurable, barren, parched. Every rock lay like a trap in Radar's path. Alert and anxious, he chewed the bit as if it were gum, a sign he had lots to think about with so much stimulation.

I had good control, and pushed him into a trot to prove it. I wanted to run, take Radar wide-open, wanted the wind to lift my pony tail behind me like a horse carries its tail. I felt like singing, but I'd never had a singing voice, so I pulled the flute from my boot and gave it a toot.

A jack rabbit shot out from nowhere and darted in front of our horses. I jerked the reins. Radar stumbled into Dolly and I had to grab his mane to keep from toppling. Dolly lurched sideways. Dr. Ben corrected, but lost his hat. Radar stomped it flat.

Brett rushed forward and pushed me upright, then swooped down for the hat, which he passed to Dr. Ben.

The tips of my ears burned. "Sorry! I guess I wasn't paying attention."

"Don't worry. It happens," Brett said with a chuckle.

Dr. Ben smacked the hat back into shape and stuck it on his head, then wagged a hand for me to move forward. I shoved the flute back in my boot and pulled alongside. "Don't let your guard down," he warned. "And don't take your hands off the reins to play your horn. A horse can bolt in a flash—you almost saw it." The hat sat cockeyed on his head, flat on the top where it once had a crease.

"I know. I'm sorry." The sun beat down my neck. Radar wore a smattering of lather.

"Another thing, we have to dispense with this doc stuff. Call me Ben like my folks named me."

"Thank you...Ben." I grinned.

Brett added, "There's lots of things to keep in mind...every little one worth your attention. Like, do you know that sound?" He looked at me brightly, cocked his head.

I turned my ear to the strange mix of noise that charged the quiet. "That?"

"Roadrunners, in the mesquite tree. See?"

Three birds gawked from the branches. I'd never heard a roadrunner's shrill call, which sometimes clicked, sometimes barked, but never beeped like in the cartoons. They crooked their heads as we paraded past. Brett' piercing whistle fluttered Radar's ears, and the birds scattered, their tiny heads jutting.

I chuckled. "Did my flute start all that?"

If he lived in Seattle, would he look at me twice?

Ben said, "If you remember, we left the ranch this morning moving east. Can you tell which way we're going now?" I shrugged, *no*. Every direction looked the same: panting and rocky. He tapped his wrist, pointed up to the sky, then down. "Keep an eye on the ground."

I fished my eyes over the dirt. "What am I looking for?"

"Shadows," Brett said.

"Ah! Shadows." I analyzed the scrubby grasses, the rocks. "I don't see any shadows."

"It's easy to lose track of time when you're out here," Brett said. "The Staked Plains aren't easy to navigate. When you don't know the landmarks, look for shadows to help you get your bearing, or estimate time and direction. Like now...what time do you suppose it is?"

I whipped my phone from my pocket. "Eleven fifty-five."

"That's cheating! What if you don't have a phone?"

"What if I don't have a *shadow*?" I answered his doubtful look with one of my own. "Seriously. Where I'm from it's always cloudy."

"You're not in Seattle. It's easy to get turned around on the plains. Knowing which direction you need to go can be a matter of life and death." He pointed to the slice of shade beneath Radar. "This time of day, you have to look under."

"Or," I said testily. "I could wait until sunset, then I'd definitely know which way was west." I squinted into the unexacting plains. "Speaking of...I guess somebody knows where we are, right?"

"There—" Ben's glove brushed the air. "—just ahead is the old homestead where your Pap grew up."

A pocket of trees once promised shade to the sun-bleached wood house. Two were still standing, leaves the color of olives. Two were dead. One had crashed through the roof of the porch. The house was a remnant of a life past; time had shattered every window.

"Only a skeleton of a place now, but it's still part of the ranch. Heat and cold and howling winds take over a place like this pretty quick." Two rabbits popped out from under and jetted away. "Varmints move in when people move out. It looks pretty bleak, but, actually the frame's still intact. Good bones, so they say."

"Pap grew up here?" I could imagine a mean little barefoot Pap, just a boy, scattering hens as he ran through the yard.

"Fred's what we call old-family in these parts. Your mom and I used to ride out here just to scratch around for treasures. Never found more'n rusty nails." He chuckled. "We were too afraid of snakes to go digging very deep. It's good for you to see this 'ol place, though." His eyes scanned the colorless roof, the tattered *bones*. "Can't help but know yourself a little better when you see where you come from."

Where I come from...I never knew I came from anywhere.

We guided our horses around a fallen fence, its wood posts tangled but still attached, the barbed wire coiled back on itself, like a spring.

"Why did they move away?"

"Drought. Every family in West Texas has a common history with water, or lack of it. Back then, folks hung on and on and on, until there was nothing left to hang onto. A couple'a years of dying livestock, people couldn't survive. Old-timers lost everything. Folks had no choice but to get out."

"Why didn't Pap go, too?"

"Ha! Those old stories aren't buried. Everybody knows, Fred wasn't going anywhere. By that time, he'd married your grandmother and, somehow they stuck it out through the worst. Fred leased up sections of land for a few dollars—neighbors were glad to let him have it. His herds survived, then began to thrive. Things returned to normal. Eventually, he bought up much of what he had leased. When he could, he built a new home for your grandmother...where he is now. That's where your mom grew up. Comanche know how to live on the land."

"Did Mims grow up nearby?" I'd always felt sensitive toward Mims, weighing her as my one real, true grandparent, since Pap was never given credit that way.

"Not anywhere we can visit."

"It's not there anymore?"

Brett brightened. "I remember her! She's the one that made those huge chocolate chip cookies."

Ben laughed. "That's her! It took a catcher's mitt to hold one."

I could see it: Young Mims with her long black braid. Old Mims with her gray, shoulder-length bob. Those gnarled hands had made cookies?

"C'mon," Ben said. "As long as we've come this far, I'll show you something you'll really like, if there's anything left in it. It's been years since I've been there, but Fred's never closed off the other gate, the one that folks use to get here."

* * *

The sun beat like a brick on our heads. Ben circled the sandstone hills that flanked the old house. We rode single-file, skirting tumbleweeds as tall as Radar's withers. I adjusted the wide sombrero that shaded my shoulders and raised my collar against the burn.

How would I look in a hat like Brett's?

At a bend the land changed again. Dolly grew fidgety, tossing her head, flaring her nostrils. Radar broke into a saucy trot. We rounded vertical stone walls and entered a tawny-colored fortress-like bowl of limestone walls. Dolly's hooves popped on rock. The splash was a surprise. Radar followed her in.

"An oasis!" The pool smelled almost tropical. Even from his back I could feel the cool water.

"Fossil water bubbles up from under the ground. Not much to it any more." Ben sized up the cache. The pool hardly covered the horses hooves. "With the dry season in full swing we're lucky there's even a puddle. You can see by the watermark how high it can get." He pointed to a pale ring scored in the stone. "At best, it gets deep enough to swim in. Growers tend to over-use water for crops and it pulls down the water table. Still, it's a nice place to water the horses."

Brett dropped from Madden's back. "I've heard my folks talk about this place." Ripping off his boots, he rolled his jeans and led the horse in. That's all it took for me to turn Radar around, shed my boots, socks, the flute and follow him in. Ben clipped the horses together with a long rope, turned them loose to pick through a spot of high summer grass.

We chuckled as he crooked a leg up to jerk his boots off, laughed as he yelped on delicate, unseasoned feet. We hooted over the big toe that stuck through a hole in his sock, and then howled when he waded in, socks and all.

* * *

We dried quickly. Brett pulled warm colas from his saddlebag. Sunshine blinked through a willow tree where limbs teased the water.

"This waterhole is where your Pap and Mims met," Ben said between bites. "It's always been a popular spot with the young folks. Our ways of having fun here in no-man's land are a lot different from the things you do in Seattle."

Brett said, "You probably have plenty of places like this where you live."

I thought about that. "Where I live, the lakes are chilly—a nice place to picnic but too cold for a swim, even in summer."

"What would you be doing now, if you were home?"

I saddled my sunglasses back on my head and drank in the landscape: no clutter, no clamor, no commotion. A dragonfly flittered above my head. "I can't think of a single thing I do at home that I wouldn't trade it to be right here, right now." I bit into the sandwich. The ham was smoked, the bread cottony, the mustard way too thick. "If you'd asked me that question three weeks ago, I might've said something different." I shooed a fly away, wondering that it could find us this far out. Probably hitched a ride on Dolly. "You said you and my mom came here?"

Ben nodded. "Every summer, many times. It was the only way to cool off back then."

I tipped a toe in a warm pocket of water trapped in a shallow dip of rock. "What did you mean when you said my mother broke your heart? Was she your girlfriend?" He dug in a pocket and pulled a picture from his wallet. I reached for the worn photo. "That's Mom?" The two were holding hands, dressed to kill. "Aren't you the looker!" I laughed over the dated clothes and phoofey hair styles. "The posing!"

He fixed a sweet smile on the snapshot. "My senior prom. I left for college shortly after this picture was taken. Your mom was a couple years behind me. That's the last picture I have of her." He lobed off a huge hunk of his sandwich.

"Why?"

"She met your dad after that."

"But you still carry the picture?"

He shrugged. "It's just a little spot in my wallet."

I lingered over the photo. "My dad swooped in and swept her off her feet, did he?"

"Something like that." He tucked the picture away, shoved the billfold in his pocket.

I passed the canned sodas around. "I guess that was sad for you."

His gaze shifted. "I...lost my smile for a while."

"But you went on," I said, not a question.

One side of his grizzly mustache turned up in something of a forced smile. "We all do. Though I'd never dreamed of life without her." His eyes looked depleted when he talked of Mom.

Darting, darting, the dragonfly landed on a branch just above our heads. I watched it watch me, its large eyes bulging, its wings translucent. I knew not to make any sudden movement or it would fly away. "Did she feel the same way? At one time?"

The smile evaporated. He shrugged it off, a tight blink. "We'd talked."

"Why didn't you marry her?"

His brows pricked. He drowned his thought in the cola, wiped his mouth. "Guess I waited too long." Another empty shrug.

"Did you ever marry after that?"

He took a deep breath. "Nope."

"Why?" I couldn't read the lines that pulled at the corners of his eyes, but sensed the pain of watching something impor-tant drift away.

"Yeah, why?" Brett added.

"You two ask too many questions."

I felt the distance, Texas to Seattle, where my mother was living like a ghost among the dead. How had she ever survived this country? Survived Pap? How did she ever fit in Seattle? Maybe Dad was right—maybe she *is* just a country hick. I wished parts of my dad were more like Ben. I liked country hicks.

"It's not too late!" I spurted the words and the dragonfly zoomed away. "She isn't married any more. Soon it'll be official." I had to cut my eyes away, embarrassed when he left the words to dangle. Attorneys were the only link between them, and documents always left the house poisoned. "You know when you told me about the bridle?"

"Yeah."

"There was also a sheepskin saddle blanket, but no saddle."

"Kyle's death changed everything," Ben said.

Kyle—

"Kyle. I've seen his picture."

"Great kid. Awful what happened." The heavy breath came loose like a long, seeping leak. "Nobody's fault, really, when she ran over that boy."

The remark stunned me. It must've surprised Brett, too, because he flashed me a look, eyebrows cocked. "She?" he asked.

"Sweet Sal." Ben hesitated, eyes fixed on the water. I nibbled the edge where ham hung loose. "Miriam had just finished a workout and moved her to the stall. Before she could even get the saddle off," His words came fast now, not a breath between them. "—something spooked Sal. She tore out of the stall, out of the barn. Kyle was in the corral practicing his lasso on a ewe. The horse ran right over the boy. Killed him instantly."

A chill slipped down my back. I drew my knees to my

middle, clutched my arms around them. "And Pap?" I whispered. "I imagine—" The bite grew in my mouth.

"Well, of course. It crushed Fred, you know it did." He winced. "He took it too far, blaming Miriam for not latching the gate. He grabbed his rifle and shot the horse right then, right in front of her."

The sandwich stuck sideways in my throat. I'd almost witnessed such a scene over Radar. Pap had lost a son. But then, how was that different from Mom losing a brother?

"It was a thoughtless reaction. He dragged the poor animal off with the truck, still in her saddle. Miriam saw it all."

The ghosts rolled back in: How long would it take for me to forgive Dad for taking off like he did? What did I do? If only he didn't hate the smell of sheep. Hate the heat. Hate Pap. Blame Mom for everything Texas. Was it really just six months ago—January...the beginning of the end?

By February he was picking her apart: for serving him chicken, for burning the toast, and, most of all, for acting like a country hick around his so-sophisticated Seattle friends. *Give me a break.*

March came and Dad went, leaving everything behind—Mom and me, a car that guzzled gas, and a pile of bills that meant she would double her work hours just for us to survive. A month later, the paperwork met her at the door.

Nobody knew the fierce loyalty I felt to my mom. I defended her as insanely as I'd defended my April decision to come to Texas, settling the kid-home-alone problem with a short telephone call.

"Geez," Brett gave me a look that apologized for the message.

Ben shook his head. "Drained the life out of the ranch. Changed everybody. Putting that horse down...it didn't help anything. Miriam spiraled into a deep, lonely place. Fred bowed out of everything. Only your grandmother seemed to handle it with any grace at all."

He shoved the crusty edge of bread in his mouth, licked his fingers, sloshed a hand in the water and washed the mustard away, then dried them on a sock. "She knew she had to be strong enough for everybody. But then, she'd always been able to look at a problem from every angle."

He pulled the stained socks over his feet, stood, and stomped one heel into his boot. "Anyway, that's the last horse to ever set foot on Fred's ranch. Sure...there's the work animals, the mule and donkey, but they're Sabion's responsibility, and no little'uns to have to think about." He punched the other heel into its boot, bounced a glance off me. "Except, you, now. Radar coming has raised a lot of guilt from the ground."

"If that's all news to you, now maybe you understand a little better why Fred won't ever love this horse. Doesn't want him here. Won't keep him." He mopped a sleeve across his forehead. "I can't help but think things would've turned out differently...I mean with...well, if none of that happened."

Brett swished a leafy branch across the sandy stone, a wrist crooked over one knee. "Did that end her riding?"

Ben wagged his head, *yes...no.* "Pretty much. She never went to another rodeo, not even to attend the big events. Oh, we managed to slip out from time to time. We had a meeting place a'ways from the house after all that happened. My family's home was a couple miles from the ranch. I'd bring a horse for her and we'd take a trailhead and disappear for the day. Miriam...she was made from the earth. She wanted to ride to the end of the world. I guess that's what she did. Just not with me."

I felt the squash in my heart. *Would I ever be loved like that?*

"I'd never have come back if it had been me!" I yawped.

"Aw, we were just dumb kids." The dragonfly lit on a branch and cocked its head.

"Pap didn't look too happy when he saw me with that blanket. Dragonflies painted on everything."

"Your grandmother was a legend around here, too. Good medicine, her people called her."

"Her people?" I tried to make sense of that. "Who would call someone a name like Good Medicine? It sounds so—"

"Native American?" I nodded. Ben laughed. "Of course. She was full-blood Comanche."

I snapped eyes on him. A spot of mustard still clung to his mustache. He might as well have said Radar could fly.

Mims? Comanche? Heat crept up my neck. The raven hair. The bronze skin. The radiant smile. I'd hoarded the precious box of letters since I could read—tight penmanship of long drooping f's and tails on her g's. There was never such a word in our house. I wanted to shout at him: *I don't know what you're talking about!* Surely I would've known *that!*

Yeah, like I knew about Sweet Sal—

"It's a shame you never got a chance to know her," he continued casually.

"So my mom's—*Comanche?*"

A slip of a laughter. "Of...course. Half. It's hardly a secret."

I glanced away. *I guess it is...*

'What about that, Mom?'

'Oh, dear. Did I forget to mention?'

I touched fingertips to my face. "I'm...Comanche?"

"Well, that would be right. At least one-quarter." He looked perplexed.

The sun gouged my back. I saw a jigsaw puzzle, half the missing pieces found under the rug, and tried to think back... flashed through everything I'd ever heard about Mims. Comanche wasn't there.

What *was* there, was the memory of coming to the dinner table with a full face of makeup. My dad called it war paint.

Mom had given him a hard look. I thought it was that he didn't want me to use makeup. Now, I think that wasn't it at all.

Brett crinkled his sandwich bag and held out a hand for mine. I gave him my half-empty root beer, half-eaten sandwich, and watched him pack the trash away in the saddle bags. I thought about Pap's strange expression when he saw the barrel unpacked. Maybe Mom didn't bother to mention Comanche to me, but then, neither did Pap. Why? It's not a thing to hide. *Unless it is.*

Ben said, hesitantly. "You...you didn't know?"

The pulse of Comanche blood throbbed in my neck. I shrugged. "Everybody but me," I said, a little too indifferently.

He studied me a moment. "There was a time your mother took a lot of pride in that."

I knew that strong, confident mother; it wasn't so long ago. I was convinced she could see through mud...before she found that quiet niche where she went to escape, when she'd given away her character. What didn't make sense is why she kept it from me. I felt like the kid who learned her family had another family. "I guess she's changed."

Ben's eyes lolled over the wide plain. "There's a lot of history around here. See those three mounds in the distance?" He pointed to the red, rocky ridge of stacked boulders with smooth tops, somewhat flat. "The tallest is Comanche Mound. There's an ancient cave high, high on the cap...a spectacular view. It's a place that's special to the Comanche. That's why when you asked if Mims came from around here, I said, 'No place we can visit.' Comanche Mound is a cairn. A burial ground, many centuries old."

It lit a fire. "Take me there!"

"No!"

"Don't cut me off, Ben, like everybody else does. Show it to me!"

Raising his hands and shaking his head vehemently, he snapped, "Absolutely not. Miriam and I shouldn't have gone there the one time we did. There's always been talk about the Mounds. We were young and didn't realize that cairns are sacred grounds. Your grandmother had plenty to say about it when she found out we'd been there." Ben turned away, he knew he'd said too much. Mom couldn't fault him for blabbing. He didn't know what I didn't know.

"But...if I'm—" The words tripped over each other, everything coming through me at once.

"Then your mom will have to be the one to take you. And before you go getting bent all side-ways, give her a chance. There may be a good reason you didn't know. The desert holds its secrets close. It doesn't give them up willingly."

The white trail of a jet streaked through the blue so far above that there wasn't as much as a wink of noise. He squatted beside me and murmured close to my ear, "A strange flower grows at the highest elevations. Unnoticeable and inconspicuous, it hides from the sun under the shade of shrubs, and struggles to survive until, on a single summers' night, the temperature drops and a bloom unfolds—an exquisite white flower opens and emits an intoxicating fragrance...the smell of sugary candy cooking. So sweet it'll turn your head. Then it closes forever...before the sun begins to rise."

I blinked, trying to visualize the flower, the scent. I'd never heard of any such flower.

"They're so rare and so short-lived that you count yourself lucky should you ever find one in your entire life. They call it Nightflower.

"Have you seen one?" I asked.

He nodded. "The bush is gnarly, like a lizard. But seeing... smelling that flower, " His eyes twinkled. "—is as special as finding Cinderella's glass slipper. Nothing you'd ever expect out here in these parts. The flower is so tender it can even get a sunburn. I guess that's why they last only one moon-lit night. Every living thing has a purpose, and there's a purpose for the Nightflower. Let it be a lesson to us: We only have so long to find what we must do." He handed Radar's reins to me.

"Thank you, Ben, for bringing me here." He couldn't know how special this day was to me. More important...I considered... more important than any day since I was born. I felt like I'd grown into my hat.

Comanche—that's pretty significant. *This* would change me.

* * *

We rode home in polite silence, as if nobody could think of another thing to say, or knew better than to try. Ben had said it right: It's good to see where we come from. We can't help but know ourselves better when we know our roots. He'd meant it of Pap's old homestead, but it applied to every stitch of my life. Today, only today, I discovered my roots.

Saturday was my birthday. Mom would probably call instead of the usual Sunday call. I jumbled everything together I might say, what I didn't know, what I wouldn't ask, puzzled over how little I actually knew about the most important woman in my life. The little town of Quitaque had formed her, but Seattle had reshaped her. Maybe it all got lost in the transformation.

* * *

There was smoke spilling from the house when we curled over the hill. Ben kicked Dolly to a race. Brett was right behind.

Radar sensed a change in my position and picked up his step. I couldn't take him very fast, but pushed him more than I ever had. When I finally turned at the corral, Pap was sitting on the porch, gaping at the pan in the dirt.

"What happened, Pap? Are you okay?"

"He's fine," Ben chuckled. "But you don't have supper."

"The house has to air out." Brett's eyes laughed.

I looked from Pap to the chicken in the dirt to the smoke pouring out the kitchen door. "Airing out?"

"He baked the chicken in its plastic wrapping."

Chapter Twenty-Three

How did I know sixteen would feel so different? Not exactly the being-another-year-older thing. Everything had changed. Everything was different. I was the mouse that got kicked over a hill. I wasn't the same as last night, or last week, or six months ago.

I checked the clock—five o'clock Seattle-time. Good! She'd still be sleeping. Time for me to get out of here. I didn't want my day ruined. I wasn't ready for the heart-to-heart I'd prepared, and I wasn't going to give her a pass.

I folded the thin curtain back. Not a cloud in the sky. The pen was empty, the sheep gone. Radar was drinking at the trough. A beautiful day for a rodeo, though Pap still hadn't said we were going. Brett and I had made a hurried plan anyway, just in case: we'd meet at the concession stand. I had the schedule.

There was no sign of Pap. Maybe I'd fix an egg. The house still smelled like burnt tires. How could I know he wouldn't take the plastic off the bird before he sealed down the foil? Even Rowdy wouldn't eat the chicken.

I rounded the corner into the kitchen, rocked back a step, clamped a hand to my mouth. A large rectangular box sat in the middle of the table. I glanced around, peeked out the screen door. Pap didn't know it was my birthday, *did he?* There was no pot of cold oatmeal left on the stove. Did Mom send the package? If she did, *now* Pap knew. If she didn't, obviously, Pap knew.

I walked into the living room, stuck my head out the front door, called, "Pap?"

Sabion, maybe? *Naw—*

The box was wrapped in wrinkled pink and green birthday paper. Orange twine tied up the clumsy folds at both ends. It had been left here for me to find. I circled the table...was I supposed to open it? I backed against the sink and stood there to think. Did Pap want to be here?

Of course not.

I shoved the box nonchalantly with the back of my hand as if it might jump up and bark. Tilting one corner, I picked up the box and shook it, turned it over. A slip of paper was stuck under the string. I recognized the bold handwriting from the letters back home in the shoebox under my bed. It was Mims' writing. *Impossible.* It read: *We leave at noon.*

A shuffle in the hall, I spun, the little note still clamped in my hand. Pap stood in the doorway, his eyes focused, intense. It *was* from him. A lump rose in my throat. "I didn't know you could write."

"Now what the heck makes you think I can't write?" he growled. "Of course I can write."

"Can you read?" He cocked his head, battle-ready. "I mean, Mims was always the letter writer, so I thought that you...couldn't—"

He blinked rapidly, scratched the back of his head, grunted, "She...she might've had a little trouble with it. We worked together on a lot of things. Go on—" He locked eyes on a place on the ceiling. "Figured you'd need something to wear to the rodeo."

On the verge of squealing, I lunged for the drawer with the scissors, grabbed the box from the table, snapped the string, stripped away the wrapping, ripped the lid off the box, tore through the layers and layers of tissue, and snuffled back a sob... too stunned to snatch the dress right out of the box.

"Well?"

"Oh, Pap!" I pinched the narrow straps between thumbs and forefingers and tenderly plucked the cocoa-brown sundress from the box. The folds unfurled to my calves. Thick swirls of turquoise, red, and yellow stitching spiraled down the dress from trunk to hem. "It's gorgeous!"

I ran to the large living room window and pinned the dress against me, tucking the straps under my chin and clamping the waist with an arm. "I've never seen anything so beautiful!" The dress had a western flare without being denim. Such a dress called for swaying—I swayed, and the dress swerved with me.

"I'll wear my boots with this! A little spit-shine, and they'll look wicked. Don't go away!" I carried the dress in my arms like a baby and charged to my room.

The bodice clung to my torso; the skirt flared, adding shape at my hips. I stepped into my boots and stomped back to the window, giddy and giggling. "I love it!" I twirled. "I love it! Thank you!"

Pap scratched the back of his head, his face expressionless.

* * *

The rodeo would draw a lot of folks, the perfect place to get answers about Radar. Time was running out. Somebody might be looking for him right this very minute, probably had been looking for him all along. Nonetheless, it would be my last opportunity to find him a home before I left Texas. Surely somebody knew something.

I tore sheets from a pad and started making flyers:

LOST APPALOOSA GELDING — BLIND!
GREY WITH DARK MANE AND TAIL
FOUND IN THE CANYON AREA

I tapped...tapped the eraser. I couldn't have people calling Pap, but everybody knew Ben. He wouldn't mind. I added:

FOR INFORMATION, CONTACT
DR. BEN LUND, QUITAQUE VETERINARIAN

I had no way to attach Radar's picture to the flyers, but if I found somebody who knew something there were plenty of photos. I'd send them all to Ben, then when they contacted him he'd be ready.

I dressed carefully, letting my hair fall to my shoulders rather than clipping it back. I still couldn't believe that Pap even knew it was my birthday. The dress was vintage, but classic. Sophisticated and stylish. When I shined the dust off my boots, they were much the same color. Awesome!

Ten minutes 'til noon.

I leaned into the mirror. Freckles rose up like dirt on my

nose. I tapped on a light coat of rose lipstick, blotted my lips, stood back to look. And blushed.

On a whim, I lashed the beaded belt around my waist, amazed that it fit. More than fit—it completed the dress. I tucked the flyers in my purse and banged out the door where Pap waited in the truck.

Gathering my dress carefully, I settled in. It wasn't lost on me that Pap's eyes wavered over the belt, though he said nothing. The truck belched into gear. Pap bumped over the cattle guard, then hit the gas. I leaned with the curve.

I curled my hands around the belt and said, "I wanted to ask you about this."

"I saw."

"I found it in that barrel with the bridle and blanket. You've never said anything. Do you remember it?"

"Yep."

"Whose was it?"

His eyes kept firm on the road. "Nobody's."

"It fits me."

His eyes scanned the fence that ran like a heartbeat with the highway, each shaping the path of the other. "So I see."

"Was it my mom's?"

He gave me a stern look. "She wore it."

"It's very pretty." *I knew I shouldn't have worn it.*

I'd come to learn it wasn't the using of things that disturbed Pap, but speaking of them. I unlashed the belt, rifled a fingernail over the bright dragonfly, and laid it on the seat between us.

Life in Quitaque was such as I'd never seen anywhere. Trucks and stock trailers, horses and sheep. And the people! It seemed the whole county had turned out. I fairly jumped from the truck.

Pap shouted, "Charley!" I startled. It was the first time Pap had ever used my name. I turned veiled eyes to him. The skin was tight around his mouth. "You forgot your belt."

* * *

It was a carnival atmosphere and I was right in the middle of it all! Pap and I walked among tightly crammed trucks and trailers that filled the weedy parking lot, horses tied alongside. Chatting people, shouting people, laughing people smiled and nodded greetings to one another. They stopped to shake Pap's hand or welcome him with a slap on his back, and greetings like, 'So glad to see you out here, Fred'; 'we've been missing you, Fred'; 'need to come to town more often, Fred'; 'Where've you been, Fred'? Always, their eyes swimming over me.

Fred Kotes was a different man than Pap. It surprised me that he visited with everybody who passed, and pleasantly, too. I felt their interest, saw their whispers. I was stylish among them. Funny, how a dress can give you confidence. I blended in naturally, like I belonged. Like the bridle did for Radar. Fred Kotes was the Pap I wanted to know.

I handed out flyers to anybody who made eye contact. One woman introduced herself as the neighbor I'd called weeks before. She said how much she missed my grandmother, what a lovely lady she was. Then she patted my shoulder and shook her head. "You look just like your momma. And more like your grandma than I could've ever imagined." Then she turned and gave Pap a big hug.

The dress swirled around my knees when I turned to Brett's shrill whistle and located the arm waving high over his head. He rushed to meet me. "I'm glad you got here early. Wow, you...you look really...great. I almost didn't recognize you."

I laughed. "That's the nicest thing you could've said. All you've ever seen me wear are boy jeans and man shirts!"

"Don't complicate things. I'm trying to impress you." He smiled—I felt my lipstick melting. "C'mon. I want you to meet my friends." He took my hand and pulled me along to a circle of pals who knew my name before I knew theirs. Brett helped me pass out the flyers in my hand, and the conversation turned to Radar, how I was training a blind horse. They studied the sheets carefully before tucking them away in their pockets.

"Hi, Brett!" We all widened the ring as a beautiful palomino pressed into our center. A pretty blond rider smiled down from its back, her long hair the same color as her horse. I was tempted to shout, *Rapunzel, Rapunzel, let down your golden hair.*

Brett said, "Hey, Lee Ann."

Lee Ann flicked her head, peeled a flaxen strand of hair away from her glossed lips, and urged the horse forward another step, then another, until I was forced to back away to make room.

"Charley," Brett spoke from under the horse's neck. "Lee Ann is one of our best barrel racers, but that's just skim off the cream. She's tops in the Reining event."

I smiled. "Hi!" The horse's whiskers tickled my cheek.

"Whatcha got there?" she asked, eyes flickering from me to the flyers in my hand. "Invitations?"

"Lost horse leaflets. I'm trying to find the owner of this horse." I handed one up to her.

She reached out, but let it slip between her fingers. "Oops!" Our eyes touched, briefly. I held out another, but she shook her head. "Save it. If Brett has one, that's enough. We'll share." She nudged her horse again so that I had to back another step. "Sorry," she said, unconvincingly.

I knew girls like her. They were never sorry. They did things on purpose and excused themselves with coy apologies you knew they didn't mean. I didn't know they lived in Texas, too.

Brett took hold of the palomino's bridle with one hand and pushed the horse's shoulder with the other. It took a step back.

Lee Ann shrugged indifferently, looked at Brett with a smart grin. "Some of us are meeting up after the rodeo." She raised an eyebrow and added, "There'll be fireworks. You coming?"

He looked at me, said, "We might."

Lee Ann's smile faded. She slapped a mosquito hard enough that I was glad I wasn't one. Her eyes flickered over me as if seeing me for the first time. "Okay then." She twisted the reins hard; the horse wheeled. I pounced back another step.

It occurred to me that maybe I'd come off as snobby, but before I could consider it further, a loud speaker screeched overhead and we all grabbed our ears.

"Sign ups end in five minutes," a rusty voice blared. "Five minutes." The loud speaker squealed one more time and everybody disbanded. The entry window bustled.

Brett squeezed my hand. "I'll see you after—"

* * *

I left some flyers at the concession stand where Ben's office assistant was working behind the counter. "You're still trying to find an owner for that horse?"

I nodded, shrugged. "Not having much luck."

"Oh, I'm sure you will, honey. If it belongs anywhere, somebody'll come scratching."

The clerk from Larry Littleton's Dollar Store recognized me immediately. "Hi, darlin'. I'm glad to see Fred managed to get that dress cleaned. It's just beautiful." She leaned in. "You look just like your momma in it."

I smiled. "Thank you. It was a surprise. Are you Brett's Mom?"

"No! Do I look that ancient? I'm his oldest cousin. There's a bunch of us, but don't hold that against me." I smiled. She was friendly after all. "You tell Brett to bring you by the house some time." Her head bobbed over the flyers. "And good luck with that."

As I was pinning a flyer to the bulletin board, a woman touched my arm. "Actually, we talked on the phone. You asked me about that horse." I brightened. "Well, I don't know anything more about that," she said, "but I just wanted to say I'm happy to meet you. We sure do miss your momma. I can see why Vernon said, 'It's just like seeing Miriam all over again.'"

I found Ben perched at the rail, elbows braced against the rail. "You better find a seat. Rodeo's about to begin," he said, cocking his head. "Don't you look nice."

As the horses paraded out, Brett and I locked eyes. He waved, so natural-looking on his horse. I raised a hand, then glimpsed Lee Ann behind him. Her dark scowl read: 'He's my guy. Back off.'

I took a seat on the bleachers next to Pap.

* * *

The rodeo started with a bang. Literally, a gunshot! The loud speaker blared at a decimal that called for cotton in the ears. The gate sprang open. A flurry of sheep scampered through, each with a pretty bow tied to their tail. The gate exploded behind them with small boys and girls chasing after the bows.

It was a pretty funny event that set the mood for what

would come: young kids rode sheep like broncs, hanging on for dear life. Who could stay on the longest?

I'd never been to a rodeo. The events were exciting, sometimes heart-throbbing as riders fell or were thrown from their mounts. I jumped to my feet every time a roper threw his calf, squirmed uncomfortably as they cinched their feet together, cheered when Brett and his partner out-performed every other roper team by a landslide, and snickered as Pap mumbled his opinions of riders and horses under his breath.

Lee Ann rode like an alley cat. I admired the way she leaned into each turn, clinging like gravity to her horse as they circled, and saw my mom in her. If I'd been raised on the ranch, would that have been me?

At intermission the arena turned into a torrid of activity. Trucks hauled loads of dirt into the arena and dumped it here and there in not-so-neat, not-so-little piles. Tractors dragged the ground to smooth it out or push it together. Bushy plants in plastic containers were added around the piles of dirt...not like landscaping.

Another crew hauled boards in, and quickly, efficiently assembled an arching bridge with a narrow divide. Another crew set up the props: standing poles, laying logs, temporary fences. They placed barrels strategically, then dragged out wooden statues: a fierce-looking bear, a crouching cougar. Somebody ran a few young calves into a newly assembled fence, and the arena turned into an obstacle course. My hands and feet itched to be part of it.

"Here it is, folks. This is what you all came for: The Art of Reining. Rider command, ladies and gentlemen. Competitors showing their horsemanship skills, and their horse's talent and capabilities. Who's got it? They're not just stepping out here, folks. No sir-ee. This isn't just a challenge of speed. These riders will put the horse though a maze that tests the skill of both horse and rider. That's right, folks. Awareness of everything makes a great horseman. And the first contender is—"

A buzzer blasted and a girl shot out of the gate. She ran her horse through a hoop, between stacked barrels, across the arching bridge, over the teeter-totter, and into the fence that held the calves.

"Will that horse shy away from those calves?" the announcer squealed. "Or— No-sir! No-sireee! That mare's already got one picked out."

Another cowgirl shot into the arena. "Look at that girl ride! Good control of her horse," blared the speaker as the girl urged her horse over the tottering bridge. "Up and over. Makes it look easy. This horse isn't intimidated!"

It was exciting, and I found myself rooting for the young rider as she yanked the rope that would pull a long piece of heavy timber behind the horse.

"Judges are watching, seeing what she can make that big horse do. She has to drag that big chunk of wood around those cement blocks without losing the rope or tipping a marker or touching the horse's rear legs on the turn—expertise of a working horse."

She dragged the log-on-a-rope around several markers, then threaded back through them without touching a thing. "There it is, folks. She's got it rolling!" She dropped the rope and turned the horse to the dirt mountain, lunging up one side and leaping off the other.

"Flying through the maze now," he said as she circled the arena and was gone. The speaker announced her time, but I didn't know if it was a good time or bad.

One after another team players raced through obstacle course. Suddenly the talking head yelled excitedly, "Here comes Lee Ann Worthington, folks! Lee Ann holds several past championships and just gets better every year. Ladies and gentlemen, watch out for *her*!"

Lee Ann blazed through the gate decked out in a fresh pink shirt that matched her horse's same-pink saddle blanket. She lost her hat along the way, but it only glorified her—nobody could miss the fluttering blond hair.

"Real smooth. Consistent. Sits her horse good— Posture is everything," the loud speaker blared. "She's got the look, doesn't she, folks?"

Her friend threw herself into the rail to shout, "Go! Lee Ann. You got this!"

Lee Ann kicked her horse hard, lunged up the dirt mound, then over the bridge. The horse never shied from the narrow make-shift span like so many of the other horses had, but trotted easily over it, then pranced into the huddle of calves where she successfully cut one from the herd and held it like a possession so it couldn't return to the others.

"Cowboy the cows," the speaker yelled. "Show 'em your horse isn't afraid of them!"

Lee Ann raced from the pen. She showed us all how easy it was to make her horse place all four feet on a small wooden stand raised off the ground.

"Step up. Step down. That's what they call putting your horse on a platform. Whoa!" He whistled. "360 degrees on a pedestal, folks! That's worth some extra points. Now for the turn. She'll have to back her horse between those six barrels. Judges like to see the control...discipline."

I was riding the wave of the thrill. I found myself holding my breath as Lee Ann stopped her horse quick, whipped her around, jerked back on the reins...back, back, backing her horse until it walked through the barrels in reverse without touching a single barrel.

"Real smooth, folks. She makes it look easy—she's going to be a challenge."

* * *

Dusk was closing in when Brett plopped down beside me. "I'm looking for a cute girl in a pretty brown dress. Have you seen her?" He craned his neck to look around the bleachers. "I know she's here somewhere."

I laughed. "Thank you—"

"I'm starving. C'mon, let's grab a hot dog before everybody hits the concession stand." He leaned across me to Pap. "You want one, Mr. Kotes?"

"No. One is all I can stomach."

I shrugged bashfully. "We had one." Then thought better of it. "What am I saying? That was hours ago. I feel like I've been riding every one of those horses! All this action has made me hungry. Yes, thanks!"

"You're staying for the fireworks, right?" Brett asked, "They don't start 'til dark."

I looked to Pap for the answer.

Pap wiped a palm across his whiskers. "Be at the truck as soon as they're over."

* * *

Brett found us a spot at a picnic table. Mustard oozed from my hotdog. Just as I bit into the bun, Brett flipped the tip of my nose playfully. When I jerked back, a huge drop of mustard landed on my dress.

"Ooh. Sorry. I didn't mean for that to happen." He grabbed a cluster of napkins and handed them to me.

221

Tapping only made the smear worse. I finished the dog and wiped my hands. "I better wash this off before it stains."

"I'll show you where." He delivered me to the ladies restroom under the stands. "Meet you back where we were sitting."

I plowed through the door. The restroom was empty. I bent at the sink and swabbed at the mustard with a wet paper towel. The door swung open. I glanced at the mirror as two girls stepped up behind me, one on either side.

I smiled, straightened. "Lee Ann! Hey, congratulations on your win! Brett's only half right, you're more than pretty darned good. You were fabulous."

"Mm."

"Mustard," I raised the wadded yellow towel, a guttural sound rising in my throat. "Can't take me anywhere."

"Did somebody take you somewhere?" Her voice was cool, humorless. Her eyes see-sawed up and down my dress. Something about the look made me flinch.

"It was a figure of speech."

Lee Ann turned to her friend and said in a baby-voice, "Tsk, tsk, tsk. We got us a messy little stain on our pretty dress. Too bad. So sad. Isn't it, Dani?"

If she was trying to goad me, it was working. They were pretty girls...cocky and certain. The kind that always get what they want. "Not a problem," I said cheerfully to their reflections in the mirror. "In this heat, it'll be dry before I step out that door." I'd dealt with crass girls in my new school.

Lee Ann flipped her pretty hair over one shoulder. "I'm looking for Brett." Her eyes blinked rapidly. She focused on my chin. I didn't want eye to eye combat either, and didn't bother to turn. "He said he wanted to meet. Before the party."

I forced a smile. "He certainly isn't in here." Girls like her didn't like being pushed in a corner.

The fake smile blew away. She stared boldly, chest heaving. "You're an Indian," she blurted, an accusation.

My hands froze over the mustard spot. I fixed on the zit between her eyes. "Native American," I corrected, my tone level. "So?" I shrugged. "Maybe I am." I surprised myself. Yesterday I cared. Today, I didn't. Maybe it was just easier talking to a mirror.

She looked one way. I looked another. "Then this won't be hard." Lee Ann snapped her fingers. Dani-girl opened her purse. There was a flurry of movement at my back, then a sudden cold, hard press of metal against my shoulder blade. Before I could wheel, a quick tug on my strap—the *pffft* of the knife as it cut through material with a single, shocking stroke.

The severed shoulder strap flew apart and flopped over my right shoulder. I spun, "Wha...what did you *do!*"

"He doesn't *like* you!" Lee Ann bit off the words. "He's just *doing* what Ben told him to do!" With a smug expression, she added, "He said so."

Tears sprang to my eyes. *Hold on. Don't cry. Don't cry.* I couldn't give them that satisfaction. I grappled with the dangling strap that left my dress hanging, broken, cockeyed, and sobbed a breath. "Bre...Brett is...only trying to help me—"

"You're about as welcome as a bug around here," Dani grunted. She looked at Lee Ann, who nodded, flicking her wrist out, palm up. Dani placed something in her hand.

Lee Ann's fingers closed around it. "And I've never met a bug I liked. All I ever do is swat or dodge or step on it!" Lee Ann took a step back, held up her right hand. "Hello, Bug." She hit me in the face with a squirt of mosquito spray.

I gasped, inhaling the ballooning mist up my nose, and broke into a choking, sputtering, gagging fit.

In a voice too-animated, Dani said, "*That's* how we take care of bugs around here."

Breathless...wagging my arms in panic, I whipped to the sink where water was still flowing and dunked my face under, quick. With one hand I scrubbed my eyes, with the other I pawed for the paper towel canister—the mist like sawdust in my eyes. When I couldn't find it, I just let the water pour across my eyes, over my face, my nose, my hair, while they snickered.

"Everything will be normal when you leave." Lee Ann shrilled. "So *leave!*" She shoved me from behind; my head bumped hard into porcelain sink. "You don't belong here," she spat.

"That's kinda extreme," Dani mumbled. "Enough—" She tucked a couple paper towels in my empty hand.

Lee Ann sniffed. "So? She's nothing to me."

Where I'd once seen rich chocolate fabric and colorful swirls, now I saw only red and a long streak of yellow. I couldn't blink away the anger. I snatched my purse and swung it wildly.

Dani dodged, but Lee Ann didn't see it coming. The metal buckle clipped her cheek.

Her hand flew to her face. She leaned to the mirror to examine the paper-thin slice, saw a dot of blood and became hysterical. "Look what you *did!*" she wailed. "I didn't cut you. Just your fancy Indian dress!" She turned to Dani and whined, "Is it bad?" Then whipped back with a yawp to scream, "You'll be sorry!" They scattered with a *humph!* The door banged closed.

I waited for the burn to slow, the blur to ease, the tremor to calm. I was alone but for the thumping carnival of laughter and echoes outside that beat through the walls. I looked in the mirror. My eyes, red and swollen, my face was crimson, the freckles now scarlet. My beautiful dress hung misshapen on one shoulder, the hem drooping and cockeyed. I reeked of chemical stink that clung to my hair that I could taste in my throat and smell in my nose.

Ripping a new clutch of towels from the canister, I wiped the wet dress furiously.

You don't belong here—Lee Ann's voice rolled through me. I felt small and foreign. Forgotten. I dropped my forehead to my arms on the sink and started sobbing, and couldn't quit.

* * *

Brett was waiting under the stands, a view of the door. When I finally came out, he closed the gap quickly. "There you are! I didn't know what hap— Whoa! What happened?"

That's all it took—the concern in his voice. A fresh batch of tears exploded. I held up the severed strap.

"It broke?" he asked.

I shook my head. My hair was soppy. I knew I looked a sight. "Those girls—" I wailed. "They... cut...they cut my dress!"

"What!" He straightened, searched over my head, his eyes slashing left and right. "Who?" He grabbed my arms. "Tell me exactly what happened."

I was torn, because I really liked Brett. But guarded, because I really liked Brett. How could I tell him Lee Ann did this? These were his friends. He'd known them all his life. I'd be gone in a couple weeks and never see any of them again. He would forget me as soon as school started. I teetered on panic. "My *dress!*"

"That was stupid and petty. The mustard was all my fault. I shouldn't have been horsing around."

My voice shook. "No, you didn't mean to. Those girls...they *meant* it!" The strap was just an inch wide, but my shoulder felt naked.

Brett turned me around, pushed his mouth close to my ear, but I still had to strain to hear him. "Word's gotten around, there's a new girl in town, and it's Fred Kotes granddaughter. Among these folks, that's a big deal."

"Why?" I cried. "What's so big about it?" The spray left a horrible taste in my mouth.

He shrugged. "Small town. Like Ben told you, we hold onto our history. People around here are curious. They see you, and it's like going back in time."

"Back in time?" I searched his face to understand. Loud speakers squawked, something about the fireworks. "For what? They don't know me. I have no history here."

"They *do* know. Stories get told and re-told. Look at all these folks who come to see this." He splayed a hand at the crowd, picked up my hand and pressed. "Most of them are probably here to see you. Pretend like it's nothing. That'll drive 'em mad. Don't let those jerks define you."

Native American. That's how they defined me. And they'd be right. Ben said it—I'm part. But to people like Lee Ann and Dani, any part is whole.

My eyes burned. I wanted to close them. I felt myself crumbling. "I'm going to the truck and wait for Pap. You go. Watch the fireworks." It irked me that this should make Lee Ann happy. When Brett began to balk, I answered him angrily, "I can't walk around like this! I don't even want to face Pap! This dress—" I shrugged. "It's a birthday gift from him. It's my birthday today. I'm sixteen."

There! It was out. As if my face could color any more—

He brightened. "Why didn't you tell me! I would've bought ice cream instead and we wouldn't even have had this mess!" He grinned. "At least vanilla would wash out easier."

It called for a chuckle, but I had no chuckle in me. "Sixteen isn't so—"

"A rocky start calls for a stony finish, which is what they'll get when I find out who did this to you. And I *will!*" His face inches away, he stuck a caramel chocolate in my mouth. "You're infectious, you know that?"

"You're just being nice."

"No. I'm smitten." Without warning, he leaned in and kissed me. A quick, soft, warm plunk that left my lips sticky. "A sweet sixteen kiss."

I felt a blush, swiped the bangs that had grown into my eyes. *My first kiss.*

"Look—" He took a hesitant breath and glanced around as if nothing had just happened. "I've got sisters. I'm going to get you out of here. Will you follow my lead?"

Salty tears were dry on my face. I felt a mess. What else was there? I nodded.

He locked an arm through mine. "Here's what we're going to do. We'll walk lock-step straight through this crowd to the parking lot. I'll hold your strap up so your dress won't hang all whompy. Okay?"

I shrugged, not sure how this would work. "Okay."

Curling an arm around my shoulder, he whispered in my ear, "Put the strap in my hand."

I raised the strap to my shoulder; he crushed the severed end in his fist. I felt the dress straighten, the hem rise. "Pretend nothing happened. On the count of three, step out with your right foot. We're gonna walk real slow, and nobody will know anything but that you're with me. Okay?"

I took a ragged breath, nodded.

"One... Two..."

Conscious of the comfort of his arm, the pull that lifted the hem of my dress, I stepped out with my right foot when he said, "Three." We strolled casually, matching our steps past the bleachers. Heads started turning. We made it to the entry post, where he zigzagged left through the gate. We walked slowly through the parking lot without a hurry in the world.

As we approached Pap's truck, Brett whispered in my ear, "Your grandpa isn't back there watching fireworks. He's at the truck. He's staring right at me. And, *yeow!* He looks mad."

Pap's eyes narrowed at our approach. A tic twitched his right eye. I sucked a breath. Brett dropped his hand and my strap fell forward. The dress drooped.

Pap's frown deepened. Even in the twilight I could see his face redden. Veiled eyes flitted from my bare shoulder to the hanging strap, to Brett. "Boy—" he started.

"Mr. Kotes," He pumped air with his palms. "Wait, it's not what you think."

"Pap, it's not his fault. My dress...came apart. Brett had nothing to do with it. He tried to help."

Pap winced. A muscle twitched in his jaw. "How—" The word stretched. His chin did likewise. "—does a dress come apart?" I lowered my eyes, feeling the pebbles under my foot. How could I explain a girl like Lee Ann? "Get in the truck," he said. We took a couple steps. He growled, "Not you!"

Brett stopped. "Mr. Kotes. Please, I need to explain."

"Boy, I think you better *git* back to your horse." Pap turned, and hulked toward the truck.

I'd seen this kind of anger before. Pap wasn't reasonable when he looked this way. "Pap, he was only trying to help!" I gushed again, but Pap never turned. "Pap?" The door squeaked open, slammed shut.

Brett whispered in my ear, "I'll call you tomorrow."

I wanted to cry out, *'He didn't do anything!'* I wanted to shout, *'It was those girls—they did this to my dress!'* But he'd started the engine and his knuckles were white on the steering wheel. He'd decided what he wanted to believe.

I would never come back to Texas!

Sixteen sucks.

Chapter Twenty-Four

Pap's silence stretched all the way to the ranch. I cowered on my side of the truck, watched the fireworks from the side mirror.

He's a hateful man. I don't like him! I will never talk to him ever again. Ever!

And I wouldn't break. *He* was the stubborn one! Not me! My heel tapped an unstable beat. I wasn't stubborn...I wasn't stubborn! I chewed the inside of my cheek. *My dress—*

The phone was shrieking when we walked in. Pap collapsed on the couch. I grabbed the phone off the hook. "There you are!" Mom's chipper voice sang in my ear.

"Yes, here I am." My voice was flat.

"Happy Birthday, Sweetheart!"

I took the ice tray from the freezer and smacked it on the counter, plunked chunks into a glass, and filled it with tea while she blathered.

"Yeah. No. Oh that's nice," I'd answer, struggling to bite

back the words I knew would make her head wobble. I was angry. Too fresh with horses and barrel racing and reining and trophies and fireworks and...and my ruined dress!

I plopped in a chair, propped my elbows on the kitchen table, spun the picture cube—young Pap with sparkly eyes and a mouth that turned up—and stifled a yawn. "Pap doesn't say, 'Hi,'" I said meanly. I knew he could hear me from where he sat in his recliner massaging his temples.

"I went on a picnic to your water hole the other day." I was ready for her now, the list lined up in my head. I rolled the icy tea glass across my forehead.

She laughed. "Oh, boy! You must've loved that."

The cut strap dangled on my lap. "Yes. Tons. I learned so much Texas history!" Attitude took over, which I knew she could hear because I sure could. I shouldn't have to be the one to bring this stuff up in the first place. I should already know these things. My stomach twisted. Mom and I had always walked away from conflict. Now, I was running straight at it. A thought, like a warning shot: *Maybe I'm more like my dad than I realized.*

I twirled the phone cord. "Ben—" I said. "—*your* Ben and *my* friend, Brett trailered their horses here last week. I rode Radar." I hesitated hardly a nano-second before blurting, "I didn't know you had a horse. Tell me about Sweet Sal." My heart beat savagely through the silence.

The screen door slammed, and Pap was gone.

"I know you're there," I said at last.

"I'm here," she said with a fake enthusiastic note.

"I would've loved to have been a part of a ranch with a horse and barrel racing and rodeos and...and a brother named Kyle." *She's probably clutching the neck of her shirt.*

"Did...did Pap tell you?" While her voice simmered, mine rose.

"No! He doesn't even talk to me most of the time. He scatters if I ask a question!" I tried to keep control of the conversation. "But I understand there's not many secrets in this town. Why didn't you tell me you rode barrels? Won trophies?" There! Splat-splat! I pitched the words a thousand miles. "In sixteen years you never told me you had a brother. Why not? How could you keep a thing like that from—"

"Obviously you know now," the flippant words pissed me off.

"I would have liked to have heard it from *you!* Not Ben. Do you know how stupid I felt?"

The silence ended. Her voice dropped an octave. "He had no business—"

"Why? He didn't know we had secrets. He was just being honest; he's the only one who *is!*" I ripped a fingernail with my teeth. Static wafted heavily through the phone. "Why do I have to hear these things from people I hardly know?"

"It was a long time ago, Charley. You were too young to understand." That came through clear and crisp.

I stretched the cord deeper into the kitchen and lowered my voice to a harsh buzz. "Try me. There's age-appropriate details you could've shared. I mean, geez, we're just talking about a horse here. Just a rodeo...just a brother!"

"I...can't...talk about it," she said.

I rolled my eyes, tipped my ear to the phone, and asked as calmly as I could muster with the pulse that beat like drums on my temples. "Why didn't you tell me I'm Native American?"

She gasped. "He— Um." The words faltered. The porch rocker creaked annoyingly.

I'd struck a nerve. Before I came here, I'd convinced myself Pap wasn't anything like Mom described. Now I allowed that he was. Maybe *she's* more like *him* than she cared to admit.

My fingers tightened around the handset. "Ben was

surprised...no!...*shocked* that I didn't know I'm Comanche! That it's my life blood." I wiped away the heat that stung my eyes, cupped the phone to keep my voice low and level, but the edge was already built in.

"Why don't I get to belong? Why wouldn't you tell me something so important? Who hides that from their kid? That's why you didn't want me to come to Texas, isn't it? Afraid I'd find this stuff out? If I'd known any of it, this entire visit could've been different."

I'd have been ready for Lee Ann.

I slipped a hand down my leg to scratch a mosquito bite until it bled. "I could've come with questions, gotten answers." I sniffed, still an off-taste. "I would've been part of something!" I flipped the strap harshly over my shoulder.

"Charley, please." I imagined eyes that would look away rather than accuse. "Let's not get into this right now. I have to get ready for work."

"Work? Again? This late?" I ached for her. I missed her. Craved the smile I knew she reserved just for me. My face was hot. I wished she could wrap me in her arms—she told me I'd never be too big.

"They called me in. People don't show up for their shifts. You know we need the extra."

"You're always at work!" It ticked me off that her job controlled our lives. I hated that she had no choice but to clock the hours, come home out of breath...always tired, always on the lookout for something she might have forgotten to do. I liked her to be there when I came home from school. I hated the empty gloom of the strange apartment—a pot on the stove or in the oven. A note. No one to ask about my day, whether I wanted to tell it or not. Nothing but the drip, drip, drip of that leaky faucet that couldn't care less how irritating it sounded.

"We'll talk about this when you come home. I'll tell you everything."

"No!" My throat tightened. "Now! I want to talk about it now." The fleeting silence left an ache in my jaw.

"I've got to go."

"Mom, no!"

"I'll call next Sunday."

"Don't hang up—"

The line died to a steady bleep. I smashed the hand piece down in its cradle, slapped that mosquito, wanting it dead in a thousand pieces. I had no control! I stormed to my room, slammed the door, threw myself on the bed. A headache had started.

Such a fake.

Would she always treat me like I was eight? Pretend I didn't hear her and dad argue? *This* was like *that*—hiding behind doors.

A tiny lightning bug played in my room, its beady little opaque bulb lighting up here, then there. *How did it get in here?* I wanted to go home, except for leaving Radar behind. I had to fear that, too. What might become of him? Radar was my anchor. He'd made life here tolerable. Pap would never change his mind. My only hope was for Ben to find him a new home.

I buried my face in the pillow. Who was I fooling? My friends had forgotten me. They weren't wondering why they couldn't reach me. A text was simple enough. I could've answered it as soon as I got to town. Who doesn't have cell reception these days?

Pap.

I'd have a lot to talk about when I got home. So would Mom.

Chapter Twenty-Five

By morning I'd made my decision: it was time to go home. I'd angered family from Seattle to Quitaque. What difference would another couple weeks make? Pap wasn't going to change his mind. I got what I came for. In fact, more than I'd ever bargained for! Brett would call; I would beg him to talk Ben into taking Radar...Radar would be like a rock star at the clinic. Ben would find him a home if anybody could.

I needed to believe it.

The hardest thing would be calling Mom again, after our conversation last night. Ha, that wasn't a conversation. It was an ambush. It would be better if I called the airlines directly and handle the plane change myself. People make travel changes all the time. How hard could it be? They have people to help you through it. Then, when I knew she was at work, I would leave the message with the time to pick me up at Sea-Tac airport.

I pulled the suitcase and backpack from behind the chair and tossed them on the bed.

What if the airlines charged a reissue fee? I didn't have a

credit card, or even a debit card. I'd have to go to Pap for the money.

Ha! He'd happily pay it just to get rid of me. *Yippee!*

I dumped the clothes from the top three drawers on the bed. I would promise to send his money back with my babysitting earnings; the apartments were full of young families who needed a responsible teen. I would put up flyers in the common areas: at the office, in the club room, and go door-to-door if I had to.

I picked through the clothing and chose an outfit for the plane, but since I hadn't bothered to repair the hole in the camo-pants, I settled on the same milkweed-blue skirt I'd worn on the trip down here. I held back a fresh T-shirt for tomorrow, just in case there was any kink in the departure schedule.

Within minutes all the clothes I'd brought to Texas were stuffed in the luggage. It wasn't the careful kind of packing I'd done to come here. That seemed a lifetime ago. The clothes were dingy from washing with water stirred in red West Texas soil. It didn't matter. By next summer, I'll have outgrown them all anyway. I would leave the clothes Pap bought, here. Sabion could probably wear them. After all, they were men's.

Bundling the jeans neatly, I placed them in the empty drawer, then folded each shirt carefully beside them. The one I was wearing would have to work another day, if I'd be here all day. Then Pap would have only the clothes I had on to wash when he found them in the laundry.

Or burn them.

The mismatched flip-flops were all that remained of my shoes. I checked under the bed. *Nope.* Only the photo album I'd rescued from the barn. I stepped into my boots, rammed the flute down the inside shaft. I'd wear them home. I liked my boots. A Texas souvenir.

I slid the bottom drawer open. *Was it mine to take?* The

dress would never be the same. The memory would. *Could Mom fix it?*

I snatched up the dress and threw it at the suitcase.

A last look around: bed made, stuff packed, I tucked the photo album under one arm and headed out the door. I'd make that call right after I fed Radar. It was the right decision, I was certain.

* * *

Sabion had left a bale by Radar's stall, which meant he'd already fed him his morning oats. The hay was my job. And I would enjoy this last morning with my horse.

There were phone calls to make. One would be to guilt Ben into a trip to the ranch. Fitting Radar into his bridle, I plunked down on the bale and thumbed through the album.

Photos didn't lie. And didn't die. There were happy pictures of Mom clutching trophies, ribbons, awards at every age:

Junior Rodeo Queen.

Barrel-racing superstar.

Goddess of the rodeo—

Bright smiles, happy and confident—Ben staring down at her, a crinkle in his eye. And the boy they called Kyle. Real faces of real people that told a completely different story than the one I'd been fed all these years. It didn't look like it had been all bad.

If I'd never come to Texas, I'd have never known that the tree on the other side of the hill was Mom's tree, that Pap had planted it there the day I was born. Mims had groomed it in a place where nature wouldn't grow it, hiking that hill like Pap did now, to nurse it along all these years—a story I'd never have heard.

If I'd never come, I would never have known that those long, skinny legs dangling over Mim's head belonged to Mom perched on a limb above. It gave me a spirit of familiarity. Last week I'd stepped into the fork of that very tree.

There was a photo of young Mims, her shiny black hair pushed away from her face in a long, matronly braid. What it didn't do for style, it made up for by accenting the most genuine smile I'd ever laid eyes on. Another, an older Mims, her gray hair cropped off at her shoulders. Her hands, planted on Pap's shoulders, were rough and tanned and weather-beaten, like you'd expect from living in such a scorching, hammered place.

I flipped through the album until there were no pictures left, as if all the chapters had been written. They stopped when Mom ran away with Dad? Fragments and contradictions needed to be sorted out, though one thing was for sure: I would never be in this book.

An ancient picture I'd shoved sideways between the pages slipped to the ground. Picking it up, I turned it longways. The indigenous woman had a serious face with wincing eyes and skin the color of the hills. She held a child wrapped in a colorful blanket. I turned it over. "Little Old Woman. Who's Little Old Woman?"

"Your great-grandmother—" I jolted. Pap stood in the doorway.

"You scared me."

"The child in the blanket is your grandmother." He ignored my jitters.

"Mims?" I said. "But she's just a baby."

He flopped a rope over a rail and shuffled past like a slug. "Yeah, well, we all start out that way."

I studied the photo. "Little Old Woman was Mim's mother? She looks so young." There was no humor in that jutting chin. A scribble, Grey Hawk, was written beneath a faint outline where a picture used to be. "And Grey Hawk? Is he—"

"Stories. Bah!" Pap threw a hand as if shooing a fly. "He had the head of a woodpecker...whomping it up against the impossible." His brows knitted together. "You remind me of him."

I closed the book carefully. He gave my eye an irritating tic that I could feel but couldn't stop. 'We judge with our hearts what we hear with our ears,' Sabion had once told me. I was judging with my ears because there was nothing in my heart. Pap wasn't ready to hear what *really* happened to my dress. The opportunity to explain had closed. He just didn't know it yet.

Pap clomped down the flagstones with the limp that made his steps uneven. He threw a shoulder into the doors and blocked them open.

I cut the baling twine and offered Radar hay from my hand. His nostrils quivered and flared over it. He turned away.

I grabbed the pitchfork, stabbed the bale, brought up a knot of hay and threw it over the rail. Radar's tail clamped; he shuffled backwards with a throaty groan. "What?" I said. "This thing? I'm not going to hurt you with a pitch fork!"

Radar snorted, flayed his head. I buried the fork in the bale. "Okay, there! It's gone."

Radar cut his eyes downward in an angle that left the eyes coagulated and glaring. Tension packed the corners of his eyes.

Pap yelled from the doorway. "Get away from that horse!"

I plowed through the gate. "He's scared of you!" I shouted over my shoulder. I took hold of the bridle; Radar's feet chopped the ground. *Pap* was the reason Radar was nervous. He remembers last time, remembers what happened.

Froth formed on Radar's lips. He thrust his head forward and wavered it back and forth.

"Get back from him!" Pap rushed to the rail, his eyes vacant. "Get outta there!" Pap bolted to the small cabinet next to Tessa's stall.

Radar turned a wild circle, swung his rump side to side. A

hip whacked me, and I went down. When he raised on his hind legs, hooves overgrown and ragged and dangerous, I drew my legs under me, coiled in a ball, and tucked my head in my arms just as the front feet crashed down, striking the bottom rung, splitting a board in two. He turned swiftly and charged rearward. One kick, and half the side boards flew away. A gaping hole of sunshine filled the barn. From the halo of dust I saw Pap swivel. He brandished a shotgun. Loaded and cocked, he swung it around.

"*No-o-o!*" I rolled sideways just as the shot rang out. Radar careened through the hole in the back wall. I hustled to my feet, painted Pap with a frantic glower of exactly how I felt inside.

He sucked air through his teeth. "You're making me—" But I'd already plunged through the wall after Radar, the blast still ringing in my ears.

Radar stomped at the gate, neck stretched out, ears laid back. His whole body trembled.

I flicked the reins over his head. "Pap's not going to get a second chance to shoot you! We're outta here!"

I seized a thick wad of mane and vaulted onto his back without a struggle, kicked the gate wide, wrapped my legs tight around his ribs, and leaned hard into his neck. We tore out of there as fast as his four legs would carry us.

Chapter Twenty-Six

I forced back the raw odor of terror and sweat and gathered the nerve to glance for a dust trail behind, but Pap wasn't chasing.

"He doesn't have the guts to come after us!" It felt good to shout, to turn all the hostility loose. The blast still peeled in my ears. "We'll never go back! He can't make it right. Not this time!" The words fell on terrain that held no echo, as if the wadded clouds were blotting it out.

Radar's coat glistened. I felt the same heat in my boots, and eased him down from the pummeling canter that left us both heaving. He slowed to a trot; I adjusted my posture to relieve the pang that seized between my shoulders.

He felt the shift and jerked forward. "Whoa!" I fisted the reins and reeled him in. "I know, boy." My voice had a flutter. "I'm nervous, too. Let's not make things worse."

I knew how important it was to stay in control. He would have to rely on me.

I'd always planned to take him out, just us two, but this wasn't the way I thought it would happen. I'd left with nothing: no sunscreen, no sunglasses, no shade hat. Only the clothes I had on and the clunky flute in my boot. But then, this wasn't a plan. It was a reaction.

I regarded the range before us. "I don't know where Sabion took the sheep today, but we're not going there, either. He'll only try to make everything okay, and everything's *not* okay." Talking put us both at ease.

We veered off the sheep trail into the rough, uneven desert that made navigation difficult. The wind didn't breathe. The sun cast an orb twice its normal size. How could a week drain the color from the rocks?

"Spring flowers, Mom? *Really?* Ha! If this dry wasteland ever flashed spring flowers into bloom, the sun bakes them right back into the ground."

I prodded Radar in wide swaths around the weedy bushes, coaxed him around burly rocks where lizards scurried and from where jack rabbits fled. Picking my way among obstacles wasn't the same as following around them with Ben in the lead. The ground I'd thought flat, was riddled with gouges. I scouted the rust-red earth with an uneasy eye for anything that slithered.

The path ahead was layered with grooves—dips and swells I didn't remember. With all my focus aimed at Radar's feet, I needed a break, and walked him into the umbrella of a Mesquite tree, cautious of the nasty thorns, the slender leaves more grey than green. We disturbed a family of birds that flittered to the top of the tree to peck busily under their wings.

Such a desperate land that grows snakes and lizards, but coughs out only thin, thorny trees for the birds to rest.

I unsnapped my shirt, wiped my face on the sleeve, checked my phone...we'd been gone more than an hour. We had a long way to go. "We don't have to hurry any more, but we need to get going."

Keeping us parallel to the east-west ridge, the terrain turned stonier. We came to a dry riverbed Ben had warned me away from. It wouldn't matter now; there'd been only that spit of rain the day of the barbecue. Even Ben would agree it was more important to make Radar's path easier. I pushed him into the soft, sandy bed.

The ravine was dry and deep...I couldn't see out of its banks. Willowy brush grazed my legs and arms as we passed. I watched that a snake wasn't laced around a limb. It made me nervous.

I drew out the flute and blew a long, distressing note that made Radar's ears flutter, but it sounded too much like a mama's bellow when calling her lamb. No telling what may be lurking around the next bend. I shoved the wooden rod in the hollow of my boot, and nudged us out of the ravine at the first low crossing that would pour us out.

The sky wore a milky tint, like a balloon-thin cloud stretched tight to cover the blue. My cheeks were stinging. Radar's head was beginning to droop. I felt a split in my bottom lip where my tongue liked to go, so I was careful to keep my lips crimped in.

I wished for a hat like I wished for water and wished for sunscreen. I would pay for not using it this morning. As long as I had a wishing rod, I wished for a normal family with a Dad that wanted to be with us, and a mother that had told the truth.

The ridge curved south. I jerked, and Radar's head came up. "The waterhole!" His ears doled. "This is the way to the old homestead!" My words filled the silence like spackle. "When we get there, the spring pond is just beyond!" Why didn't I think of that before? I could already feel the cool.

What could I use to carry water in, my boots? Brett had scooped water in his hat. It felt empty without Ben and Brett. I added the wish that they were here, too.

I tapped Radar's flank lightly, prodded him forward with a cluck. "We'll be there by noon. It won't be long."

But since I had nothing to do but think, another thought took form:

What will we do when night comes?

We would camp by the pond and Radar can eat buffalo grass and we'll have plenty of water.

"We're pretty close, now. I'm sure of it."

I squinted into the wavering land, watchful for the stand of dead trees that proved nothing survives forever.

How on earth did the Comanche etch out a life in these rocky knolls that divided the land like hard-baked crusts of bread? I couldn't imagine how the women grew food in this puzzle of caked soil.

I mopped the overgrown bangs off my forehead. *Where did they camp? Where were their springs? Maybe the pond was theirs.*

A dragonfly lit on the tip of Radar's ear. It cocked its head and stared with a chunky look, as if to remind me of a life once planted here.

I shouldn't believe in myths.

We approached the house from a slightly different angle. The dead trees looked a little more dead, their trunks crooked at the ground. The sun burned through my clothes. I wrangled my red neck against the collar to wipe up the perspiration, and wondered at the ghostly, unpeopled house roasting in the sun, its battered porch tilting on one end. Windows weren't just broken, the frames were empty...all the glass gone like the fade in Pap's eyes. Oh, how the land vaporizes its own. When Ben brought me here this place had seemed almost tranquil. Now, the desolation was creepy.

The collective stillness kept me quiet. We slogged around

the fallen fence that once claimed a yard, each step a snare. Barbed wire could do some real damage if Radar's feet were to tangle in it.

Two large buzzards hopped from the top of the fragmented chimney, and my heart stopped. They stood on the stoop and stared haughtily, like Dad—all menacing and showy in their own importance.

Bitter lay in my throat.

"He's a bully." I could see that now. The way he shoved people around. Sad, when even your own kid sees it for what it is. I'd never been a crier; Dad broke me when I was nine: *If you don't quit that sniveling, I'll give you something you'll really cry about!*

I didn't cry, but couldn't prevent the tears that poured down my face. No wonder people came and went from his life. I never admitted it to him, but Sabion had nailed it: Some people are very good at hurting those who love them best.

I whipped out the flute and blasted the birds. Extending their wings, they beat the air until it lifted them up, their flight a singular sound.

"You know what, Dad," I yawped after them. "Sometimes people need to cry, and it's okay, no matter what you say!" I licked my hand with a dehydrated tongue, like a dog cleans his paw. I didn't know why I did that—to push the flavor from my mouth? It felt like something I should do.

The sun trekked higher, searing my head. We moved soundlessly among the thick, thirsty, stubby plants that grew by sheer will. Radar's mouth worked; mine felt equally tender. I swung my legs, hoping to scoop up a whisper of ventilation that might penetrate the sweaty jeans. I wanted to toss the boots!

* * *

When Radar's hooves clomped on shale, I sat taller, hurrying him around the circle of rock into the vertical tower of limestone that trapped the pool.

His hoof dragged over the powdery stone. Swinging his neck side to side, as if he could see what wasn't there, I gawped at the depression that held zip, nada, zero.

"The water dried up in five days?" I clamped a hand over my raw nose and swallowed the thickness that lay on my tongue. I felt like a slab of meat.

I stared stupidly at the dry hole and thought of Pap. 'Quit your belly-aching,' he would've said.

I wish it were you *out here by yourself, Pap. On foot!*

My mouth was gummy, my mood stuffy, the sun, heavy. I would *never* smile at Pap again.

The castle of rock embraced us like an oven. "We can't stay here." We had to get moving again, away from this boxed sink-hole. "We'll find the other gate Ben was talking about. We'll go to town, and I'll talk to him, myself, about a home for you. And Brett won't mind taking me to the airport. The luggage is worthless. He can burn that, too." The sun bored to the backs of my eyes.

Sure. Fine. I'll do that just as soon as I figure out where another gate might be. Which way to town? I was talking crazy.

Three small birds flew by hurriedly just a foot off the ground, rushing...racing. A current of hot air trickled past, the first breeze I'd felt all day. Radar felt it, too, and halted. He wheeled his ears out, his mouth worked a chew.

"What's got you spooked? The air's turned around, is all."

He thrust his nose to the rifling breeze and opened his mouth wide, but not in a yawn. Ligaments bulged on his face as he pulled in long drafts of air and blew them back out in a loud flutter. It would've been funny any other time, but I didn't know what it meant. We were a long way out. The towering walls suddenly felt like a trap, with its limestone rock the color of mountain cats. Radar might be blind, but there was nothing wrong with his nose. He sensed danger.

He broke forward but I was ready and held him back. He side-stepped and stumbled. The reins broke from my hands. I lunged, but not in time…the straps lay on the ground pinned under his right foreleg.

I didn't want to get down. I was running out of energy; I'd never have the zest to jump back up. I slid off, cupped his face in my hands, laid my forehead against his cheek.

"Okay, Old Man. You've got my attention. You want out of this pothole. Me, too. We have to go to the windmill. *That* tank won't be dry."

I pulled out my phone. One-thirty. We'd been out more than four hours. "It's either that, or go back and face Pap." I could imagine the look in his eye when he saw me sneaking back. "Okay then. To the windmill."

There was plenty of daylight, but we couldn't get water too soon. "It's not too far, I don't think. We'll backtrack to the home-stead, then follow the ridge to the tank. Maybe Sabion will still be there, if that's where he took the sheep. Maybe there's a short cut."

Aligning Radar beside a hefty rock, I climbed, stepped onto his back, nudged him forward with a tap to his ribs.

He balked, swung his rump side to side, his whole body tense. If he kicked, then where would I be? I felt he could bolt.

"No!" I thundered, and thumped his ribs again. "We're getting out of here!" It wasn't the time to test me. I popped down hard to move him but he rolled his ears back and leaned rearward.

It was middle of the day but nothing made a shadow. The sky cast a slurry on the prairie—no movement, no sound. The scant breeze had already stalled, the air wooden, as if a giant straw had sucked all the oxygen out of the world. Two weeks earlier these hills were tinged in brown and pink and shades of beige the color of wheat, the flavor of bland. Now they looked brick-red...purple-blue. Muted. Distorted. Unnatural.

Nothing scurried.

Nothing flickered.

Nothing slithered.

Nothing pestered, not even a deer fly.

The grass didn't stir.

I know when a day's not right.

The western horizon had turned frothy, a flat shade of brown. A thin white pigment separated the brown from the sky, almost no color at all. A tingle started in my toes and shot through my fingers like static. I knew the thing coming.

"Sand!"

Chapter Twenty-Seven

Radar's nostrils closed in a squeeze that sent ripples up his face like a backward sneeze. I tightened my grip on his bridle. "I know."

What I knew: the ranch lay somewhere beneath that butterscotch sky. Another thing I knew: the sandstorm was heading straight at us!

"We can't go back to the ranch." My voice broke. My heart hammered. Even if I could force Radar around, we'd never make it. It took half a day to get here. Forget the windmill. Forget the old homestead—that certainly wouldn't shelter us.

The bloom deepened behind my eyes. I had no idea how fast a sandstorm could move, but if the power of sand was anything like the force of water, not only would it mow us down...it would bury us forever. We had to get somewhere safe.

Where can we go? My thoughts stumbled over each other. *Who can I ask?* If only somebody could make the decision.

"Think like Sabion. Think like a cowboy. What would Sabion do?"

Something else nagged at me, something that wasn't right. Something besides the eerie silence that made me shrink. I slashed at the pasty strands of hair that clung to my face. "Your mask! You don't have your *mask!*"

I dropped, shucked the shirt, wrapped Radar's eyes, tied the long sleeves under his jaw. Then it hit me. "Comanche Mound! There's a cave!" Ben couldn't go there. He's not Comanche.

"But I *am!*"

Shading my eyes with the back of a hand, I searched the rocky ridge where Ben had pointed. *Three mounds.* I couldn't make out shapes from here, but if Ben said there was a cave, then it had to be there.

The sandy squall began to move like a shoulder roll, rotating up, and over, changing color from honey to amber to rust. My heart beat faster than I could breathe. Had it already passed over the ranch? Were Pap and Sabion okay? The sheep?

Were they worried about me?

How far was it to that ridge? A mile?

A wide, open plain lay between us and the ridge. I pulled my phone...*low battery*...killed it, rammed the dead thing deep in my pocket.

"You're not going to like it, Radar, but you have to trust me on this." My mouth was dry and tacky. "We have to find that cave!"

I wrapped the straps around my knuckles and wrenched the reins. Jabbing my heels in Radar's sides, I whooped, "Go! Go! Go!"

Radar took off in a jarring, stiff-legged trot, grunting with each step.

* * *

The air was heavy and stagnant. Radar trotted with his mouth gaping. The barren floor tasted thick, the humidity, tough enough to ride.

I divided my attention between the ridge tops, watchful for three mounds, and the ground under his feet, alert for anything that might trip him.

Behind us, sand had changed color and shape. I could no longer tell where the ground ended and the sky began—the atmosphere a color of brown sugar. The stark plain I rushed for turned out vast and sweeping, and I couldn't see that we were making much progress at all. Brush and rock and tumbleweeds reshaped the ground into an obstacle course. Jack rabbits startled from every rock and scrub, stirring new frights. I ushered Radar right and left, not knowing for sure where we'd land.

Half way across, mid-day turned an ominous shade of dusk. Clouds in the north brewed a dense, sickly green, like an ugly bruise. Lightning sailed sideways out of the soup and splintered overhead. I whipped. Radar stumbled. A thunderous crack spliced the air.

Two storms?

I forgot to be thirsty.

I could hear Ben's voice in my ear: 'Stay out of the gullies— storms hold lots of rain. On this desert floor, rainwater can gush from miles away without warning, and dislodge anything in its path.'

The land was a different kind of wilderness than any I'd ever known: No stellar clusters of thick, dripping rain forests. No outdoor hike in a mountainous adventure. *This* wilderness was savage and stark and soul-destroying.

Death by vicious predator.

Death by severe heat.

Death by extreme thirst.

I had a cramp in my leg. "Please, Radar. Pick up your feet." I clutched the reins tighter, stuck my leg in a pose to relieve the muscle, booted him into a hard trot with the other. I bobbed on his back, urging him to make time, keeping watch for three peaks...mounds...points...something. *Anything!*

The once fawn-yellow limestone had darkened to a nasty blend of deep colors. It helped me spot them: red and rocky and rising in a spiral...flat at the top. The mounds were right in front of me all along. Not like what I was looking for—nothing like the mountains back home. These mounds were squatty and angry-looking, decorated with chunks and slabs of fallen rock.

Horse dung, Ben had said the ancient Comanche had called them. From the bottom, I could see them that way...as if the mounds had fallen out of the sky and landed with a giant, flattening thud. I'd never figured horse manure as a gob or a splat or a mesa, but my eyes would never have picked them out if he hadn't described them that way.

From the base of the ridge, the slope was so steep it unnerved me to ask Radar to climb. I found a place assessable enough to enter the hill. His muzzle was drawn, his breathing rackety. A long fold of slobber swung from his lips. He was suffering. He needed a break. He needed refreshment.

"We'll stop when—" A colossal crack of thunder knocked that right out of my head. "We're going...there!" I breathed out the words as if they were my last.

Radar laid back his ears. His mouth sagged open. Yielding to the urgency in my voice, he lunged at the hill, planting his feet like on stair-steps, but the next step confused him and he stalled.

Heat pushed through my socks. "Yes!" I tasted blood; I'd bitten my tongue. I was thirsty and hot and soggy and sunburned and smelled like horse dung myself. My jeans were soaked with Radar's sweat and hair.

I looked behind—the western sky was lit like a forest fire. I could no longer tell where the ground ended and the sky began. Northward, rainclouds the color of lead, closed in. Both had spread wider, climbed higher. My scalp was the tender shade of dynamite.

I leaned into his neck and picked the way carefully, guiding him around crumbling limestone and low-lying scrub. His hooves rasped on the rocks as he leaned into them and rammed forward, pushing blindly with his back legs one gruelingly step at a time.

The hill steepened. I pressed harder, bounced to add thrust, no longer trying to conceal my panic. With each splinter of lightning that shattered the sky, each cackle of thunder, Radar's hind legs buckled, while I twitched and jerked and ducked as if a boogey man was chasing.

He staggered, jerking the reins out of my hands. I hopped from his back, slipped my fingers through the bridle, and pulled, grappling with my footing and bracing a boot against any root or rock solid enough to keep me upright.

A large stone tumbled loose and crashed down the hill. An unidentifiable noise behind me made me turn.

Radar's teeth were chattering! He was stressed over the top, his tail clamped tight.

Every muscle ached. The air wore the odor of fever. We were both exhausted. How would we find the cave when even *breathing* was an effort? The thought of getting caught on the side of this hill terrified me. The wind alone would sweep us right off the side.

I spotted a trace along the ground that ran horizontal to the hillside and inched upward as it went. *A switchback!* I'd hiked enough to recognize an animal trail—it would lead somewhere. A clean trail will be easier for Radar to follow.

Halfway up, the slope turned even more treacherous. The air felt dried to death. Loose gravel made the scramble dangerous.

Keep your eyes on the trail! Don't look down.

I looked down. Fear shot through my socks.

The switchback turned, sharper this time, ran under a thick protruding mantle that extended to make a ceiling above us. *Was it the top of the mound?*

Radar went down on one knee behind me and struggled to regain his footing. Each time he tripped I thought of Pap. Radar would never be the same. How could he ever trust me again? He'd only remember me as *that* girl.

The inky sky was the color of grim. A low grumble rippled the air, and echoed rock to rock without a whistle of air to carry a sound, or a wisp of wind to capture a breeze.

"We're getting there," I tried to mumble, but my mouth was too stale to cluck. I jostled the reins to keep him moving, squeezed my eyes closed to fight back the alarm.

The soil was unstable. Thick chunks of rock lay spread in our path. *Keep your eyes fixed on that ledge! Don't lose sight of it.*

An explosion of lightning, and Radar's back legs collapsed. I shrank, as if I'd caught him in my lap. I wanted to run, but could barely crawl. My arms were clammy and raw. A touch to my lips busted the raw tissue.

A chilling noise like a speeding freight train rode over us. The spinning sand feathered into the black thunderstorm and turned the sky a ghoulish shade of black-green, like a dense kettle of stew. The two storms were poised to converge some-where overhead.

We're not going to make it—

Chapter Twenty-Eight

The trail passed under the ledge. Such a perfect snake-nesting spot if I never saw one. I probed the crumbling soil watchful for anything that slithered, my ears tuned to a rattle or hiss. We didn't have poisonous snakes in Seattle. Brett said they could get as long as a man.

Hesitant, I led Radar into the shade. Thunder boomed over the ridge and echoed through the rocks. Radar was way over-heated; froth coated his mouth. He pressed the long of his face against mine. His cheeks had no fat. Deep grooves ran between his brows like one who carries too heavy a load.

"Only a…minute." The overhang wasn't enough. I clenched my throbbing head. I'd never known this kind of thirst. I never knew what it would be like without water. How long was too long? Radar groaned pathetically. "You'd been…better off…if—" *if you'd never found me.* Every word was a slur, my lips so swollen they didn't close. We had to find that cave. "Have… to… go higher." *Can't stop now.* We were almost at the top. I might never get him moving again.

I readjusted the shirt, combed the lather down his neck. If I couldn't be strong for myself, I would be strong for him.

My feet were on fire. Every muscle screamed. I stepped out, went down. Searing pain shot through my foot. Radar's ears pricked to my cry. I clutched my left arm; the touch drew blood. In no time a knob formed on my elbow.

What? *That?"* I turned my ankle on that *stob* of a root?

The wind whistled like a distant foghorn. The sky hung like a sooty ceiling over our heads. *Get up! We can rest when we get there.*

Brushing away the dirt and grit, I squeezed the dull from my eyes. My hand scraped the raw blister on my nose when it made a pass. The ankle already felt thick in its boot, my legs felt like tree trunks.

I stood, craned to see above the ledge. The cave would be up there. Too dry to lob the signal to spur Radar on, I clung to a handful of hair at his wither and hobbled away from the safety of the shelf. I tried not to favor the foot as I lunged at the grueling hill, but each step was a struggle. There was definitely a stone in my boot. How did I get a stone in my boot?

Limping around a rocky approach, I could see the top! The cave had to be, *"just there!"* Radar's head drooped. Just one... big...step...up. Up though that slanting shaft of pinching rock!

I crawled upward until I was almost at the same level with Radar's head, then wrangled the reins for him to follow. Sensing me higher, he tucked his hips and leapt.

There were no congratulations. No smiles. No pats or claps. And no cave. A gigantic boulder blocked our path forward.

Tall slabs of limestone encircled every side but one, the one that spilled off the rim into an endless pocket of air. The lump blew apart in my throat.

I prowled the enormous boulder like a bug, walking my hands over it, smoothing every crack, feeling for a split...pushing, as if Abracadabra could move it, and fell, wheezing, against it.

No cave!

No way around the mound! No way off this wailing mantel of limestone!

I wanted to shriek or howl or bawl; a dark, raspy laugh backed down my throat. I'd delivered us to the end of the world —a wasted, rocky crag at the top of nowhere. I couldn't think, couldn't breathe. *This* was my designated *safe place?*

The dense black soupy storm pressed overhead. 'The earth places no value on rebellion.' *Who'd said that? Pap? Sounds like something he'd say.* I felt betrayed, and blamed him.

A low, yowling whistle moaned through the rocks. The first scatter of wind kicked up like death on a doorstep. I tried to swallow, but my tongue wouldn't shift in my mouth. I saw Mom in that moment, slinging a spatula over the pancakes and telling me matter-of-factly, "Things always go wrong. It's how you fix them that matters."

This wouldn't be a good memory. The only way to fix this was to find that cave!

I couldn't ignore the stone in my boot any longer. The ankle was throbbing. I crooked one leg over the other. Just as I yanked, a white bolt of lightning splintered the sky. The boot soared topsy-turvy through the air and landed on the brink of the ledge. The flute tumbled out. I wailed, "My—" It toppled over the side.

I traced the tender whelps on my palm, my heart anxious. I had to get it! I had to get the boot! How deep was that ravine? I needed it! My hand found a rock the size of my fist and lobbed it over the side, but I never heard it hit.

Do it! Get it!

Nipping back a curse, I dropped on all fours and crouched like a lizard toward the ocean of sky that melted my backbone. It would be better if I couldn't see that paralyzing drop.

I wheeled onto my back and scooted—a foot, an arm, a hand —until, finally, my fingers poked leather. Grabbing the boot, I flung it to safety and quickly rolled away. When I unfurled to my feet, the awkward turnaround left me face to face with an unseen side of the limestone ledge. A dogleg slit broke the rock in half, leading into a passageway I couldn't have seen from anywhere else.

I'd never have seen it if I hadn't gone out on this rim...if I hadn't almost lost my boot.

Chapter Twenty-Nine

The wind moaned, the sound a living thing makes, like pushing air down a hole. Radar swiveled frantically, as if searching for a place to run. The shirt had slid again. His eyes flicked side to side...anxious, alert, overwhelmed. Tiny muscles winked at the corners.

I was torn: back up and fix his mask, or follow that narrow ledge! We needed the protection of the other side of this mound.

Think!

The squall was closer, slurping up the desert like a vacuum, spinning like a Ferris wheel instead of soaring like a cloud. I couldn't see the beginning from the end. A vein pulsed in my neck. No time to question. We were stooges on this hill, completely exposed. If we didn't move it, we'd be swept off the mound! Where could the path lead except to the other side—the side away from the storms?

How would I negotiate that narrow ledge?

I didn't think my ankle was swollen, but it throbbed as if it were. I had to be able to feel my footing. Working the boot off, I tossed it with the other one, peeled away the socks and stood, testing its sturdiness.

I will step flat and not flex my ankle.

The first wave of grit blew in—tiny pellets that stung like ant bites. I raised a hand to shield my eyes, but couldn't see past my fear. Sabion would've prattled Jennie and Tessa with sweet talk until they did anything he wanted. I didn't have time to prattle.

Lightning shot horizontally from the thunderhead. Radar's hoof struck rock, *chop, chop, chop*—each thwack punching the boulder like a sledgehammer. *Pow!* A clap of thunder hit so close I fell to the ground. An unnatural charge rumbled through the hill when the two storms merged. The colors changed: black to green, orange to brown. We were about to get clobbered. The mound was swallowing us up, piece by piece.

I knew what I had to do. I was frightened to death to follow that narrow ledge, scared to death not to. I had no choice.

In my rush to get to Radar I tripped on a fist-sized stone, and my big toe folded. I cried, a husky, guttural noise. Radar pushed his nose in a nook of rock, as if *that* would save him. How could I be strong for both of us when I hardly had the pluck to breathe?

I hobbled on my heel. "Don't be afraid." I tried to say, but my words couldn't compete with the wailing wind.

I pulled him to the rim, his uneven steps a weight on my knees. My fingers trembled as I loosened the bridle and fastened the straps like a halter around his neck.

A loud sucking sound rode the air with the intensity of something coming full-throttle. Hair whipped over my head and flogged my cheeks. I tried to shove it aside, but it blew back faster than I could push it away. I could see trash swirling in the sand as the wind whooshed it up, possessed it for a time, then sent it crashing back to earth. I had to protect my eyes!

I fumbled with the jeans...the zipper. I would tie the legs around my head like the shirt around Radar's and look out through the zipper slit.

The hem snagged my toe as I fought to step out of the pants. I slung them around my neck, but before I could tie a knot, the wind yanked them out of my hands, and the jeans flew away like a tumbleweed, the way the wind carried everything that isn't rooted in the ground.

"My—*phone!*" My only link to the world in the back pocket, now a kite!

I was empty. Exhausted. Lost. Burps of laughter bubbled through me. *Who was I going to call anyway?* That phone hadn't worked all summer. I chewed on sand. *You're a cowering rabbit—*

With each *Boom!* I crouched and covered my head.

Be bold! Be assertive! I was hungry. My mouth, a dry gulch. I longed for water.

I stood at the pathway, Radar behind me, his back to the storm. The vertical wall rose at my left hand; the right side dropped away into the same void that owned my flute, and now my jeans.

I didn't want to think about what I'd been thinking about: Radar's weight...whether the ledge would hold him. It was hardly wider than the hallway in Pap's house. It would be nasty, like walking a plank. One bad step and we'd be in a bottomless tomb. One gust could send us right off the side. Was I this desperate?

Yes.

There was no room on this ledge for a screw-up. I raised the straps to bring his head up, folded them over my left shoulder, and wobbled onto the ledge where nothing was certain. Radar immediately pulled back and crouched.

I clutched a knob of wall to stabilize. "Don't—"

Please. Please. Please.

I was more frightened than I'd ever been in my life—more afraid even than when Dad walked out—and fixed a hand on his nose. I'd never had to think about dying.

Don't look down. Don't look up.

My heart thumped. I wouldn't think that the whole pathway could give way. *I won't think that—*

One baby-step, I leaned into the wall and drew my fear alongside. The ankle felt the size of my neck. A sideways-shuffle, I committed to the ledge, parked my feet spread-eagle, and urged my legs to settle. I made the mistake of glancing down, down, down, nothing beneath us, and reeled. I looked up instead. Shouldn't have. Air currents swirled speedily backwards, as if time were reversing.

Radar unlocked his knees, and faltered unsteadily into the netherworld. I pulled his head so that it would loll toward the wall, and shuffled again.

There was no turning back.

Three...four. My feet felt for stones or pebbles...anything that might cause us to stumble. The sound of the storms hounded us—if only I could hold the roar from our ears. I wished for cotton balls to stuff them, even cotton straight from the field—dry and seedy.

Folks would be shutting their houses, hiding from the storm like a night-closing flower. Towels were probably stuffed in all the window sills. Mom used to say, 'Sand and water can find any crack and fill any hole.'

Even the raisin cookies I made yesterday? Oh well, Pap won't mind. He chews on grit every day. He and Sabion were probably sweeping the house out right now.

I replayed the harsh words he spat at me yesterday: 'A fool who scoffs at rules is chained to failure and defeat.'

Why should I keep thinking of him?

Five...six. Radar was positioned fully on the ledge when he tried to pull away. Every nerve in my body seized. I gripped the straps hard, but he was trembling. What would I do if he tried to turn? My mouth wouldn't close; it took all my energy to breathe.

I rocked with him, swaying like a slow dance as spits of sand swirled around and around and around. The sky was getting darker. Soon, every sneeze of light would be wiped away. A gazillion pounds of sand eagerly awaiting our burial.

The cave. It has to be there!

Seven. Eight. Nine. The wind shrilled like a boiling tea kettle—not an earthly noise. I couldn't see over Radar to know what was happening behind us, and the craggy curve blocked my view of what lay ahead. I set each foot down cautiously and tried not to wonder: Is the ledge narrowing?

What if it...stops?

What precautions should I take in a sandstorm? I knew the rules in a blizzard: take cover, hunker down, stay put. I'd broken every one of them.

I leaned forward just a little to catch a glimpse of how the ledge curved, but the sensation of toppling heels over head drew me back quickly. If only that pond had had water, everything would be different. I needed something to swallow, and promised to remember this thirst if I should ever taste water again.

Ten...eleven...twelve. We clung to the side like mountain goats, exposed and defenseless. Radar's side scraped the wall, but from where I stood it looked as if he was hanging in space. There was blood on my fingers where I'd seized whatever indentation or knob my hands could find. Jagged stones scratched the elbow that was already missing a piece of flesh.

Lightning mapped the sky. I startled, jamming the damaged toe against a ragged edge of rock. A thunderous clap followed fast after it. The mound shuddered from the tremor. I refused to look down at the toenail I knew I'd torn.

Keep your eyes straight ahead. Keep your eyes on the wall.

One misstep would be a tumble into somewhere no one would ever look.

With each *c...c...c...crack,* I shrank. My limbs felt not my own, each pinned to a nerve. I wanted off this howling ledge! The sand rotation had grown monstrous, and it hasn't even arrived!

I hate this place. I hate Texas. I hate—

Thirteen...fifteen, sixteen. Thunderous clouds blanketed the sky. I watched the path closely, my toe barking. The T-shirt wasn't enough. My teeth chattered. I'd never before wished for those jeans back, *but now—*

Be strong—

That's what people say when they feel the weakest. That's why the last steps are always the longest.

Eighteen...twenty...twenty-one. The sand pummeled from behind. We were in the curve when Radar pulled back, and everything in me curdled. I halted with him, a sickening image of tumbling off this cliff. Just as bad, the thought of being left all alone if he were to take the dive.

I shuffled a circle to face him. "Don't...kick!" A deep groove ran between his eyes. He pressed his face into my t-shirt; slobber bled through. I reworked the covering and rotated back like through a cramped revolving door. How could I calm him when I didn't even believe my own words? When had I become such a scaredy-cat?

Yet, who'd expect otherwise when I didn't even know how to use a wall phone?

Twenty three...twenty-six. I inched through the curve, feeling for a knob of stone to cling to, but, here, the wall was smooth. Sand bites eased some after the bend, the towering wall a protective buffer between us.

Thirty steps. I sponged the grime from my eyes with the pad of a fingertip. There was light ahead. The wide rock shelf ahead looked like the one from where we started. Or had we made a complete circle?

No. I could read the surroundings: the sandstorm was west, behind us. The thunderstorm was north. The light in the sky ahead was neither of those directions—we were definitely on the east side of the mound. A few more steps and we could be off this deathtrap. I felt hope for the first time. The cave?

Careful. Don't be rash. Don't be hasty. False hope is no hope at all.

Thirty-five. Bulging, bloated clouds boiled overhead. I pushed for longer strides because we seemed to be moving in slow motion. Radar chose not to step at all—he was frozen in the spot. I tugged the straps four times, hoping he would realize it was a signal...*four steps,* but he wouldn't budge.

Pressure built in my ears; goose bumps covered my legs and arms. The world was hostile and broken. I would've liked to kick a hole in the rock wall! "But we're so...close!"

The wind shrilled like shoving furniture over bricks. A zip of lightning shaved two years off of my life. Radar's head shot up. This time he followed—stiff legged, tail twitching angrily.

Thirty-nine. A tight clutch on the reins, I edged onto the open shelf with all the unsteadiness of feet that had just removed their roller skates. Radar staggered forward and dropped his head. His coat was sudsy. If he sniffed the ground and laid down, I'd never get him up.

My hands were scratched and bleeding. Darkness would soon cover us. I was shivering. How could it be so cold in Texas in the middle of summer?

I scraped the scale from my tongue, wiped the blood from

my lips, and took a feeble look around. It would've been comical if it wasn't so terrible. Of all the blood-letting steps that had steered us here, as the crow would fly, if we'd been plucked off one side and set down on the other, the difference was probably no more than rope-throwing distance away. We were one big boulder apart from where we started.

The wall angled away, where we stood, but there was a pleat in the wall, as if something were cut in stone. I cranked up as much energy as I could muster and crept toward it, forcing Radar along. Maybe it was a shadow that made that rock look sunk in. *Maybe a hole?*

A hole that...maybe—

The rock was rent apart. A large gash gaped like a broken mouth, its craggy opening taller than it was wide. My toes felt nailed to the spot.

The cave? The cave! It's the cave!

I hurried forward, but recoiled. *If something lived inside...*I dropped to a crouch.

My mouth was spongy with gunk too thick to taste. I was thirsty enough to suck dew from a stem, if only I had one. Was it a lair? The lair of a mountain cat?

Quit quivering like a stupid rabbit. It's the cave! Look behind you! Look above you! Make a decision. Move! Move! Move!

I picked up a lumpy stone. If something charged out, we'd make lots of tasty meals. Squeezing my eyes tight, I hurled the stone through the opening, positioned to dash. It plunked, rock on rock. Nothing moved.

We staggered into the cavern like into the jaws of a great fish.

Chapter Thirty

Radar's ears whisked over the chamber. The cave was cold, but the sand was warm, its texture soft as flour sifted through a sieve.

Fatigue washed over me. I had no help left. My legs would hardly work. I blew on my hands, buried my toes in the beach-like floor, and waited for my vision to adjust to the pale light that shrouded the cave like a spiderweb: strong for its weight, a snare for the foolish, a meal awaiting its prey.

My eyes were blinking closed. I had to hurry, plant Radar as far from the entrance as possible, not chance that he might wander.

Leaning in, stumbling forward, I forced him back and sandwiched him against the wall, removed the halter with trembling fingers, and peeled away a thick glob of gunk that crusted his nose. He groaned like an exhausted puppy.

I brushed the grime from his face, smoothed the boney ridge between his eyes, burrowed my hands under his mane, twisting the hair into mittens...and tried to feel grateful we were out of the storm. "Morning...will be—"

Hot again.

My knees tried to buckle. I willed the pounding in my head to slow, even as the shivering ratcheted up. This place would smile me into the sand.

I collapsed on one of the large, rectangular stones that formed a circle around a center, like stumps around a fire pit, and pulled my knees into the T-shirt. The rock was warm from the days' heat, and I welcomed the comfort of this desolate place where no one could live.

No one, except maybe Pap. I pressed the heels of my palms to my eyes. *When had I determined to have my own way?* I had failed. I would be the grave mistake that proved him right—a judgment I'd wear through the night.

Balling my hands into fists, I tucked my thumbs into the cocoon of fingers and lay back to listen to the wind, and search the cave for hope.

I can't help Radar. I can't help myself. So this is what Pap had warned me about.

The cavity dwarfed me. The cave rose tall as a two-story building. I couldn't smell the charr on the ceiling, but could see that fires had burned here. Where would the wood have come from to build such reaching flames when there were no trees around at all?

A screech sat me up. A hawk soared past the window of the cave with feathers fluffed out like the brown garment of a monk, close enough I thought I saw a glinting eye flare at me. It wasn't the hawk that took my breath away, but the enormous chasm he glided over. I had to remind myself to breathe. A faint haze painted the abyss like breath, flavorless as egg whites. Below, beyond, the purple shade surely took in half of Texas! The other side of the mound wasn't the bottomless pit. *This* was.

The chamber was notched with images of deer and rabbit— the hunters and horses and bison were distinct. I shuffled around the circle, reached out a finger to trace the blood-brown drawings crackled with age, lengthy drawings of rivers with water.

Water. I never knew water was such a thing of value.

Ancient spirits had honored this place for hundreds, even thousands of years. The Mighty Ones, Ben had called them. A thin place now, like the shadow a sparrows wings make.

This was a Comanchaire burial site.

My birthright.

My people.

My heritage.

Was I a treasure dragged in? Flint-hard hands had designed this cavern, a legacy they would leave behind—a sanctuary cave to preserve life, to preserve history, to preserve a culture and a time. A fortress cave. A thirsty place. Did they come here to find rest from the heat? The cold? A storm such as this? Or was this merely a grave the color of bones to swallow me up?

At my elbow was the red stain of a small handprint. I stepped around shards of broken pottery protruding from the sand like bleached memories, and laid my fingers against it. It was tiny compared to my own.

I felt the presence of warriors, keepers of the Llano Estacado, envisioned a sad procession of a proud people climbing this mound to deliver up their dead, understood the soft whimper of a spouse who'd lost a worthy companion, of children who would never again feel a father's strong arms to guide them.

A vapor.

An illusion.

A half-breath.

A small clay jar sat in a niche grubbed out of the wall. I carried it to the scant light at the entrance to read the chiseled inscription:

The mind justifies, the heart perceives.
Grasp the meaning of your life.

There were markings beneath that I couldn't decipher. I sensed stale breath on my neck—a sensory, like seeing with my ears and hearing with my eyes.

The storms had grown quiet, a silence as complete as the ocean floor. I stood at the cave entrance listening to the eerie moan echo from the deep grow like a siren.

The temperature plummeted. Thick, black clouds poured over the gorge like a train derailing—splintering...screeching... crashing. Numbing cold crashed over me, drove the air from my lungs. Sand slurped over the wall and whipped at the cave's opening as if it couldn't decide how to get in. With a great sucking sound, the floor shifted, billowing and swelling like bad breath.

I dropped the urn, raised my hands against the blowing particles, but the silt lifted and swirled the way bees swarm— around, around, up from the ground, lobbing sharp bits in my eyes.

I couldn't see to move, couldn't see to turn.

I wiped at my eyes but the effort made it worse. I tried to blink, but the tissues were too delicate, like grit in a window. My ears clogged; I joggled my jaw to clear them, but that didn't work. I might well be screaming through gravel. My teeth wouldn't quit chattering. Once I started shaking I couldn't stop.

The sand knocked me to my knees. I got up, tried to back peddle, but the wind whipped me around so that I hovered in place in the moment like a bird clinging to the lashing limb of a willow tree. A heavy spray threw me off-balance again.

Get inside! Stay on the ground!

I began to crawl, mindful of the crashing thunder that

echoed from the canyon, mindful of the driving rain that pelted my legs. I wasn't sure which way to go.

"Ra-dar?" I wheezed, choking and spitting and crawling blindly, my eyes clamped shut. *C'mon! Make a noise!*

The smell of the wind changed, or was it the sour in my mouth? Was I swimming the right direction—away?

I clawed my way to my feet and thrust my hands out. A wall! I tried to feel my way across it, one hand over the other, but the whipping wind and the whooping rain and the stinging sand bit at my arms and face and empty legs and rolled me in an unstable whirl that distorted every sound. I couldn't catch my fall.

A flash of pain.

A dull ache. Warmth trickled across my face. The metallic smell of blood was nauseating. I pressed a hand to my forehead —a knot the size of a peach filled my hand.

I drooped slowly, like how a flower fades—first its color, then its pedals, one by one. Finally, the stalk turns brown. For just a drop of water. Now I know. Rain can wash sky. Wind can shift the earth. I floated somewhere between, listening to crickets sing in my ear—they never shut up.

Be strong!

My head throbbed. I could see nothing—not the storm, not the blackness, not my way. I raised on all fours and tried to puke, but nothing came up. "Need..."

Tiny noises leaked from my belly, like that of a small, insignificant bee. *Honey bee, or bumble bee?*

So...cold.

My fist, cold and damp and tacky, found a hard, flat stone a hand-size wide. I began raking the sand...raking and raking, every pass like an electrical current snapping the air. My mouth held a foul thickness, the taste of the cave.

Howling wind chased over the mound. A gust surged across

the floor and blew blips in my face like naughty children who throw sand.

I rolled into the shallow hole I'd dug, and, with my last pound of strength, stretched out a hand to pull the warm sand over my legs, my belly, my chest. I lay perfectly still, like on a beach, in my tepid body armor, only my hands and shoulders and head exposed, and dug at the sand in my nose.

Nobody knows where we are. Nobody to come for us— How will we get off this horse dung mountain?

Another mighty gust of sand rolled over me, bleeding under my eyelids.

Oh, yeah. How many days can a body live without water? Did I figure that out?

A memory crept over the floor like a bug: The desert doesn't give up its secrets willingly.

Who'd said that? Something about a flower.

What had I gained by running away? I had run far, but not away. The very narrow line that separates life from death is thinner than I'd guessed.

My head hammered. My chin quivered. My teeth chattered.

I'm going to die here. Buried to my neck in sand, no one to find me. No name to remember. The same bones that brought us here, one day for someone to discover?

In a month?

In a year?

A hundred years?

Who will it be? A hiker? Explorer? In another age? Another civilization? A death prison...my reward.

I thought up the headline: 'Remains of teenage girl discovered in a T-shirt and undies found alongside a horse with a snap-down shirt tied over his bleached-bone head.' *How would they prove who I was?*

Is it okay to cry, now, Daddy? Now that I have no tears?

My tragic, fractured family. What worked for one, didn't work for the other. It's not that lies were ever told, it's that truths never were. Whatever went wrong, remained unspoken.

* * *

Forms walked among the rocks. Figures hunkered at a warm fire. Voiceless shapes hid in the dark with studying eyes... *paired with eight legs? Crawling lizards and slithering sn...* "Don't—"

Please don't let me be here when it turns night.

This siege tower that some called empty, the Comacheria knew how vast and brimming. My ear caught a whisper of it. *The vase—why should I think of that now? Where did it go when the storms collided?*

A twitch tickled my hand. The same quiver I'd known at the pond, and on the ledge when I clung to the rock. *It followed me here?*

"Mims—" I gasped. She was such a beautiful young girl. Shiny, cascading black hair around a tender, wise face.

Where were you when I needed you? When I needed direction?

I swiped at the crust on my face, worked to open one grainy eye just a slit. It hurt like a pokey finger in the peeper... The tender behind it thrummed.

Radar is moving!

Clomp. Clomp. He staggered through the rocks and nickered over my head. His muzzle brushed my hair, drafts of slobber on my forehead, a warm puff in one ear.

"Sure," I slurred. *Go ahead, step on my head. Make this day perfect—*

The same drumbeat resounded, over and over and over.

How long will it take to die? I don't want to hurt. I'm tired of hurting.

My tongue was swollen and seasoned. The Comacheria—*how many others are buried here?* What if they're right, the ones who say eyes watch over us? How many are lost?

If the ancients are watching, will they watch over my grave, too?

"I'm...Com...anche."

Thoughts of my mother, how she haggled me to be safe, to take no chances. She knew she could only control me so far, then she had to trust. She didn't deserve this. I could see the fatigue in her face when she dragged home from work. How I'd slit my eyes toward her, but never acknowledge her, not let her see me look up from the television.

"Mom—" She will look for me, but never find me. The pulse throbbed in my forehead. I felt her tears. *I'm...sorry. I felt so needy, and all the world knew it.*

I wept for my wrecked mother, my missing dad, my lost self. My poor horse. I could have done things differently. Thirst has a way of curing a hard head. Now, nobody would ever find out.

I held onto consciousness as if it were clasped between my hands, squeezed for a bit of its strength, but the drumming pebbles and snarling wind and pounding rain lulled me in and out of uneasy sleep.

I dreamed of bubbling springs, spontaneous laughter, pounding hooves. I dreamed of angels and warriors—many, many warriors, prowling among the stones—angel-warriors who uttered odd chants without pitch, like intonations of a song, each sound fused to another.

They stood around me, not touching, their contemplative faces lit by a homey fire. Their painted horses waited to be ridden through that enormous expanse of sky and land.

Sweet sleep is good company. Dreams of ice cream in a bowl

with a bent spoon. Knocking…like bare feet running through a feeder trough. Streams of fresh water splashing into pools that pucker the earth like a land-feature map. Lines coursing through my palms. They all had boundaries.

I dreamed of a blue dragonfly roosting at the birthplace of the wind. Dragonfly—keeper of dreams. The dragonfly can strip away all pessimism.

I listened to the night spirits softly whisper. They resided in certainty, among laws that never hid truth, and asked harshly, "In the history of the world, who are you?" I shook my head, a seizing at my breast.

Nobody.

I'd neglected my own set of rules. How could I prove who I am?

Murmurs filled my bones like marrow. I forced an arm through the sand and stretched out my hand. Sand jelled on the sticky blood between my fingers.

The same hand that injures can also heal. It scolds, then sets free.

I sensed the dragonfly flitter.

Why is it easier to tell a lie than to accept a truth? *I never knew the truth,* I might've answered. How could I when nobody will even answer my questions?

Truth must be found.

Mims held the hand of a young boy. They sat beside me, their appearances swelling with care and watchfulness. I sensed their piercing silence.

Groggy, without anchor, as if the air had changed shape, I tried to move, but didn't have the spark to struggle. The sand warmed my neck.

Mom had once said, "What do you do when it's dark and you're scared? You light a candle."

I hadn't forgotten. She didn't think I was paying attention. She never thought I paid attention.

Such quiet. So still. *I am Charley. Is it my time to die?*

The tips of my ears were icy enough to break. I had no lick for my tongue. I laid perfectly still in the thick, black quiet and thought about how foolish I'd been. Now I was trapped and alone. Alone—the very thing I'd always feared. Abandoned, like the poor lamb Pap used for bait.

How can a father leave his child? Why couldn't I have a brother or sister to share the anger, the pain? A selfish thought. Why would I wish my ache on anybody?

A giant leveling stick roams the world, and when it points to you, you know it.

Darkness crept in like vapor.

My head, my head...I dared not shift my eyes.

I fought for more than a shallow breath, wrestled the weakness thirst had left me with. I could no longer hear the wind, and dug at the sand that packed my ears. I might've been on the beach hearing the ocean through a sea shell.

I had deceived myself. I chose the life I felt I deserved, not the one that I really did. I had wrapped myself in Mom and Dad's troubles. It didn't begin in January when Mims died. That's just when the light shined on it. Their lives were like wearing a hat inside a hat...it didn't fit. Their stories were their own—I could see that now.

Mom's life had crashed and burned, but I couldn't fix it. Only she could. I rewrote her story. She would bounce back like a ball of Silly Putty, that strong, resilient mom of mine.

Of Dad...he had his secrets. Nobody will know what he doesn't want them to know. He was on his own.

Mims was easy. Her parts didn't need revising.

I rewrote Pap fifty times. It was exhausting. I'd never known anyone like him. If only he'd wanted to include me. If we accidentally stumbled together, he was quick to set us apart. Yet, he did me no harm. He was...Pap. I would find a way to love him. He'd said it, 'When you give up, you're lost.'

Too late, Pap. I'm lost. Just not how you meant it.

I found peace, turning them loose. The kind of peace that let me know I would never be alone. The kind that assures everything will be okay, no matter how it turns out. That moment was like walking through a refining fire. Weight lifted off me as with wings. Their problems had no more hold over me.

An awareness stirred the fog of my mind. I dreamed of running streams...fresh-water springs. Of scooping water into my shirt. Would morning come for me? Even if, then what?

I wanted to live, but feared the end would be worse than the beginning.

I would never leave this place.

Chapter Thirty-One

Something disturbs me—something loud, pumping, whomping, booming, beating, like steel wings, far, far away. My head is pounding so hard I don't want to move a finger. A thunderous scream fills the air.

I know that bellow! Radar—

I whine, *Don't shoot, Pap!* but my voice can't make the words.

Something topples, the tone of its crash, rock upon rock. Radar is moving, flat feet crunching. A cry rises in my throat, *Come back, Don't leave me!* But something keeps it inside.

A brilliant light pours through my lids. My eyes refuse to breathe underneath. Sand grinds like glass if I merely shift an elbow. I can't cut my eyes, and don't dare squeeze them, so I have to turn my head away.

I thought the storm was gone, but a sprinkling is stinging my face once again. *The storm turned back?* I arch a shoulder with effort, but can't lift it from the sand. It hurts to part my lips. *Now I know—a sandstorm never ends.*

Yawning, reverberating rumbles spill through the cave in

booming waves. A calm voice fills the chamber: "Charley. Charley, I can see you!"

I suck a scant breath. *God...is calling me!*

I'm dead? I don't remember dying. *No wonder I feel so stiff.* My head aches bad enough to be dead.

I can't think. As I try to recall that scream, the voice wafts through the air again.

"Charley, we know where you are. We're coming to get you!"

Coming to get me? What does that mean? I should know.

The deep, beating echo retreats, its brassy whomping growing slowly distant. Tranquility and peace once again fill the cave. My breathing is short, ragged, uneven, as I wait to be taken.

I'll go back to sleep.

I struggle to remember what the voice had said.

Something yelps from the ledge. Radar stomps noisily. A rustle, a bark, the chinking noise is close.

Radar...can bark?

The sharp yowling that follows seizes my heart. The mountain lion has found me! A grunting, panting, wheezy clamor rushes at me in a flurry of yelps.

Stop! I scream in my throat, and drop my face to the sand as if to make myself invisible. I hold perfectly still, waiting for the pounce. I'd never been bitten before.

But I won't feel it! I'm already dead.

A foot scratches my head, scrapes my scalp. I'm too paralyzed to breathe.

Hurry. Get it over with!

It slobbers on me, falls across my sandy grave, licks my face, my cheeks, my lips. Hurting my busted lips...tasting me. *I didn't know a mountain lion licked their meal first...*

Writhing over my sand, it twists, stands, and shakes the grit all over me, then digs its nails into the grave, raking one sunburned arm free. I lift the limb like it can protect me. Just as quickly, the cave is silent again. The monster, gone. I perk my ears to the quiet left behind.

I had imagined it.

Radar steps delicately among the stones and dips his head to my freed hand. I brush his soft nose with a finger, his prickly whiskers.

I'm sorry, I want to tell him.

He makes a great noise of tumbling to the ground...first to his knees, then, with a heavy grunt he collapses beside my head.

Bells. I strain an ear toward the pleasant jingles tickling the air. I've always liked bells. *The call to come home?*

I'm...here— I think.

The bells grow louder. The air cackles with squawks and static and faint, far-away voices. Rough hands touch mine.

"We have her!" a voice croaks to the hiss of snapping static. An angel kneels beside me. Hands cup my chin.

"Charley! Charley, dear girl..."

Angel's voices—

There's much shuffling. A light floats, flickering the way a dragonfly moves, zip...zip, back and forth, back and forth...left, right, over my face, turning my hurting eyes inside out. Fireflies? Bright little fireflies soaring between the jumble of murmurs.

A voice rings out, "How in the world did she—"

"Get back!" The angel shouts. "Make room!" The bulk settles beside me. "We're going to get you out of here, Charley!" it says kindly. "Thank *God* we found you."

I pause to form the thought. Words have taxed my strength. "Are you—" I cough, choke. "—the...warrior angel?" I murmur like with gravel in my throat.

Laughter breaks out behind. The one kneeling answers, "Can't say as I am, Missy."

"The warriors...came!" Mine is the vacant voice, a whisper. "They're still here."

"Oh yeah? Wish I could see that."

"I...*hear*...them." They hover in the crust behind my eyes. I choke on a whisper, "One...plays a...flute." I grasp the reaching hand. "Are you...proud of me, Daddy?" Eyelids dare not shift.

A gentle squeeze on my arm. "Very."

The cave lights up like mid-day; the brightness penetrates my lids. Unrecognizable, busy noises fill the chamber—irritating clutter...distant, like traffic, except without the horns. Many hands begin to scoop at once.

"We've got you, sweetheart." They lift me from my warm bed of sand.

My teeth began to chatter. I shake uncontrollably.

A crinkling blanket goes around me, tucks in and under, and sets me down carefully against a rock. Fingers press into my neck. Others on my wrist. Water wipes down my face. I seize the hand and grope the water to my tongue. It sloshes, cold on cold. "Yes, yes. Just a little in your mouth, and spit." The trickle starts again, and stops. I want more. Water ticks down my cheek, over my lips.

A rough, dry tongue licks my arm. "C'mon, Rowdy. Move over," the angel scolds.

Rowdy? He's dead, too?

A large hand clamps the top of my head. "Charley, are you wearing contacts? I need to know." The angels's voice is grizzly, commanding, strong, reassuring.

Contacts? I know what that is.

"I need to irrigate your eyes." My head falls back. Sand washes from my hair, down my neck.

He will lift the scales from my eyes?

I stick out my tongue again—a tongue that feels like somebody lost it there—and try to swallow, but gag. It feels like spit is running down my chin. The hand pulls back. "Just sips." A soft sponge is tapping on my face. Something wraps my arm. I push the hand away.

"I know. I know." The hand pats. "But I have to see what we're dealing with here. That's quite a knot you have on your forehead. How'd you do that?"

I can't answer. Can't think. Can't stop shivering. The smell of something antiseptic stings. "...warrior horse—" The thought flies away.

Hands walk down my arms, hesitate at the elbow, squashing, nipping. There's probing pressure on my knees, down my legs, over my feet. When they come to my toe, I yelp— The fingers linger there. The voice turns away. "Nothing's broken."

Radar— Something about Radar that I have to remember. My whisper is raspy, urgent. "Radar...he can bark, you know—"

"Mm—" Wiping. Wiping. Wiping. "We all knew he was special."

"Radar. Give..." but the voice is in my ear again.

"You can let go, now, Charley. Sabion is taking care of Radar. Let somebody else be brave for him."

"Si, Carlota. I am here! I am here!" The words knock back and forth, waiting to settle. "You take good care for Radar. Now I will take good care. Little Jennie has come for her friend. She is like the mountain goat, that one. You can be certain she will lead him safe down the hill where you papa waits with a trailer. So you see, already you papa and Jennie make a plan."

Pap?

Fingers touch, tap, poke. "Heart rate's slow," the warrior

murmurs. A calloused hand flashes a tiny beam of light, a probe that hurts the most. "Try to open this eye—" A touch on that side of my head. "—when I say." Wet hands cup my head, one over each ear, and turn my head to the side. "Now!"

A finger pulls the eye slanted. A steady stream of water trickles over it. "Okay. Blink for me, Charley. Over and over and over again. Keep blinking." I blink, but he says, "More. Keep going. Blink. Blink. Blink." The water runs and runs and runs. "Great! Can you open, just a little?"

I can't. Cold runs through my hair, down my T-shirt. The grit under my bra has made my skin raw. I am uncomfortable, but do as I am told.

"Okay Charley, you're doing great." More frigid water, in tiny bursts. "Now, blink, blink, blink. See if you can open, any at all."

There's too much going on around me. I can't keep up.

"Charley...Charley!" the voice thunders, but every time I hear my name it's like from farther down a well. There's pressure on my arm. "One more time. Look left, Charley." A tap on that shoulder.

I try, but my eyes can't do right. Nothing is important any more. All I want to do is go to sleep. There's murmuring like from a bee-hive somewhere above me. There's a horrible squeeze on my arm.

"Blood pressure's dropping. Breathing's shallow."

The angel voice changes...brisk, impatient, growling. "Shock. We can't wait. Have to get fluids in her faster. Start the IV right here. Now!" He bends to my ear. "Charley, it's Ben. Listen to me." The voice is slow, deliberate, composed.

I nod. *Funny, it sounds like Ben.*

"Charley? Charley!" The bellow is almost angry, "I need you to listen..."

It's warmer in my sand. It's hard to pay attention. "I tried to fix—"

A bark, "Hurry up with that saline!" Something heavy drops. A zipper rips. A thick figure fills the space. Tight rubber grips my arm, then there's a hurting snap. "You're going to feel a little pressure." Fingers prod, pressing, tapping up and down my arm.

It's so cold.

"Stay with me!" Hands urge me awake.

My head lolls sideways. Something tightens on my arm.

"Stay here, Charley!" the voice demands. I taste the alcohol rather than smell it through the gunk in my nose. "A little stick, now, and we can pour fluids in you quicker this way."

I don't feel anything.

More patting. More pressing. "Hold this." I try to raise a hand. "Not you—"

There's smothered laughter. Tape rips. "Tourniquet's off," one says, like into a radio.

I can't stop shaking. Murmurs fly around my head; someone shoves my feet into warm socks, as cold flows though my veins. I stifle a sob. My angel scoops me up like a lamb, and rocks me against him. I clutch his pocket, my throat broken with bleats.

"Go ahead, sweetheart." His voice is gruff, as if Pap's oatmeal is in his throat. "Cry that sand right out of your eyes. Tears are about the best thing for you right now. You'd be surprised what all they can wash away."

I cry for my dad who would never come get me, as I cling to the man who did.

I cry over everything I never knew, and now, over the things I do.

I cry for Radar. He deserves better than me. What have I done?

I cry over something lost, while I cry for something found.

And finally, I cry for what only I can know: that I've left my childhood behind.

My angel holds me close like my dad hasn't since I was twelve. He tucks the blanket under my neck and whispers close to my ear, like to a kitten left on a doorstep, "Outside the mouth of this cave is a Nightflower in full bloom. Even now, I can smell its fragrance."

I lock on his voice, racked with grief.

"To see such a flower is very, very rare. The sun is just about to break. The bloom is drooping. Its work is done." He whispers for only me to hear. "Nightflower, I think I would choose for your Comanche name, if you were my little girl."

Chapter Thirty-Two

"Basket's coming down," a squawking voice announces. The hand is heavy on my arm. "Ready?"

I shake my head and whimper as the bandage is wrapped around my head and what's left of my senses is closed off. "How can I—"

The answer comes with a squeeze. "It takes time."

I mash my teeth as he lifts me and carries me onto the ledge where I hear the same thumping, booming drum of my dream. "Just a feather in my arms."

Sand grinds into my skin. There's the piercing squall of a hawk passing overhead, as if nothing unique had occurred to change his world—he flew above the storm.

I have mixed feelings about leaving these ancient people who, somehow, I knew never left me. The walls were their record. There's a certain order about it. The hand of nature that pursued me here almost won.

Almost isn't good enough.

I am not ready, no matter what came out of my mouth. I clutch the nylon jacket. "Wait!" I sob. "Wait!" My throat is like tar. He halts. I squeeze the arm that's carrying me. "What... what do you...see?"

He pivots slowly. His sigh is deep. He turns, and I turn with him, eyes and arms holding me are one, working together. "The sun is beginning to rise...chasing away a large, round, pink moon. The canyon is thick with particles suspended in the air. It'll take awhile for everything to settle."

A cackle and squeal announce other-worldly mumbles. "Hospital's on standby. They're waiting for us! Let's go! Let's go!"

"A minute!"

"Ten-Four," the static voice bawls, like ducks clucking. "Standing by."

He lays me carefully on a hard, flat surface—web-like, rather than a cushion. "We can't bring the helicopter to you," he says. "It would stir up more sand. They had to set down on top of the mound. We're going to winch you up vertically, take you up in a basket. Reverse rappel."

Hands arrange me, tuck me, strap my legs, my arms, my waist so that I can't move even my head. Fingers busily snap and cinch and bind me.

"Harnessed. Basket's ready," he says to someone unknown. The hands leave me. "And...backing off."

Deep, booming beats rumble through the radio—a slow rotation of whomps strike the air. Wings beat faster. Drums bang in my ears. The sound of metal snapping onto metal, something locking in place.

It alarms me! I brace against the straps. "I can't—" My voice is strangled against the noise. "Please. Don't—*leave*—me."

A hand touches my face. "I have to send you up first. Don't worry. I'm right behind you. The folks in that copter, they're very careful. It'll be the ride of your life."

Every limb turns icy. Panic floods me. "I've—" *already had a ride of my life!* I can't answer. *I don't want another!* I clutch the fingertips that touch mine. "A girl...can't know...every...thing."

He pats. The transmitter cackles. "Ready, then?"

I'm seized with fear. I gasp for breath. "I'm...not strong—"

"Get 'er out of here!" he shouts.

I'm pinned to a basket on a ledge that lives in the sky. It lifts, swings out, and terror fills every branch of me. I've seen the endless drop from this cliff, the hollow pit where wails reside.

Every nerve and fiber inside me scream at another ride of my life!

Chapter Thirty-Three

My life has split in two: the world before the storm, and the world after. I tried to recall the tomb with its heavy stones and limestone walls, and the Comanche companions that shielded and watched over me.

I'd pressed my palm to the handprint of an ancient child and traced drawings with my fingertips, as if interpreting the language recorded by another culture, in another time.

I stood alone on a high table of rock like a hawk on a ledge, and discovered new colors—a canyon soaked with brushstrokes only a storm could deprive of color.

My time in that cave taught me that a broken spirit is a torn soul. It's a force that has to heal from the inside—the heart and mind must work together.

I'm holding onto my roots with tight fists. I thought I had to go outside myself to find peace, but what I found was choice: It was already living inside of me. I'd survived in spite of the thing that made every attempt to suck away my life.

It was a difficult passing. My life was required in order to find it again, like the little lamb whose life was needed to save the other sheep. A second chance? What would I do with it?

Never again would I believe in my own significance. I was no more important than one of the ancients who came before me. Would the day come that I'd be glad I went up that mound?

These were my thoughts as I lay in a stiff, plastic bed not my own, and listened to beeps that reported from somewhere behind my head—a tangle of tubes to pour life back into my body.

I raised a hand and traced the wrapping on my face, drew a finger across bandages that sealed off my sight. It felt weird to be wrapped like a mummy—only my ears and mouth exposed.

I took slow breaths, drawing air in, spilling it out luxuriously. There was the scent of flowers. I tapped at my lips, gooey with balm, touched my forehead and discovered a huge, tender knot. I was raw all over. I itched. I ached. My arms and neck tingled with a thick, sappy gel. I didn't want to shift my eyes. Would I ever see again?

"About time you woke up," Pap said gruffly.

I shrunk, flung the sheet over my head, and cowered like a stupid ostrich. How could I face him?

A chair scraped the floor. He didn't say anything more, so I trained my ears to his movement: shuffling boot steps, a door that opened and closed...paper crinkling on a tray...the stirring of an icy drink. And over it all, the sweet scent of flowers.

He sat down hard beside me. The sound of air escaping its cushion filled the room's hush. He plied my hand off the sheet like peeling a root from the hard, calculating ground until I released the cloth that hid me.

Taking my hand with a thick, gnarly paw the size of a grizzly bear, he clutched with one hand and stroked with the other, then dragged his fingers through my hair, picking, pulling. He was Mom in that moment, and I could not be moved to pull away.

"Pap," I wailed, my voice broken and raspy. "I won't give up on you, like you gave up on Mom." I choked on tears and had to clear my throat.

"Hm." He refilled his lungs and let it loose with a loud sigh. "A body grows weary, but it's never without hope." He sounded tired. "I never gave up. I just let go." My shoulders bobbed with the distress that wouldn't seep out. "I've just been sitting here thinking," he said slowly. "I have to quit this—"

A wretched mewl climbed my throat like steam seeping from a pot—a pitiful moan I couldn't hold back. "I'm sorry, Pap! I'm sorry. I am so, so sorry. Please—"

"What!" he exploded, ramming the chair back so hard it screeched on the floor. "I don't mean you! I wasn't talking about you! It's me, it's all me, Charley. I'm such a fool."

It was the third time he'd said my name. A wave of hiccups pumped my chest.

"I've been a fool for so long...until...until...I didn't know how to be any other way." He got up. Hard leather heels ground unevenly to the door.

I sat straight up. I couldn't take another walk-away. "Please, don't go!" *Don't abandon me, too.*

He spit and growled, "I'm not going 'til I say I'm going, and I've got something to say, so I'm not going!" His words mushed together across the room. "I've been hiding. You just don't know. And neither did I realize...you made me see that, dad-gummit! I never wanted to get to know you!"

I croaked, a painful moan. "Why?"

"Because—" He paused. "Because." He spat gruffly. "Because it would hurt too bad to see you go away. I know all about that. I have a knack for driving people off. I'm afraid the years have turned me crusty."

There was true regret in his voice, and it swallowed the thorn in my throat—the thorn that he'd never talk to me again.

That I would never again ride in his sweaty, stinky, oily old truck.

"You just didn't have enough misery in you to stay on your side of the porch!" He fell into a coughing fit and I flinched. "I've wasted a lifetime despairing my losses. But...it seems we're more alike than we are different. The likeness makes us family. The differences make us individuals."

He ruffled my cover and folded the sheet back. "Sometimes all we see are the differences. They kinda overlap. We'll have to sort those out."

I inched back a sliver of elastic wrap that covered my eye. The blurry room was full of blurry flowers: on the nightstand, on the tray, in the window, beside the television that snarled through an old western with no sound.

Pap looked different. Besides being an orb floating in my vision, and though not a hair on his head had changed, *something*...somehow, he didn't seem as old.

But then, I knew. I was different, too.

The blur of his steely blue eye challenged mine. "You were right," he said. "I am an 'ol coot. My roots are firmly planted in this dirt." He wrangled my finger away and the bandage snapped back in place. "But I'm your ol' coot, and you're stuck with me."

I knew what I had to say. "I'm sorry, Pap. I'm sorry for everything. I'll never take off again. I want to be just like you, worn out knees and all—up that hill, hobble-hobble." I was rambling. "And not only that, I'm sorry for a whole lot of other things, too, like, I'm sorry about—"

"Okay, okay. Stop!" He lifted my hand and kissed the back of it. His lips were warm and squishy and the kiss disarmed me. "We're just a couple'a sorry...mm, never mind. I suppose what we both have to work on is, stop doing the things that make us have to say I'm sorry. I will if you will." He shrugged. "Heck, I need to work on it even if you don't."

In the awkward silence that bloomed, I was afraid to ask, "Radar—"

"And I wasn't shooting your blasted *horse!*" He punctuated the word. "If I hadn't pulled that trigger, things would've been a whole lot different. I killed the rattlesnake that crawled out of the hay. There wasn't time for a lot of wishy-washy sweet talk."

I sat up. "You weren't trying to...shoot him?"

"My aim's a heck of a lot better than that. Radar's a pretty big target. If I'd wanted to shoot him, I'd have hit. I'm surprised you didn't see it. Radar knew it was there. He's the one who alerted me. You gotta pay attention to how animals are acting. They're trying to tell you something."

"Radar's...okay?"

"Yep. Jennie brought him down the mound with those blasted jangling bells...I could hear'em coming for a mile. Sabion and I loaded him into the trailer and took him to Ben's clinic. He's going to be fine. Nothing serious. Dehydration. Some cuts and bruising. Like you. Hunger. But then, he's always hungry." His hand lingered on mine. "Like you."

I threw the cover, flung my legs over the side of the bed, and threw myself blindly into Pap. His whiskers stabbed—I had to draw back, but I couldn't let go.

"Alright, then. Alright." He eased me off my feet, sat me back on the bed, and straightened the plastic tubing that had knotted around my arm. "Darn horse didn't have to knock the barn down though," he muttered sourly.

"I'm in a hospital?" Nobody actually said.

"Yes. In Lubbock."

"How long have I been here?"

"They brought you in yesterday morning. Do you remember the helicopter?"

"Kinda. Slightly. Not really." I recalled the fright.

"Severe dehydration. Shock. First and second-degree burns. A dump-truck load of sand...and that bump on your head. Your ankle and toe took a powder. You've been sleeping ever since."

"Does Mom know?"

"She does. Feared she'd scream me off the phone, so I let Ben handle that. I'm scared of her."

"I'm kinda like Mom. My tongue is my downfall."

The gruffness returned. "Well, now, that makes it a family heirloom, kinda in the same corner with burned toast." Things shuffled on a tray. A sound like paper unwrapping. "You've got a meal getting cold, here. Hamburger. Lucky you."

Pap fit the burger in my hand. It smelled like a Dairy Blast burger. "And, I mean to see you eat every last bite of it. Put some meat on those bones."

The door whooshed open. "Hey, now. This is a good sign."

"Hello, Doc," Pap snarled. "You here to squeeze a few more bucks out of me?"

The doctor didn't answer. I felt a flurry at my bedside. "Hello young lady. Glad you made it back to us. And I mean that literally."

Damp, spongy hands picked up my arm, tucked it against starchy fabric. A blood pressure cuff coiled around one arm. Another voice, a female this time, said, "Open your mouth for me, dear."

I refolded the foil over the burger and let her slip a thermometer under my tongue. She pressed two fingers into my wrist and relayed the information across me. "No fever...blood pressure's good."

"Great!" Doc announced. Intravenous tubes rattled. Fingers thumped the bag. "These'll be done soon," Doc said, and pushed a straw to my mouth. "We've been pouring saline and electrolytes into you. You're fully loaded...hydrated, but I still want you to drink."

I nodded, slurped.

"Let's get you out of these bandages, then you can finish your lunch, okay?" He snipped. One side of my bandage fell away. He peeled off the pads.

I squinted through slits...at the room, at Pap, whose mouth scrunched grimly. Flowers sat on every flat surface. My eyes felt like gristle. My arms were bright as lobster tails against the white sheets.

The doctor smiled briefly, eyes close to mine. "So nice to see you."

"Everything's fuzzy."

"It'll take a while to heal. Sand has scratched the cornea." Palming a laser light, he leaned over, flicked a light right and left, and whispered so only I could hear, "You're very lucky, you know?" He brought his face to mine, pressed my hands as if delivering a message in Morse Code. "Don't you ever do that again." He tilted my head back and put a drop in each eye. "Do you feel strong enough for a cool shower? I bet that would feel nice."

I nodded, shifted in grit that had slept in my bed.

"Which brings me to one other thing that needs clearing up. I have to ask, what happened to your clothes? ER said you came in with only your underclothes, and some very serious sunburn."

I was embarrassed to talk about it, but I scraped through the recall: "My horse didn't have his mask. I had to use my shirt to protect his eyes. Then the storm got so bad I had to use my jeans to protect mine. Except, the wind ripped them out of my hands before I could get them tied. I lost my flute. I lost my phone. I lost my boots." It hurt to talk so much. The memory hurt to relive it.

"I see."

There was panic in the hallway. Something dropped. A loud bang followed, and I heard my name like an explosion. The door blasted open. Dr. Ben held it, Mom ducked under his arm.

Pap jumped to his feet. "Miriam!"

"Mom!"

She wore a look that silenced the room. Whether from anger or from happiness, I knew all hell was about to break loose.

Ben quietly closed the door behind them. Even in a blur, I could see her eyes were red and swollen. She hadn't bothered with makeup, or if she did, it was long gone. Her clothes were a mess, her hair, almost as bad as my own. She saw the melon on my forehead and broke into a long, reaching sob. "What has *happened* here?"

"I'm okay." I hurried to say, but the scratching grate of my voice set her off again.

She garbled words at me, "No...you're...not!" The pain in her eyes brought up a jag in my throat. Ben held out a box of tissues. She yanked one, two, three, four...five, and shook her head, dropping a hand on my arm.

"Ouch!"

She jumped back like I'd slung french fries. "I'm so sorry!"

"It's just...the sunburn, Mom. It's okay."

The roots of my hair were on fire. Of course I was glad to see her, except her coming reminded me that I'd never outgrow my mommy. The little bit of fizz I had left drained right out of me. "What are you doing here? I mean, why did you come?"

"Why! Why?" She turned an accusing glare on Pap and shook a little pointy fingernail at his nose. "You didn't answer the phone! You haven't returned my calls!"

Pap shoved his chair back. "I've been...here. Ben was taking care of it. I knew he could do a better job of explaining than me."

Her chin trembled. She spat through gritted teeth, "I couldn't get here any faster! Air service to Lubbock...*oh my God!*" Her dark eyes filled with tears and she wiped furiously. "Then the pilot refused to land. Refused! All because the runways were too hot! Have you *ever?* Can you *imagine?* Runways melting because of the *heat?* In *Texas?*" She sucked back a breath, buried her nose in the tissue and blew hard... wiped the wet from her nose. "You'd think by now they'd get that right!"

"The pilot re-routed." Ben explained. "I drove to the Dallas-Ft. Worth Airport to pick her up. That's why we're so—"

She lifted her thick hair and fanned the back of her neck. "Otherwise, I'd have been walking!"

"Good morning." Ben smiled that smile I'd come to appreci-ate, the carton of tissues still boxed between his hands. "Bandages came off? Good!" He squinted into my face, into my eyes. Inspected the bop on my head, the red blisters on my ears, all without a touch.

"Mom," I said non-combatively. "Pap is taking good care of me. I'm fine. Really."

The doctor stepped forward with an amused grin. "Miriam, it's been a long time. Good to see you home." Turning, she, looked him over as if he'd just blown through the window. "She's going to be all right," Doc said, his smile genuine.

Mom judged with huffs of doubt. "Going to be—What about her eyesight? Any damage? What about—" Her eyes melted over me, up my neck, down my arms. Her arms flared.

Ben glanced from the doctor to Miriam...whispered in her ear. She nodded. Coupling her hands over her mouth, she allowed him to gently draw her back.

She stopped at the end of the bed, lips clenched tight, black eyes snapping from Pap to the doctor. "How long will she be here?"

"She can probably go home tomorrow," the doctor said. "She's on antibiotics to stave away any infection."

"Anti...biotics." Mom repeated jaggedly, then blew again into the tissue.

Doc nodded. "Our bodies are pretty miraculous machines. She'll heal in no time. I'll send the gel home with you, too. For the burn."

"Burn? What burn?" Her eyes flashed back at Pap.

"The sunburn," Ben reminded. "She was out there a long time." Mom cheeped a muffled whimper.

"Use it generously," the doctor continued. "Several times a day. It's a bad sunburn."

Mom nodded quickly, her mouth in a twist. "Gel. What about that knot?" She bit off the nib of a nail.

"Nothing time won't make better. Call me if there's pain or tearing in her eyes. Redness...difficulty opening her eyes." He dropped a business card on the tray. "There may be a deeper corneal scratch. Follow up with an eye specialist if her vision continues to blur—I can give you some names."

Doc stood over me. "You'll be uncomfortable with light for a while, so I brought these." He pulled a wad from his pocket. "I want you to wear these very *un*-cool sunglasses for at least two weeks whenever you go outside." He fitted them over my ears. "At the very least."

Now Radar and I look just alike.

The doctor patted my hand. "Understand? Everywhere you go. Use them inside, too, if you feel any eye strain. You'll know."

"Two weeks," I croaked, and closed my eyes. *Where I'm going there's very little sunshine to hide from.*

"Promise? You can tell your friends you're starting a new

trend." He laughed at his joke all alone. "Okay, then. And stay out of that desert unless somebody's with you!"

I felt like a bobble-head, nodding—too much, too soon, too many—so much to everyone. Jeans, boots, long sleeve shirts, wide brim hats, sunscreen...and ridiculous sunglasses.

Until I'm gone.

"And I want to see her in my office in two weeks," he told Mom as he passed.

I wouldn't be here in two weeks. *I'll leave it all in a drawer.*

He quietly closed the door behind him. You could've dropped a mouse and it wouldn't have squeaked. Everybody stared at the door, as if he were about to shoot back through and yell, *Just kidding!*

Pacing, pacing, Mom stopped in front of Pap. "What were you thinking, letting her go out there like that? She's not a rancher. She doesn't know the ways of this life."

"She's—got it in her," Pap said. "That's enough."

Mom sipped air from the corners of her mouth, her stare cold. "I guess I know what's best for my daughter." She forced the words out.

I pushed the sunglasses over my eyes.

Pap tucked his arms and met her scowl, his shiny eyes holding. Hooking a boot heel on the roll-away tray, he wheeled it out from between them. "She been looking for something she knew was here. Time for speaking will never be better than right now."

She glared at his knee. "Frankly, I never thought she'd make it here all summer."

I'd thought that myself. "There's probably things we can all do differently," I said. They both turned their silence on me.

Ben floated behind them in a blur. I was ready to break up the match. "Ben, how did you find me?"

"Your phone. We'd have never known where to look except we got a ping from your phone." He looked at Mom. "Your mother and I knew exactly where to look. There's only one place you could've gone—that cave is positioned just exactly right for reception from a brand new cell tower they put up last year. You had the best rescue outfit team in all of Texas at your service, miss. Well-trained, highly qualified. We coordinated to move out as soon as the sand storm passed—a team on the ground, and one in the air." He covered my hand with his. "The longest hours of our lives."

The bed sagged. Mom sat beside me. "I was so scared." I could barely hear her.

Ben said, "You have to tell somebody when you're going off—no matter how mad you might be—where you're headed, when you expect to be back. Take a buddy if you want to explore. West Texas is a tough place to get lost in. Luckily, it turned out all right. Being head of the rescue team, I can tell you how often it doesn't."

"I didn't know there'd be a sand storm."

He nodded. "They're not common, but a thing like that can whip up pretty fast. By the way, how'd you know to dig that hole?"

"I was so cold! The sand was warm."

"Well, it likely saved your life. No matter the elevation, in a storm like that, temperatures plunge."

"West Texas isn't for the faint-hearted," Pap barked. "I told 'em all, 'She's smart. She's my granddaughter, isn't she? The land is in her blood.'"

I drew a scant breath. Such words were all I'd ever dreamed to hear from Pap.

He tipped his hat. "As for that horse—" The heart monitor blipped. A dismal wound to open the past and fuel the future.

His eyes held a twinkle. "Radar's here to stay. When a blind horse can learn the things you taught him, well, Sabion said it: He belongs here."

He settled the glasses back over my eyes. "But, I'm holding you accountable. I took you for a kid who would disappear inside a week and never look back. Radar will expect you here next summer, and the one after that."

I forced a smile, but my throat was narrow as the straw. I hid behind the glasses so he couldn't see the tears. They weren't tears of joy—returning to Seattle was the last thing I wanted. I'd be going home to a place I'd discovered I no longer belonged.

I wanted everybody to just go away and quit looking at me, like there was no place else to look. I blocked the chit-chat from my ears.

I am strong. Mim's blood runs in my veins. Though it took all summer to find her, suddenly, I knew where she was. Mims was in Mom. She'd been there all along. The words formed on my mouth. "I am Night...flower." Nothing came out, though I knew Ben read my lips.

A slight knock, the door opened a crack...then a hand-width wider. An urgent whisper, "Can I come in?"

"Yes. Brett," Ben said. "Come in." I whipped the silly sunglasses away. Brett's gaping mouth assured me how awful I must look. I shoved them back on.

He tiptoed, a tall, thin, gawky slow-dance across the room. His eyes flickered over my gritty hair, lingered on the lump on my forehead, shuffled down my willowy red arms spread out on the white sheet.

I didn't hate *his* eyes.

He clung to a big box of chocolates, a shy look of uncertainty. "I brought you —" He laid the box on the bed next to me. "Caramel-chocolates." He shrugged. "Or, chocolate-caramels."

I smiled back. "I'm glad you came."

He scanned the room. "Do you like the flowers?"

I flicked an indistinct look around. "You sent these?" He nodded. "All of them?" He smiled. "They smell nice."

His eyes strayed to Mom, who leaned dangerously into every word, and yawped, "You're—"

She reached over me to shake his hand. "Miriam. I'm Charley's..."

"I know who you are! You look just like the pictures in my mom's album. I grew up knowing you!"

She twinkled. "That was a long time ago."

"Just the same, you're a legend. I'm glad to meet you." He gushed into overdrive about her accomplishments—the photos, the trophies, the record.

I turned my head to the window. Why wouldn't everybody leave? Except Brett.

Ben caught Pap's eye. Taking Mom by the arm, he said, "Let's go get a sandwich. Let them visit."

Pap made a big production of dragging out of his chair, clomping across the floor with that flat-footed shuffle of his. Mom turned back to look three times in a distance of six feet, just in case I would want to stop her. Ben pressed her gently forward. When the room was quiet, I blew a huge sigh of relief.

Brett took Pap's chair and reached for my hand, careful not to touch the goo on any part of my arm. His eyes traveled over my face. I'd seen the knot in the mirror over the sink. It was hideous...all cranked up like somebody had smacked me with a golf ball. Blood vessels speckled every inch of it. "How *are* you?" he asked.

I didn't want to answer that question one more time, and looked away. He squeezed my hand. "Truly, how are you?"

I lifted a shoulder that didn't shrug—a movement that made my skin feel like it might separate from the bones. "I'm okay."

He tore a straw from its wrapping, dropped it in an icy

carton, pressed the cup to my mouth. His eyes poured into mine. "You scared us all."

Tears welled without warning. "I know. I'm sorry. Scared me, too."

"Please don't do that again. You don't know your way around this country."

Same thing over and over...he didn't know how it happened that I took off. I nodded, closed my eyes, but felt him watching me.

"I know it was Lee Ann and Dani who did that to your dress," he said. "And I've taken care of it." I flashed a look at him. "It was immature. She was jealous."

I shook my head. "It's not worth losing a friend over." Growing good friends is hard enough. "You've known each other far longer than me. I hardly know either of you."

"We've never been anything more than friends, and we're not even that, now."

Lee Ann was the last person I wanted to talk about. Had she been on that ledge with me, how good a friend might I have been?

Chapter Thirty-Four

"Does that hurt?" Mom asked for the tenth time as I sat on a stool in a lukewarm shower and let her wash my hair.

More than you know.

The sand trickled down my back, puddling on the shower floor rather than washing down the drain. Even the power of water couldn't flush away what the wind sent home with me. I closed my eyes, shook my head, too weak to respond. All I wanted to do was crawl back to bed.

She helped me dress, a slow, deliberate shake of her head. "You've grown. How can that be, in six weeks?"

Six weeks. Is that all it takes to change a life forever? When she tried to teach me, I wouldn't listen. When I was ready to listen, she wasn't there to teach me. When I desperately wanted a different life, I was powerless to change it. Now that I'd changed it, I was helpless to keep it. This had changed me. Now I walked like Pap.

"It's the room. Everybody looks bigger in a tiny room."

"No," She wagged her head, dropped the few articles I

never wanted to see again into a plastic bag. "I definitely see a difference."

* * *

I left the hospital in half breaths, more fragile on the outside than in, for once. Pap left ahead of us, said he had work to do, though I hadn't seen him work all summer.

I climbed into the back seat of Ben's big red truck and stared quietly through the dark sunglasses at the destruction that spewed out before us.

We drove without speaking, everybody mentally frazzled. Scattering buzzards feasted on antelope and deer that laid dead everywhere. Miles and miles of jack rabbits lay tossed against fences or in the ditches all the way from Lubbock to the ranch.

A bleak sight.

Ben and Mom glanced back and forth at each other, but never at the same time.

When we drove onto ranch property, I peeled the shades away, my whole body tense. Cream-colored sheep were strewn across the grassland like discarded clothing, bodies swelled in the heat, legs like prongs, reaching for the sky. Dark glasses couldn't hide the death, or change it back.

Ben's eyes found mine in the rear-view mirror. "The storm took its toll," he said gently. "Sand packed their noses and mouths. They couldn't breathe."

I shut my eyes to the ragged scene. No justice. I knew what they were thinking in the front seat because I was thinking it in the back: It could've been me. They might never have found me.

Ben parked as close to the front of the house as was possible. Sabion met us at the truck. He opened my door, my boots in his hands. "See what we find for you!" He held my boots out like precious things. "I find them, they stick up from the sand. Jennie walk on one, I am sorry."

It took seconds to reach for them, though I could never muster the words to thank him. I turned to the barn, feeling their eyes on my back.

How can they act like it's just another day when everything in the world has changed? So much slaughter. *And it's all my fault.*

I walked through the gate left open and entered the empty corral. At the barn doors, I saw Jennie was in her stall. She flicked her tail at me. Tessa munched hay with her eyes closed.

I sat on the stoop in the doorway. The emptiness felt all wrong.

Rowdy appeared out of nowhere and laid down beside me to pant. I hugged him, and he let me.

I didn't notice Sabion until I smelled the manure on his boots...the sweat on his hatband, Jennie on his jeans. He squatted beside me. "How are you, Carlota?"

Tears sprang to my eyes. His inquiry was genuine, the result of a lifetime of understanding nature and humans and animals. It wasn't a question.

"I am very grateful to see you home safe. I mean, I pray and I pray you will be okay." He shook his head. "It was very bad here." His eyes swarmed over the empty pen with over-whelming sadness.

"Sabion," I whispered. "Do you remember when you asked me what I wanted, what was my dream?"

His shoulders rolled in. "Yes, Carlota. I remember." He lowered his head and waited through my deep, racking cough.

"I know now." I met his gaze. "Peace. I want peace. That is what I dream of. I found it in that cave. It got me through when everything was wrong." Talking gave me hiccups. "I'm just," I felt it coming, the tears. "—worried it's not mine to keep."

Sabion listened attentively, giving it weight, the way Radar listened. He cocked his head and shrugged. "It belongs to you already." Then he knelt and looked candidly into my eyes. "Because, you see, now you know what it is. When you recognize such a gift, you will not let it slip away."

* * *

I dragged myself to the house, to my room, and shut the door. Someone had opened the window. The curtains cupped back like bat wings. A mist-like vapor hovered in the room. I stood at the window, watching. Sabion hadn't moved from where I'd left him. Lifting his hat, he scratched the back of his head and contemplated the empty corral. At the nothing that was left.

Mom was in the kitchen. There was endless clatter before I smelled the chicken frying. I hadn't had fried chicken since I left Seattle, yet my favorite meal repulsed me rather than enticed.

The house had been closed tight against the sand, but the flavor of silt still milled in the air. The bed was turned down. Traces of grit clung to the bed cover. I flopped in its middle, no matter the heat.

Seattle. When would we leave?

I tried to go to sleep but every time I closed my eyes I felt the mound...the scalding heat, then searing cold, and ached all over again.

I should have done things differently.

I felt myself floating away only to awaken with a storm's growing whistle steeping through my dream. I refused to answer the calls for supper.

Three times someone came to my door.

Three times I heard the door creak open.

Three times a silent head peeked in as I pretended to sleep.

Murmurs from the kitchen buzzed...the clinking of dishes, chairs scraping the linoleum. I let the din roll right over me; I didn't care enough to listen.

At dusk, there was a loud knock on my door. I still didn't answer, didn't want to see anybody, and rolled the pillow over my head.

"Charley? Mind if I come in?"

I wanted to shout, 'Go away!' but I couldn't say no to Ben. I tossed the pillow aside. "Okay."

The door cracked open. I sneaked a look at the silhouette framing the doorway. "Mom—" Behind her, Ben pushed her in and gently closed the door.

Soft-soles slipped across the hardwood floor with hardly a sound, crept to the bed I'd pushed under the window to keep an eye on the stars, even as they guided the sneaking coyotes along their trails. Mom stood silent over the bed, her long hair pinned back and caught in a clasp.

I had a chill, but my eyes were hot. "It's all my fault. The sheep—" I had no tears left to fall, yet my eyes swam.

She touched my forehead, smoothed aside my bangs. "That's not so. The storm would've taken the sheep with or without you. They would've died regardless."

I waited for the clench to go out of my muscles, afraid my voice would betray me. "Why does growing up have to be so hard?"

The mattress slumped where she sat. Her fingers touched my head. The room, the house, the yard, the barn were deathly quiet. "I suppose because there's so much to learn." I opened the blanket and she folded in beside me. We huddled like spoons smashed together. She stroked my hair, picking, pulling while Rowdy whined under the window. "My life would be over if I'd lost you." Her voice was anguished, like the ewe at the rail who'd lost her lamb.

"Why did you leave Texas? My life could've been so different."

Warm breaths infused my hair. She laced her fingers with mine. A short swish of breath hovered at my ear. I imagined a hint of a smile. "My life still wouldn't have been your life. My childhood was nothing like yours, partly because of the generation, partly because of living in such a remote place."

"Partly because you're Native American?" I unwrapped it for her. She didn't know what I knew. I wanted to hear it from her, but she dismissed my outburst with a short, singular click of her tongue.

A cooling breeze passed through the window. "There's so much to understand."

I untangled myself and sat up. "You kept it from me. How can I understand who I am if I don't know where I come?"

I didn't realize how much I missed her eyes. She turned to face me. Holding herself straight and still, she steepled her hands to the tip of her nose, fingertips pointing skyward. I'd never seen her do that. "I am Comanche. I am Dragonfly. My feet are formed from the desert dust."

"Dragonfly, you?"

"Native Americans parents choose fitting spirit names for their children as they enter different stages of life. Dragonfly is my *noon-day* name, my middle-life spirit name. Dragonfly is thought to be good medicine for change. It represents protection and rebirth, the symbol for water. It was once thought the dragonfly could fly in two directions at once."

I tried to show my understanding. "Ben said Mims knew medicine."

"There are many kinds of medicine.

I remembered the vase in the cave, how it felt in my hands. What had happened to it? "There was a dragonfly vase in that cave. Is it Mim's ashes?"

"It is the ashes of my little brother." The air left the room. "Kyle?"

She nodded. "His life was cut short when something spooked my horse one day and she bolted. Kyle stood in her path."

"Nothing was ever the same after Kyle died. I was thirteen—such an impressionable age. When I needed my daddy's hand the most, he couldn't reach. Sabion had to step in."

I understood such a loss more than she could ever know.

She shook her head as if shaking away the memory. "I couldn't know how bad it was for him." She pushed a slice of hair behind my ear. "Kyle's death changed us all. But Pap, he just...just evaporated. Mims tried to soothe him, but Pap could not be consoled. He'd lost his boy." She clasped her hands. "I lost them both."

"That's the reason you left Texas?"

She shrugged. "Maybe it set things in motion. I blamed myself for Kyle's death, just like you're doing now for all the sheep lost in the storm. I was still mourning Kyle years later when I met your father." Tension showed in her eyes. She blinked it away. "I suppose I was desperate for attention, and your dad showered me with plenty...back then. I quit school and ran off with him. It seemed the answer at the time. I thought it would take me out of the pain." She shook her head. "It only moved the pain around."

She stopped, a look or horror. "I never wanted you to know because I didn't want you to make the same kind of mistake. How could I be real with you when I couldn't be honest with myself? She smoothed the bedspread between us. "The dragonfly cautions us to look for the deeper meaning of life. I had lost my way. It took your Dad leaving for me to see I'd thrown aside everything I believed in, just to believe in his vision."

"That's no reason to hide your heritage."

"Though I never saw myself as anything different from him, he did. He had particular...beliefs, about the Native American culture. I told myself, We fell in love didn't we? He wouldn't have married me if my being Comanche mattered, right? If it wasn't love, I never wanted to know."

I nodded.

"No. Denying my heritage was the first step of a big lie. That I was Comanche mattered very much to him. And I believed what mattered to him should matter to me."

"You could've told me that!"

She shook her head slowly. "No, I couldn't. First, I was instructed *not* to tell his family I had Comanche blood. Then, I wasn't to tell his friends. When you were born, he forbade me to call you even one-fourth Native American—that he would *not* have a squaw daughter!" She chuckled softly. "Though that's exactly what he had."

"How do you change your complexion? How do you change the shape of your nose, chin, style of your cheeks? Even an outward change can't remake what's inside, who we're created to be. Shame on me for ignoring signs that were certainly there."

I'd always thought my mother was beautiful, but now I peeled her apart: the prominent cheekbones, the thick, black hair, the bronze skin...proud chin. She'd always held herself straight and rigid. She , and flowed when she walked. I wanted that strength. "I wish I had more Comanche blood in me."

"I've asked myself many times, Will it make a difference to Charley, knowing she's Comanche? Would it bind us together, or drive us apart?"

"Why would it drive us apart?"

Her shoulders locked a shrug. "It made a difference to him; what if it mattered to you? I couldn't risk it. I couldn't change it, like pushing toothpaste back in the tube. It was all on me. I had to remember how to love myself again."

Sad, that Dad looked at me and could only see Comanche. That Lee Ann could only see Comanche. I'd been wrestling with a patchy kind of incompleteness and didn't know why. Now I knew.

I said, "It's kinda nice to know you're not perfect. Perfect is terribly hard to live up to." She wrapped her arms around me. I laid my chin on her shoulder. "Is Pap Native American?"

"No. He grabbed the next best thing. He married your Mims."

It's difficult, being responsible for someone else, like I had to be for Radar in the storm and Mom had to be for me after Dad left. She couldn't stop living any more than I could give up in the desert, even when I thought there was nothing more I could do. Life is a climb up a spiral staircase. I learned a thing I'd never known before: I'm made for this country.

"It's a struggle," I said. "Finding yourself."

Nodding, she took a new breath. "Speaking of finding, your dad called. He knows where you are. He had nothing to say about that. He knows we've moved to the apartment. When he's ready, he'll know how to find you."

I should have felt something, but just thought, Sometimes bad things have to happen to make room for something better.

I'd left behind the person I no longer wanted to be. Dad had to leave and Mims had to die for me to live. Really live.

While we huddled under the billowing curtain in the room where Mom grew up, I wrestled to find a way to say the thing most on my mind. Every time it surfaced, I shoved it back down. "Mom?"

"Hm?"

"I don't want to go home."

The sharp intake of her breath gave me goose bumps. She pressed four fingers to her mouth and fixed snapping eyes on me. I remembered those eyes from a long, long time ago. She asked, "What...exactly...do you mean?"

I searched her face, the full realization taking shape in my answer. "I don't belong in Seattle." Her eyes fluttered and I rushed to say, "I know, I know. I'm only sixteen. What do I know?"

The rapid blink sliced away. "No. No, that's not what I'm thinking."

"Mom, I understand more than you think I do. Standing on that ledge, huddled in that cave, I didn't think I would survive. Now that I have, I'm ready to live. I don't want to go home." I was exhausted for keeping it in.

The house was quiet. Did Ben leave? Where was Pap?

Mom's eye-lock broke first. "Me, too." The whisper barely made it to my ears and I wasn't sure she'd spoken at all. Her eyes flashed around the room, settled on the doll on the chair. She nodded, repeated, a hand half-covering her mouth. "I want that, too."

I squelched a gasp.

"I've wanted that for years. When I came back to bury Mims, I knew, then, that I'd be very happy to come home—I never thought you would!" She flung a hand. "Still, we don't have that choice. Jobs are very hard to come by in such a small town."

"Ben would hire you! I know he would! You know so much about horses. And—"

She shook a finger in my face. "Wait a minute! Don't go thinking—"

"I see the way he looks at you!" I teased.

"Ben and I have known each other our entire lives. I know how he thinks, the things he believes, his values."

"What more can you ask? He'd probably even help us move here. Before school starts."

Why, hello Lee Ann. Surprise!

A tap on the door, it opened a chunk. Ben spoke through the crack. "It's kinda noisy in here. Is it safe to come in?"

I glanced at Mom, who flustered. She shook her head, *No*, but I rolled from the bed and flung the door wide. "Yes! Yes, Ben. We have to talk."

He closed it behind him. I said, "Mom and I were just discussing how you two can go back to Seattle and pack up our apartment and move us back down here!"

"Charley!" Mom scolded.

"Well? School starts in a month! I can't go. I've got a lot to take care of. Besides, I can't leave Radar."

Wide-eyed, Ben scanned my face, then Mom's, his expression shifting from shock to surprise to confusion, then blooming into an over-the-moon grin. "Yeah, sure! I can arrange that."

I pulled Mom from the bed. "It's settled, then. C'mon, let's give Pap the shock of his life. Right now, while he's so agreeable.

Pap's mouth puckered. We waited through the scowl. The sunlight painted his cheeks more worn and sun-pocked than I'd noticed before. I said, "I'll start sweeping. Get this sand out of the house."

"Sabion and I already swept."

I ran a finger across the television. "You did a lousy job. I can still taste it."

"I'm confused," he said to Mom. "I thought you were both too good for Quitaque."

"Did I ever say that? Now, did I?" She laid a hand on his shoulder. "A dragonfly can move two directions at once if she had a mind to, so I guess I can change my mind if I want to." She gave me a wink.

"It's a pretty good offer." Ben admitted.

She picked up the picture cube taken so many years ago and turned it in her hands. "I've missed the place. I didn't even know how much until…"

Ben said, "I happen to have a couple'a cats hanging around the clinic who'd love to live in your barn."

I swooned. "We can give them a home, can't we, Pap? There's plenty of room. I've always wanted a cat."

"Hm." He laid a hand on Rowdy's head. "Mm…yeah." *Pat. Pat. Pat.* "I think Rowdy would really like a…couple a'*cats*." He hissed the word.

I rolled my eyes.

He narrowed his eyes at Ben and asked, "About that vet bill…Are you gonna give me a discount with that horse?"

Ben's head wavered slowly, shoulder to shoulder. "Sure, Fred. I'll give you a discount." He shrugged. "Actually, I wasn't expecting to charge Charley anything for Radar's boarding and care. But if you'd rather, I'll give *you* a discount; I can certainly arrange it."

Pap reached for the jar of raisin cookies I'd made when the world looked different. One bite, and he spit it out. "I said I don't like raisins!"

"Good!" I smacked off the light. "Cause we don't have any."

It would still be daylight in Seattle.

Acknowledgments

I am grateful for the input of family and friends who helped this book along. Foremost to my husband, James, whose edits have fine-tuned several western-specific details, and whose endless encouragement helped propel this book forward.

I wish to thank writer and friend, Melody DeLeon, whose keen eye helped bring every chapter together. Thank you for your constant support, counsel, suggestions, and direction. And to author and friend, D'Ann Mateer, whose guidance, encouragement, edits, and advice moved this book to print.

Special thanks to Society of Children's Book Writers and Illustrators (SCBWI) contributors and co-conspirators, Bridgette Booth, Lisa Hardwick, Liz Soutendijk, Marisa Schouten, and Melissa DeCarlo, whose broad strokes of insight contributed to the early formation of *Nightflower of Comanche Mound*. And to beta-readers who sent me flicking through the pages time and time again: James Bates, Melody DeLeon, Linda Shelton, Marc Weise, Mackie Squires, Susan Wingo, Jessica Ferris, Stephanie Bates, and to Roger Ferris for direction in the book cover design.

It was an honor to interview Mr. Carney Saupitty, Jr., Cultural Specialist at the Comanche Nation Museum & Cultural Center in Lawton, Oklahoma. On his advice I read his great uncle's book, *The Life of Ten Bears*, which illuminated the Comanche way of life.

A significant shout-out to Rockwall Christian Writers

Group (RCWG) authors D'Ann Mateer, Mary DeMuth, and Leslie White who set me on the *proper* writing trail so many years ago, whose long-time devotion to writers has generously educated, instructed, tutored, and encouraged so many.